BEAR

LEILA JAMES

CREDITS

Editing: Krista Dapkey

www.kdproofreading.com

Photography: Michelle Lancaster

@lanefotograf

Cover Design: Lori Jackson

www.lorijacksondesign.com

Interior Formatting: Shauna Mairéad

@shaunamairead_author

Model: Eric Guilmette

@etfitnesscoach

PLAYLIST

"I Want To" Rosenfeld
"Who Do You Want" Ex Habit
"HSYEH" Dutch Melrose
"Therapy" Voila
"River" Bishop Briggs
"Know Better" Josh Levi
"The Wall" Patrick Reza
"Sex and Candy" Alexander Jean
"Please" Omido, Ex Habit
"You Put A Spell On Me" Austin Giorgio
"Body" (Slowed & Reverb) Rosenfeld
"I'll Make You Love Me" Kat Leon
"Lips On You" Maroon 5
"Thriller" (Stripped) Jessie Villa

"I'm Yours" Isabel LaRosa

"Locksmith" Sadie Jean

"Yes Girl" Bea Miller

"In The End" (Mellen Gi Remix) Tommee Profitt,
Fleurie, Mellen Gi

A NOTE FROM THE AUTHOR

BEAR IS the second book in the Bastards of Bainbridge Hall trilogy, centering around three men and one woman. MMFM

WARNING: This trilogy contains dark elements, graphic content, and situations that some readers may be particularly sensitive to. If you have triggers or are remotely unsure, please check out the Content Warnings, available at my website.

https://www.leilajames.biz/content-warnings

ALSO, be aware that I don't always know how a series will end or all the underlying secrets until they reveal themselves in the writing process, so you may need to check content warnings for each book in the series as they come out.

ONE

MASON

Vivid blue eyes full of naked fear stare at me. I blink. *Fuck*. Lennon needs to stay so very fucking far away from me. I can't appropriately handle the guilty what-ifs that creep through my mind. They'll drive me insane if I dwell on them because I can't exactly control when my brain decides to hiccup and confuse me. I know I become irrational, unfocused, and unable to distinguish dreams from reality. I'm aware of my issues, and I don't foresee anything changing the way my twisted-up mind comprehends things.

What if I'm truly tangled up in the past and I *hurt* her?

My eyes drift to the side, scanning the assorted sketches plastered all over the attic—proof that my head is a very dangerous place, most especially for Lennon. What if I flip the fuck out on her like I did that day on the balcony, and no one is around to stop me? How far would I go? Would I push her over? Would I even realize what I was doing?

I swallow hard, blinking some more. My gaze reconnects with hers. Wild panic fills her eyes. *Fuck.*

Like a lightning bolt has cleaved us in two, I release my vice grip on Lennon's neck and stumble backward, my head a confusing fucking mess. Dragging in great lungfuls of air, I give myself a shake before surveying the damage I've inflicted on Lennon.

She's collapsed onto the floor in front of the railing I had her pressed up against, the clothes she'd been clutching to her before I'd gone after her, scattered at her feet. Her face is a splotchy red and pink, cheeks wet. She's shaking badly and gasping, each breath she takes labored.

Agony roars through my body as my eyes crash shut. I hate myself. I fucking *hate* myself. I drop to my knees, clutching my head between my hands. I shake my head as the pain from what I've done to her seeps from every pore.

Her lip wobbles as she stares at me. "W-what the fuck are you talking about?" she chokes out, her voice raw. I did that. I squeezed the fuck out of the slender column of her neck with my bare hand. I just wanted to make sure she understood how dangerous I can be. My chest fills with an agonizing ache, terrified of the havoc I could wreak on people I care for.

Lennon was beginning to sneak past my defenses. I was beginning to feel something for her.

Now you'll be next—that's what I said to her. Deep inside my twisted heart, I believe it to be true if she and I continue down this path. My chest heaves, and I look blankly at her. I can't allow this girl to think she can somehow fix this. Fix me. I can't let her get any closer, no matter what. I will cause her unimaginable pain. I might *destroy* her.

But fuck, I *want* her. And I know I'm being foolish thinking I can break the connection between us so easily. I wish I could give her my heart. I'd rip it out of my goddamn chest and hand it to her if I thought there was a way, if I thought it'd be enough for her. That way I could keep my distance.

My eyes flick around the attic, once again taking in all the emotional damage on display. How is she not running scared? I force out a sick laugh, glancing at her. I can't give her more than a cursory look or I'll beg her to forgive me. I'll want to touch her. Hold her.

I wet my lips, infusing a coldness to my tone as I snarl, "What am I talking about? You wanted to know so fucking bad what was in my head, why I am the way I am. Well, now you fucking know, don't you? You know exactly how sick I really am, what I've done." A vision of my mother tumbling over that balcony rail skitters through my brain as it does so often. I see it in slow motion. My hands on her, her scream as she tipped over the edge. Her descent and the finality of her impact on the stone below.

I choke back vomit. I can't get it out of my head, and it's fucking torture. I rake my teeth over my lip as I watch Lennon struggle to draw a breath, misery flowing from her eyes. Shaking fingers stroke up and down the skin of her throat, assessing the damage.

She said she wanted all of me. I don't have it in me to believe her. To hope.

"M-Mason." She shakes her head, lip trembling. "You can push me away, but I still see you."

My jaw hardens, and I arch my brow. "I think you like the idea of it. How many times do I have to put my hand around your throat before you recognize there's something really wrong with me?"

She stares at me, all traces of emotion leaving her face. Softly, but with menacing conviction, she murmurs, "If you think you're the first person to put their hands on me like that, you're wrong. You don't fucking scare me at all. I told you—I *see* you." Her words are like a cannonball, plowing a hole straight through my chest. "But if that's how you feel, I'll believe you." Exhibiting frustration with every swipe of errant tears from her cheeks, she heaves out, "I'll fucking go." Before I can say a word, she's on her feet, clothing left behind. She races down the stairs, her footfalls thundering in my ears.

"The fuck!" My heart clangs around behind my rib cage. I shoot to my feet, following. "Lennon!"

She glances over her shoulder as she gets to the bottom of the steps and throws open the door. "Leave me the fuck alone, Mase," she grits out, like her words are being dragged over gravel.

Goddammit, what did she mean I'm not the first? I catch her as she's shutting her door, slamming my hand into it, then reach in and take a firm grip of her forearm. My chest heaves as I back her into the room. "Lennon, what the fuck?" My mind takes a sick spin, trying to make sense of what she said, and my gut—fuck, it's telling me something I don't want to believe. I grip her upper arms, any composure I had beginning to slip. The air rips from my lungs like razors scraping along my throat. I shake my head, my lips pressing together in disbelief. *"No."* But it's there in her eyes. The truth. And from the angry look in her eyes, I'm unsure if she intended to tell me at all. Or maybe she simply regrets she did now that she has my reaction.

This girl ... she's more damaged than I'd assumed, and everything I've fucking done to her— Tension stretches across my shoulders, and my jaw hardens as my eyes flick over her features, checking to see if there is any sign that I'm imagining things. *Fuck.* My brain spirals. Forget the nightmares she has while sleeping, I've—

Oh god. What have I done?

"Mason!" Her panicked voice snaps me back to her blazing eyes as she desperately attempts to tear away from me, but to no avail. "I said leave me alone," she gasps. "Let me fucking go!" She renews her efforts, but I can't seem to loosen my hold. Each breath I take hurts like the fire of a thousand hells, spreading through my chest. A low wail escapes her, verging on a sob. My jaw clenches as I stare into tear-soaked eyes. "Why won't you let me go?" Anguish slides over her face. She draws in a sobbing breath before she shrieks, "Get your hands off me!" Heart-wrenching sobs burst from her lips, her entire body shaking. "Let me go." Her chest heaves. "Just let me *go.*"

"Tell. Me," I grit out, the need to know a live beast within me, roaring. I can't sever the connection between us. I'm incapable of letting her go, can't do it until she explains herself.

"The *fuck's* going on?" Duke shouts from behind me. His hand comes down on my shoulder, trying to pry me away. There's no hesitation from him, despite the fact Lennon and I are both completely naked. I ignore him, even as his fingers bite into my arm.

Lennon's response to Duke's arrival is a raspy cry, betraying what I've done to her. "H-he won't let me g-go."

Duke turns to me, gritting out, "Stop, Mason. Whatever's going on. Think about what you're doing. This isn't helping anything." His blue eyes bore into mine, as if ... as if he's desperately trying to find me inside this hollowed-out shell of a person I've become.

I blink, staring at him, my chest rising and falling so fast, I can't catch my breath.

"The fuck." Bear appears in my peripheral vision on my other side, and I glance at him for a fraction of a second as his big hand comes down on my other arm. "Enough, you fucking maniac. That's e-fucking-nough."

Duke hesitates for a moment before gripping the back of my neck and forcefully turning my head, but I refuse to meet his eyes. His other hand clenches my arm with fierce intent as he insistently whispers, *"Mase."*

The intensity of his tone has my gaze swinging wildly toward his. I blink rapidly, then focus on the girl in front of me, really trying to see her. She's in a worked-up state, her face flushed and agitated. Upset. With me.

This wasn't my intention. I didn't mean to do this, but the idea that someone in her past has put their hands on her, it sends me right out of my goddamn mind. *Fuck. I'm such a walking contradiction.* On a choked exhale, I release Lennon's arms and stumble backward. Duke catches me, then grabs hold of me when I lunge in her direction again, yanking me against his chest and locking his arms around me. I clamp my eyes shut, the storm raging inside me isn't dissipating at all. I need to find out what she meant. Lights flicker behind my eyes and sound crashes in my head.

Bear's deep voice growls from very far away. "Do you have him?"

Duke's breath hits my cheek. His arms tighten around my abdomen. "Yeah." I pry my eyes open again and look on in agony as Lennon huddles against Bear's chest. "Come on. Let's go," he murmurs in my ear.

I don't want to leave her, and my feet remain rooted to the floor, but Duke is strong enough to drag me backward until I have no choice but to move with him.

Faint whispers in the hallway tell me we aren't alone. *Fuck.* We've roused half the house. Out of the corner of my eye, I count at least three people standing there watching Duke pull my naked ass out of Lennon's room.

Fuck. Fuck, fuck, fuck. The rumors that are going to fucking swirl around this place ... I don't even want to contemplate.

Without looking in the direction of the open doors down the hall, Duke grinds out, "Get the fuck back into your rooms." He throws his door open and hauls me with him into his bedroom. I'm too fucking stunned to argue or stop him, and far too upset over what I've done and what she implied to make any decisions for myself, anyway.

Duke kicks the door shut behind us. For a long moment, which extends into several more, we pause in the middle of his room. My eyes flick around, taking in the space. It's much the way I remember from that disastrous first week at Bainbridge Hall, mostly neat and void of anything too personal, with two glaring exceptions. There are framed photographs on top of his dresser. The first is one of Bear and me with him on high school graduation day, all of us in caps and gowns. Tristan took it, if memory serves correctly. It'd been a rough year, but we'd made it.

The second was obviously taken at a dance—him and Juliette. Junior prom, maybe? They're in the middle of the dance floor, eyes locked on each other, smiles beaming. That would have been only months before she died. *Fuck.* With everything else, I completely dropped the ball and didn't ask Lennon about the mumbled questions that had left her mouth earlier. My mind rolls back to when I first encountered Lennon in the throes of her nightmare.

"Why are you so scared? Who is he? Wait. Who is he, Juliette? Wait!"

TWO

DUKE

"If I let you go, are you going to wig out?" I murmur next to Mason's ear, unwilling to release my hold on him until I know for sure he *isn't* going to freak the fuck out and race right back to Lennon's room.

The wild, distraught look in his eyes had been both terrifying and gut-wrenching. And Lennon, fuck. She's actually a little bit harder for me to read, but she'd been more in a state of panic than anything else. Not that I blame her, because fuck, he had not wanted to let her go. The first thing I'd heard when I ran into the room was his dire, desperate request for her to *tell him* something. Fortunately or unfortunately, I have no idea, she hadn't ever answered him. And he'd not let on why he'd lost it and wouldn't—no couldn't—let her out of his sight.

My arms flex as they band around his middle, my

front molded to his back. I've fisted one of my hands at his abs, the other is firmly grasping the wrist and locking Mason against me.

I breathe steadily, trying to ignore the erratic jumping of my heart and the tormented thoughts that whirl through my head as I hold him. The last time he was in my room, he'd been just as naked. Trying to shake myself free of the anguish in my head, I patiently wait, knowing he needs me right now.

Several moments later, he slowly nods, though when he speaks, his voice cracks. "I-I'm good." He takes several deep breaths, and I automatically inhale and exhale with him, almost as if my body needs to remain as close to his as possible; I need the connection, even though I shouldn't want it. I drop my forehead to his shoulder. I hate my hesitation in releasing him, hate that he can feel it, too. Because I know the potential for him to lash out at me, insert the knife and twist—it's high in these circumstances.

As I unlatch my hold on him, I watch him warily, the muscle at the back of my jaw twitching. "What the fuck was that?"

His gaze connects with mine, and for a moment he says nothing. My chest clenches, my lungs forgetting how to function. His dark eyes pin mine, chaotic and dangerous. Despite the fact I know Mason well, sometimes I don't have a fucking clue what goes on in his head. He thrusts his hands into his hair, then tips his head to look at the ceiling rather than let me in and share his thoughts.

"I'm no fucking good for her. I needed to push her away."

"I hope you mean emotionally, because physically, you were doing the opposite two seconds ago." I step into Mason's space, firmly grasping his jaw. He stutters out a choked gasp at my touch. I bring his head forward so I can look him pointedly in the eye. "She said to stop. To let her go. What the fuck, man?"

He wrenches himself from me and backs up a step. His gaze slips down to my mouth, where it stays for several seconds before he finally takes a deep breath. "You're judging what happened in there based on the thirty seconds you saw." He shakes his head, his eyes finding mine, searching. "Have you ever picked out a movie based on a snippet of a trailer, and you think it's going to be about one thing, but then you watch the entire thing, and you're floored because the actual movie is nothing like what you fucking thought you were going to be watching. Like, 'Oh, fuck. This is a thriller. I thought I was getting something different because all I saw was the one sexy-ass scene in the teaser.' That's how you're approaching this situation. Because what you saw in her room versus the whole of what went on between Lennon and me tonight are distinctly different." His jaw clamps shut, teeth grinding. After another moment, he mumbles, "Still kinda messed up. But different. I told her things I shouldn't have."

I stare at him in astonishment, wondering what the fuck he's talking about.

"She knows way too fucking much about me. And I'm not responsible for telling you what you don't know about your messed-up stepsister, but there's something seriously fucked-up going on with those nightmares of hers. Maybe you should try getting to know her, try to figure out what the fuck is setting her off, if you're as concerned for her well-being as you say you are."

Way to put my brain in a blender and hit puree. And I'm so distracted trying to figure out the meaning buried in his words that my eyes roam. They follow every dip and groove of my former best friend's body, causing my breathing to go shallow.

I blink and focus on Mason in time for him to grab the back of his neck with both hands and cautiously change his stance, cock swinging proudly between his legs. Because, yeah. Mason's still standing buck naked in the middle of my room, completely comfortable in front of me. I can't say I feel the same, but some sort of curious unease slicks down my spine. He watches me from under hooded eyes but doesn't say a damn word. But that knowing look he gives me has me shuddering.

I allow myself one more moment of insanity, then I tear my gaze away, spinning on my heel before crossing the room to my dresser. Standing in front of the drawer I've opened, I spend several extra seconds poking around at the clothing inside before finally picking out a pair of joggers. I ball them up, spin around, and chuck them at Mason. They hit him square in the chest, and he brings up his arms to catch them before they can fall to the floor.

He looks down at the dark-gray joggers and smirks. "Afraid to have me naked in your room again, Duke?"

I press my lips together as I cross my arms over my chest. A protective stance. I can't allow him to mess with my head. Because that's what Mason does. He mixes me up. Confuses everything I thought I knew about myself. Studying him for a moment, I finally huff out a breath before giving him an unamused smile. I shake my head. "Fuck off. Leave me out of your crazy." His brow arches, and I let out an exasperated breath, steering the conversation away from me. "And no matter what happened between you and Lennon—because I'm sure there's plenty that you didn't mention—it's obvious it wasn't good. Once you've calmed the fuck down, you should think about apologizing."

He snorts out a little laugh, his full lips stretching into a grin. "Leave the dad stuff to Bear and stick with being the dick. We all know you're good at it." He bends to slip into my joggers and hikes them up.

I feel an immediate sense of relief ... and if I search way down deep, a flicker of disappointment.

"I don't know why you dragged me in here with you." He blows out a hard breath. "You could have just as easily opened my door and shoved me into my own fucking room." He lets another smirk cross his face. "But I think you like me here." His brow hitches up on his forehead in challenge.

"Just sit the fuck down," I groan out in frustration as I gesture to the couch on the far side of my bed. I shove his shoulder as I walk past him to claim a seat. I find when I get over there, I need to keep myself in a position of power and right now that means perching high on one of the arms of the couch with a foot up on the cushion. If I put myself on his level, it's all over. I wait, drawing in one ragged breath after another, watching him approach out of the corner of my eye. Somebody needs to calm down, but it's not necessarily Mason at this point, and that pisses me right off.

He shakes his head as he circles around the side of the couch. For a moment, he stands there, sizing me up. I worry a lot that Mason can see right inside my head. My eyes slam shut for a moment, not wanting to consider all that that means. When I open them again, he's seated himself sideways on the couch, leaning back against the cushioned arm and stretching his legs across the couch. Lazy. Easy. He gives me a good glare.

I glare right back, scrubbing my hand over my stubbled jaw. "Talk to me."

An annoyed smile twitches at his lips. He shifts his gaze to the side for a moment before bringing it back to mine, his dark, sinful eyes locking on me. "I don't have a single fucking thing else to talk to *you* about."

This shift in attitude doesn't surprise me. It's classic Mason. And he might be able to flip his switch fucking fast, but so can I. My expression goes hard as I grasp the back of my neck with one hand, fingers digging in and massaging the tight muscles. Every time I deal with Mason, it makes me tense. Well, time to make him feel a little of that as well. "Mason, how long's it been since you've seen your therapist?" My brows lift on my forehead as I wait for my words to sink in.

As I thought I might, I've caught him off guard with my question, and his true feelings are written all over his face. As far as I know, I'm the only one who knows that he's ever seen anyone for his issues. He laces his fingers, resting them overtop his head, putting on a false front.

"Couldn't fucking tell you." His response is flippant, but his eyes flick to mine, and his teeth positively grind.

I throw out a hand in his direction. "Look. I know we haven't been particularly friendly in a long time—"

"Not my fucking fault," he spits, not even allowing me to finish my thought.

"I'm trying to fucking help you."

"None of this is helping." He rolls his eyes as he throws up finger quotes around *helping*.

I draw in a breath, eyeing him carefully. Two can play this game. "I'll tell you what. Either you fucking talk about what the hell triggered you tonight or ..." My lips press together. I really didn't want to have to play this card, but he's leaving me no choice.

"Or what? You fucking threatening me now?"

I grimace. "Look. I have a responsibility toward Lennon. And if you're going to continue with your psycho tendencies—which, that's my guess, something got you freaked out—I suppose I'll have to talk to my father about it. And you know that means he'll put in a call to yours. I mean, who knows how the fuck he'll handle it." I let that bomb drop, knowing he won't like the idea of Murdock Mikaelson being apprised of the situation over here.

He freezes, staring daggers at me, probably wishing I

don't know how to push his buttons so fucking easily. But I do.

I chuckle low and dirty. "He'd send Hunter." My head bobs, knowing I have him. "That'd suck for you, wouldn't it? You hate him."

Knowing Mason like I do, he won't allow me to have the last word. He slicks his tongue ever so slowly over his lower lip as his gaze wanders over me. "You want to know more about what happened in the attic? I fucked Lennon. Your stepsister's pussy is the stuff fucking dreams are made of."

I don't doubt he railed her, but that can't be what caused whatever set him off. I narrow my eyes on him, suddenly very worried about the glint in his eye.

He huffs out a laugh and unleashes on me. "Too bad you won't ever know because you can't get over yourself and admit you want her." My forehead pulls into a deep scowl, and just when I think Mason's done, he goes in for the kill. "Tell me, Duke— since you want to talk tonight—what was it like, standing there between the stepsister you can't admit you want to fuck and the guy who's already fucked *you?*"

THREE

BEAR

"LENNON? ARE YOU OKAY IN THERE?" I stand at the door of her bathroom, fingers hooked on the top of the doorframe, my forehead pressed against the door. After Duke hauled Mason out of here, I'd simply held Lennon for several long minutes before she'd said she felt like she needed to clean up, but she'd made me promise not to go anywhere, so here I've stayed. Because, yeah. Like I would go anywhere if she asked me to stick around.

The shower stopped a while ago, but I haven't heard much movement beyond that door since. She's making me nervous, hence my position right at the door. I don't know how much longer I can stand it. I rap my knuckles lightly against the door before returning my hand to the doorframe. "Can I come in?"

I let out a sigh of relief when soft footfalls approach the door. A moment later the door cracks open. My Little Gazelle stares out at me, her eyes glossy. I can't quite tell if she's been crying in here by herself or whether this is leftover frustrated tears. Without her telling me, I don't want to automatically assume anything about her current state of mind. She's not a weak girl. She's dealt with quite a lot where Mason's concerned in the last week. And despite what Lennon told Duke that one morning in the kitchen—we won't break her—*everyone* has a breaking point. So ... yeah. I don't know what to think.

She pushes the door open a fraction wider and grimaces at me. "I was surveying the damage." Her fingers clutch the towel between her breasts, holding it closed.

My brows shoot up, and my jaw locks in displeasure. I put my hand on the door and nudge it until she has to back up, at which point I push it all the way open. "Show me what you're talking about before I flip my fucking lid."

Her wide eyes seek mine out. "I—" She stops to swallow, her free hand creeping to her neck. "I'm marked up and red in spots from getting manhandled at the stadium. Some of it, I think I may have done to myself, banging around inside the locker against the wood.

And ... well, a little bit of it is a result of—" She doesn't finish, but it doesn't take more than a flick of her eyes upward for me to gather that Mason contributed to her injuries today.

My eyes dart to her reddened upper arms. Probably a combination of her attacker and Mason. I heave out a sigh. "I want to see the rest."

Lennon stares at me, bold trust in her eyes. She drops the towel, but holds her arms drawn up in front of her breasts. Her skin looks soft and dewy from the shower. I close my eyes for a moment, dropping my head down to stare at the marble floor. Starting at her toes, my eyes drift upward, slowly sliding over her curves, noting angry redness on her knees from being jammed in the locker. Before I can look everywhere, she begins a slow turn, and I notice more areas that will likely become bruises. A nasty spot on her hip makes me wince, but it's what I see when she scoops her hair out of the way that has me wincing in sympathy for her. "Fuck." I suck in a breath, and step closer, hesitating to touch her. Her spine is dotted with marks where she must have scraped herself raw trying to find a way out of that locker. My eyes shift upward to a spot on the back of her neck, just under her hairline, that is red, like something rubbed against it. It looks a bit like rope burn. My stomach gurgles as my fingers gently brush over it. That's because it fucking is. Whoever tied that bag over her head is responsible for that.

"The bag. I pulled at the front, trying to get it loose, and it roughed up my neck."

"Yeah, I see that." Now that I'm closer, I turn her in my arms to explore her neck. I take her jaw in both of my hands, tipping her head back so I can get a better look. "Goddammit, Mason," I grit out, wrenching my gaze from four fingerprint-like marks on one side and what looks like a thumb on the other. "He had you by the neck again. The fuck." It's not even a question, just a bitten-out exclamation of frustration. "I'll never make excuses for him, not for this."

She sucks in a breath. "I know it. And I know I should walk away, but I can't. Couldn't explain it if I tried." Her shoulders lift in a confused shrug before she quickly wraps me in a strong hold, pressing our bodies together. She shudders in my arms and mumbles, "He told me some shit that—" Cutting herself off, she shakes her head, the color leaching from her face. "I won't betray what he told me. He was out of his head, distraught. But I understand him better now. No one lives through something like that and ..." Her voice wobbles, and she never finishes her thought.

I feel her rough swallow against my chest, and it's like a knife to my heart. I can only assume Mason said something to her about his mother. "Lennon, is there anything else I need to know about?"

She looks up at me with wild eyes, her cheeks turning cherry red. "Um. No. Not really. Some things happened when we were—"

"Fucking," I supply for her with a grimace.

Raggedly, she murmurs, "Yes. There's a mark on my breast." When she looks into my eyes, I don't hide my irritation. "It's not a big deal. I-I wanted it."

Seeking calm, I reach for each of her forearms and draw them from around my waist and force her to take a step back. Her chest caves in, shoulders rounding. My eyes fixate on her breasts. Sure enough, one nipple has a distinctive bite mark around it.

My heart thunders in my chest. I knew—not only from things I've seen and heard from Mason, but also from the way he'd touched her when he joined us on the yoga mat—that he has some serious carnal knowledge of Lennon. But seeing this, not knowing how it all came about, and not completely trusting Lennon when she says she wanted it—it makes me a little unhinged.

"You let him hurt you, Lennon. Why? You can't tell me you don't see that. Don't feel it. Fuck, you have the evidence of it on your body."

She struggles to get her arms free of my grasp, and I immediately let her go, not wanting a repeat of earlier.

But then she dives forward, nestling her body close to mine as she wraps her arms around me. She sucks in a stuttered breath, tipping her head back to look up at me. "I told you. I wanted it," she whispers softly. "I understand him. We have this connection, and when I'm with him, we both kinda— I can't explain it. We get each other, and— Fuck. I can't talk to you about this. You wouldn't understand it."

My jaw clenches. "Lennon, he's my friend, but fuck that. Even if I ignore everything else—he tried to choke you. He *hurt* you. You can't tell me you're okay with that."

She takes a deep breath, and with surprising calm, she states, "He wanted to push me away. He tried to scare me. But I don't scare that easily."

My head scrambles, trying to understand what she's telling me. "So he pushed you away, yet somehow ended up completely unable to let you go. Literally refused to take his hands off you."

"I wish I could explain it." She chews on her lip. "He was fine until I asked about his mother. I wanted him to tell me more about her. He didn't like it. And then he kinda ... lost it. But I'm telling you, I understand him more now than I did before." There's a glint of determination in her eyes—one that tells me whatever they are to each other is definitely not over.

So, I was right. Discussion of what happened to his mother played a role in what happened. And the odd thing is, despite the fact that she says he lost it when prompted to talk about Lily—he obviously told her *something,* but I wonder how much. I don't like this. Their relationship is volatile at best. Fuck. I don't know how to help them.

I'm so distracted by my thoughts I don't realize Lennon has slid her hands around to my back until they're dipping under the waistband of my joggers. Air punches from my lungs as she kneads my ass cheeks, and for a moment everything is perfect. Gorgeous girl. Hands in my pants. Cock quickly hardening. *Fuuuck.*

I inhale sharply as warning bells begin to clang in my head.

"Lennon, wait." I skim my hands from her upper arms over her shoulders before carefully sweeping them up her neck so I can cup her face between them. "I need to ..." I work my jaw to the side, trying to figure out how to say this without offending her.

She looks up at me, that trust I'd felt earlier still shining there. "You need to what?"

"I can't." *Fuck.* I release a ragged breath. "I need you to know that you're beautiful, and I'd like nothing more than to lay you down and make us both feel really good."

Her brow furrows as her teeth come down on her lower lip, worrying the skin there. "But ...?"

Does she have a clue what my concern is? "But you're hurting. And the physical bruises are only the tip of the iceberg. It's been a rough day for you emotionally. Fuck, it's been hell for me, too. And I don't want us to fall into a pattern where you're hurting about something Mason—or *fuck,* anyone else—has done, and I become the one you seek comfort in."

She looks up at me from under hooded eyes, a prominent flush creeping onto her cheeks. "Could you explain why that's a bad thing?"

I take one unsteady breath and then another. Her hands haven't moved from their position on my ass. My dick would like to know why I'm saying a goddamn thing. And maybe I shouldn't, but fuck. With my heart thundering in my chest, I murmur, "Because I don't want times like this to be the *only* ones when you come to me. I love that I make you feel safe. But that can't be all this is. Not for me." At the wounded look on her face, my eyes crash shut. "I'm sorry. I have way too many areas of my life where I deal with secrets and untruths and outright lies. I don't want to keep things from you."

"No." She nibbles on her lip again. "I see what you're saying. I didn't mean to make you feel like that."

Her hands slide out of my pants to rest lightly on my hips.

Needing to occupy my mind with something other than the tempting nakedness of the girl in my arms, I murmur, "I'm happy to take care of you, though—and I actually think the first thing we should be addressing is your back."

With her teeth clenched together, she groans, "It's that bad?" She cranes her neck around, trying to see into the mirror behind her.

"There are a few spots along your spine that look a little raw. It could use some antibiotic ointment and a couple of bandages." I dip my head down, catching her chin in my hand at the same time, brushing my lips over hers. My heart is a wild stampede of horses in my chest. The way this girl makes me feel is unreal. "Gonna grab a few things to fix you up. I'll be right back."

I duck across the hall to my room, taking a moment to breathe. This entire situation is fucked. I'm going to wring Mason's neck. I grit my teeth as I sort through the medical supplies in my bathroom drawer, gathering what I need. I don't even fucking know how to handle him. I hope Duke was able to fucking deal with it without them getting into it again, because I'm not going to be there to tear them apart this time. If that's how they decide to handle things, then they're going to have a good go at each other.

I take a moment in the hallway between our rooms to listen, but I hear nothing, so I continue back to Lennon.

She's crawled into bed but is sitting up with a sheet drawn to her chest, waiting for me. I set a small pile of bandages on the nightstand and sit down behind her. "I should have thought about this earlier."

"It's okay. I'll live." She turns her head, offering me a small smile. "I'm made of sturdy stuff."

"That you are." I shake my head, chuckling a bit as I open a package containing an antiseptic wipe, then slowly and carefully blot it over the first open spot on her skin.

She immediately pulls in air between her teeth, and her back arches, trying to get away.

"Sorry. Does this help?" I lean in and blow over the spot. "I do this to my knuckles when I bust them up."

She nods. "Yes. Thank you. I should have guessed you'd know what to do."

I grunt a bit, thinking about the fact that I have something important to talk to her about, considering I'll be seeing my father for fight night. *Fucker.* I work my way down her back, cleaning four different abrasions on her skin. I turn, picking up the bandages and begin to open one after another, applying a dab of the ointment and placing them over the wounds. "Let's wait and see what the rope mark on your neck looks like tomorrow before we do anything. I know it probably stings, but it's not open, just roughed up."

"Okay."

I stand, heading to her dresser. "Which drawer has T-shirts? Got anything oversize or loose around the neck?"

From behind me, she murmurs sleepily, "Yeah. Second drawer down. There should be something."

I dig around for a second before coming up with a good option. I turn and hold it up so she can see it.

"That'll work."

All of a sudden, not only does she sound exhausted, but she looks it, too. "Arms," I murmur as I return with the shirt. My chest tightens. Why the fuck does the act of helping her dress almost seem more intimate than taking her clothes off? I shake my head, laughing internally at myself as she holds her arms up, poking them into the sleeves before I finish by pulling it over her head. I must be the only fucking college-aged dude who turns down a girl coming onto him and then sticks around to fucking help her get dressed. This is how I know I'm in big fucking trouble. This girl is going to rip my heart out if I let her. With that thought in my head, I carefully sweep her hair out from under the collar as she pulls the shirt down over herself.

"Thank you. You're really good at taking care of people." Her smile is disarming, hitting me right in the gut, despite the fact that I know she's about to fall asleep sitting up.

I nod. "I try." Clearing my throat, I pull the sheets down so she can get situated in the bed. Without much inner debate, I turn off the light, then circle the foot of the bed and get in on the other side. I lie flat on my back, and Lennon doesn't hesitate more than a second before she turns over and tucks her body into my side, resting her head on my shoulder. She fits just right, here at my side, and it's odd, but ... I breathe easier with her near me. And especially after the last twelve hours, I hardly want to let her out of my sight. Fuck, I'm so screwed.

I let way too many minutes pass by, staring at the ceiling and inhaling Lennon's scent before I break down and whisper, "Are you still awake?"

She shifts in my arms. "Yeah. I'm so tired, but I can't shut my brain off. Why, what's up?"

I hesitate. "Tomorrow night. Or, shit, I guess it's tonight at this rate. Anyway, I have somewhere I have to be."

She props herself up on her elbow. Her eyes glitter like diamonds in the dark. "Can I come?"

Huffing out a small laugh, I give her a perplexed grin. "I'm surprised you want to go anywhere with any of us after what you just went through, and I actually do think you'd like it, but …"

"But what?"

"My dad will be there."

"Oh." Her mouth snaps shut.

I stare steadily into her eyes. "It's okay if you don't want to tell me exactly what happened, but I intend to talk to him. Whatever he said upset you, and that's why you took off from the VIP suite in the first place, leaving you open to getting assaulted afterward."

A breath shudders out of her, and her gaze drops to my chest. "I don't—" Her face is unreadable. She shakes her head. "The words don't so much matter, it was just mostly some crap about me living with a bunch of guys. Insinuations. And then, he spouted some more BS when he put his arm around me." Her lips press together. "I hesitate to say this because he's your father, but I got the idea he could make even the most innocuous sentence dirty in some way."

She's not wrong. And rather than push Lennon after the day she's had, I'll ask the bastard to his face. Fucking asshole perv. I have plenty of ideas as to what he might have said to her. My eyes crash shut. "It's a fight, by the way."

"Wait, what?" Her eyes search mine. "But how do you do that and football? Don't you have to choose one sport per season?"

I squeeze my eyes shut for a moment. "It's not school sanctioned. It's not for sport. My coach doesn't know. Can't know. My dad runs these fight nights. It's a whole gambling set up ... and I fight for him."

"But"—her brows knit together—"isn't that dangerous for you? Like from a collegiate-sports perspective?"

"I ..." I wet my lips and simply finish by shaking my head. It's more dangerous than she knows. Not only because I'd get kicked off the football team if they knew, but also because sports gambling is currently illegal in Georgia. It's fucking stupid and reckless and a whole lot of other shit, too. She's fuckin' smarter than any of us gave her credit for.

Does Derek Pierce give a shit that it could be career ending for me? *No.* All he knows is that I'm his cash cow, and he has me over a barrel. If anyone ever found out what I did ... well, it'd all be over. Every minute, every hour, every day of my life. Every football practice, every time I puked from working so hard. All the blood, sweat, and tears that I've poured into my career. It'd all be over in an instant.

FOUR

LENNON

THE SUNSHINE STREAMING into my bedroom tells me I've slept in well past my usual hour. I figured I would, considering the sheer insanity of the last eighteen hours or so. Exhaustion had been like a heavy weight pulling me under the surface, but it's best that sleep had found me, because I'd so badly needed the rest. And by some miracle, I hadn't woken up to a nightmare either.

I wince at the soreness radiating throughout my body as I roll over in search of Bear's warmth. Finding cool sheets at my fingertips instead of his skin, I frown. Then it hits me. *Right.* He got up early to get a workout in. I remember now, he told me he was leaving. That must have been hours and hours ago.

I cover my eyes with one hand as my mind sets all of yesterday's events on replay and forces me to relive them, one after another. The ick from the OG Bastards at the football game. The abduction. The locker. The nightmare. Mason's attack—physical and verbal. The shit he told me about his mother. *I fuckin' killed her. Me, Lennon. I pushed my mother off a balcony.* I take a breath, remembering the rest. *You shouldn't have clawed your way into my heart, Kintsukuroi. Now you'll be next.*

I force my lungs to work, pulling air into my body and exhaling heavily. I'm overwhelmed. Completely and utterly crushed and beaten down by all of it. A *balcony,* like the one we share that he'd held me up against when I was so out of it, I couldn't fight back. How the fuck I'm not curled into a little ball and rocking myself after that ordeal is an excellent question. Everything hadn't even been going that great, but this weekend took the cake. What a disaster. And now ... I don't know what to think. Whether I should stick it out or run.

I press my fingers against my eyelids, struggling to understand my own thoughts, my feelings. *Fuck.* If I stay, I don't know how to handle Mason. What the hell do I say to him? How do we begin to interact with each other after the way he came after me? And worse yet, when I think back to how he'd fucked me free of that nightmare ... I seriously wonder if I'd turn him away if he came in here right now. There is something so twisted up and wrong about the way I feel when I'm with him. Yet,

I can't escape the pull I feel toward him, the connection we have. Two damaged souls trying to make each other whole. I feel the closest to him that I've felt to anyone in my life. He sees my broken pieces. The problem is sometimes he puts them—*me*—back together ... but last night he'd torn me apart.

It'd been Bear who caught me when I fell. Bear who'd held me and made sure I was okay. But also Bear who'd put his foot down when I tried to seek comfort through sex ... and despite the fact that I made him feel like I was using him, he'd still taken care of me. Fuck. I hate that I made him feel like that. I never in a million years would have thought he'd say no. But when he explained what was on his mind ... I guess I kinda get it. The guy hasn't said it in so many words, but I think he has real feelings for me—and he doesn't want to be the type who continues to say, *Fuck it, she's offering herself up to me, I should take advantage of that.* This time, he hadn't let us go there. And I'm not entirely sure how I feel about it.

Setting that aside for now, I pull myself out of the bed, moving gingerly, and head directly to the dresser to pull out some clothes. Once I have a pair of cutoffs, a tank top, and underwear in hand, I slip into the bathroom, peel the T-shirt I'd worn overnight off, and set everything else down on the counter. As I get a look at myself in the mirror, my eyes widen, and I gasp. *Oh, shit.* I scan my body with nervous eyes, concern mounting at every visible bruise and scrape. Turning around, my gaze drifts over the bandages that Bear had so gently applied last night. On the whole, it's worse than I thought it was going to be, which totally sucks. Usually, I'd just be like, fuck it. But wow.

Damage. Injury. Hurt. I'm a fucking mess—and all this? It's only the physical battering I'd taken. It'll take far longer to recover mentally. And knowing myself as I do, I'd love nothing more than to try to pretend none of it ever happened instead of dealing with it. I've been doing that for years with my abhorrence for small spaces. But there's no way I can live here with Mason and ignore what happened. It'd be uncomfortable for both of us and only come back to haunt me later. *Ah, fuck.* A cold sweat breaks out over my skin. I really don't want to deal with any of this. My heart rate accelerates until my head begins to spin. I slam my eyes shut, gripping the counter for balance.

Breathe, Lennon. This is temporary. *Most of it, anyway.* I give myself another five seconds, then do my best to shake free of the spiral I'd almost gone down. I'm gonna be fine. As I pick up one article of clothing after another, I fumble a bit as I get dressed, my hands trembling. *Get it out now, girl. Don't you dare show any of these brothers—whether it's Mason or any of the rest of them—a single sign of weakness.*

I glance at my reflection again. There's no way I can go downstairs looking like this, but maybe if I wear something with long sleeves, it will make my injuries not quite such a glaring issue. I head for the closet, turn the knob, and swing it open. My gaze narrows on the clothing hung there, and I almost immediately see what I'm after—a lightweight hoodie, the kind I like to wear at the beach for sun protection. I lunge into the closet and grab it by the sleeve. It pulls off the hanger no problem, but then my eyes fixate on that hanger while it swings wildly. A shudder shakes me to my core, but I blow out a hard breath and pull the closet door firmly shut behind me.

Leave it to me to give myself an immediate reminder that small spaces are never going to be my jam, especially after being trapped in a locker. I've hardly put any of my clothes in the closet, instead opting to keep most of what I brought in the dresser. The first day I got here, I thought for a moment I'd be okay with the fancy walk-in closet since it was within my bathroom, but nope. I fucking hate it.

I take a few moments to braid my hair over my shoulder, then slick a little lip gloss on and sweep mascara over my blond lashes. Good enough. As far as I know, I can hang here all day to catch up on the hellacious amount of reading I have to do for my psych and history classes.

I tug the hood over my head to ward off as many questions as I can and jog down the staircase, noticing with every bouncing step how quiet the house is. Suits me fine, seeing as how I'd rather not be interrogated about the handprint on my neck. I would imagine most of the brotherhood is resting or getting homework done for tomorrow's classes, so hopefully I'll be in the clear to grab something to eat.

In the kitchen, however, I come around the corner and almost run smack into Tucker. There's a moment of uncertainty as he bobbles his plate of food, and I stumble, but he manages to both save his food, as well as grab my arm to steady me. I flinch hard, jerking myself out of his grasp. *Fuck that hurt.*

He doesn't seem to notice anything is amiss, or if he does, he doesn't explicitly say so. He sits at the island with his food, even though I swear he was on his way out of here a moment ago. Much to my dismay, he appears to be getting comfortable. He tips his chin in my direction. "I didn't hear you coming."

"That's okay. I didn't know anyone was in here either." My gaze travels from Tucker's raised brow to where Warren is visible sitting at the dining room table, sandwich held up to his mouth. He takes a bite, never lowering it back to the plate as he frowns down at the assignment that seems to be stumping him. He taps his pencil on the table. Then, almost as if he senses I'm watching him, he looks up and lifts a hand in greeting— the one with the pencil, not the sandwich—but then goes right back to whatever he's working on. I refocus on Tucker. "Where is everyone, do you know?"

He glances down again, then back up, squinting at me, and I can't help but feel self-conscious. "Out of the house, mostly. Pierre is in the pool. Quincy and Arik got sent on some errand for next weekend. Something about masks that were special ordered." He shrugs, putting a chip in his mouth and chewing slowly.

He must be talking about the auction. Not really any of my business. I fully intend to make myself scarce that night, if possible. Pushing all of it out of my mind, I head over to the counter where the fruit bowl sits next to the fridge and select a shiny apple, then open a cabinet where I'd spotted an industrial-size jar of peanut butter earlier this week. Taking it over to the island across from Tucker, I rummage around in a drawer and then a cabinet until I come up with a knife and a cutting board. Quickly and quietly, I begin slicing the apple, but the entire time, I can feel Tucker's snakelike gaze slithering over me. It's almost as if he's waiting for a good time to strike.

Finally, I stop what I'm doing and glance up to see him semi-leering at me. "What?"

His gaze drops from my eyes to my throat. I give my concentration back to cutting up the apple, but a moment later, find myself adjusting the collar of my hoodie. He chuckles. "Goddamn, girl. Who've you been getting on your knees for? That's the first thing I noticed. They're all red. And your neck. Fuck." His lips twitch into a knowing smile that's designed to make me feel filthy.

For several seconds, I go right on with what I'd been doing. I pull a butter knife from the drawer in front of me and jam it into the peanut butter jar, scooping some out to put on a paper plate—there always seems to be a stack on the counter—and I let his words sink in. Slowly, I raise my eyes to his, giving him the most uninterested look I can manage. "Don't be a dick." He obviously thinks he has a shot with me. I have no idea how he always seems to be with a girl. Don't they see right through this?

The asshole gets up, circling the island until he's standing no more than a foot from me. He casually rests his hip against the counter as I slide my apples from the cutting board to the plate next to my peanut butter. He leans in, totally invading my space. My skin prickles with distaste, and he's so close I can feel his hot breath fanning over my face. It smells like potato chips. My heart picks up speed, but not in a good way, more like an irregular, nervous jumping around inside my chest. I glance over my shoulder through the doorway, but Warren is consumed by whatever he's reading.

As if I'm watching from outside of my body, his hand reaches up, and his fingers trail over the discolored skin on my neck. My body shivers violently, then in the next second I bat his hand away with a sharp slap. Meanwhile my other hand closes around the handle of the paring knife. I continue staring at him. He has no idea who he's messing with. The confidence in this prick is astounding.

"You like it rough." His eyes hold a dangerous glint. "So, let's stop this back-and-forth banter shit and get to the good stuff." His gaze slides over to the pantry door as he puts an arm around my back and pulls me against his beefy frame. "How about we step in there, and I'll let you get on your knees for me. I'll leave your neck alone, promise. But you can choke on my cock for a bit instead." He has the audacity to wink as he leans in close to whisper, "Your knees still have another round or two in them. Show me what I'll be buying this coming weekend."

I ease back a fraction with a fake smile on my lips, tipping my head up so I can stare straight into his eyes. At the same time, I get a firm hold on his shirt so he can't get away, then bring the tip of the paring knife up to poke into the soft flesh under his chin. "Go ahead. I dare you to say another fucking word," I grit out. "One. More. Word." My head buzzes as I wait for his answer.

"Warren. This bitch has a knife to my throat. Would you give me a hand? Text Duke. I'm sure her stepbrother would love to see what she's getting up to."

"What the fuck?" From the other room, a chair screeches as it's heaved back. A moment later, Warren approaches from behind me. His hand is both gentle and cautious when it finds my shoulder. "Lennon?"

I ignore him, shrugging off his hand, in favor of digging the knife's tip deeper. "Listen up, you awful fuck. Don't ever come onto me like that again with your lewd suggestions and insinuations. You don't know me. You won't ever know me, especially not like *that.*"

He outright sneers at me. "You don't call the shots around here, you crazy sleepwalking cunt."

Huffing out an amused laugh, I shake my head, and allow my eyes to bore into his. The longer I wait to respond, the more he seems to regret his words. My eyes flick downward for a split second. It could have something to do with the knife's blade that now has blood dripping down it. "You know what, though, you arrogant asshat, at this very second, I'm in complete control because I'm the one with the fucking knife. One false move from you and this 'crazy sleepwalking cunt' will flick her wrist and spill your blood all over the floor."

Warren clears his throat behind me, almost like he's trying to remind me he's there, but whether it's because he's on my side or Tucker's, I can't be sure. I simply don't know him well enough.

"What do you think? Is this what you thought it'd be like if you got close to me?" I cock my head to the side, studying the fear sliding over Tucker's features.

"Warren, what the fuck man." His eyes are wild as he looks past me to the guy he joined the brotherhood with two years ago, someone he should know well, I would think. But apparently, he didn't click with Warren, because he gets zero response. Maybe Warren is here to back me up, after all.

He leans in close to my ear. "This dickhead isn't worth it, Lennon. But I'll help you clean up the mess no matter what. What can I do to help you right now?"

I draw in a relieved breath and shake my head. "Nothing. I'd just like a witness who knows how pathetic this douchebag acted the second I didn't agree to give him what he wanted." I glare daggers at Tucker. "I didn't give in, didn't fall to my knees for you, so you automatically decide that makes me a bitch. You'd better not cross me again." I pull the knife away and in the next instant, shove Tucker hard to get him away from me.

He stumbles back into the cabinet, probing the spot I'd poked into his skin with his fingers. They come away bright, bloody red. "I'm reporting this."

"You do that," I spit, sparks shooting from my eyes. If he knew what I've been through in the last day, he'd be more careful with what he says to me or the next time he crosses my path, he might find that the paring knife slides a bit deeper. I must look pretty fucking scary because he turns and hurries out of the room. I wait a moment for my chest to loosen its hold on my lungs, then take a deep breath. My face is hot. In fact, all of me is a little overheated. Agitated. *Angry.*

"Don't worry about him. He deserved that. I'll back you up if there's any backlash." Warren's voice comes from behind me.

Exhaling hard, I pivot on my heel toward him, and his eyes widen as they drop to my hand. It shakes violently, the knife still clutched in my grip.

Warren's gaze flicks from the blade to search my eyes as he slowly brings one hand up to wrap around mine, steadying me. I see nothing but kindness and concern in his expression. As my heart pounds and pounds, he slowly brings a second hand up, covering mine with his. "You okay? Let me take that for you."

I nod, swallowing, and that's when my hoodie falls back off my head. *Oh, shit.*

If I thought his eyes were like saucers before, that was nothing compared to what they look like when his gaze drops to my neck. "Holy shit. What the fuck, Lennon."

I suck in a stuttered breath, my hands coming up under my chin to cover my throat. I blink at him, completely incapable of doing anything else.

"Lennon—" He stops himself, mouth snapping shut. "Fuck, I—" Closing his eyes for a moment, the struggle he's feeling practically screams through the quiet kitchen. When his eyes pop back open, he exhales harshly. "You can totally tell me to fuck off if you want. I saw some, uh ... stuff last night. Things I know I wasn't meant to see in the hallway. But shit." He pauses. "Sorry, I'm really having trouble with this. Um"—he lowers his voice as he turns to the counter and plants his hands on the granite—"I know we don't know each other that well, but if you don't feel safe here, I want you to know you can come to me, and I'll help you. I don't know what the fuck I'd do, but—"

"Thank you. You don't need to say anything else. I'm okay for now. I'll"—I tilt my head to the side considering the fact that I might have an ally in the house—"let you know if I need anything." I give him an apologetic smile. "I'm sorry you got dragged into this bullshit with Tucker. It kinda came out of nowhere."

He presses his lips. "Are you kidding? That was classic Tucker. Duke, Bear, and Mason aren't around? He figures he can pull rank and do whatever. Keep that in mind and be careful because I doubt he's the only one who'd like to get his hands on you. Why any of them think that's okay, I have no fucking clue, but they consider you fair game. Or maybe it would be more appropriate to say they consider women pawns in whatever games they like to play."

It disgusts me, but he only speaks the truth. I begin to walk away, but then I stop, turning on my heel again. Warren glances over his shoulder from where he was rummaging in the fridge. "You okay?"

I inhale deeply. "Yeah. You don't happen to know where Mason is, do you?"

He eyes me steadily, and I see the war behind his eyes over whether he should answer or not. "If he's not in the attic or in his room, you might try the pool house."

FIVE

LENNON

THE HEAT and humidity of the day hits me full in the face as I step out the back door. I glance cautiously in the direction of the pool. Pierre's at it again, swimming in the nude. I can make out his tanned ass cheeks below the surface of the water. What the fuck is this dude's problem? I shake my head and carefully avert my eyes as I give him a wide berth.

"Hey, sweet thing, wanna come for a swim?" He glides through the water to the deep end, coming up and resting his arms on the pool's edge.

"Yeah, no thanks." I wrinkle my nose, trying to play off the fact that I'm weirded out by his naked swims. It pains me to imagine how his buoyant man junk is floating about in there. "I'm not wearing a swimsuit."

"You don't have to wear one. Or any clothes, for that

matter." He gives me what I assume he thinks is a sly wink. Dude's definitely got a lot to learn about flirting in particular and women in general.

I press my lips together and shake my head as I keep walking. "I'll pass."

"Figures. Can't see a good thing when it's right in front of you. Instead you're fu—"

Stopping in my tracks, I pivot. That was one step too far. "I'm what, Pierre? May as well spit it out. I'm tired of the bullshit around here."

He snorts to himself, running his hand through his wet hair, pushing it out of his green eyes, which take a leisurely tour up my legs, making me wholly uncomfortable. "Yeah, I bet you're tired."

My head rears back. "I'm sorry, what?"

"I've heard you've been fucking *busy* entertaining the guys on that end of the hall—or busy fucking? Maybe I've gotten that part confused. But if you want a really good time, you'll bring that pretty cunt down our way." His brows lift, anticipating a response, but all I can do is laugh.

"Pierre, you're a huge dick, you know that?"

"Yeah. I do." He grins, then reaches down into the water, grabbing himself.

Ick.

I walk closer, squat down, then peek over the edge

into the water where he's fisting his hard little peen. "Hey, baby. You know what?"

Eager, the idiot smiles widely at me as he strokes himself.

"I said you *are* a huge dick, not that you have one." I roll my eyes skyward. "Like I'd be interested in that microscopic pencil you're packing, Pierre." I stand up and walk away, ignoring the ugliness he shouts at my back. *Jesus.* Warren wasn't fucking kidding. Fucking entitled assholes.

Before I can get to it, the door to the pool house opens. "What the fuck's going on out here?" Mason ducks his head out, eyes keenly and quickly assessing the situation. Thank fuck it's one I was able to handle on my own.

I don't bother turning around as Pierre sputters, "Sorry for shouting. I was just asking Lennon if she wanted to swim."

"And I'm pretty fucking sure I said no."

Mason shakes his head grimly, brows tugged tightly together, eyes focused on me. "You good?"

I roll my eyes, glancing over my shoulder toward Pierre, who has resumed swimming ... only this time he's doing a backstroke, and his miniscule erect cock is like a tiny man bobbing along, struggling to keep his head above the surface. I stifle a laugh. "Yeah. I can handle his kind." My gaze swings back to his dark eyes, which are pinned on me, curious. "I was looking for you, actually."

Mason bites down on his lip, scraping his teeth over it as he considers me. "You sure you want anything to do with me after last night?" His breathing is surprisingly steady, and he watches me with his head tilted to the side, a bit of a devilish attitude emanating from him. "I was pretty brutal."

The sweep of his sinful gaze over my body makes shivers roll down my spine—and not necessarily in a bad way. I get the feeling that how we handle this exchange might influence the future of whatever relationship we have. Enemies? Friends? Lovers? There are only so many ways to take what he did. He put his hand on my throat and squeezed hard enough to discolor my skin, hard enough that I struggled to breathe.

He crosses his arms over his chest, arching a brow at me, and I can't help but think he's doing it again. Trying to get me to retreat, albeit in a calmer fashion in the light of day. I'm getting a very distinct *Come on girl, you can't be this dumb* radiating from him. It pisses me off enough that my jaw locks up. My eyes flutter shut for a moment, disappointment hitting me hard. I hadn't held out much hope, but I thought there was a slim chance we could get past this. There's no way to do it, though, if he's going to reinforce those walls around his heart.

"Don't do this, Mason. Please." Drawing in a breath, I glance over my shoulder. We now have an audience. Kai, Brendan, and Pierre watch with interest from twenty feet away. "I think the least you could do is talk to me and try not to act like a complete dick. Can we go inside?" I point toward the pool house doorway. "I doubt you want any of those jackasses to hear some of what I have to say."

His chiseled jaw works to the side and to my surprise, he mutters, "Yeah, okay." He steps back inside, gesturing that I should follow. He closes the door behind me, but instead of coming further into the room with me, he leans his back against it. Out of the glare of the sun, I notice the dark circles under his eyes. He hasn't slept. Not a wink, if I had to guess. Doesn't make him any less striking, though. Women would kill for the definition in his cheekbones. Perfect fucking lips. Casually messy hair that looks good no matter how many times he runs his hands through it. It only gets better from there, but I refuse to let my gaze wander over his body—a body I enjoyed very much last night. My heart stutters. But I shouldn't be thinking about any of that right now. I need to focus on the things he said to me and find out if he was yanking my chain or if there was any truth to it at all.

I also absolutely refuse to hide the bruises he put on

me. Peeling off my hoodie, I set it down over the arm of a spacious couch that sits in front of a television screen. Then, without offering him so much as a glance in his direction, I go a step further, tying my long hair in a knot at the back of my head so it doesn't hide my contused neck.

Maybe it's a little vindictive, but I want him to get a good look at what he did to me with those beautifully artistic hands of his last night. He deserves to be held accountable.

I feel his eyes roaming over me as I walk around the place, taking it all in. It's furnished almost like a small apartment or a guesthouse, which I find kinda bizarre, but there are also two different bathrooms visible from here, and a shelf near the door loaded with neat stacks of fluffy towels. At least that part screams pool house.

"Kintsukuroi," he gasps out as I turn around to face him. Something like remorse weighs heavily on his shoulders, dragging them downward. His eyes scan and inventory every visible inch of my skin. "I—" His hands grasp the juncture between his neck and shoulders, like he needs something to hang onto as he pushes off the door. Step by step, he crosses the room until he's standing close enough that if he reaches out, he could touch me.

My breathing falters, lungs constricting, before I get

ahold of myself. I have to maintain control here. I raise one brow. "You what?" I glance down at the purplish splotches on my upper arms, then lift one hand to carefully skim my fingertips over the bruising on my neck. I dampen my lips. "To be fair, my arms were already a mess when you grabbed me last night. But the marks on the sides of my neck? Those are definitely your doing."

He bows his head, slowly shaking it while staring at the hardwood floor between us.

Is he shaking his head because he disagrees or because he can't fucking believe what he did? I'm hoping it's the latter but won't know for certain until he talks to me. "Are you just going to stand there?"

When he finally lifts his head and meets my gaze, the shell-shocked look in his eyes knocks me for a serious loop. He's disturbed by what he's seeing on my body ... much like I'd been disturbed by what he said last night about his part in his mother's death. And I know, deep down, that I added to the problem when I told him he wasn't the first to hurt me like that. I can't believe I even said that to him. I've never told anyone.

"Lennon ..." His jaw goes rigid, and I don't want him to reach the point where he flips his shit on me again, so I don't quite know what to do.

I lift my hands to the sides of my head, pressing my fingers to my temples and moving them in slow circles while I think. "Mason. I like you, but I don't know where we go from here if we can't talk about this."

He takes one deep breath. Then another. "I need you to—" His eyes squeeze shut. *"Fuck."*

I take a slow step closer, unsure whether he's closer to a wounded animal or one that might strike. I'm directly in front of him; there's no chance to get away if this goes terribly wrong. "Mase," I whisper.

The poor guy jumps a mile, but his eyes flash open, staring at me with such confusion that my insides flip over. He heaves out a breath, his expression dour. Forbidding.

I refuse to let him try to scare me again. "Don't."

I touch my hand to his abs, gently ushering him over to the couch. He lets me guide him, but hardly sits, immediately moving as far forward as he can go. His elbows rest on his thighs as he jams his hands into his hair. I get the feeling he's ready to fucking take off at any second, decide I'm not worth this.

I choose not to sit at his side. I need to be able to look into his eyes, so instead, I sit on the coffee table across from him. After a moment, he growls, "I don't know if I can accept you being nice to me."

"Poor choice of words—maybe it's more like you can't believe I'd be kind. But then that doesn't say a whole lot about what you think of me, now does it?"

He grits his teeth. "That's not how I meant it."

Giving him a small smile, I shrug. "I'm acting with compassion because I can tell you aren't some psychopath who hurt me for the fun of it. There is obviously something driving you to behave like this. And it's the same thing that gives you nightmares, causes you to get confused. I've told you time and time again—I get it. Sometimes life fucks us up."

He peers up at me, a heavy breath falling from his lips. And then another. "If we're going to talk about this, I need to know that you won't tell anyone else."

I nibble on my lip, weighing the potential consequences of making him a promise like this. It seems like an easy decision, one that in the past has gotten me in trouble. I inhale slowly and deeply, eyeing the anxiousness sliding over his features. "I would never tell anyone something that you told me in confidence." I hold up a finger so he knows I'm not done. "Not unless I felt I was in danger or thought you were somehow going to harm yourself because of whatever information you shared." I shake my head. "Because I won't have that on my conscience. I can't." *Not again.*

He worries the inside of his cheek with his teeth while his hands continue to claw through his hair. Finally, he gives a sharp nod. "Okay. Same. Will you tell me what you meant last night?"

I meet his eyes, a hand sneaking back up to my throat. "You mean ...?"

He nods. "You told me someone in your past had hurt you, put their hands on you just like I did—that I wasn't the first." His breath hitches, forcing him to stop and regroup before continuing. Chest rising and falling fast, he murmurs, "I know it sounds fucking psycho of me to change gears so fucking fast. I mean, look at what I did to you." He pauses to wet his lips. "I get that I scared the shit out of you, following you back down to your room the way I did."

"At least you aren't in denial about it."

He hangs his head. "I'm not. But, Kintsukuroi, I need to know. Being in the dark about it is messing with my head, tearing at my heart, consuming my every waking moment and thought. I haven't slept. Haven't eaten. Just—" He heaves out a breath. "Please tell me who hurt you."

I wet my lips, searching his eyes for any sign that he won't keep this information to himself. I see none. "One of my mom's boyfriends. He was supposed to be watching me. He didn't want to. He put his hands around my neck and squeezed. I woke up later, completely out of it." I shrug, then look at Mason from under hooded eyes. "I thought I had died or something. I couldn't remember at first what'd happened."

Horror washes over his features. "How old were you?"

"Little. I was five. It was terrifying. I'm a little foggy on the details after all this time, but I've never told a soul." I wet my lips, taking a shaky breath. "I remember waking up dazed and in pain. In a closet."

"Fuck. *Fuck.*" His jaw stiffens, loosely leashed fury flowing through his body, as if any second he's going to leap up and try to avenge what happened to me so long ago.

I close my eyes, gathering myself. The more I think about it, the shakier I become. So, I stuff that memory away with all the things that hurt me. My eyes flutter open to see Mason tussling internally with the fact that I've shut down that line of questioning. He drags in a labored breath. "Understood. I won't say another word unless you come to me about it." He grimaces, throwing out a hand. "Do you remember his name?"

I nod. "Yes. But only his first name. I have no way of knowing where he is." Searching his eyes, I don't miss the anger simmering there. "Leave it, Mason."

His teeth clench hard together, jaw twitching as his eyes pierce into mine. "You can trust me."

"I do." I press my lips together, closing my eyes for a moment. "Not even my mom knows exactly what happened. I refused to speak when she found me." I take a deep, calming breath. "So, I hope you take that to heart and can trust me, too." I stare steadily at him as I psych myself up for the question that's been festering inside me since last night—one of them, anyway. If I'm honest, I have so many, but ... I swallow past the nervous lump in my throat. He knows damn well what I want to know, but he waits, watching me with those deep, dark, knowing eyes of his. I rub my clammy palms on my thighs before I murmur, "Did you really push your mom off the balcony, Mason?"

I can practically see the sweat pop out on his forehead. He blinks rapidly, his hands reflexively making fists. His exhales are audible pants, and I'm scared for a moment that he will refuse to answer me, and we'll move backward in this sick little game of Truth or Truth we're playing. But then his eyes connect with mine and he nods ever so slightly. "Yes." The word comes out ragged and raw, so full of pain, I want to leap into his arms and hold him tight.

Remaining as calm as I can, I wet my lips. The rapid beats of my heart threaten to crack my chest wide open. "Tell me," I whisper.

His jaw twitches. He's looking at me, but almost right through me. If I'm not mistaken, he's lost in the memory. "My parents were fighting on the balcony outside their bedroom. I had to help her. I ran at them."

He scrubs his hands over his face. "I swear, I thought I was helping her, but I pushed her right over the railing."

The furious pounding in my chest stops for a split second, and my eyes bug out, but I quickly school my features, because Mason's hands are visibly shaking. He's gone deathly pale. I can't bring myself to ask any more questions, even though I have plenty. The most glaring and worrisome one is why he told me *I'm next*.

But the scared little boy he once was looks through his eyes at me, and all I can do is give in, climb onto his lap, and hold him as he trembles in my arms. "It's okay, Mase. That's enough. You don't have to tear open any more wounds for me today. I know this stuff is hard."

"I don't want to hurt you," comes his gasped admission.

I shake my head, holding him tight. "You won't."

His body quakes violently. "But I might."

SIX

MASON

O UT ON THE patio late in the afternoon, I drop onto a lounge chair beside Bear. Duke sits across from him, sunglasses on, blond hair looking even more sun-kissed than usual in the direct light. I tear my eyes away and focus on Bear instead. "Is Lennon around here somewhere?"

I feel like I need to put eyes on her. Make sure she's okay after our talk. It'd shaken me in more ways than one. The bruises I'd put on her, the things we'd discussed ... but I should have said more. I should have fucking apologized. And here this girl was, holding me together while I cracked in half.

And worst—it almost felt as if I'd threatened her all over again. I don't know if that's how she took it. But when I thought about it later, saying I *might* hurt her?

Yeah. I should have clamped my damn mouth shut. There's something about Lennon, though, that makes me want to tell her shit. To be the most honest version of myself that I can be. For her.

I'd seen her at the dining room table, working on some English lit assignment with Warren after we spoke, but haven't seen her since. She should really approach Bear about helping with that class. The man has an entire library in his fucking room.

"I kinda doubt she has anything to say to you." Duke gives me an odd look.

Bear blows out a breath. "If she fucking says no, you listen, Mason."

I work my jaw to the side, not letting on that she and I have already spoken. Who knows what they'd think if they knew. Duke would probably freak out that she was alone with me. And Bear would go all dad mode on me. "Got it."

Speaking of the big guy, he exhales heavily, then jerks his head in the direction of the house. "She found herself a spot in that plush chair in the sunroom and has been curled up reading for one of her classes ever since I came home, lollipop in mouth, crease right down the middle of her forehead. Seemed like she was deep in concentration, so I didn't bother her—I felt like she deserved a normal, quiet day."

That's a nice subtle jab, but I'll take it because I deserve that and more. It's probably for the best he doesn't know her day was, in fact, not quiet at all because of me. And now, Lennon is one of the few keepers of my most heinous secret.

Propping his sunglasses on top of his head, Duke eyes me, but doesn't say anything directly to me. Looks like I fucked things up with multiple people last night, and his silence is all it takes for my head to divert from the current conversation. Instead, I replay all the things I'd said to Duke last night in his room. I'd pissed him off with my taunting, but to his credit, all he'd done was point to the door. *Get the fuck out.* Probably for the best, or we'd have gotten into it again, and who knows what would've happened. I've still got a bruise on my cheekbone from the last round of punches we exchanged.

I give myself a shake. I need to tune in to what Bear and Duke are discussing. Duke's head bobs in response to whatever Bear said. "I heard they're bringing in some brawler from Gamma Chi tonight."

"Yeah. He's young, a sophomore I think, but supposedly a beast in the ring." Bear shrugs, rubbing his hands over his face before staring off toward the light flickering off the surface of the pool. "I'm not worried."

He's not lying, but he always needs some time to talk through upcoming fights. He likes to be able to think through strengths and weaknesses of his opponent, kind of size them up in his head. Whatever works for him. I've been in fights before, but I don't know if I'd be able to do what he does, willingly step in there, especially knowing that everyone is gunning for Derek Pierce's son. And Bear? He just doesn't lose. With every win under his belt, he becomes more of a temptation to every fighter out there. To win against Bear Pierce would be huge. No one expects to do anything but lose when they step into the ring with him—winning is an impossible dream. And no one bets against him because it's fruitless. It'd be quite the upset if Bear were to lose ... and Derek would lose his shit.

My lips twitch with a private smile. I might like to see that, actually. Bear's asshole dad thinks he can do no fucking wrong. He'd do well to remember that all this shit is illegal. If he's the least bit careless, he'll end up in the prison cell next to my father.

Sometimes, I see a look in Bear's eye ... like he wishes he could be anywhere else but that ring. But I can't fucking figure why he doesn't stand up to his old man. Then again, I'm sure that's easy for me to say with mine locked away.

Duke crosses his legs, resting his feet on the glass-topped coffee table. "Okay, so let's talk through this. What are his strengths?"

Bear grimaces. "Heavy hands, so I want to stay away from those. He's quick. But if we end up on the mat, it's pretty much over for him. I'm aiming to trade no more than a few punches before going for a lightning-fast take-down, grapple, and submission."

I sure hope Bear makes this fight a fast one because he looks fucking exhausted—and that's mostly my fault. I hope the interrupted sleep doesn't affect him too bad tonight. It was my crazy ass that'd woke him up by hollering at Lennon. I shake my head. What a clusterfuck.

My head is so mixed up, fight night will probably do me good, if only as a spectator. It's usually a pretty good adrenaline rush to watch Bear go to work on someone. I can only imagine what that surge of chaotic energy is like for him. Must be insane. "Good. Sounds like a cakewalk again." I steeple my fingers together, leaning forward on the lounger.

"I'll do what I have to do to win." His gaze meets mine and then Duke's, in turn. "I told Lennon she doesn't have to go. I don't want to subject her to my father again. I'd rather leave her home."

Duke nods, eyeing Bear. "I think you get the deciding vote, since it's your thing. Can't say I liked the way Tristan treated her yesterday, either."

I raise my hand. "Agreed, if you want my opinion.

And yeah, definitely one of the two of us doesn't attend the fight to stay with her." It should probably be me going with Bear. That leaves her here with Duke. I hope he can fucking handle it.

Bear takes a deep breath, shoving his hands through his hair and scrubbing his fingers over his scalp. Finally, he nods. "Yeah. I think that's for the best, even though it threw me off last week to not have the two of you there with me. Whether you like it or not, you're part of my routine." He grimaces. "I doubt she'd take off if left alone, but this week has me questioning what we're dealing with, you know? I'd think she's safe enough here, but ..."

My jaw works to one side, and I throw a hand out in irritation. "Yeah. Tristan can say she's got issues all he wants, but at this point, I totally don't think it's her fault." I lock eyes with Duke. "I think you nailed it last night when we were talking it through. These nightmares and the sleepwalking—he sees it as a growing mental instability when I'd bet money it's a trauma response to shit that's happening to her. Those are two very different things. And it's fucked up is what it is." I pause, meeting both Bear's and Duke's eyes as they nod their agreement. "You, uh ... Did you tell Tristan about some of this shit that's gone on with Lennon?"

His lips twist. "I assume you aren't talking about *your* antics."

I roll my eyes at him. "Or yours? You're as unpredictable as I am where she's concerned. Maybe if you admit—"

Bear gives a shake of his head cutting me off. "Let's focus, please. I can't handle the two of you fucking arguing at every turn. Not today."

Duke gives me a mildly perturbed look. "To answer your question, no, I haven't told him a thing since the sleepwalking incident."

I hold up both hands in front of me. "I thought you were talking to him about her yesterday. I guess I was mistaken."

"Nope, I told him things were fine and steered the conversation elsewhere." He shrugs. "I have to go with my gut. I was going to say something and then ... I couldn't. Something isn't sitting right."

We're quiet for several moments. I don't disagree with him at all, for once. Someone is definitely out to get her, and I don't fucking understand any of it. She's not the pain in the ass Tristan made her out to be, either.

Duke takes another swallow of his drink before shaking his head. "Frankly, I'm concerned what my father's next steps are if he thinks for even a second that there's a problem." He looks pointedly at both of us.

"Do either of you want him to yank her out of here?" His chiseled jaw clenches, and at our lack of response, he finishes. "Yeah, that's what I thought. But it'd help if there wasn't drama here, too." His eyes flick to me.

I cross my arms over my chest, feeling his accusation. "Yeah, well. I don't know what to say that I haven't already told you, Duke."

Bear grimaces, catching my eye. "Look, I heard her side of it. She felt like you were pushing her away. Trying to scare her." He presses his lips together. "You know what I think? I think she scares *you.*" He shrugs and arches his dark brow at me. "But what the fuck do I know?"

I don't know how to respond to that because I agree, so ... I don't.

Taking a deep breath, Bear leans in and lowers his voice. "I don't know how much either of you paid attention to the state of Lennon's body last night, but I hadn't realized until you two were gone—her back got totally fucked up inside that locker. Rubbed raw in spots. And that's the stuff no one will see. I didn't get a look this morning to see how bad everything else is, but I did notice she's wearing a hoodie. Considering it's ninety degrees today, I can only assume it's to hide the worst of what's visible on her arms and neck."

I drag my hand down my face and reach for the

vodka and Coke. I take a sip. And then a longer swallow. Bear's right. I said some scary shit to her. And I made her hurt. I hate myself for it. After our talk earlier, I fully admit to myself that I don't want to let go of her, even though it's dangerous for her the closer we get. I've already proven that. My toxic heart will ruin everything. "I spoke with her earlier." I lift my glass, the ice cubes tinkling lightly, and rub the cold glass over my forehead.

Duke's brow arches. "I'm confused. I thought you were going to talk to her about how you terrified the ever-loving shit out of her. But you're saying you already did."

"We talked. But I can't help it—I feel like there's probably more that needs to be said. I saw what I did to her. And yes, I feel fucking sick about it." I grit my teeth.

"I'm surprised she let you come anywhere near her after you fucking lost it on her like that." Duke cocks his head to the side, eyes disbelieving.

"She sought me out. And I'm fine now." I grind out the words, trying to force them into reality, to be the truth, even though it's only a partial truth.

Bear purses his lips, peering at me. "Is that like a girl's 'I'm fine' that's terrifying as hell or a *real* 'I'm fine'?"

"Fuck off. I'm good." Exasperated, I flip him off with a smirking smile.

Duke catches Bear's eye. "Leave it. If he says he's fine, he's fine."

My head swivels in Duke's direction, and my mouth drops open for a split second before I snap it shut. I wasn't expecting him to defend me. And from the stunned look on Bear's face that he tries and fails to mask, it caught him off guard, too.

Duke doesn't give me a chance to question his motives, as he clearly has more he's sifting through than just shit pertaining to me. He clears his throat as he sits up, resting his arms on his thighs. "In my mind's eye, I've had the scene in the locker room on repeat. Lennon out of it and so fucking panicked." He exhales sharply. "And I know you both think I have issues with her, and I mean, maybe I do, so why the fuck would I care, right?" He hesitates for a moment before vehemently shaking his head. "I'd never wish what happened to her at the stadium on anyone. I'd like to be the one to stay behind with her, if you don't mind."

"Agreed. I'll go with Bear. It's fine. I'll try to talk to her before we go. Or after. I just—" I don't know why I'm trying to explain myself, except that I'm embarrassed by my behavior.

Before either of them can say anything, Duke's phone lights up on the coffee table, vibrating against the glass. The three of us look at each other, apprehension thick in the air. If the three of us are together, there are only so many other people it's likely to be on the other end. What are the fucking odds that we'd been discussing the devil and he'd call minutes later?

With a stony, clenched jaw, Duke leans forward and taps to answer, then puts it on speaker.

Tristan, without pretense or greeting, barks out, "Son, how's it going?"

Duke's head is bowed, and he rubs his temples with one hand extended over his brow. "Fine," he bites out, "I won't be there tonight, just so you know. I'll be staying behind with Lennon."

"That's fine. She'd probably hate fight night."

I almost laugh aloud at that. I actually think our fucking feisty girl would love it. Tristan doesn't seem to know Lennon very well at all. Despite not being well-acquainted with football, she'd still loved watching Bear on the field—you know, until Derek bothered her. I happen to think she'd enjoy this sort of event, too. Hard to say if it's because of the sports aspect or if it's Bear himself. She gravitates toward him when sometimes I wish it were me she wanted instead.

Tristan's deep voice cuts through the speaker again. "And is there anything I need to be aware of? Pertaining to Lennon, I mean?"

My eyes dart to Duke's, then Bear's. I press my lips

together. Fuck, all I can do is trust that Duke's going to continue to go with his gut. I don't trust any of our fathers as far as I can throw them, especially not where Lennon is concerned.

Duke takes one heavy breath, then another. "No, not at all. She's been acclimating well to classes and the brotherhood. We're good to go. I'll let you know if anything comes up. Gotta go." He leans in and jabs the End Call button.

I give both of them a grim look. "I guess we'll see if that bites us in the ass later."

SEVEN

BEAR

I WATCH the minutes tick by as we edge closer and closer to the time Mason and I need to leave. We're due to arrive at the warehouse where all my old man's dirty fights take place no later than 10 p.m. It's far enough on the outskirts of town that it mostly goes unnoticed, except by the people who are in the know and are approved to be there. It also doesn't hurt that my father has an in with the police department. Strangely, there are never any patrol cars in the area on Sunday nights. Ever.

I stop next to Mason, who's sitting on the arm of one of the couches, on my way through the living room. I nudge his arm, then point one finger upward. "I've gotta shower and change. I'll meet you down here in twenty."

He nods. Looking down at his own attire, he huffs

out a laugh. He has smeared charcoal down the front of his shirt. "Looks like I'd better fuckin' change, too." Mason glances at Duke. "Text if you need anything tonight. I can always come home."

"We'll be fine," Duke grits, staring off at nothing in particular. Something's got him distracted, which isn't what we need. He said he wanted to be the one to stay with Lennon, so I hope to hell he shakes this mood. There's a chance he's beginning to spiral about the impending anniversary of Juliette's death tomorrow. Mason and I have been watching for it to happen, and Duke's definitely been a little out of whack the last few days as we expected him to be, but nothing major. So. Either he's going to be okay this year, or he's going to crash hard tomorrow. I guess we'll fucking find out as we continue to live through the aftermath of Juliette's death with him.

But Juliette isn't the girl he needs to focus on right now, and I'm about to open my mouth and point it out to him when Lennon's screams reach our ears plain as day all the way from the second floor. Duke, Mason, and I freeze in place, eyes wildly staring at each other as the heavy slam of a door sounds. My heart lurches, and everything seems to stop for a moment, like we're in a vacuum. A void.

And then, like I've been slapped upside the head, it

all comes roaring back. Duke growls out "What the fuck," and we're off in the next second, plowing through the living room. In our mad dash, I plant one foot on the couch cushion and leap over the back while Duke hurdles the coffee table. Mason knocks into Kai and Brendan coming out of the den and shoves them out of the way.

"What the fuck's going on?"

"Holy shit, where's the fire?"

None of us stop for even a second to answer their questions.

We take the stairs two at a time, my mind pushing me faster than my body would normally ever allow me to go. I charge down the hallway in front of Mason and Duke, throwing the door open to her room.

Lennon stands stock-still, staring at the bathroom door on the far side of her room like she's in a mother-fucking trance. As my heart pounds in my ears, I approach her. "Lennon, what the—?" But I don't finish because I can't tell if she even knows I'm here. Duke and Mason enter the room a second later, coming to a rather jarring stop because what's before us is definitely ... odd.

A moment later, Lennon snaps out of it, draws in a deep breath, and pivots to face us. Her face is pale and the light in her eyes has dimmed. "Someone's been in my room."

Perplexed doesn't begin to describe my confusion.

"How do you know, Kintsukuroi?" Mason steps forward, reaching for her, but she shakes her head.

I looked that fucking word up once it became clear Mason wasn't going to drop the habit of using it for Lennon. Kintsukuroi is the Japanese art of repairing pottery by mending it with gold. Within our imperfections and our flaws lies the potential for beauty and strength. Once the broken pieces are put back together, we are sturdier and more beautiful than we were before the damage was inflicted. I can see why Mason's chosen that in reference to her.

I give myself a stern shake, focusing on Lennon again, only to find her brow furrowing as she backs up a step.

"No." The plea is clear in her eyes as she stares at us, for all the world looking like she's about to completely break down. "You wouldn't have done that. Would you?"

The truth slams into my gut. Lennon doesn't want to believe that we'd do whatever has upset her ... but she's also nervous as hell that we have. It makes my heart plummet to my feet.

Mason looks at her with wounded eyes. "I didn't do anything. Promise. The last time I was in your room, you were with me. We all were."

Her lips press together tightly. Her chest is rising and falling way too fast. She needs someone to calm her down, and it kills me that she doesn't seem to know if she can trust us.

Duke rubs one hand over his jaw, eyeing her. "Stella Bella ... what are we talking about?"

Their blue eyes connect—his wary, hers fearful. "Duke. Tell me you didn't do it."

"Do what?" he grits, but he's frowning, and I can read him well enough to be positive he doesn't have a clue what she's talking about either.

"You know how I am. Small spaces. Closets." She huffs out a disturbed laugh, her arms flailing wildly around her. "And I guess we can add lockers to the list. But this is—" Her eyes crash shut, and she shakes her head. "It's so fucking wrong. It was my favorite."

Before I can ask her favorite *what,* she shifts, grabbing my hand and leading me to the bathroom. I side-eye her but twist the doorknob and open the door. At my side, she jumps a fucking mile, which startles the shit out of both Mason and Duke. If it were possible for someone to physically come out of their own skin, Lennon would have done it the instant I opened the door. I warily glance at her again and clear my throat. "You want me to go in there?" My voice comes out all gruff, betraying my concern.

"Yes. I can't. It's hanging up inside."

Craning my neck, I can see the cavernous closet in her bathroom standing wide open, but I can't tell what she's referring to. I look over my shoulder, meeting Mason's eyes, silently pleading with him to do something for her.

"Lennon. Come stand here with us." Mason holds a hand out to her.

Surprisingly, she does, but turns right back around so she has eyes on the bathroom door. "It freaked me the hell out. There's no way I would have left the closet open like that, no matter how tired I was today. No way. And then ..." A shudder runs through her entire body.

Mason slips an arm around her back, tugging her close to his side. To my surprise, not only does she let him touch her, but Duke's hand finds its way to her shoulder, and he gives it a squeeze and doesn't let go. Lennon stands perfectly still with a hand pressed over her heart while I turn and disappear into the closet on her behalf.

What. The. Fuck. It's immediately obvious what's got her so freaked out. There's a pretty black dress made sordidly ugly by the red paint dripping down the front from the haphazard letter *w* that was drawn on it.

My brain clicks back to tenth grade English class. *The Scarlet Letter.* Poor Hester Prynne was made to wear a red letter *a* on her clothing, which stood for adultery and was meant to shame her for her sins. If I had to make a guess, I'd say whoever did this was thinking along those basic lines. So ... *w* for whore?

I will put my fist through the face of the prick responsible for this. My stomach roils, and I take several deep breaths as I stare at it, not wanting to bring it out of the closet. But at the same time, Mason and Duke should see this bullshit, and we need it the fuck out of her room.

With my jaw locked, I pluck the hanger from where it was hooked and emerge from the closet. "This is pretty fucked. She's right. Especially when you add in that whoever did this likely knows her well enough to give her the one-two punch of the closet shock on top of this bullshit." I give the dress a pissed-off shake as I turn it around for them to see. "And this didn't happen on campus. Some sick fuck was in our house. In her room."

"What the fucking shit?" Mason grits out, his eyes ablaze as he takes in the ruined dress.

"Fuck! Seriously? Who the fuck does something like that?" Duke's face burns red, an impressive scowl gracing his features.

At their outburst, Lennon flinches between them. Her gaze finds Mason's, first. "A-After that day you drew on me, I wondered for one agonizing second if I should do something like this to all my clothing and walk around the house like that. But … I know better. And this does nothing but make me sick to my stomach." The paint drips slowly from the letter, making it look like it's bleeding.

"I don't know what the hell to think." Mason's hold tightens on Lennon, and I'm surprised for a second time when Duke inches closer on her other side.

Is this Mason's fault that someone would think to do this? Is it Duke's? They've both slung that word—and worse—at her. Fuck. What a mess. And who? Who had access to her room and this fucking house except one of our own? My stomach pitches at the thought.

"You didn't do it?" she asks, her head swiveling to meet each of our gazes in turn.

Mason shakes his head. "I was up—"

"No." She stiffens, eyes flashing. "I don't need to know where you were. You don't need an alibi. I need you to tell me to my face that you had no part in this. I'll believe what I see in your eyes more than I will any explanation."

Unable to handle the idea that she'd think for one second I could have done this, I hang the dress from one of the knobs of the dresser, then come over to stand in front of her, tip her chin up with one finger, and stare steadily into her eyes. "I did not do that to you," I rasp.

Duke grimaces, his fingers flexing into her skin until she turns her head to look at him. "I've said some shitty stuff, but no." He shakes his head firmly. "No. Not a fucking chance in hell, Stella."

Fuck, I hate that someone thinks it's okay to continue jabbing away at her like this, and even worse that this person, whoever it is, has gotten under her skin on our watch.

Mason presses his lips against the side of her head. "Kintsukuroi, look at me." She turns her head, and his eyes bore into hers. "Doesn't matter what hasn't yet been said between us. You know me. You do. This was not me."

Lennon's lips curve the slightest bit at his words, but then she nods and draws herself up. "If I choose to believe the three of you ... and something inside me says I should ... then that means someone else is doing this to me because I sure as hell didn't ruin my favorite dress on purpose or lock myself in *anywhere.*"

"It makes me really fucking uncomfortable to say so, but this was done by either someone in this house or someone with access. We have a real fucking problem."

She winces, her gaze darting to each of us before her eyes close and she shakes her head. "I was trying to blow it off, but yeah. This could have been Tucker. Or Pierre. And that's just based on today."

My head cocks to the side like an animal trying to decide whether or not to pounce. My fuckin' teammate better not have had anything to do with this. "Why do you say Tucker? What's that little fucker done?"

"First of all, the only one who could get away with calling him little is you, and you know it. But second, I embarrassed him in front of Warren earlier. I, uh ..."

"Stella, spit it out." Duke's positively bristling at her side.

"He implied that my red knees must mean I was getting on them for the brotherhood. And he saw the bruising on my neck, too. Suggested I show him what he'd be buying at the auction."

Fury pounds through my veins, and my fists clench so hard my knuckles turn white. The level of aggravation makes my words scrape up out of my throat, gritty and raw. "Tucker. That prick is gonna get his ass beat when I get my hands on him. Might happen here. Might be at practice. Either way, he'll regret it."

Lennon's eyes go wide. "I happened to be cutting up an apple at the time. I think it took him a little by surprise when I held the paring knife under his chin." She gives us a worried look. "I made him bleed. It was running down the blade. I thought it was the right move at the time. But now ... maybe not."

Mason grits his teeth. "Fuck. Pierre was acting like a

dick earlier, too. Trying to coerce her into the pool with him."

I growl. "What the fuck did he say?"

Lennon dampens her lips with her tongue, almost as if she's stalling for time, trying to decide how much to tell me.

"Stop."

Her eyes flick to mine, registering the anger rising inside me.

My voice comes out sounding lethal when I murmur, "I need for you to tell me what that asshole thought he could get away with."

"Let's just say he was very suggestive, and he was touching himself while talking to me. I wasn't going to say anything—thanks, Mase—because it wasn't as big of a deal. He's obviously caught wind of whatever everyone thinks went down last night and implied the guys at the other end of the hall would like to show me a good time. Wait— I think it was more that they could show me a *better* time. In any case, Quincy and Arik are also constant assholes to me, and Kai and Brendan aren't much better. I don't know how we could ever pinpoint a culprit." She bites her lip with a shrug.

Duke's blue eyes have gone hot, like there's a fire raging in there. "Stella," he huffs before stopping to scrub his hand over his cheek, "you've gotta fucking tell me when this shit happens. It *is* a big deal. All of it."

She wets her lips again, tongue slicking over them slowly as she considers him. "And you'd do what? Join in with them?" The challenge—the dare—is clear in her eyes.

My eyes flick between them and then to Mason, who lifts his shoulders ever so slightly. He recognizes it, too. The tension between Lennon and Duke is a palpable thing. Heavy. Vibrating. Intoxicating. Raw. They don't have a clue how to handle it, either.

I let out a hard breath when neither of them says a damn word. "I can't decide whether knowing exactly what went down today will be distracting for me or whether it'll fire me up enough to knock this Gamma Chi kid out with one punch."

Agitation washes over Duke's features as he looks down at his watch. "Fuck, we don't even have time to sufficiently deal with any of this right now—"

Mason shakes his head, interrupting. "This happened under our noses with all four of us here. With this unresolved BS, there's no way in hell we're splitting up tonight." His eyes connect with Duke's. "You should come with Lennon."

I nod. "I'd feel better knowing no other crazy shit is

happening while I'm trying to concentrate on not getting knocked out. You okay with that, Little Gazelle?"

"Yes." She gestures to the dress hanging from the knob of the dresser. "I need time to get this out of my head. Can— Can someone get rid of it?"

"I'll take care of it." Mason hooks the hanger over his finger. "Meet all of you downstairs in five."

EIGHT

LENNON

MY EYES ARE WIDE as Mason pulls the SUV up to an old, run-down warehouse. I'd never guess what goes on inside—not that I'm one hundred percent sure what I'm getting into, but I think I have an idea. Fights. Gambling. *Definitely*. Drinking? Drugs? *Quite possibly*.

And while I want to check all this out and learn what these fight nights of Bear's entail, me being here is kind of a problem. Tristan and Derek will no doubt be present, which is why the guys didn't want me coming tonight in the first place. Not after the shit show in the VIP box. Tristan talking about me wearing a jersey to show off my feminine form ... Derek suggesting I'm fucking the entire brotherhood ... and then putting his arm around me while telling me his son doesn't like to share? *Get the fuck out, old man.*

But I have no wish to stay home, either. Someone is out to get me—someone who knows way too much and has access to me all the time. I've been attacked after class, at the football stadium, and had things in my own damn room defiled. There simply isn't a safe place for me, and that thought makes my head pound and my skin crawl. So yeah, I get why the guys are freaked out.

I force myself to take some deep, cleansing breaths, my gaze moving over each of them as Mason puts the SUV in park. They've promised me that they aren't responsible for what's going on. And I believe them. I do. But that doesn't mean I'm not still scared shitless. Possibly even more so because I can't fathom where the threat is coming from. At least being here keeps my mind off how the hell I'm going to sleep alone in my room tonight.

Mason and Bear roll quickly out of the vehicle. My eyes follow as they meet at the front of the car, their heads immediately together in quiet conversation. I frown. Game plan, maybe? I try to read their body posture and facial expressions, but I'm not getting much out of it other than the fact they're both tense and keep looking my way.

Mason catches my eye and winks. Maybe he sees the tension in me, too. I wouldn't have thought after last night that Mason and I would even be approaching okay, but here we are. There's definitely more buzzing around in that head of his, but I knew what little he'd shared had been huge to him. It makes me wonder how much detail Bear and Duke have. Do they realize the exact circumstances that led to Lily Mikaelson's death? I glance at Duke from the corner of my eye. I'd ask him, but if he doesn't know everything, I'd feel like shit for even opening my mouth and putting focus on it.

As I reach for the door handle, Duke touches my forearm, bringing my attention to him. "Here's what we're doing, Stella." I scrape my teeth over my bottom lip, my eyes flicking to his. *Bossy.* "We'll enter through there"—he points toward the old rusty-looking door we'd pulled up next to—"and try to keep out of sight. Bear's dressing room isn't far, and I figure we'll stay there for the most part, you and me. I don't want to alert my father that either of us are here after I told him earlier this afternoon we specifically wouldn't be."

"I won't get to see the fight?" My heart does a little dip, and I know I'm pouting, but I can't seem to stop myself.

Duke smirks, his lips twisting. "No promises. Once things get going, I can see if there's a spot out of the way where we can watch some of the action. We have a ways to go before it even starts, though. There will be a preliminary match before Bear's, which is the main event, and during that time, we help him get ready. Kinda get in the zone, wrap his hands, get him all suited up."

"Okay, that all sounds fine."

"You and Mason ... You're good? He's made it clear he has more stuff he wants to talk to you about." His concentrated blue stare makes me wonder how many details he knows about my attic misadventure last night, but also ... it's shaking me that he seems to truly care.

I look out the windshield at Mason, who is animatedly gesturing as Bear says something to him. "Yep. We're fine for now. Kinda? Weird, I know. Hard to explain." My gaze slides back to Duke's, and I smile awkwardly. "So, how about after the fight? What happens when it's over?"

Duke's shoulders lift a bit, and he shrugs. "He celebrates in whatever way he chooses. He usually comes back to the dressing room for that. And then when we want to leave, we'll sneak you back out the way we came."

I can't quite tell, but I have a gut feeling Duke is leaving a little something out of his explanation, but there's no time for questions because all of a sudden, he gets a signal from Mason and jerks his head toward the door. "Let's go."

I tug on the door handle, but before I've managed to

deal with the heavy door, Duke's right there, pulling it open, and he holds his hand out for me, helping me from the vehicle. I gingerly step down onto the running board. I look up to find him frowning as he watches how awkwardly I'm moving.

"Hurting, huh?" He studies my fiercely wrinkled brow as I ease myself down to the asphalt.

I press my lips together, giving him another small smile. It feels weird to smile at him, I'm so used to defending myself and scowling at him. "Yeah. Achy. I look like a piece of rotten fruit under my clothes. I'm covered in bruises."

His expression darkens, and from the way his gaze darts downward, he'd like to examine every inch of me, taking an accounting of all my injuries. And I don't know why my mind goes where it does, but I imagine what it would be like if he found the person responsible. All the havoc he'd wreak to pay back the asshole for each and every fucking bruise on my body. It definitely feels like an odd thing for me to consider. Especially since part of the injuries were inflicted by Mason. I absolutely won't be bringing it up. I'm not a fan of rocking a boat unnecessarily, and the two of them have been the tiniest bit nice to each other this evening, which is an interesting switch for them. I don't want to mess that up, even if I think it's strange as fuck and throws me off kilter.

I take a deep breath and watch as Mason gets back into the SUV and drives off, leaving me here with Bear and Duke. "Where—" My eyes follow the vehicle as it rolls away.

"Just to the corner where there's an old parking deck. It's less obvious than everyone parking right here," Bear answers, collaring my neck with his big hand and guiding me toward the door. "He'll meet us inside in a few minutes." His eyes flick to Duke's. "You brief her on what to expect?"

"A little. She's not going to get the full experience, anyway."

I shrug, eyeing both of them. "You really think it's bad if they know I'm here?"

Duke grits his teeth, and I can tell he's mulling over something in his head. "My father seemed far too relieved for my liking to find out I wouldn't be here. Makes me wonder what shit these fuckers are up to tonight. It's probably for the best that I am here, in case things get hairy."

What the fuck does that mean?

"You're not wrong," Bear agrees in his deep-throated growl before grazing the side of my forehead with his lips.

With that, Duke yanks the door open. The hinges protest loudly, and he turns and lifts his finger to his lips before we enter. When I move to follow, Bear holds me back. "One sec."

It seems like we wait forever, but it's probably more like a minute before Duke pokes his head out to wave us inside. I follow him with Bear bringing up the rear. There doesn't seem to be anyone around, but I'm grateful to Duke that he'd thought to come in and check things out first. We hurry down a dimly lit hall, only one bulb dangling from the impossibly high ceiling. It casts strange shadows on the walls, making my heart jump inside my chest. But there's no one in sight, and at the end of a hall, Duke throws open a door and ushers me into a decent-sized room. I glance over my shoulder to see Bear thump his hand on Duke's shoulder as he passes.

Duke closes the door as he steps into the room, automatically heading for a cushy-looking chair and dropping into it. It's clear he's comfortable here.

Bear stops when he reaches me and drops his bag on a table before slowly pushing the hood off my head. "Even though it wasn't planned, I'm glad you're here." His warm hazel eyes search out mine. He smiles, then before I see it coming, he grasps either side of my head, tilting it back. He crushes his mouth to mine, catching me by complete surprise.

At the onslaught of Bear's lips, I melt against his chest, my arms circling his back. With bold, greedy strokes, his tongue licks into my mouth, kicking my heart into overdrive. Ah, fuck. I inhale his clean scent. I like it a whole lot, but I'm actually looking forward to post-fight Bear. I've had sweat-slickened chest, breath heaving, eyes-only-for-me Bear on my mind the entire way over here. It might be some crazy fantasy, but the idea of him in beast mode just does something to me.

A noise off to my right reminds me we aren't alone in this room. It sends some fiery, wild thrill through me to know Duke's watching Bear kiss me—watching and not throwing a temper tantrum. And whether that's because he's getting used to seeing us together or perhaps because he doesn't want to screw with Bear's pre-fight mojo or some other reason entirely, I may never know. But I do know that it lights me up inside, the same way it did that night when I watched the sorority chick suck him off. He'd watched me as well, tracking everywhere Mason's hands had roamed over my body. I know if I turn around, that same heat will be radiating from his eyes. The same want. The same desire.

Bear groans, drawing my attention back to him. Our breathing is labored, hot, heavy. His thumbs stroke over my cheeks, and he worships my mouth, the licks of his tongue sensual and sure. He pulls me close to him, letting me feel every toned muscle. As is always the case when Bear kisses me, I could go on and on, not realizing the passage of time. With Bear, I'm able to just let go. There's no place for trepidation with him. There's no anxiety or uncertainty. We simply *are*.

A knock at the door has me clutching Bear's waist tightly. We freeze in place.

"It's just me."

Mason. Thank goodness because I wasn't sure whether I was supposed to hide behind the door or what.

Duke shakes his head at the two of us, then gets up from the chair he'd crashed into to let Mason in. As soon as he opens the door, he groans out, "Just a warning, there's a lot of lips and tongue action going on in here."

Mason slips through the doorway, turning to lock it behind him. He throws Bear a sly wink. "Just be careful, man. You don't want to fight with a hard-on."

I ease back and give Bear a teasing grin. "Oh, shit. I don't want to interfere with your usual pre-fight routine." I look over my shoulder, for the first time noticing the couch on the far wall, and point. "I'll just sit over there and watch you do your thing. I'll stay out of the way."

And so I do, curling up and watching as Bear strips out of his shirt and drops the joggers he'd worn over. *Fuck me.* The compression shorts he has on don't hide a damn thing. That monster cock of his is a prominent bulge in his stretchy pants, and I suddenly wonder if Mason was really joking all that much about the hard-on and how he's going to manage the beast in his pants during this fight. My questions are answered when Bear rummages in his bag and comes up with a cup that he tucks his junk into before he secures it with the strings attached.

My brows dart together, watching the process. "Wow. That's impressive. But also a little weird."

"Gotta protect things. If you've ever taken a full-impact groin hit, you'd know why." Bear shoots me a grin before knocking his knuckles against the hard cup. "Can't feel a thing."

I bite the corner of my lip, watching as he pulls on another pair of shorts over what he's already got on. Tight shorts. Damn. There's hardly anything left to the imagination. My mouth waters.

"Help me wrap my hands?" Bear's question is aimed at Mason. "I hated not having you here to do it last week." He walks over and takes a seat at the same table where he'd dropped his bag.

"Aw, Bear." Mason smirks. "Are you saying what I think you're saying, big guy?"

"Shut up, Mason, and get them wrapped."

Mason's grin at Bear's barked command—it's something that I haven't seen often, and to be honest, the pureness of it is shocking. He crosses to where Bear sits and quietly begins the process of securing his hands for him. It's obvious from the ease with which Mason goes about the task that this is a long-standing tradition between them.

They're midway through the second hand—we're already hearing the screams and shouts from the first fight in progress—when there's another knock on the door. I lurch upright, my heart jumping into my throat. *Oh, shit.*

NINE

LENNON

DUKE'S GAZE darts to Bear and Mason, and they both shake their heads. "Over there, Lennon." He points toward a small bathroom in the corner of the room, but immediately cringes realizing what he's asking of me. "Fuck. Shit. Um. You can leave the door open. You shouldn't be visible from the doorway."

"Okay." I suck in a breath and launch myself across the room. Once I'm sequestered in the bathroom area—I stand right at the doorway because it's a small, small room—Duke strides over to the door.

"Who is it?" he barks.

"It's just me. I wanted to wish Bear good luck."

Me is the owner of a decidedly feminine voice. My hackles go up, and I can't logically explain why, except—

I hear the door open, then Duke's voice. "Hey,

Morgan. Um, Bear is kinda in the zone right now. Not taking visitors."

I lean forward to catch a glimpse of who the hell he's talking to. This Morgan girl stands in the hall right outside the room, big boobs stuffed into a tiny sports bra and rocking a pair of stretchy shorts covered in sequins. She's curvy and gorgeous. And much to my dismay, my jaw tightens and my hands clench into fists. The other thing I notice? This girl's eyes, complete with sparkly eyeshadow that matches her shorts, are positively glued on Bear.

"Oh, come on, can't I say hi? I'm his lucky charm." She gives Duke a beguiling flutter of her eyelashes.

I stiffen, my lungs seizing up, which doesn't really matter because I'm mortified to find I'm holding my breath. My eyes flick to Bear where Mason is finishing up with his second hand.

He finally glances up and offers this girl a reluctant wave with the hand that's already wrapped.

The small smile she'd been wearing goes megawatt at his perusal, her entire face lighting up with it. "Good luck, Bear!" She subtly shifts, showing herself off to her best advantage. They obviously know each other. "I'll be here after the fight to help you cool down." She tosses him a little wink.

He smiles back with those same lips that were on

mine not twenty minutes ago. He looks at her with eyes that I could have sworn only saw me. I take a step back as an uncomfortable, sick feeling slithers its way through me. *Jealousy.* This chick is straight-up pissing me off, and I don't know why because odds are very good that she has no clue I exist or what Bear and I have been up to this week. Fuck, am I the other woman?

I edge forward again so I can take a better look at her. She's got long red hair—what is it with these guys and redheads?—that falls in beautiful waves over her shoulders, a smattering of freckles over her pert little nose, and pretty brown eyes. Eyes she only has for Bear. I swallow hard.

Or maybe I'm feeling this way because Bear is currently ignoring the fact that I'm standing here listening to his, what? Girlfriend? Ex? Ringside chick? Or by her own words, his fucking *good luck charm* go on about how she's going to take care of him after the fight? Is she insinuating what I think she is? Because fuck that.

Ignoring our interloper for a moment, Bear checks in with Mason. "How much time do I have?"

Duke glances over his shoulder at me, and our eyes connect. I'm waiting for him to say something smart, something he knows will sting if he lets it loose. Something that will tell Morgan I'm here. And being made to fucking hide myself. No fucking thank you. But all I see in his eyes is a warning. Don't fucking do it.

Ignoring his advice, I step out of the bathroom and into view of the girl at the door, my brow arched and a sassy smile on my lips. "Hi." I cock my head to the side and watch the smile fall from Morgan's face. "Have we met?"

Her mouth opens, then closes again with a snap that I'm surprised doesn't rattle her teeth. "Who are you?"

I laugh. "Me? I'm the upgrade, bitch."

She looks flabbergasted. "Wait, what? Bear?"

His gaze meets mine, his golden eyes alight with curiosity.

Without looking at her, I jam the knife in deeper. "Oh, and Morgan? Don't bother coming around after the fight. I'll be taking care of all his cooldown needs."

His brows hike up on his forehead, interest radiating from every part of him.

Morgan heaves out what sounds like an exasperated breath, but that's simply a guess, because I can't tear my gaze away from the man in the center of the room, the gleam in his eye intensifying the longer this carries on. My lips twitch, but I try to hold back my smile. She flat-out whines a moment later. "Where the fuck did you come from? I don't get it."

"Straight outta your worst nightmare, honey. And

don't you forget it. Now, get the fuck out." I take a breath, my eyes flicking over to the doorway. "Duke? Could you shut the door for us so we can continue with Bear's fight prep?"

He practically chokes on his own spit. "You got it." He pushes the door shut in her face, then turns around to lean against it, arms folded over his chest. "So much for us keeping quiet."

"It's not like I told her my name."

Mason is trying hard not to laugh. "Are we allowed to call you 'the upgrade'? Because that was funny as hell."

"No." I roll my eyes. "How else was I supposed to handle that?"

Duke shakes his head. "I was waiting for you to tear her throat out, honestly. I'm impressed that there was no bloodshed. Especially now that we know you weren't afraid to hold a knife to Tucker's throat."

"Hey, the night is still young. She comes back around, and it'll be"—I drag my pointer finger across my throat—"all over for Sparkle Pants." I joke, but I'm also mildly concerned what my reaction will be if I'm forced to deal with her again.

Mason snorts with laughter as he gets up. "I'm going to check and see where they're at out there. Be right back." Duke steps aside and lets him exit, then shuts the door behind him before crossing the room to take his seat again.

Bear crooks his finger at me. Of all their reactions, his is the one I'm most concerned with. This is his event. His fight. In the moment, I thought I was doing the right thing. But now I'm nervous. This is awkward. We've fucked. We like each other. But it's not like we've made any sort of commitment to each other. It's not like I've staked a claim ... nor has he. In fact, I've been with Mason, too, so who am I to say that Bear can't—

I stop my internal battle to cringe at myself. He can do what he wants. And now I wonder if I've pissed him off by sending someone away who is part of his fight routine. My face heats. Oh god. I messed up.

Sometimes I forget what a big guy he is until I'm confronted with him directly. He holds out a hand to me, and when I place mine in his much larger one, he tugs me into a straddle position on his lap, the steel cup meant to protect him during the fight hard between my legs. Air gusts from my lungs, and I try to draw another breath, but it hitches as I look into his eyes. Bear pulls me closer and whispers in my ear, "Holy shit, Little Gazelle. I can practically see the wheels grinding inside your head."

I aim a worried half smile at him. "How badly did I fuck up?"

His hands slip from my waist upward, until his thumbs are brushing the sides of my breasts. "I don't know yet. Did you mean what you said when you were trying to get rid of her?" He shifts, lifting his hips, the cup dragging right over my clit.

I blink, an electric jolt crashing through me as he does it again. And again. My mouth drops open. "W-what do you mean?" Pinpricks of white-hot lust burst inside every cell of my body. He runs his hands down, cupping my ass, and guides my movement. My toes barely reach the floor, so I'm forced to hold onto his shoulders as the intense feelings riot within me. I breathe in his air and stare into his gold-flecked eyes.

"You said you'd be taking care of my cooldown needs. Did you mean it?" Our lips are only a hair's breadth apart, and I close the distance with my tongue as I flick it over his bottom lip. I can imagine what "cooldown needs" might entail. The thought of it makes me hot all over. He groans and catches the back of my neck with a hand, his mouth slanting over mine and delving deep in his exploration of my mouth. His tongue delivers lick after wicked lick, sending me half out of my mind as I grind my clit against the cup. My panties are dampening at a rapid rate, and my thighs begin to shake with the uncontrolled, desperate need to come.

When I tear my mouth from Bear's so that I can take

a breath, my eyes open ... and connect with Duke's over Bear's shoulder. He's watching us with what I'd call an entire fuck ton of interest, his hand resting on top of his cock. And now, with my eyes on him, he palms it, stroking roughly while his hips thrust.

Out of nowhere, the orgasm strikes, blinding pleasure coursing through me as the tight knot in my lower abdomen unfurls. Wave after wave hits me, threatening to take me under. Bear nuzzles my neck, licking and sucking at my skin, and Duke, he just keeps fucking watching. His face is mostly unreadable, the only thing I'm truly able to pick up on is the heat in his eyes.

"Ah fuck, I leave for five minutes, and this is what I miss out on?"

My pussy continues to intermittently throb as I look over my shoulder. Mason strides toward us, hooks his hands under my armpits and lifts me off Bear. "Baby sis, the man has to be in the ring in the next five minutes."

I grit my teeth, giving Bear an apologetic but saucy smile.

He stands up, hips shifting, with one hand to the cup. "Wrinkly grandmas, pea soup, baby bunnies, fucking creepy tarantulas," he hisses, then breathes slowly in and out. In and out. He gasps again, "Fuuuck."

"Is there a reason you're still calling her *baby sis,*

asshole?" Duke gives Mason the side-eye as he gets up to rummage in the mini fridge.

"It bugs you, and you know I can't help myself when it comes to fucking with you." Mason shrugs. "I don't hear you protesting *too* much."

"Whatever," Duke grunts, coming up with two bottles and handing one off to me. "We'll see you back here when the fight is over."

Bear stalks my way, grabs the back of my neck, and hauls me close. His warm breath fans from my ear down to my neck. I shiver in response. His voice gruff, he murmurs low enough that only I can hear him, "You still didn't answer me, but I assume you meant to say '*Yes, Daddy.*'"

My eyes widen, but before I can say a damn thing, he's out the door. Mason shakes his head. "You riled him up. We'll see how that translates in the ring. See you in a bit." He gives me a dirty little smirk and follows our fighter, the two of them practically taking all the air in the room with them.

TEN

DUKE

When Lennon turns around, I grunt, "We'll wait a little bit, then I'll scope things out." She nods at me, catching her lip with her teeth and worrying the tender skin. I'm certain I don't want to know what Bear just said to her because it must have been positively indecent to make her face flush like that.

Fuck, or maybe the color is still high on her cheeks from all the grinding she'd been doing in Bear's lap right in front of me. My eyes scan her face, taking her in. I'm going to think of that color as "orgasm blush" for the rest of my life.

And it'd been me her eyes had been locked on as she came like that. Those two going at it had me rock hard over here in the corner, and I'd contemplated pulling my dick out and giving Lennon a show right back. I don't know if I should be weirded out by the fact that the thought of it turns me right the fuck on. As it was, I'd stroked myself through my pants—and she'd definitely seen me doing it. She may be my stepsister, but it's not like we grew up together, so ... yeah. I'm having a whole lot of trouble denying the fact that I'm attracted to her.

Mason and Bear seem all too aware that I'm in the struggle of my life. Mason even thinks it's funny. Bear? Hard to say. Sometimes I catch him watching me, and I wonder what he's thinking. I'm ninety-nine percent sure he and Mason have both been with Lennon. I don't know for sure about Bear, but that's my assumption. At the very least, he knows how her pussy tastes and that's enough to drive me to the brink of insanity.

If only Lennon didn't remind me so goddamn much of the days when Juliette was alive. Whenever I look at her, I remember the first time I peered through the window at Stella's and watched the two of them in their cute waitress outfits walking from booth to booth, taking care of their customers. Lennon had been young but pretty all the same, though I only ever had eyes for Juliette.

Until now.

It's hard to say whether that bothers me because the anniversary of Juliette's death is tomorrow or if it's that

I've let Lennon take Juliette's place in my thoughts more and more often.

It frustrates me.

I head over to the small table next to the couch and hook up my phone to a speaker dock. Scrolling through my Spotify account, I pick a playlist I think Lennon might like. Turning around, I reach into my pocket and pull out the cinnamon lollipop I'd shoved in there before we left the house.

Meanwhile, Lennon has come over and taken a seat on the far end of the couch, pulling her legs up onto the cushion. I hold out the bright-red lollipop between us and gesture that she should take it. She tilts her head to the side, studying me with a curious look.

Heat hits my cheeks. Maybe I made a mistake. I shrug, playing it off. "I thought it'd help occupy you if things got weird."

Her brows drag together as she pulls the wrapper off the candy. "Are things any weirder than usual?" She slips the sugary goodness into her mouth and twirls it around.

My dick twitches. Fuck. This was a mistake.

I can imagine how the cinnamon flavor would burst on my tongue, and what it might taste like if I were to kiss her right now. Jesus. *Help.*

I follow suit, joining her on the couch, and sit sideways like she is, facing her. Pulling one leg up onto the cushion, I keep the other planted firmly on the floor and eye her while chugging half the bottle of water in my hand. Way too much time has passed since she asked if things were weirder than usual, so I clear my throat. "I guess not. But I brought it for you all the same." My traitorous eyes fall to her lips where they've closed around the lollipop stick before she pulls it slowly from her mouth. My eyes follow.

"Everything okay?"

I nod, and a long, hard swallow works its way down the column of my throat. I feel like I could drink ten bottles of water, and my mouth would still feel parched. It's then that my gaze dips down to her neck and locks there.

Her lip trembles the slightest bit as she watches my eyes travel over the now purplish bruises. My voice is full of grit and gravel and something else I can't quite pinpoint. "Mason does like his hand at your throat."

"I don't know what he told you, but he was trying to freak me out. It worked. For a hot minute." She lets go of her lollipop for a moment, touching her fingers to her skin.

I'd been so worked up after the discovery of the dress in her closet that I guess I hadn't paid enough attention earlier. It looks tender, and I wince at the thought of how that happened. "Yeah, but I mean that wasn't the first time he's done it." I shift closer, leaning one elbow on the back of the couch and resting the side of my head in my hand.

"No, you're right. It wasn't." She pulls the candy from her mouth, resting it against her lips for a moment as she stares into my eyes.

Hers are a bold, vivid blue. I could so easily get lost in them. Drown. Because of that and combined with the fact that I don't have a fucking clue how to deal with her, I shoot her a smart-ass smirk and let my next words fly with a teasing raise of my brow. "You'd think I'd be the one to want to strangle you." My eyes drop to her mouth just as "Sex and Candy," the version by Alexander Jean, begins to play. *Fuuuck.* I laugh internally.

I wonder if she'd deny it if I pointed out that it does, indeed, smell like cinnamon lollipop ... and *Lennon* in here. *Fuck,* I like it way too much. She shifts on the cushion, tugging at the neckline of her hoodie, then drags in a breath before exhaling sharply.

Desire flares to life in my blood and I wonder if she can see it written all over my fucking face. I want her. It's a good thing I have superhuman control.

A flicker of interest crosses Lennon's face, a tiny bit of devilish intuition that makes me think she can tell exactly what I'm fucking thinking. I work my jaw to the side, staring at her as I let a fantasy play out in my head ...

I'd lunge forward, brace myself over her, peel those shorts off—along with the fucking La Perla underwear I'd bought for her—then bury my goddamn face in her sweet pussy. I'd lick her until she screamed for me. And I wouldn't stop, not even if Mason and Bear walked back in. My turn, fuckers.

I blink, coming back to myself to find she's frowning as she taps the sticky lollipop against her lips, then slicks her tongue over them. I tear my greedy eyes away from her and stare over her shoulder. After another moment, though, she gestures with the candy. "What do you think, have we waited long enough?"

My gaze darts to hers. What is she talking about? *We?* "Sorry, what?"

"Can we try to see the fight now?" An amused expression slips over her features. "What did you think I was talking about?" She tilts her head to the side, studying me way too carefully.

Fuck. Nope. Not fucking telling her that I thought she meant we'd waited long enough in an entirely different way. "Nothing, sorry. I was preoccupied. Wait here, and I'll check things out. I'll be no more than a minute. Don't open the door for anyone. I have a key." I get up and stride out of the room, locking the door behind me.

I'm edging more and more toward pissed off at myself.

I can't even imagine how we'd ever not be biting each other's heads off. Setting the Juliette stuff aside, Lennon drives me crazy on a regular basis, and I can't even seem to resist messing with her. A holdover from my preconceived notions—shit I got into my head based on watching her mother with my father. One thing is very apparent at this point. She is not her mother's daughter. Sure, biologically she is. But in all the other ways it counts, Lennon is nothing like her mother. I hang my head. It's what she's been trying to tell us since the moment she got to Bainbridge Hall. And some of the things she's said ... it makes me wonder what life was like growing up with a mother like Nikki Bell.

I'm equally curious and hesitant to find out what happens when Lennon and I reach a boiling point and everything we feel spills over and into the open. So much time has been spent with the two of us at each other's throats. What would happen if we were to flip the script and stop fighting each other? I let out a shuddering breath. We're ripe for an explosion of epic proportions, but it's shitty-as-hell timing for me, personally.

Gritting my teeth, I cautiously give a look around. I think we'll be okay if we stand behind these big dudes at the end of the hallway. My father is holding court in his usual seat with Derek beside him. A bunch of high-stakes gamblers surround them. And ... well, that's fuckin' bizarre. Morgan sits on Derek's other side. My brow furrows for a moment before my gaze slips to Bear, who toys with the Gamma Chi brother. I'd better go get Lennon in case this is over as quickly as I think it might be. Moving stealthily, I creep back through the spectators in the standing-room-only area, and down the hall to Bear's dressing room.

I let myself in, and Lennon is immediately on her feet, an excited glint in her eye. We slip back down the hallway together, and without thinking, I take her hand. It's small in mine, and to my utter surprise, she hangs on tightly as I tug her along behind me. We weave through the crowd, not stopping until we come right up behind the big guys I'd seen standing here earlier. Lennon goes up on tiptoe, but it's obvious she's straining to get a look.

"Shit. You can't see much can you?" I squeeze her hand when she doesn't answer.

She glances at me for only a moment before she goes back to the dance she's doing on tiptoe, trying to catch a glimpse of Bear.

I release her hand, then turn a bit, patting my shoulder. "Hop up on my back."

Her brows pinch together. "Really?"

"Yeah. I've seen plenty of fights. You deserve to see

one. Come on. Quick, before he knocks this dude out and it's all over."

With only a moment's hesitation, she nods, and coming in close, she puts both hands on my shoulders. "You're sure?"

"Yes," I grit out. Motherfuck, I hope I can handle Lennon's body draped over my back, because the mere thought of it is making my dick twitch excitedly in my pants. "Jump on three." I pause only a second before I count under my breath for her. "Ready? One. Two. Three."

Lennon jumps, leaping easily onto my back, and at the same time, my heart jumps into my throat. I clasp her smooth thighs near the knees while she grips my shoulders and shimmies upward. I'm rewarded with a waft of coconut and mango drifting up my nose. Fuck. It's going to drive me batshit crazy, just like it has on every other occasion I've had her close like this. At least it makes things a bit more pleasant—this warehouse stinks like sweat and greed.

With her scent cocooned around me, we watch as Bear plays with this guy. The Gamma Chi dude is big, but he's clearly nowhere near as muscular as Bear. He's also a good three inches shorter, which usually translates to a shorter reach. From the looks of it, he hasn't gotten many hits in, and not only that, but he's sluggish. Bear is fast on his feet, an absolute powerhouse. His body was made for this, in the same way it was made to perform his position of tight end for the KU Lions.

I sure hope he knows what he's doing, continuing on with fights like this. Normally, I wouldn't voice my opinion, but fuck, he needs to be done with this before it lands him in a whole heap of trouble. If I were him, I'd get in Derek's face and tell him this is it. No more. Even though I'm envious of Bear's football career and the potential he has to go pro, that doesn't mean I want him getting removed from the team for something his dad forces him to do.

Just then, Bear plows his hand into this guy's face, then immediately brings a left hook around. I wince, my body jerking at the impact. Lennon clenches me, both at the shoulders and around the waist with her thighs. I might be in heaven. My brain scrambles with thoughts of my dick in her pussy, and her legs wrapped around me and holding on tight. Fuck. Focus on the fight.

My eyes flick over to Mason where he's going apeshit on the outside of the caged fighting area. He shouts encouragement at Bear and throws his fists into the air with every landed punch.

"You okay?" I grit, giving her a little bounce to hike her up a bit higher on my back.

"Yeah. Do both of you usually do that?" Lennon points toward the cage.

My gaze darts back to Mason, and I chuckle. "Mase is the only one who acts like a lunatic. But yeah, I'm usually at the cage with him."

"Sorry."

"Don't be. It's fine."

"It's definitely my fault you aren't over there with your friend." She lets out an aggravated sigh.

"Again, not a big deal. He's doing fine."

A minute or so goes by before she asks another question. "Why is this guy not trying to hit him back?"

I study Bear and his opponent for a moment before answering. "It's kinda strange. He's supposedly a striker, but he's got a pitiful defense tonight. Not looking so great, to be honest. Probably should have prepared better before going up against the likes of Bear. He's only embarrassing himself."

While watching from the corner of my eye how Bear circles his opponent, I let myself see what Lennon must see, the sheer insanity of what's happening before our eyes. There's raised seating all the way around the caged ring, absolutely full of spectators. The lighting isn't the greatest, but the dimness only adds to the already unsavory atmosphere. It's quite obviously a curated crowd, meaning only those who can pay the price of admission are invited to participate. And these rich men, supposedly the pillars of society, get off on knowing they're doing something illegal.

"What's that over there?"

"The ticket-window-looking thing? That's where bets are placed. That'd be the biggest source of revenue." I swivel a bit with her on my back. "And then there's the bar that does nonstop business. I don't even fucking know if they have a liquor license. If they do, Derek must have bought someone off in the Georgia Department of Revenue to get it so everything looks above board." The bar does crazy-good business on fight nights, and it's currently slammed with people ordering drinks.

Bear hooks his leg around the back of this dude's knee and down to the mat they both go.

Lennon whispers, "I don't know much about this style of fighting, but I can tell Bear still has the upper hand."

I grunt my agreement as we watch them roll around a good bit more.

Lennon lowers her head to whisper in my ear again, her soft breath tickling my skin and sending my pulse racing. "I noticed you and Mason were pretty good at this stuff, too."

I glance over my shoulder at her with a wry smile.

"We'd have to be. We're his sparring partners when he wants to work on certain skills at home."

"Oh, like practice buddies?"

"Yeah." I huff out a laugh. "Practice buddies."

She's quiet for another minute, but now that Bear's taken this guy to the mat, she squirms a bit with each move they make, trying to see better now that his opponent is practically pinned on the floor. I'll be honest, with her body molded around mine, I'm not paying attention to this fight. I don't miss her quick intake of breath when Bear lands a blow, nor the way her thighs tighten on me ... in excitement? Fuck, I don't care why she's doing it, but I have the insane urge to spin around and pin her to the wall.

Instead, my eyes roam over the crowd, and things are just fine until Lennon spots Tristan and Derek sitting there, drinks in hand, wearing their expensive-looking tailored suits to a cage fight. It's as if all the air's been knocked from her lungs. She claws at my shoulders. "Tristan," she murmurs, "and Derek. Over there."

I briefly squeeze her thigh. "I know. I saw them. We're okay."

"No. I want—" She tucks her face against the side of my neck and whispers frantically, "Turn around. Go. Now."

I dislike the nervous energy rippling through her. I

do a quick pivot and speed walk back to Bear's dressing room, throwing the door open. I shut it behind us, then spin, leaning back to catch my breath—with Lennon sandwiched between me and the door. I can't tell which is making my heart beat faster, the fact that the mere sight of my father and Bear's has caused Lennon to panic or that I've pinned my stepsister's soft curves against my back with her legs tangled around me.

After we calm, I tap her legs, and she releases the vice grip from around my hips. She slides down the length of my back until her sandaled feet hit the floor. When I step away and turn around, I note that she continues to use the door for support. Stepping close, I brace one forearm over her head and lean in, my chest rising and falling at a steady pace. "Did they see you? Is that why you're upset?"

"I-I don't know." She clenches her teeth tightly together, the look she shoots me is full of wariness. "I spotted them, and a few seconds later, Tristan's head turned. But I have no idea if he was looking specifically at me or at that row of big dudes in front of us. Did he really say they didn't want me here for some reason? I mean, I know why I didn't want to see *them.*" She shudders, unable to stop the involuntary reaction.

It makes me want to tear through that room and drag either—or both—men into the ring and pound on them. Is she scared that she'll be pulled out of KU? I shake my head before I answer. "No. It was more of a feeling that I got from my father. It was nothing he explicitly said."

I can tell that explanation doesn't make her feel much better. I grip her chin with my fingers, tipping her face to mine. "Don't panic." My heart begins to pound an even fiercer beat. "It's not that big a deal. I'd prefer they hadn't seen us, because I didn't like the vibe I got earlier or the way you're reacting to seeing them. But if they did happen to see us, we just say we decided to come at the last minute. It's as simple as that. Let me do the talking if they come looking for us for some reason. If we're lucky, they'll be too caught up in what's going on out there to bother."

I don't know which I find more disturbing right at this very moment—considering possible reasons why the OG Bastards wouldn't want Lennon here or the realization that if it comes down to it, I'm on Lennon's side. I would protect her with all that I am.

I sure as fuck didn't see that coming.

ELEVEN

BEAR

I'VE ALMOST GOT HIM. I ignore the roar of the crowd as I grapple on the mat with the Gamma Chi, trying to focus on getting the job done. This asshole may occasionally manage to get the upper hand, but never for long. Sweat drips from me, my muscles scream, but this is it—the match is almost over. I can feel it. He's allowed me to get him on his back, trap him with my legs—one over his neck and the other clamped over his waist. I've got a good grip on his forearm and begin to maneuver it tight to my chest so I can execute a classic armbar. Pulling his arm flush against my chest, I finish him off by arching my back until his elbow begins to hyperextend.

It only takes two seconds of that before he's gasping in excruciating pain and taps out. At the ref's quick signal that the match is over, I release him and roll away, standing up on the mat. I stare down at the guy, my heart still racing. From the look of exhaustion on his face, I'd say he's relieved the fight is over, no matter the outcome. The crowd surges to its feet, wildly clapping and shouting, but I hardly hear the cheers. They don't mean a goddamn thing to me anymore.

In the beginning, it used to be such a rush to walk into the ring and show everyone what I was capable of. I was young and dumb. Didn't think through the ramifications. But now I get why these fights are such a stupid thing to be excited about—because every fucking fight I take, I'm putting myself and my football career at risk. I need out from under my dad's control in the worst way. If only I'd never fucked it all up in the first place, I could simply walk away. But I can't.

My jaw twitches as my gaze finds my old man in the crowd, talking with some of his cronies. They're always here for fight nights, and it's the same group that's generally at the big poker games my father throws once a month. Only alumni are allowed to attend, and what they're like is all very hush-hush. It's a social thing for some of them, but it's all about the gambling for my dad. It's what he excels at. I've seen the evidence in his bank accounts, both personal and business. Too bad it's all fuckin' dirty money.

I don't know if it makes me an awful son, but hopefully this bullshit won't last forever. Eventually someone will open their mouth when they shouldn't and this entire kingdom my father and his friends have built will go up in flames and be nothing more than ashes.

It won't matter to me at all. I get nothing in exchange for these fights except my father's silence. Fighting is the only way I can be assured that he'll keep his mouth shut.

I don't miss how similar our situations are. One word breathed in the wrong ear about what I did, and it's over for me.

I'm shaken from my disturbing thoughts by the announcer booming my name and the ref grabbing my forearm to hold it up. Victory. Again. My eyes connect with my old man's, and he nods. No smile, no cheering, no nothing.

"Fuck yes, Bear! That's how it's done!" Mason's bellow as he climbs the outside of the cage, arm pumping in the air in recognition of my win finally puts a smile on my face. Mason, Duke, and I may be a dysfunctional family, but at least we fuckin' support each other when it counts. I shoot him a smirk at his antics as I wait for permission from the ref to exit the ring. We always make sure the crowd is dispersing before we leave the safety of the cage. Gamblers can be fucking ruthless sometimes. I'd be more worried if I were the other guy tonight, though.

As I stand trying to catch my breath, my eyes scan the arena. I don't fucking like what I'm seeing ringside. Heated words being exchanged between my dad and Tristan have me on high alert. My eyes connect with Mason's, then shift, trying to get him to pay attention to what's going on behind him.

My concern registers with him, and he turns, glancing ever so slightly over his shoulder to take a look. The moment the ref lets go of my arm, I shake hands with the battered Gamma Chi and smack his sweaty bicep with my palm. "Good fight," I grit out, then hurriedly make my way out of the ring.

Mason meets me, holds his hand up to grip mine. He brings me in close, other hand clapping on my shoulder. I duck my head as he leans in, knowing he's going to brief me on his observations, and we need to keep our thoughts on the down-low. "It sounds like they're aware Lennon's here. I don't know what the fuck to think. Whether they saw her with Duke, I don't know. I'd assume so."

I nod stiffly. "They were out here for the fight?"

"Just for a couple minutes." He gestures with his chin toward the back hallway. "They were well hidden. I was watching for them, or I don't think I'd have noticed." Mason scans the crowd. "Oh, fuck."

My jaw locks up at his tone. "What?"

"That bitch Morgan. Look at her. She keeps looking from us to your dad and Tristan."

Out of the corner of my eye, she smoothly moves closer and closer to Tristan and my dad, wearing a smile like the cat who swallowed the canary. "What the fuck is with that look on her face?" She stops only about a foot from my dad with her hands clasped behind her back, pushing her breasts out in what I'm sure most people would agree is an enticing manner. But when it's my old man she's putting herself on display for, it hits a whole lot different. "What does she think she's doing?" I growl under my breath.

Mason huffs out a disturbed laugh. "I have a fucking guess, but it's going to piss you off and make you want to vomit all at once."

Stunned, I search his eyes, glance at Morgan, then at my dad, and finally Tristan. "Oh, hell."

"I bet you when Lennon told that entitled, crazy bitch to get the fuck out that she went directly to Derek and Tristan and pouted about it until they gave her some"—he pauses to make a yuck face—"reassurance."

"She probably blew both of them to make herself feel better."

Mason snorts with laughter. "Well, if that's what it takes, at least she wasn't pounding down your door."

"Truth."

"Ah, fuck. Your dad is waving us over. He seems ... displeased."

"Well, that's great because I'm not pleased with him, either. I want to know what he said to Lennon yesterday."

Mason's teeth clench. "I get that. But is it worth knowing? Or is it only going to piss you off?"

"Both. Come on." I throw my towel around my neck, hanging onto the ends with both hands and stride purposefully over to where my dad and Tristan wait for us, out of the way of the exiting crowd. One thing about these fights, they happen and then people make haste with their winnings or gripe on their way out the door about their lost money. Either way, they don't stick around.

I can't tell from the tight set of my dad's jaw what he's thinking, but Tristan is eyeing me like he may want to take my head off. What'd he do? Bet against me? Lose a shit ton of money?

There's a dangerous glint in my dad's eye when we join them. "Son. Nice fight." He turns to offer Mason a bob of his head before his gaze rolls right back to me.

I can't make heads or tails of what the fresh hell is going on.

Beside him, Tristan gives me a tight smile. "Yes. Good job out there. Liked that armbar at the end. Thought you could have gone after him a little harder, though."

My control for the moment must be pretty good because I keep my eye roll in check and instead simply lift my brows at the suggestion. What'd he want me to do, break the guy's elbow? Warily, I size him up, knowing it's best to save my comments for the shit that's surely coming our way, judging by the smug look on his face. But I can't fucking help myself. "Thank you, sir. But what good would it do to have embarrassed him further? Or for that matter, why would I risk injuring myself?"

He presses his lips together, completely ignoring both questions as his eyes scan the emptying warehouse. "My son couldn't make it tonight, huh?"

I glance quickly at Mason, whose brows have pinched together. It's always best not to lie unless absolutely necessary. "Actually, he's here. He's with Lennon in my dressing room."

Dad raises a brow, a look of unmistakable interest slipping over his features. "Is that so? Huh."

My blood begins to heat. *Oh no, old man. Get*

thoughts of her out of your fucking perverted head. I draw in a calming breath, eyeing him carefully. "One, I think you already knew that they were here, whether you saw them or not." My jaw twitches as my gaze lands on Morgan for a fleeting second. She seems perfectly happy to stand near these two wealthy men and witness this exchange when she has no real reason to be here.

Dad nods with a wicked smile. "And two?"

"What the fuck did you say to her yesterday?" I growl. "There's a reason why she's not out here. She didn't want to have to deal with you." Out of the corner of my eye, I watch Mason pull out his cell phone. I hope like fuck he's telling Duke to get Lennon out of here. His gaze slides to mine, and he gives me the barest nod.

"Respect, son. Watch your mouth." He shoots me a steely glare. "Unless you're going to tell me that she's not already involved with at least one of you, then I didn't say anything to Lennon that was unwarranted." He beckons Morgan to his side.

"Did you need me, Mr. Pierce?" she practically purrs as she shoots him a smile, and my stomach turns. Why the fuck does she seem so comfortable around him?

He loosely collars the back of her neck, pulling her close to his side. He leans down, whispering something in her ear that makes her flush from head to toe.

What. The. Fuck. I blink rapidly, trying to wrap my head around this development.

In the end, though, what the fuck do I care if Morgan wants to suck my old man's dick or anyone else's?

"Morgan, here, was telling us earlier that there was a mouthy young lady who told her in no uncertain terms that you didn't need her ... services ... after the fight."

My gaze shifts to Morgan, who eyes me with interest. I'm sure she wants to know more about her competition or whatever she sees Lennon as.

"Having your choice of women after a fight is a winner's perk you shouldn't pass up." Tristan's brows lift. "Unless you're saying you intend to use *my daughter* for those purposes, instead? Is that what's going on here? Because that's *not* an option."

At his words, Morgan lets out a huffed exhale and leans closer to my dad. "That's what I took it to mean, Mr. Valentine." She gives him what I can only describe as a beguiling smile before she turns and pins her viper eyes on me.

I could lash out at her, but I won't. She's not worth my time. Tristan, though? This prick needs a wake-up call. "Oh, please. Lennon is not your daughter, and if you cared two shits about her well-being, you wouldn't have sent her to live in a house full of men. Don't kid yourself, *sir*. She means nothing to you, and we both know it. We *all* know it."

Tristan's jaw twitches, but he doesn't deny the truth of my comments.

"But like I said, I wasn't far off in my assumptions *or* what I said to Lennon after all." Derek throws his head back, laughing. "I'm glad you've at least confirmed that for me."

My jaw pops as it shifts to the side, fury rushes through me at his audacity. I bore my eyes into his as I let the rage at my own father's words seethe from me. "You know jack shit. Keep Lennon's name outta your goddamn mouth." And I don't think, I simply plow my fist into his jaw, then turn and walk away, the sound of him crashing to the floor a distant noise in my buzzing head.

OUTSIDE, Mason and I hustle to the car deck. "Fuck, I never thought I'd see the day." He shoots me a wicked grin. "That was fucking awesome."

I grit my teeth, the violence still not having left me. It flows through my blood, surging and crashing in my veins. "He had it coming. Didn't he?" We'd only stopped long enough in my dressing room for me to pull on shoes and grab my bag. I'm covered in sweat and walking to the parking deck in my compression shorts. I don't fucking give a shit.

Mason glances over his shoulder, and I look too, but no one is behind us. "I'm not saying you did anything wrong. I'm fucking proud of you that you stood up to that asshole. And really, I was on the verge of letting loose on Tristan for some of his snide remarks. He's putting on a piss-poor daddy act. I see right through it."

I exhale heavily. "This is going to be really fucking ugly." My fists clench as it sinks in what I've done. What I've brought down on our heads.

We enter the parking deck, which is all but empty, and head straight to the SUV where Duke and Lennon wait for us. He stands outside what has now become our getaway vehicle and Lennon sits sideways on one of the back passenger seats, long legs dangling out the open door. I press my lips together, fucking hating it even more now that I have confirmation of the sort of garbage my dad said to her. It was one thing to have her hint at it and another to have him admit it to my face.

And the worst part is, I'm betting he made her feel fuckin' awkward, considering she *has* actually slept with two of us. Now, why it's okay for a man to fuck around all he wants and not a woman is beyond me. The thing is, I will take whatever pieces of Lennon she wants to give me. I love her take-no-shit-from-anyone attitude ... even if I know sometimes it's a show. Sometimes she does care. She just hides it well. It makes me want to dig in deeper with her and find out more.

Of course, that means she will likely want to do the same with me, which scares me to death. The idea that she could ever find out the sort of person I really am. It's a conundrum—but one I will fight tooth and nail trying to find my way around.

"What the hell happened?" Duke approaches, eyes darting from me to Mason.

"Let's get in the fucking vehicle and get out of here," I snap. "I made a goddamn mess of things."

Duke huffs out a laugh, tucking his phone back into his pocket. "Yeah. Sounds like maybe you did. But also, I bet it felt fucking good."

I assume Mason has already mostly filled him in via text. I give a brief shrug. "Yeah, maybe."

Mason points at Duke. "You drive this time. I'll take the front. Bear, in back with Lennon. You know that's where you want to be anyway."

I give a stiff nod, noting that in the few seconds we took to arrange that, Lennon has hopped out of the vehicle and approached us. "What's going on?"

My jaw grinds, but I tuck my fingers into the front of her jean shorts and tug her close. I cup her cheek with my still-gloved hand. "Sorry, Little Gazelle. We've gotta run now. There'll be time to talk at home. I just need a few minutes on the ride there to decompress."

Her blue eyes search mine, but she nods as she lifts onto her toes, her hand resting on my sweat-slickened chest, and plants a kiss on my chin. "Okay. Let's go."

TWELVE

LENNON

On the way home, I'd helped Bear out of his gloves and wraps while Duke drove. He hadn't been kidding about needing to decompress. He'd been silent the entire journey, as had Mason and Duke. The two of them seemed to understand the situation, but I'm still very much in the dark. But—I'm also not that girl. I'm not going to beg for details. Besides, I'm certain from the way the three are behaving that it's all going to come out sooner or later. Probably sooner. The tension in this SUV is far too great to think some sort of explosion isn't imminent.

I know Bear and Mason were with Derek and Tristan immediately following the fights, so I can only assume that's when everything went down. Whatever happened to make Mason send us out to the SUV early and had

Bear hauling balls out of the warehouse without showering and changing had to have been kinda crazy. Like so stupid crazy I can't even come up with a scenario in my head that fits.

Oh god, the more I think about it, the more this has Derek and Tristan written all over it. My gut twists and roils at the thought of them and what they might have said or done, but— I suck in a breath through my teeth. Maybe I simply don't want to know. Did it have to do with me? I can only assume so, and that's why the guys are quiet.

Really, how much more am I supposed to take?

We pull up to the house, and no one makes a move to get out of the vehicle right away, all of us lost in our own thoughts. My eyes flick from Bear to Mason, and finally to Duke. All three are mentally exhausted, that much is easy to pick up on. I glance at my phone. It's almost midnight. We have classes tomorrow. How the hell does Bear do this so often and not completely wear himself out? And tonight, in particular, we obviously left more quickly than he normally would have.

I blow out a breath. "Well, that was fun."

Mason peers into the back seat at me, his dark eyes glinting at me with what I sense is amusement. He huffs out a laugh. "Kintsukuroi, you worry me sometimes."

"Just trying to lighten the mood."

He nods, his jaw twitching. "Yeah, I get that. I'm too fucking tired to rehash any of this tonight. I might go up to the attic for a bit, but maybe not. I'm ready to crash." I don't miss how he's keeping a careful eye on Duke in the driver's seat. My eyes flick back and forth between them, trying to figure out what the hell I'm missing.

"Ditto. I'm—" Duke abruptly stops speaking as his eyes glue to the fancy touchscreen display at the center of the dashboard. "Fuck." He rubs his hands over his face, a hard exhale leaving him. "Fuck," he bites out again, the sound of it harsh and full of ache. "I can't deal with anything right now." He grasps the handle, opens the door, and launches himself from the SUV.

Mason clenches his teeth together as he points to the date in the corner of the screen. "It's September 5."

"Oh. Oh, no." My heart gives a violent tug as my eyes follow Duke's retreating figure as he bolts into the house. I hadn't forgotten. It'd simply been in my head that tomorrow would be difficult. It hadn't even hit me that technically the anniversary of Juliette's death arrived the moment the clock struck midnight.

I scramble to unbuckle and follow, as do Mason and Bear. Up ahead of us, the door to the house slams shut behind Duke. One shared, disturbed glance later, and the three of us charge up the front steps together. I'm desperate to get to him, though what I'd do or say if I caught him is beyond me. This can't be fixed. Dead girl-friends are just that—dead.

Mason reaches the door first and throws it open for us. As we enter, I spy Duke turning the corner at the top of the stairs. My heart sinks, a tiny fissure opening because of the pain that emanates from him. It vibrates in the air all around us, stealing my breath and making me ache for him.

I'm about to tear up the stairs after him when Mason clamps a hand on my shoulder. "Wait. Probably better if only one of us goes." He shrugs, taking a deep breath with his eyes focused on his hands. He works his jaw to the side, finally meeting our gazes. "I can talk to him."

My brows pinch together. It's probably not even my place so say a damn word, but I can't help myself. "Are you sure?"

"Yeah. He needs the straight truth right now. We might not always get along, but I know what's in his head. It's fine." He glances from me to Bear, who is still in his skintight compression shorts looking like he's in need of some serious de-stressing himself. Surprisingly, in this moment, Bear would be my last choice to send up there to talk to Duke even though he's usually the most even-tempered of us.

Proving my point, Bear rakes a hand through his sweaty hair, making it stand on end. Unlike anything I've seen from him before, he's a horrifying mix of pure frustration and absolute wreckage. His lips pinch together for a moment, as if he's waging an internal battle with himself over not being the one to take control. Finally, he nods at Mason. "Okay. If you're sure you can handle him."

Interestingly enough, I'm picking up on some big irritation from Mason. Like he's pissed Bear is uncertain of him right now. Less so with me, but it's still there.

Mason throws us a bitter smile through clenched teeth. "I've got it. Bear, you don't need this right now. Not after dealing with your dad. And frankly, *Stella,* I'm a little unsure how Duke'll handle being around you today." Mason's usage of Duke's nickname for me grabs Bear's attention.

"Why are you calling her Stella?"

Mason's lips quirk into a twisted smile. "Because it's an important piece of the Duke-and-Lennon puzzle, that's why." He winks at me, ignoring Bear for the moment. "Baby sis, it really hadn't occurred to you that his issue with you was never solely about your mother marrying his father?" Mason cocks his head to the side as he studies me. "I mean, there's a bit of that thrown in, the whole disgust at Nikki Bell, but ... yeah. I don't think that's really it."

Bear's brow furrows in a very definite what-the-fuck

kind of way. "This is too much for me right now," he growls.

"Yeah, I know. That's why I'm asking you to trust me with him." Mason shakes his head, shooing us away as he turns to mount the staircase. "It's fine. We can sort everything later. I could swear you two have some unfinished business, anyway. You can ruminate on it while you have a good soak or something."

I look up at Bear to find his gaze already on me, but I could swear, behind those beautiful golden eyes, he's worrying over something big on top of everything with Duke. I'm betting it's something to do with his dad. He keeps making a fist with his right hand, then straightening out his fingers, testing them.

Oh, hell. Did things get physical between them? Shit. I swallow hard. *Shit, shit, shit.*

Mason tugs me close before whispering, "Make sure he's not being too hard on himself."

My throat goes dry at his earnest tone. I shoot him a perplexed look, momentarily setting the Duke drama aside. Whatever happened back there at the warehouse, it wasn't good either.

Quietly, he murmurs, "He'll tell you about it if you ask ... and I'm sure you can figure out how to take his mind off it once he's spilled." His lips brush over my cheek, but then he eases back to look into my eyes. "You can handle him." A smirk tips his lips and his eyebrows wriggle. He leans in, brushing a kiss over my surprised mouth, then takes off up the stairs without a backward glance.

Taking a deep breath, I let it out slowly before facing Bear. I slide my hands up his biceps, my tongue darting out to wet my lips. "Letting the jets in the spa soothe your muscles doesn't seem like a bad idea, actually. And you seem tense. Maybe it'll help."

Bear arches a brow. "Yeah?"

I nod, grabbing his hand and threading my fingers through his. "Come on. Lemme take care of you for a change." I flash him a grin.

He tilts his head to the side, searching my eyes. Slowly, he rasps, "Yeah, okay. Let's go."

THIRTEEN

LENNON

BEAR and I walk quietly through the house, then outside and around the pool patio, both of us a little lost in our own head. It's a strange turn of events to have Bear and Duke being the ones in need of some help tonight, but I'm confident I can get Bear's mind off things, though my worry over Mason with Duke hasn't dissipated at all. I squeeze Bear's hand and glance up toward the upper floor of the house. "You think they'll be okay?"

His lips quirk as he gives my question some real consideration. After a moment, he shrugs. "If all else fails, it'll be a fuckin' slugfest, and we'll have to patch them up again." He shakes his head, a bit of a laugh that rumbles up from his chest escaping. "We know the two of us can take them on."

"True." My eyes land on the outdoor shower next to the in-ground spa, and I let go of Bear's hand to turn it on for him.

With that accomplished, I perch on the cool stones along the spa's edge and play with the settings, trying to keep my eyes to myself, but really ... I'm only human. And Bear is post-fight *dirty.* It's making me clench way down low and has my panties dampening at an alarming rate.

He notices me watching and tilts his head to the side, a teasing smirk playing at his lips. And even then, I can't freaking look away. My eyes are pinned to him as he hooks his thumbs into the top layer of shorts and pushes them over his hips. He takes a moment to untie the protective cup, his gaze locked on me. Those golden eyes of his gleam with a hunger that makes lust catapult through my veins. With no warning at all, he peels off the second pair of shorts, leaving him as naked as the day he was born.

He rasps, "You about killed me before I went into the ring, by the way. I was semi-hard going into that fight."

A smile sneaks its way onto my lips, and I shrug as if what he's saying doesn't affect me in the slightest, even though it does. Oh fuck, it does. My eyes drop to his dick, fixating on his long, thick length. I don't know if

I'll ever get over just how well-endowed this man is. Tapping the pads of a few fingers to my lips, I watch as he steps under the spray and slowly begins to move his hands over his body, removing the sweat, blood, and grime of the fight from his skin. "Take your time." I pull my hoodie over my head and toe off my sandals, feeling my face flush. "I wish I had a swimsuit. I didn't bring one. Had no idea I'd need it."

Bear gives me a wolfish look, water pummeling his skin, and sliding down over his body. "You don't need one. Don't worry about it. I doubt anyone is awake. Underwear isn't so different from a suit." He leans his head back, getting his hair wet, and the action makes my nipples into hard little points of desperate need. He brings his head forward again, catching my gaze. Gruffly, he demands, "Tell me what Mason is talking about with you and Duke. He was being fucking cryptic, but it seemed you knew what he meant."

I draw in a breath, my mind racing. It's hard to think with him so very wet and naked in front of me. Biting my lip hard enough to make me focus on that instead of *Bear*, I ponder what to even say. It's so fucking complicated. "Um, so I told Mason the other day—when he found me at Juliette's grave—that I used to work with her."

Bear's brows rise on his forehead, but he doesn't say

anything, just gestures that I should continue. Apparently, he was in the dark on that, too. Good boyfriend points for Duke, I suppose, keeping Juliette's secret from getting out.

"So, that's where I first encountered Duke—Stella's Diner. We never talked. I only knew him as her boyfriend who'd wait outside for her. And he knew me as the girl who worked with his girlfriend. I've tried so many times to figure out where his head's been at. Maybe because her dad didn't want her working there, it made him nervous. I know Juliette's dad didn't want her saving for college, but that's exactly what she was attempting to do. And maybe Duke was a little envious that she befriended me, and I got to spend that time with her when he didn't think she should have to work at all?" I shrug. "Duke associates me with Juliette and the diner. Mason is implying that might be the real issue."

Bear eyes me as I peel my tank top over my head, then quickly pop the button on my jean shorts and unzip, lowering them over my hips and letting them drop to the ground. "It sounds like the reminder of the friendship you had with her is too much for him some-times. Or ..." He clamps his lips together.

"No, what? Tell me what you're thinking."

"Maybe it has more to do with his obvious attraction to you. Like he feels bad ... like he's betraying Juliette? I think that makes a lot of sense." His head tilts considering. "That nickname, though. Stella."

"Yeah, weird, right? Juliette worked there, too ... so ... does Duke not mean it in the way I've always assumed he has?"

"Could be. Sounds like Mason has the same thought."

I nod, absorbing everything. Mason had hinted at some of it, but Bear's more straightforward. Duke. All this time. Feels like he's betraying Juliette? Because of me? It's a big, weird thought to digest. Quietly, I murmur, "I'm getting in." Slipping into the water in my panties and bra, I sink down, careful not to wet the bandages on my upper back.

A few moments later, I feel Bear's stare, and figure it's probably for the best that we get the other elephant in the backyard out of the way. I throw the question over my shoulder as I swivel to look at him. "What happened after the fight?" I shift myself onto the far seat where I have a view of the shower. Bear seems to be enjoying standing under the spray of water, and I don't mind watching as he slides his hands over his pecs, then up over his neck again. Despite all the crap we've been discussing, my damn mouth is watering, and I can't tear my eyes away from all that sleekly toned muscle. It takes me a second to realize he hasn't answered. Finally, I flick my eyes up to meet his.

His jaw has gone hard. "I fucking punched my dad."

My mouth drops open for a moment, my earlier thoughts confirmed. "Oh, shit. Are you okay?"

"Yeah. He ran his mouth. You already know what he said to you, so we won't go into it. I'm just a little concerned about what shit will be flung my way now. I don't have a good idea of how many people saw it happen. I was kinda in a daze. So, depending on who was there when I humiliated him ..." He blinks rapidly, water clinging to his lashes as he turns around, briefly showing me his back as he sticks his face under the water, groaning.

Fuck. The only thing that makes sense to me—because it's what I'd want, too, if it were me in distress—is to get his mind the hell off it. I unhook my bra clasp and slip the garment down my arms.

When he comes back around to face me, I purposefully wait until he looks this way to hold my bra up, dangling it from my finger. "I think you should forget about your dad right now." I drop the undergarment, and his eyes follow. I catch the corner of my lip between my teeth as his gaze zeroes in on the bubbles surging around my bare breasts. When his focus finally shifts from there to my eyes, I slip my hands under the water, and begin wriggling free of my panties.

"Lennon." My name leaves his lips on a harsh rasp. "What are you doing?"

I give him a tiny shrug, holding the wet underwear over the side of the spa, too. Releasing them from my pinched fingers, they hit the ground with a wet slap. I give Bear the most innocent look I can conjure.

He cuts off the water in the shower, running a hand through his hair. His chest heaves as he stalks over to me. And I do mean *stalks.* He's like a predator going in for the kill. I hardly blink, and he's in the water with me. He gathers me to him, one arm around my torso, and the other threading into the hair at the side of my head.

"You've decided on being a naughty girl tonight, huh?" And before I can answer, he devours my mouth, savagely plunging his tongue inside. I moan aloud. We frantically nip and lick and taste, all while our hands slide over each other's bodies. He makes my heart beat so damn fast, it's going to explode from my chest.

Breathing heavily, Bear pulls away from me, and before I know what he's doing, he lifts me up out of the water and sets me on the edge. "Hold onto something," he growls.

I gasp and grip the stone surface as best I can. He gives me a rakish grin, eyes glittering in the dark. "You're so fuckin' beautiful." He tugs me forward, tipping my hips to the angle he wants, until my ass is teetering on the edge. I'm forced to lean back and watch the show as he spreads my legs wide.

His eyes skim over my exposed pussy and a split second later, he dives down, burying his roughly stubbled face between my thighs. He's like a ravenous beast, licking and sucking at every part of me.

"Oh god," I choke out. My stomach dips and my chest heaves. Every movement of his talented tongue sends fiery sparks shooting through me. I gasp aloud as he spears it into my pussy over and over again.

He eases back for a second and grunts out, "Fuck, Lennon. Fuuuck." His lips hover over me, his breath hot on my skin.

A ragged breath escapes me as I look down my body. My nipples are taut, needy peaks and the pounding of my heart is so loud in my head, I imagine it could wake everyone in the house.

"Lennon," Bear growls loudly. "Eyes on me, baby."

I blink, my eyes first sweeping the midnight-dark backyard. I recognize that I'm very exposed here, but I suck in a breath and nod, watching him latch onto my clit and suck. All the air whooshes from my lungs, and my head goes hazy. Blinding need rolls through me. And fuck it, I don't even care, couldn't stop this any more than I could stop a runaway train.

His hand slips between my legs, two fingers sliding effortlessly into my pussy, his rough thumb flicking back and forth over my clit. It throbs at the very welcome friction. He alternates between rubbing and sucking on me until I'm a writhing mess, not cognizant of anything but the sensation building in my lower abdomen.

My legs shake hard as I approach orgasm, the feeling beginning to shimmer at my core. "Oh god. Oh fuck. Yes. Yes!"

"That's it. Give me everything, Lennon." His words mumbled against my pussy sends me flying fully over the edge into some sort of beautiful oblivion.

Deep inside, tension unfurls within me, and my hips buck, but Bear holds me tightly in place, forcing me to feel every drop of pleasure that he's wringing out of me. My heart hammers a chaotic, glorious beat in my chest, and I find it hard to breathe. Hard to think. Hard to do anything but accept what he's doing to me.

Bear rises from the position he'd been in and, as if I weigh nothing, flips me and bends me over the edge of the stone surrounding the spa where I'd just been sitting. He grasps my hips, hiking them back. He has me splayed out, ass up for anyone to see ... and I'm here for it. I yearn for him, need the feel of him filling me up. Honestly, after the way tonight went, we both need it, so we can fucking forget everything for a little while.

He doesn't hesitate. I feel his thick cock at my entrance one second, and he plunges inside me the next in one devastatingly deep, satisfying stroke. Crying out, I try to hold on, but my wet fingers slip.

"I love the feel of your pussy stretching around me. You take my dick so good, baby." His raw, whispered words send a streak of lust shooting through me. My body clenches around him, and we both moan at the intense feel of it.

I'd speak, but I'm overwhelmed with the feeling of fullness and the hot slide of his cock in and out of my body as he twists the hair at the back of my head around his clenched fist. The fingers of his other hand grip my hip. Sucking in a breath, I glance over my shoulder at him. His eyes are set to smolder, and I'm afraid he may burn me alive because this is insanely hot what we're doing out in the open.

I like it a lot. Maybe too much.

"That's it," Bear groans. "Take Daddy's cock like a good little girl, Lennon."

All the breath heaves from my lungs, and his body curls over mine as he continues to smoothly pump in and out of my body. He sets a rhythm that has me so fucking hot for him, I'm half afraid even the water in the spa won't stop us from going up in flames.

I don't know if it was a sound or movement that catches my attention, but I look up at the house. Mason stands on the balcony calmly watching Bear fuck me. I don't say a word. Our eyes connect, and I know he knows I see him because his head tilts a bit to the side. He doesn't look upset or anything. He's just there, enjoying the view. And the thing is, this was basically his suggestion.

My pussy gushes around Bear's cock. *Fuck. Oh my god.*

After a few moments, I clue Bear in. "Mason's, um … watching."

He makes a noise behind me that's half grunt, half chuckle. "Want me to stop?" His cock slides so fucking deep inside me, I almost lose the ability to speak.

I stutter out my one-word response because that's all I can manage. "N-n-no."

He plants a kiss on my shoulder before righting himself behind me. He smooths his hands down the sides of my body, squeezing at my hips. "Does it turn you on to have someone watch?" He pulls all the way out, then slowly plunges back into my pussy. He keeps up this new slower rhythm, and I'm one hundred percent certain he's got one eye on me and the other on

Mason, who is still chilling on the balcony. I don't know why he's not with Duke, but the idea that he's watching me take Bear's cock might even be a step beyond the way the two of them touched me on that yoga mat.

Fuuuck. I draw in a ragged breath, realizing I haven't answered his question. "Yeah. Maybe." My eyes crash shut. "Yes. It does. I like it."

"Okay, that's good to know." The flat of Bear's hand comes down on my ass as he thrusts, and I yelp. The sound of the smack reverberates through the air, and it's too much. Naked. Outside. Bear. Monster cock. Mason. Butt smack.

"Again," I gasp. And as Bear pounds into me from behind, he gives me another sharp smack to my ass, and I lose it. "I'm coming. Oh god. I'm coming." My pussy clenches viciously on his thick cock, as my release slams into me.

"That's it, baby. Milk my cock." He drives himself hard into me and stills with a grunt of pleasure, and I swear to god, I can practically feel the explosion of cum rocketing from him.

"Oh fuck, Bear. Fuuuck."

He curls around my body, breath gusting from him. "Gideon," he rasps. "My name is Gideon."

FOURTEEN

MASON

I KNEW when I came out onto the balcony there was a chance I'd get an eyeful of whatever Lennon and Bear were up to outside. Gotta say, I fucking love the way she simply owns whatever she's doing. Rubbing my hand along my jaw, I watch how he's got her kneeling on the seat, bent over the back of it. She's hanging on for dear life, and every time he plunges that big dick of his inside her pussy, her mouth drops open and her eyes roll back. I can hear her low moans and whispered cries from here. She's the embodiment of rapture. It's fucking fantastic.

I grip the balcony railing, a low rumble of a groan escaping my lips. *Fuck.* It's like watching wild animals straight out of a motherfucking National Geographic mating special. Totally hot. And the fact is, Bear needed her. And Lennon deserves— Well, from the little bit I've learned about her upbringing, she deserves to have whatever makes her happy. Because the more I learn about her, the more I'm convinced she hasn't had the easiest life. It wasn't good before her mother married Tristan Valentine, and it wasn't great after they wed either, but for very different reasons, the worst being a stepfather who seems to hate her. So yeah. She deserves happiness.

My tongue slides out to wet my lips as my mind circles back to the way I treated her last night. It was bad, I know it. But I'm unconvinced I'm doing the right thing by letting her see inside my head, letting her climb inside my heart. If I were smart, I would keep pushing her as far from me as I possibly can. It only seems logical to not let her in any further than I have, not let her experience what it'd be like to really know me. I'm losing my mind when it comes to her, though. I'm so caught up in her. Lost. She says she understands me. She *sees* me. I draw in a breath. I see her, too. I do. The connection we have, while potent and heady, it's also scary as hell because I *hurt* the ones I love.

Hell, I can't even handle my own shit—the evidence of that is currently imprinted all over her skin. So it seems like a dangerous prospect to allow this thing between us to go any further. But *fuck*. I want to. The terrifying part is that when I had my hand around her neck, I hadn't been in control. I'd let myself slip. Lose it.

And like I told her during our sick little heart-to-heart, I don't want to hurt her. But I might. And that'd be the end of me, I think. I'd go out of my ever-loving mind if I were to do to Lennon what I did—

I squeeze my eyes shut. I don't want to think about my mother right now, don't know if I can bear to tell Lennon any more than I already have. What I shared with her this afternoon had taken it out of me. I'd put on a brave face, a mask to hide what I was really feeling, because I knew it was important to support Bear. But yeah, at this point, I'm fucking drained.

I can't focus on me right now, though, and knowing I have other shit to attend to, I pivot and leave them to it. I chuckle quietly with a shake of my head and shut the door behind me.

For some reason, I've told myself I'm capable of dealing with Duke's Juliette freak-out. There's no doubt in my mind with the way he took off that he's wallowing in memories and regret and thoughts of vengeance. But he might also be remembering what'd happened the first —and only other—time I tried to help him on the anniversary of her death.

I let out a harsh exhale as I hurry out of my room and directly across the hall. Lifting my hand, I rap my knuckles against his door. "Duke, man. Open up." It's useless. I knew that before I knocked, before I opened my mouth.

The only thing I'm rewarded with is his silence. I'd tried to talk to him through the door when I first got up here. Then I'd pounded on it. But no go, not to any of it. Not even so much as acknowledgment that he knew I was out here.

But he knows. For sure. He's simply choosing to ignore me.

On one hand, it's obvious he's not in a talking mood, but on the other hand, what kind of fucking friend would I be if I saw him that upset and just let him drown in it?

Which is why I'm going to pick this fancy-ass lock he had put on his door over the summer. It'd taken me a minute to find the tools that I knew were somewhere in the trunk in my closet, but now that I have them, it should be a simple thing to get in there. He's going to be fucking pissed.

And I don't fucking care. I know Duke, and he'll go off the deep end without someone to talk him down, talk him through it. It only takes me a minute of messing around with the lock-picking tools before I hear things click into place. With a smile, I stand and twist the knob, throwing the door open in dramatic fashion.

I pause on the threshold, taking in the scene before

me. Duke stands at the window looking out over the front lawn of the house. He's shirtless, wearing only a pair of jeans, and his arms are braced over his head as he stares out into the dark.

He turns his head as I enter the room, his intense gaze sliding toward me. He shakes his head without a word.

Clearing my throat, I murmur, "Don't know when you started underestimating me; but you know if I get something in my head, I'll make it happen."

"No shit. And now that you're here, get the fuck out, Mase." He throws his well-muscled arm toward the door, welcoming me to take my exit.

I slowly shake my head. "Yeah, no. That's not happening."

"I don't need or want you here with me right now. I want to be alone with my thoughts." His jaw twitches and pops. The muscles in his back are rigid. That coiled tension will let loose with one wrong move.

Or fuck. Maybe it'd be the right move. To push him hard enough that he unleashes every bit of built-up anger inside him. "No. The last thing you need right now is to drop into a spiral of unending sadness and self-pity."

He turns to me, blue eyes blazing. "What the fuck's wrong with you? Do you not understand basic fucking human emotion anymore? Are you so goddamn damaged that you can't understand why I might not want to be with anyone right now?" His chest rises and falls rapidly. He throws his arm out again, this time in the direction of the attic. "As if you don't hide away on a regular fucking basis. You get all rage-y when anyone dares set foot up there. And yet, you won't give me this?"

My heart clenches hard, like it's being gripped in a vise. "We're different people. You've never done well on your own, Duke. You get all up in your head. You never let anything out. When I'm up there sketching, I'm letting it out."

"You think I'm going to fucking fall apart if I'm alone, but let's face it—I've never done so hot *with* people either. Especially not *you.*" His expression is hard as he stalks toward me, a deep line etched into his forehead and a mad scowl slipping over his features. When he reaches me, he slaps his palms against my chest and pushes me backward as hard as he fucking can.

He's strong, I'll give him that, and I stumble momentarily, but don't give up any ground. My heart trips, too, thrumming in my chest at his proximity, at the angry way he's assessing me. An annoyed, close-mouthed smile tips my lips. "Nice. Look, I didn't come to talk about us, asshole. Funny how that's what you automatically divert the conversation to, though."

Duke steps so close I can feel each of his breaths as he stares into my eyes, furious temper heating his brilliant blues. We remain unmoving for so long I'm not quite sure what the hell is running through his head, which is odd because usually I have his number. That's why it's so easy for me to fuck with him.

I cock my head to the side, taking another few moments to study him with the same intensity he's scrutinizing me. *Except, ha.* Yeah. Now I know what's ticking around in his head. I've pointed it out to him, so he's not going to be able to stop thinking about it. I quirk my brow at him, knowing full well that it infuriates him. And frankly, I'd rather have him pissed off at me than in devastation mode from feeling Juliette's loss all over again.

I slick my tongue over my lower lip, and his eyes drop to my mouth, following the movement. I can't help the smirk that finds its way to my lips. "You wanna push me around some more, Duke?" I shrug nonchalantly before I grit, "Go right fucking ahead."

We're just about the same height so the only intimidation factor he has is that he might outweigh me by like fifteen pounds. But as we established yet again upstairs in the attic, I'm meaner than he is, and if I see something I can use to my advantage, I damn well will.

It just so happens that Duke's greatest weakness, the thing I can use to taunt him … is me.

"I'm not leaving you like this to mope around all fucking night and day until another anniversary of Juliette's death has passed and you finally become human again."

He glares at me, his entire body stiffening. "I mean it, Mason. Leave, right the fuck now."

"Or what, D?" I narrow my gaze on him, purposefully letting it slip down his body. "You scared of what might happen if you let me stay?"

His eyes flash. "The only thing that's gonna happen is me laying you out, now fuck off."

"If memory serves, last time it was me who laid you out." My thoughts crash backward in time to the night he ripped me from Lennon's body, and we'd rolled around, pounding on each other. I'd really gone after him—both with my fists and with my words. I blink, noticing my comment has caused agitation to roll off him in waves.

He shakes his head, furious. "What are you trying to achieve by coming in here and getting all up in my head? You think getting in my space is gonna calm me down? If anything, you're pissing me off even more."

I slick my tongue over my bottom lip, curiosity

blooming. "Why? What is it about me that crawls under your skin?"

Duke's tormented eyes meet mine, confusion warring with something that looks an awful lot like flat-out need. He turns his back on me, running his hands through his hair and tugging at the strands. As I watch him, his broad back expands with the deep breaths he's taking. Attempting to ignore my question, no doubt. His voice gritty and raw, he rasps, "Stop fucking pushing. The past should stay where it fucking belongs. I don't wanna talk about it."

If I could just make him see that he needs to sift through these emotions, accept them for what they are, then maybe he can move on. He says he wants to be alone and doesn't want to dredge things up, but right now he appears to be very stuck in the past. "Yeah, is that why you've locked yourself in this room? Because you're *not* in here, reliving the ghosts that haunt you? 'Cause from where I'm standing, the past is exactly where the fuck your head is at."

"She was my girlfriend. I. Loved. Her," he grits out.

Exhaling harshly, I plant my hands on my hips, watching as his back heaves with the labored breaths he's taking. It fucking kills me to see him doing this to himself. "Nobody is saying otherwise, man. I know how you felt about her." I throw both arms out from my sides in exasperation. "And fuck, I spend most my nights revisiting my childhood, but I'm not the one refusing to admit the past is what molded this future. Every piece of us is forged from the moments we've lived through, Duke. Every fucking moment. Even the ones you refuse to acknowledge."

"It doesn't mean we need to fucking talk it to death." Duke whirls around, taking two fistfuls of my T-shirt, and in one violent move, he tears it practically right down the middle, then yanks me against him. Breath gusts unsteadily from between his lips.

I study his raging body from under hooded eyes. "What are you doing?"

"Why won't you leave me alone?" he grits out. Without warning, he grasps the back of my neck with both hands, and his mouth slams into mine, all fire and fury and heat.

Fuck. My brain misfires as I hook my hands over his biceps and sink into the kiss. He doesn't wait for permission, but forces his tongue into my mouth with deep, devastating licks. My head buzzes, full of memories of the last time Duke and I kissed. He'd been angry at the world. Trying like hell to get his mind off things. I'd brought a chick to his room, and we'd ended up fucking her—sharing her—but after she left, I hadn't wanted to fucking leave him because I could still see it in his eyes.

The sorrow. The regret. The anger he'd turned inward at himself.

That'd been the first anniversary of Juliette's death. We'd both been drunk, one minute laying side by side, and the next ... a furious, raging wildfire of passion.

But we aren't drunk now, that's for fucking sure. And I'm afraid all Duke has for me right now is unhinged hate. He continues to plunder my mouth with his wicked tongue, and it sets off all sorts of fireworks along my skin. I'm burning up. The feel of his hard body coming into contact with mine, his hot skin under my fingertips. The way he smells of pure, undiluted male with a hint of citrus aftershave. *Fuck.*

I let go of his arms in favor of sliding my palms over his rib cage, then trailing them along his upper back. I hold him firmly in the circle of my arms while he continues to assault my mouth. His kisses are brutal. Savage. Full of lust and a desire so profound, I have to wonder if this has been building and building for the last three years while he's been in fucking denial over what happened between us.

"I don't need you." He gasps for air as he changes the angle of our kiss, his fingers rubbing over the hair at the back of my head, the pads of his thumbs sliding along my jaw. A desperate groan tears from his throat.

Like *fuck* he doesn't need me. I slide my hands down

the firm planes of his back, roaming over sleek muscle, and rest them just above the waistband of his jeans. I swear to fuck, I've applied no pressure, but his dick is suddenly sliding along mine, sending a wave of desire crashing over me. I'd been ignoring the semi I've been sporting during our argument, but there's no denying it now. I'm fucking hard for him, just like I have been a thousand times in the past.

I let out a ragged breath, my lips hovering just over his. Those blue eyes bore into mine, so intensely angry that it almost knocks me off my feet. There's no way in hell this can be anything but his decision … but I'd be lying if I said I wasn't going to tempt the shit out of him, especially because he's the one who initiated. Sliding my hands down to cup his toned, muscular ass, I bring our lower bodies flush.

His throat bobs with a hard swallow. "I don't fucking want you." My heart beats erratically as his hands slip to my shoulders and he dives back in to take my mouth again.

I let him attack me with his searing kisses for several hot, lusty beats of my heart before wrenching my lips from his and looking at him from under my hooded eyes. "Your dick says otherwise."

He snarls, then uses his lips and tongue and his teeth

—everything in his goddamn arsenal—to drive me out of my mind. To punish me.

But I fucking like this kind of punishment, and my dick is so fucking hard in my pants, I let out a hiss every time his cock nudges mine.

He spins us, backing me toward his king-size bed, his hands grappling with the remains of my shirt until it's lying in tatters on the floor. He nips along my jaw, practically growling as his tongue darts out to taste my skin.

The back of my legs bump into the side of the bed, and we pause there as he stares into my eyes, determination lighting his. He reaches between us, unbuttoning my jeans, and draws the zipper down slowly. I swear I feel each metal tooth release as the waistband of my jeans loosens. My cock is like an angry bull wanting to escape its isolation cell. "Are you still trying to say you don't want this?"

FIFTEEN

DUKE

ONE BREATH after another bursts from me as I attempt to wrap my head around what's happening between me and Mason. My jaw is tight as I work his zipper down, refusing to look at him for a moment. I need to get out of my head. I want—

My chest clenches. I don't know what I'm saying. I don't understand what I want. My skin feels tight, as if I'm going to burst free of it. But I can't get free, and my misery makes me want to hurt him. Punish him. How fucking dare he come after me. How dare he remind me of how this went three years ago, the last time he tried to help me. For making me remember the night he fucked me until I couldn't think about anything else.

The morning after, in the light of day—no, no, no. I

hadn't known how to come to terms with what he and I had done. Hadn't known how to look my friend in the eye. So, I avoided the whole thing. Pushed him away. And I'm really fucking good at that. I told him he took advantage of me in a weak moment. And when he suggested maybe it was something we should try again, I shut him out. Told him to fuck off and leave me alone, that it wasn't happening.

We haven't been the same since.

And now, I don't know what the fuck to think. I don't fucking want him. I don't. But my cock swells at the thought of being with him, leaking onto the front of my boxer briefs. Nothing I'm feeling makes any fucking sense.

He wants this, I can see the lust in his eyes, can feel it in the way he's touched me. But he shouldn't have fucking come to my rescue. I'll make him pay for it, too. It means nothing. What I choose to do doesn't define me. And no one has to fucking know.

Fuck it. I haul Mason closer by the back of his neck, tugging his mouth back to mine. I sweep my tongue over his fucking full lower lip before we crash together again. I have a hold of the waistband of his jeans and yank him to me, letting our cocks line up. It feels so far from what I think I should want, but I also can't help the way it riles me up. A strange mixture of rage and unholy thoughts bursts through my veins and makes my head go cloudy with yearning.

Disengaging our lip-lock, I shove him onto the bed. Eyeing me without a hint of the jackass smirk I'd have thought he'd be wearing, he crawls backward. He's a fucking sight with his hair mussed, skin flushed pink and splotchy in places, and his jeans hanging open with the hard bulge of his erection pushing against the confines of his boxer briefs.

I don't know if this is right or wrong or somewhere in between, but I pop the button on my jeans, too, working the zipper down with one hand as I follow him onto the bed. I brace myself with my forearms and stare into his dark, desire-filled eyes.

A flash of the two of us that night three years ago hits me upside the head, and I search his face, wondering if he remembers it the same way I always have. I'm rocked by the recall of us totally fucking naked, cocks leaking on each other's stomachs as we writhed together on the bed. Panting. Moaning. No fucking clue what we were doing. My head had been hazy and fucking full of him.

My face goes hot and tingly as the full memory of Mason touching me hits. The feel of his cock breaching my ass. And the way we'd grunted and gasped, moving together as his dick glided in and out. I shut my eyes against it, my jaw locking up, teeth grinding.

When I open them again and search the depths of his eyes, I can't fucking stop myself. I take his lip into my mouth and bite. He gasps aloud, and I recklessly plunge my tongue into his mouth as I drop my body weight on top of him. The skin-on-skin contact is mind-bending. It sends electric shocks of pleasure down my spine. We're savage, the two of us, clawing at each other. With every stroke of my tongue, I seek to punish, and I grind my cock against his until we're pitching and rolling and shifting and straining.

I rear up, shuffling until I can pull Mason's jeans and underwear from him. His dick juts from his body, harder than hell, the tip glistening with a bead of moisture. He blinks but then is up and on his knees so fast I swear I must be out of it, because he's staring directly into my eyes as he tugs my jeans over my hips. He reaches into my boxer briefs and pulls out my cock. I hiss as his fist closes around me and groan aloud at the contact. My head twists and screams when his hand shuttles along my length. But, oh fuck, it's good. The sight of his dexterous, masculine hand working me over only makes me harder than I was before, which shouldn't be possible, but then again, none of this should be happening at all. I stutter "F-fuck" as he slides his thumb over my slit and brings it to his mouth. He licks it clean, and then pulls my mouth to his. Then this motherfucker maintains eye contact when he dips his tongue inside my mouth.

The taste of me on him comes close to making my head implode, but it also spurs me on and makes me spiral down the path to certain destruction. I ruthlessly kiss him as I glide my hand over his cock, then down to cup his balls, tugging firmly.

His chest stutters, and he draws in a surprised breath before he grasps my ass, pulling us tightly together, our dicks trapped between us. Our mouths slam into another kiss, our arms tangle, and our hands roam. And through it all, we grind. His bare cock touching mine sends me into a fucking frenzy, and he's right there with me through it all. We tear at each other as we fall to the bed, and I finally kick free of my jeans and underwear.

I mercilessly touch him, running my hands over his firm muscle and smooth skin, not giving him a second to think or breathe, because I don't want to do those things myself. Sucking on his neck, I rock my hips in time with his, grunting as more and more of our slick pre-cum mixes on our skin between us.

Rising up, I straddle him with every intention of going for the lube when the bastard throws me for a loop, lazily sliding his finger through the mess on his stomach before lifting arm and bringing it to my mouth, smearing it all over my lips. *Dirty, dirty boy.*

My tongue slips out for a taste. The salty, musky, earthy flavor of *us* sends a jolt of undiluted longing through me. I tilt my head to the side as his hand finds my hip and he tugs.

"Get back here," he grits out.

I dive back down, attacking his mouth and sharing it with him, and our tongues tangle and twist, battling in a war neither of us is going to win. I'm terrified that I'm about to lose *myself*—in him.

The heat between us, the animalistic grunts and groans, it all feeds into this chaos in my head. I want to ravage him for doing this to me, make him understand there's a price he'll pay for doing this to me again. He will cry out for mercy before I'm done. I hope to fuck he's ready for me to get him back for every sleepless night I've had. For every carnal thought of him I've had to shove down deep and ignore.

I push myself up, edging back, my mouth ghosting over the dips and ridges of his chest and abs, stopping to lick and suck on his skin, and making him gasp out in surprise and pleasure and fucking agony. And when I get to his cock, I flatten my tongue and lick him all along the underside from base to tip.

He shudders with need and clutches at my hair. I allow my eyes to travel from his dick, where I continue to flick my tongue, ever so slowly up his body until I meet his gaze. There's pure fire raging in his eyes, and the flames jolt higher when I take him in hand and begin to stroke while closing my lips around the head of his dick. I swirl my tongue, then suck, eliciting a huffed cry from his lips.

"Fuck, Duke. Where the hell did you learn that?" His face is flushed, eyes glazed over as he watches me take his dick to the back of my throat before sliding it most of the way out again. I go after him with a vengeance, making his hips lift from the mattress and his legs quake. I wet my lips, pausing for only a moment to take his balls in my grasp, firmly holding them in my hand while I go back to sucking his dick.

He's fucking squirming beneath me, panting. I'm relentless. Merciless. He's losing his goddamn mind.

And I think I am, too. The taste and smell of him floods my senses. I thought at first that I'd suck him off to within an inch of coming, but there's no way I'm stopping now. I want him to know who's in fucking control here, and it's sure as fuck not him. Not right now. He grunts, his breath labored. His stomach muscles dip and twitch. I tug firmly, massaging his balls in my hand, then slip my fingers back, rub them over the skin between his ball sac and his ass.

"Oh god. Fuck." Mason throws his head back. "I'm

gonna— Fuck." He gasps, bringing his head up again to search my eyes. "Oh god, Duke. I'm gonna—"

He never finishes his sentence as his cum hits the back of my throat in forceful spurts, and I swallow it down. I can tell from the look of utter shock on his face that he wasn't expecting me to do that. Probably thought I'd pop off at the last second and let him jizz all over himself.

I'm not giving him a single second to think this is over. While he's lying there in a daze, I grab a bottle of lube from my nightstand and quickly squirt some into my palm, stroking myself roughly. "This is what you wanted," I growl, my voice low and raspy.

His dark eyes seem almost black as his pupils have dilated, and his cock is still stiff, darkly flushed, and so fucking enticing. I don't know what it says about my current state of mind, but it turns me on like crazy that I just made him come so hard.

Mason arches a brow and takes a quick breath. "Yeah. We'll let you think that."

Fucker. How the fuck does he know what's in my head? Does he realize that I fucking know he's not coercing me? That he didn't the first time either? Tension coils within me. *Dick. Fuck, how does he get into my head like this?*

"We'll see how smart that mouth is when I shove my cock deep in your ass."

"Challenge accepted." He sits up and rolls over, getting to his hands and knees, and it's fucking on. I get behind him and smear my lubed-up fingers over his asshole. He hisses but pushes his ass in my direction. I'm not especially gentle, but it doesn't seem to matter to him, as he makes a sound that is half moan, half plea when I slide a finger inside him. "Fucking give it to me, Duke." He turns his head to look over his shoulder at me. His jaw is tight, and I can't quite tell what he's thinking, but if he's giving me the go-ahead, I'm not holding back.

I pick up the lube and squirt more at the top of his crack and let it slip down between his cheeks. I want him to ask for it. I want him fucking begging. Pushing his upper body down to the mattress, I plant my hands on his ass cheeks and spread them apart, sliding the underside of my cock through the lube, up and down the crease of his ass. My teeth grind because it fucking feels phenomenal, and my head is beginning to spin at the sensation.

His chest jerks, and he moans into the bedding beneath him. I lift one hand and smack his ass, but it's well-muscled enough that it hardly moves, but it does make him yelp. "Fuck."

"Mm-hmm." I continue to slip my cock over him. The more I do it, the more labored his breathing becomes.

"Duke." He looks over his shoulder. That lip I've found I like to bite is caught between his teeth. His eyes are glazed over with lust.

"Yeah?"

His breaths gust from him, and he pushes his ass back against me. "You talk a big—"

He doesn't get to finish because I slam forward. A wild keening sound rips from his throat as I slide deep inside. "Fuuuck." It's so damn intense, my vision begins to tunnel. I ease back just a bit, then stroke forward with a snap of my hips. Again. And again. *Holy fucking shit.* My cock is in his ass—and that's not all that has me sweating. He pushes back against me, taking more of my dick with every mind-bending thrust. A low-level buzz sounds in my head, and I can't focus on anything but me and Mason and the way his ass is clamped around my cock.

His breathing is erratic, but he spreads his legs wider, giving me more room to work. "Oh fuck."

"That's right." I grip his hips and plunge my cock as far as it will go, balls deep, then pull out and plunge back in.

His head snaps up and his fingers clutch the sheet,

twisting it in his fingers. "Harder," he groans out, meeting me halfway with every fucking stroke.

My heart is threatening to come out of my chest, pounding hard against my rib cage, and sweat pops out on my brow the faster I move. I watch how he's taking me, and my lungs constrict in my chest. My fingers sink into his skin as I keep up the frantic rhythm we've set. I lift one hand and smack his ass again. He lets out a low moan in response.

His body shudders. "Fuck. My dick is leaking all over the sheets."

"Is my fat cock gonna make you come again?" I lean forward and collar the back of his neck, running my other hand over his back.

"Y-yes. Fuck. Goddamn. Almost there."

My balls are heavy with the need to come, too. I can't even believe I've held out so fucking long because it's been a possibility I'd fucking lose it with every twitch and clench of his tight, tight ass.

Suddenly, this isn't enough. I pull out and flip him over on his back. He gasps at the sudden change, but I'm on him, pushing his legs up, exposing him to me again. I lean in, nudging his ass with my cock, and I swear to fuck, he greedily takes me back inside him. My eyes widen as I stare for the first time directly into his eyes while I'm filling him up. He stares right back, his jaw clenched. I rock into him and watch the changing expressions on his face. Lust. Passion. Absolute fucking rapture.

I take it a step further and lie on top of him, chest to chest, with his weeping dick caught between us, and our lips find each other, teeth gnashing, tongues plunging deep, like we're looking to find as many ways to be connected to each other as possible. I take his head between my hands and hold him to me, while his hands claw at my back and my ass, trying to pull me closer.

Our chests heave together as we go at it, and it doesn't take much longer before I feel the orgasm roll down my spine. My balls draw up, and I grunt into Mason's mouth as I come hard. The way he fucking whimpers, I could swear he feels me shoot my load inside him.

He tears his mouth from mine, his body quaking, and then he's coming, too, his release spurting from his thick cock and smearing between us as we continue to writhe against each other. I lean in, skimming my lips over his jawline, then bare my teeth to nip at him before sucking on his neck. He moans and shifts beneath me. It feels too fucking good. *Way* too fucking good.

I don't want this to be over. Because I'll have to go right back to hating him.

SIXTEEN

LENNON

MY STOMACH PITCHES, falling into nothingness. I wake, gasping at the sudden feeling of being submerged. Water floods my mouth, and I choke on it as I try to breathe. What's happening? Why?

Instinct has me pushing to the surface, and I come up coughing and gagging, trying to expel the chlorinated water from my lungs. *Chlorinated*. Wait. Confusion reigns.

How the hell did I end up in the motherfucking pool? I blink, recognizing the blare of the house alarm crashing through the still of the night. Oh my god, what have I done? Shock jolts through me as Mason appears at the back door. His eyes widen, horror crossing his features as he sprints toward me. Still hacking up a lung, I wipe water out of my eyes as I swim the short distance to the edge of the pool. Bracing my arms on the edge, I let my chest hitch violently in protest of my misadventure.

"Lennon!" Mason doesn't stop running until he's in the pool at my side. "What the fuck? Are you okay?" His wild eyes search mine, and he puts a hand to my back, rubbing as I continue to cough.

Mortified, I shake my head, color rising fast on my cheeks. "I don't know." I cough again, hating the feeling of being on display and how unstable this makes me appear.

A good ten seconds later, Warren arrives, followed by Arik and Quincy.

The two butthead brothers roll their eyes and stand there, but Warren hovers at the pool's edge, brow furrowed. "Do you need help getting out?"

I drag in a rough breath, trying to smile at him and mostly failing. "I need a minute." I'm hyperaware that I'm shaking. The entire thing embarrasses and frustrates me because I don't like that this has happened again, putting me in the spotlight, when my original plan was always to keep my head down. Not that these guys have let me fly under the radar at all, constantly in my face and poking at me.

Mason's hand continues to move over my back in a calming manner as he whispers in my ear. "You take your time. I've got you, Kintsukuroi." He eases back, searching my eyes carefully, then slides his thumb over my jaw. "You trust me, right?"

I nod, blinking hard and fighting back the stinging sensation that assaults the back of my eyes. I wasn't upset a moment ago, but those words. *I've got you.* They mean something to me, because when I've needed someone, he *has* been there. Maybe that's partly why I'm able to look past his other idiosyncrasies and faults and allow trust to grow again between us—he gets me, and he's been there. "Thank you. I don't—"

What would have been a feeble explanation at best is cut off by Kai, Brendan, and Pierre stumbling outside. "This is what we stopped gaming for?" Kai pushes his hair off his forehead and bellows, "Somebody cut off the fucking alarm!" They look—and sound—drunk. On a Sunday night, too. Living their best lives here at Bainbridge Hall. Inwardly, I laugh, despite the fact it brings on another coughing fit.

Someone must have punched in the code because the alarm stops sounding just as Pierre throws out a hand, connecting his gaze with mine and laughing. "Sure, *now* she wants to go for a swim."

"Little late for that, don't you think, princess?" Brendan shakes his head, lips pressed together. He seems perturbed, one of those angry drunks, and heaven forbid

I've interrupted whatever late-night gaming session they were involved in.

Jackasses, all of them. Paying them no attention, I attempt to catch my breath and close my eyes for a moment.

Sensing his presence before I see him, my eyes flick open to find Bear—*Gideon*—folding his large body until he's seated at the edge of the pool next to me. "What are you doing in the pool, Little Gazelle?" He helps me smooth my sopping-wet hair away from my face.

I blink up at him, tingles washing through my body before my gaze shifts for a split second to the in-ground spa. My face burns at the memory of what we did in there not all that long ago. "I-I don't know what happened. I should have listened to you." Because the last thing Bear had said to me before we parted ways in the upstairs hallway was that maybe, with all the bullshit that'd happened, I would be better off if he stayed with me. I don't know why I'd refused the idea, except my head had been spinning a little. Mason. Bear. Duke. All three are fighting to get to the forefront of my thoughts, and the hell of it is there's no clear winner. They're all on my mind for different reasons.

"It's not your fault, don't worry about it," he rumbles, his voice gruff and low.

I glance past Bear toward the house as Duke exits.

Before he can get to us, Quincy drops into a lounge chair poolside and huffs out a laugh, chitchatting with Arik as if the rest of us aren't right here. "I wonder if once she has the code to the alarm system, she'll punch it on the way out so the rest of us don't get awakened every time she wants to take a midnight swim."

"You aren't kidding. Fuck, man. All this interrupted sleep," Arik groans obnoxiously, but it's clear he thinks Quincy's thoughts are hilarious from the chuckle that directly follows his faked discomfort.

Fucking assholes. My face flashes hot and my jaw trembles, but I don't have to say a word in my own defense because Duke aims a steely-eyed glare at the grunts. "Looks like you dickwads will be spending another week eating at the kiddie table in the kitchen. Maybe try not to be fucking douchebags. And as for the alarm code, forget that for now. You definitely haven't earned jack shit."

Quincy's eyes widen. "But—"

"No fucking way," Arik groans. "Come on!"

"Shut the fuck up, both of you. You're just digging yourselves into a hole you'll never get out of if you keep going," Duke grits, tossing the command over his shoulder as he comes down on his haunches directly in front of me.

His face tells the tale of how his night has gone since

he took off. He looks absolutely haggard. Worse than I do, I bet—even though I almost drowned myself. *What a shit show we are tonight.* I check from the corner of my eye to see how Mason is reacting to Duke's arrival, because I'm highly curious how the two of them got on earlier. Mason had eventually made it into Duke's room after he watched us from the balcony, that much I know because there'd been heated voices coming from inside when Bear and I walked past. But after that, I don't know. I'd taken a quick shower and climbed into bed.

"Stella Bella." His blue eyes catch mine and hold steady. The nickname, when he says it softly like that, makes my heart stutter. Why does it feel different now? Does he realize he's acting differently toward me? It could be a show, so he can slap me down at his convenience. He might be waiting until I'm comfortable and not expecting the attack before he swoops in. That's what Duke would have done a week ago.

I expel a hard breath, and when he doesn't say another word, I simply respond "Duke," then look away, my eyes traveling uncomfortably over the rest of the brothers who still hang around the pool area.

My chest jerks in surprise when he reaches forward and grips my chin, steering my face back to his. "Do you want to get out of the pool?"

"I—" I glance at myself, for the first time realizing I

must have walked right out of the house in the under-wear and sports bra I'd climbed into bed wearing. I suppose I'm lucky it was this because I've been known to just wear a T-shirt and nothing else. I stare down at the white bra that's practically translucent when wet. "Fuck it. Looks like I'm giving everyone a show. Sorry." I wince, putting my forearm over my breasts where my nipples have pebbled behind the thin cotton.

Duke exhales hard. I can totally tell he's trying not to look at me at all, and whether that has more to do with the fact that I'm not wearing much or—and this is actually more likely—he's still having a really bad fucking night despite whatever efforts Mason made to make sure he was okay.

Duke pats Bear on the shoulder, urging him to his feet, then once their eyes meet, Duke gestures with his chin toward me. It's almost as if they have an entire conversation with that one movement and a certain look passed between them. A moment later, they each put a hand under one of my arms and lift me out of the pool.

"Thank fuck for the lights around the pool, huh?"

"Wish we could see better. What the fuck time is it, anyway?"

I don't even know which jackasses opened their mouths, but much to my dismay, the initial question sets off a series of catcalls—not that I wasn't expecting them when they pulled me from the water. Duke's annoyed yet concerned gaze flicks to mine, and he's quick to reach over his shoulder and pull his shirt off, flips it around, and has it over my head only a second later. I give him a grateful smile as I poke my arms through the holes while Bear pulls the hem down over my ass. As soon as I'm mostly covered, the hooting and hollering dies down, especially after the withering look Bear shoots everyone behind him.

Duke extends a hand to Mason, helping him out of the pool. There's an odd tension between them that is thick in the early morning air. I'm unsure what to make of it, but maybe it has to do with how their conversation went earlier. I can ask Mason later, when it's not dark o'clock and only a couple hours before we have to be up to get to classes.

The brotherhood has just calmed from my pool exit when a low rumble of laughter and more talk begins to work its way through the group.

My brows dart together, frowning. I can't tell what they're talking about, it's all muffled chatter and hushed chuckling. My eyes flick around the group, the crease down my forehead deepening at the commotion rolling through the group. A few point ... toward Duke. I bite my lip, turning to get Bear's take on whatever the hell is going on. I've missed something. He shakes his head, though, shrugging his shoulders. He seems as perplexed by the current situation as I am.

The dam bursts as Brendan lets out a huge guffaw. "Damn, what hellcat have you been hiding upstairs?"

And before Duke can turn to face them, there's another comment, this time from Kai. "Fuck, Duke. Whoever she was, she clawed up your back good, man." He eyes Duke with interest.

Bear shakes his head, deep voice booming. "That's e-fucking-nough."

"The fuck's going on? What hellcat?" All heads turn to the back door where Tucker finally strolls out onto the patio, rubbing his eyes before he stops to gawk at the scene before him. A wide grin pulls at his lips.

"Just shut up. All of you," Duke growls, a stony look on his face.

I wouldn't cross him, but apparently, Tucker has no such qualms. His face registers surprise, then morphs into a sick enjoyment of the topic at hand. "Wait, are they saying you and your sister ...?" His eyes shoot between me and Duke before Tucker throws his head back, laughing.

Someone else lets out a low whistle and a couple more chuckle quietly, but I'm more interested in the way Duke's face has gone pale before turning bright red. The expression slipping over his features is lethal. A muscle in his jaw twitches angrily. "No, dickface. This had nothing to do with Lennon, my *step*sister. But there's plenty we need to address that does concern her, and you'll all be present"—he grits his teeth as his gaze touches on everyone—"tonight. Brotherhood meeting. Every single one of you fuckers *will* be in attendance. There's some shit that needs to become real clear, real quick before I start kicking asses out of this goddamn house. Got it?"

Bear sucks in a breath, but his head bobs, and he barks out a final command. "Now, get the fuck back in the house. All of you. We don't need your help, and this isn't for your goddamn entertainment. It's not a fuckin' reality show."

Tucker wriggles his brows at Duke, which has Duke lunging forward until Bear pulls him back with one big hand to his shoulder. "He's not worth it, man. We'll talk about how to deal with their piss-poor attitudes and the obvious lack of obedience later."

While we're waiting on everyone to wise up and move the fuck on out, I turn and ask Mason one of the questions that's been ticking around inside my head that's only semi-adjacent to the current shitstorm. "Were you awake when I came out here? How did you get down here so fast?"

He hesitates for a moment, glancing past me toward Duke, while scraping his teeth over his full bottom lip.

"Yeah, I was in the attic and actually heard the beeping before the alarm went off because I left the door ajar. I hoped it was one of these assholes coming in drunk or whatever and forgetting to punch in the alarm code, but I didn't want to take the chance that was a wrong assumption. I got down to the first floor and was about to go to the front of the house when I saw the door to the patio standing open."

I rub a pair of fingers at each temple in tight circles. Yep. Still embarrassed as fuck but going to put it out of my head because I have no other choice. "I can't believe it happened again. I'm sorry."

With a growl, Duke huffs out, "You don't need to apologize for something that isn't your fault."

Mason grips the back of my neck, giving me a gentle squeeze as he shakes his head. "You didn't do it on purpose. We all know that. Come on, looks like the coast is mostly clear."

As our foursome trudges back to the house, I murmur quietly, "Thanks for loaning me your shirt, Duke."

He huffs out a beleaguered grunt from up ahead of us, which is all the acceptance of my thanks I'm going to get, from the sound of it. I guess no one would have seen his back if he hadn't done me that favor, so maybe he's pissed about it. I wonder when it happened.

When I glance over at Bear, he's got his lip caught between his teeth, he lets his gaze shift to Duke for a second, then back to me. His head jerks ever so slightly. I nod in response. *Got it.* It's probably best to let him be, even though I have plenty of questions surrounding his shirt, or rather, why his back is indeed rubbed raw in places. I understand the *hellcat* and *claw mark* references now that I've had a chance to get a peek.

But how? I must be too tired for this. Truth be told, I'm exhausted and don't know if I'm going to manage to pry myself out of bed to go to classes in a few hours.

Silently, we walk up the stairs, Bear and Duke leading the way with Mason and myself following. We're leaving wet footprints everywhere we step, and, in hindsight, probably should have grabbed towels out of the pool house, but it's late—or early, whichever way we want to look at it—and obviously none of us are completely with it at the moment. All the way up the stairs, I study the marks on Duke's back, but I don't dare say a word. My brow furrows.

As we get to the end of the hallway, Mason reaches out, lightly toying with my hand. "You gonna be okay, or do I have to set up camp out on the balcony?"

"Hilarious." Bear crosses his arms over his chest, surveying the three of us as he turns, walking backward the remaining distance to our rooms.

We all come to a stop, and at the teasing smirk Mason shoots me, I roll my eyes. "I'll be fine. Seriously."

There's an awkwardness among us, which isn't usually present, and I can't quite pinpoint what's causing it. "Class at nine, so see you all at eight thirty at the latest?" I throw that out there, and they nod without comment, almost as if each one is caught up in his head.

Mason's eyes finally train on Duke. "You going to class or staying home? Did you decide?"

"Don't know yet." This poor guy, his emotions are clearly all over the place. One minute he's slamming doors, the next he looks so fucking sad I want to wrap him up in my arms and not let go until today is done. Maybe it's stupid of me to have that thought in my head, but ... we got along just fine when we were left alone during Bear's fight.

"I'm going to attempt to sleep." My eyes find each of theirs in turn and they nod their agreement. Mason's still holding my hand, so I give it a brief squeeze, and he lets go. "Thanks for jumping in after me."

"Anytime."

In the dark, I can barely make something out on his neck. Curiosity gets the better of me and, leaning in, I run my fingertips over it. "Um." I frown, cocking my head to the side, truly confused. That wasn't there earlier today. I'd have noticed it. "Where'd that come from?" I meet his dark eyes and search them for the answer. "'Cause I know it wasn't me."

To my surprise, Mason gives Duke a furtive look out of the corner of his eye that I'm unsure I was supposed to see at all.

My eyes go wide like saucers before I blink rapidly. Wait, what? My brain is going a mile a minute. Clawlike marks on Duke's back. A hickey on Mason's neck. The odd look they'd exchanged. But no matter how hard I try, I can't seem to make the evidence before me compute in a way that makes sense.

"Why the fuck are all of you staring at me?" Duke's tone is ... defensive.

All eyes swing back to Mason, who simply shrugs and holds up his hands, eyeing Duke up and down. "They probably want to know who marked up your back and my neck."

Bear's brows go up at around the same time my mouth opens and closes.

Duke spins on his heel. There's no hesitation at all, he slams his fist directly into the door with a sickening crack. I don't know if anyone else is at the right angle to see it, but his face creases in pain before he rears back and punches again.

"Duke!" I suck in a breath, covering my mouth with shaking hands. I'm too stunned to move more than that.

"Duke, don't." Bear grabs him by both shoulders and yanks him back, his gravelly voice whispering in his ear. Whatever he's said seems to get through to him, as Duke expels a hard breath, his chest heaving as he faces us.

"You think you know things, but you don't know shit." He shakes his head, swallowing hard before turning to yank the door open, then slamming it behind him.

Mason's hands go into his hair, clutching at the inky, dark strands. "Jesus." He grits his teeth together. "I guess he must not have fucked all the mad or sad out, huh?" His jaw works to the side, eyes burning with something I don't quite understand, but I almost believe it's something close to humiliation. It makes my head spin to realize Mason is upset by what just transpired. Like at first, he tried to make light of it, but he must have recognized he wasn't fooling Bear or me.

He strides past us to the end of the hall, where he throws open the attic door and shuts it behind him with a sharp, meaningful snap. The kind that says, *Don't fucking follow me.*

SEVENTEEN

DUKE

ALL OF TWO fucking minutes have gone by when my door creaks open. I don't look behind me. Fucking Mason can suck a bag of dicks for all I care. I'm too busy tearing the sheets off the bed that still harbors evidence of what we did together to give a flying fuck if he wants to stand there like a creeper and watch me.

With every move I make, my knuckles burn and my heart continues to jackhammer in my chest. My attempt at controlled breathing isn't slowing down the vicious pounding, nor is simply willing it to stop racing working at all. I pause, bracing myself with one hand on the bed while rubbing the other over my left pec. Before I know it, I'm clawing at my heart, trying for a more physical approach, wanting to tear it out of there. I grimace at the feel of the fast-paced *thud, thud, thud.* It continues until I'm sure it's going to punch through my rib cage and land right here on the mattress in front of me. *Fuck my life.*

Why today of all days? I huff out an irritated laugh. *Simple. Because Mason, that's why.* Not the first time he's messed with my head on the anniversary of Juliette's death. Probably won't be the last. The question is what the fuck is his angle? Is he purposely choosing the day when I'm at my weakest to come at me like this? Way down deep, I don't want to believe that's the case. And I know ... *I know* he hadn't wanted us to be a one-time thing all the way back during our freshman year. I shut my eyes, my jaw tightening as my head spins and spins, knowing he's watching me slowly unravel.

"Where do you keep the spare sheets?" Lennon's voice is like a bucket of icy cold water dumping over me. Shock slides through my system. *Oh, hell.* Now I'm hearing shit. But then I turn my head to find I'm not imagining things, and it really is her standing there, watching me with cautious, concern-filled eyes. Eyes that are currently seeing way too fucking much.

I pick up the cum-stained sheets, my face growing hot. I squeeze my eyes shut for a moment, pressing my lips into a tight line. When they flick open again,

Lennon hasn't budged an inch and is watching me like a hawk. Without a word, I pivot and march the bedding into my bathroom, where I disappear into the closet. I'm confident she won't follow me in here, given her anxiety issues, so at least I can catch my breath for a few seconds.

Dumping the sheets into a laundry basket, I fold my hands over the top of my head, lacing my fingers together while I think. I should probably deal with the mess I made of my hand, but I'm too keyed up to worry about it.

Lennon definitely knows what Mason and I were up to earlier. I close the door to the closet for a moment, turning to look at my back in the mirror's reflection. *Holy fucking shit.* I blink, certain that my tired eyes aren't really seeing what I think they are.

Fuck me.

There are angry—not "claw marks," thanks fucking Brendan and Kai—red patches all over. Mason and I had gone hard at each other, and it hadn't occurred to me until my shirt was already off and everyone was fucking whooping that it'd be that noticeable. I shouldn't be embarrassed. It's not like they fucking know how they got there.

But I do.

"Duke?" Lennon's voice drifts to me from the other

side of the door. "Are you okay? I will absolutely walk out of here right now if you tell me to. But ..."

I grimace, then pull the door open. She stands on the other side in a tank top and some sort of stretchy little short-shorts, the same kind she'd been wearing—or, uh, *not* wearing—downstairs in the gym with Bear and Mason. She must have taken a few minutes to towel off and find dry clothing before coming to search me out.

My eyes ping over her softly curved hips, the tininess of her waist, and up to her perky tits before noticing that while she'd taken time for clothing, she hadn't bothered with her hair. It's still soaking wet.

As if she can follow right along with my thoughts, she gives me a wry grin. "I rinsed the chlorine off, but I didn't stop to dry my hair. I—" She pauses, eyes meeting my distrusting ones. Shrugging, she murmurs, "Sorry, there's no way I was going to bed without checking on you. It's already going to be a shitty day—we all freaking know that—but to add both the assumptions about you and me that Tucker made down at the pool and then ..."

And then Mason and the fucking purple love bite I left on his neck without realizing it. Or was it a hate mark? I don't fucking know which it was, just like I don't want to think about whether or not I knew what I was doing at the time. Because the answer—fuck. It messes with my head in the worst way.

I blink, realizing I have no clue if Lennon ever finished her thought, but I guess it doesn't fucking matter because I knew she'd bring up Mason, and I'm having a lot of trouble processing everything as it is. And now all her thoughts are colliding with mine, resulting in a tempest in my head that won't die down.

She continues explaining her presence in my room, gesturing a bit wildly toward me, then back at herself. "I didn't figure you were sleeping, and I'm kinda worked up from my underwater adventure, so here I am."

My jaw shifts to one side as I watch her every movement and listen to every word coming out of her mouth. "Fuck. Do you always talk this much, or am I in some weird alternate universe?"

Her lips twitch, studying me. "Maybe not to you I don't. Are you going to come out of the closet?"

My brows lift. No man who's unwilling to admit he likes dick wants to be asked that question. My jaw tightens as our eyes meet. At my disbelieving stare, she appears confused. The moment it hits her, though, her lips part, and a flood of color moves from her chest to her neck and all the way up to her cheeks where it burns a heady shade of pink.

I rest my hands on my hips, narrowing my eyes at her. "Was that some sort of bad joke?"

She picks up on my irritated tone quickly, scraping

her teeth over her bottom lip as she points one finger at me. "You're literally hiding in a closet, and I— You know how I am with that shit, Duke. You've witnessed my meltdowns firsthand." Her eyes close momentarily as she murmurs, "I didn't mean anything by it. I was going to say are you coming out, or do I have to come in after you, but yeah. We all know that's not happening. So I didn't finish my thought, and it sounded like I was teasing you, but I swear I wasn't. I wouldn't." She drags in an exaggerated breath, only—I'm actually unsure if it has more to do with her explanation or simply the closet itself. She gives me my answer two seconds later. "Can we go anywhere else to talk? I—" Covering her trembling lips with one hand, she swallows hard.

It's official. I'm a fucking dickhead. I have a right to how I feel, but she's not lying, and having seen her reaction to this shit multiple times, I don't need to use it against her. I work my jaw to the side, then grab a neat stack of sheets from the shelf. "Yeah. Sorry." When I step out and pull the door closed behind me, she visibly relaxes. I eye her cautiously. "Someday, you're going to tell me what the fuck is up with all that. And quit apologizing for something you can't control." I let out a sigh. "I shouldn't have stayed in there. I knew what I was doing."

She mulls over something in her head but must finally shake it because on an exhale, she says, "Trust me, you don't want to know more than you already do. It'd just add on to whatever assumptions you have about me, and I don't need that."

I can see the wheels ticking in her head, and it's not like I've forgotten that I called her a basket case a mere week ago. Granted, I was simply repeating what I'd been told, but that's a lame-ass excuse, honestly. And a lot has changed since then. A lot that I still need to sort in my head. Letting my eyes bore into hers, I murmur, "Maybe you don't know me as well as you think you do."

She gives a little jerk of her head like she doesn't believe that, but I gesture that we should head back into my room. She strides quickly away, leaving the closet behind, but I move more slowly. It'd be really fucking helpful if I could unglue my eyeballs from my stepsister's voluptuous ass and long legs, considering the conversation I'm positive is about to happen about me and where my dick's been lately.

Stopping at the side of the bed, she holds out a hand. My brows hitch together, and I hesitate as her lips quirk in question. "What? It's late. Let's get your bed remade so you can crash."

I blink, but then throw her the fitted sheet.

"Your hand looks like shit." She doesn't say another word about it, though, and begins the job of pulling the sheet over one of the corners at the foot of the bed, so I circle to the other side, and as I do, she tosses the other bottom corner in my direction. We're both busy wrestling with the sheet when she glances up. "You don't have to hide it from me, you know."

"Hide what?"

She rolls her eyes. "Are you telling me all the animosity between you and Mason hasn't actually been well-contained and tamped-down chemistry?"

I inhale steadily through my nose as I secure the second corner, then reach for the top sheet, flicking it open. My brain is heavy with the idea that she wants to talk about this—that she's offering me an ear. But I'm not ready to give voice to it, to admit my attraction to Mason. The minute I do, it's a real, breathing entity. Not something that I can take back. And because he's the one thing lately that I have no control over, I can't stop the insanity that roars through my head as mental images take over my mind and remembered sensations of what it was like to be inside him assail me. I'm a ship in a raging storm being pummeled by the crashing swells. They threaten to capsize me and send me to the deep, dark places inside I try so hard to hide.

I blow out a hard breath as we pull the sheet into

place, then tuck the end under the mattress. I take all that time to gather my wits about me so I can finally answer. "No, that's not what I'm saying. But I can't think about it right now."

"Was that the first time?" Her inquisitive gaze sneaks right past my barriers, and for a split second, I allow her to see all my confusion, my desire, my unending agony. Her eyes widen. *"No.* Okay. Well, you could do worse than Mason, you know."

Frustrated, my eyes find hers, and I pound a fist to my chest. "Even if I wanted to have this discussion ... even if I wanted to have it with *you*—which I don't—I couldn't, because I don't fucking know how I feel." The anger inside me battles with my confusion and my desires, and the result is downright explosive. Frustrated, I lash out. "What's right? What's wrong? What am I supposed to feel?" I clamp my teeth down on my lip to stop it from shaking, because she doesn't get to see that. *Nope.* I take a few heavy breaths as our gazes lock together. "Stella, I have too much other shit on my mind today to examine what happened, so if we could just fucking *not."* My body bristles, and my fists clench at my sides.

She stands there, hands on her full hips and shrugs. It's like she can see right inside my fucking head with every word that leaves her lips. "First, if it's easier for you,

you could let the brotherhood think it was me. I don't fucking care."

"That's what we need; rumors flying around the brotherhood that I'm banging my sister. Because that's how they'd put it. That's how they'd see us. No matter that we didn't grow up together. Just— Fuck. No. Don't tell them that." My teeth grind with frustration. Something that feels a whole lot like jealousy moves swiftly through me, but I will never fucking tell her how much it messes with me to see her look at Bear and Mason the way she does. She's given them her body, and to a certain extent, her trust. Bear has been all-in almost from the goddamn start, and she sees him as her protector. And Mason, he's the one who *gets* her and her tormented dreams, even if he's so fucked in the head himself that he's ended up hurting her. More than once.

Then there's me. I'm her asshole stepbrother.

"Fine. I won't say anything. It's your business. I just thought I'd offer myself up as an option if it would make anything easier for you." She lifts her hands, tucking her hair behind her ears. She waits a beat before expelling a harsh breath. "Then second ... Juliette. If I'm not mistaken, today's date has set half of what's bothering you in motion. Actually, probably all of it. I—" She hesitates while my chest clenches, heart twisting, a wave of emotion crashing down on me. "I wanted to say how sorry I am. I didn't get to tell you then. Losing her like that devastated me. I can't imagine what it was like for you."

I rake my hands through my hair, staring at her. The backs of my eyes sting with the untold pain that is about to leak out and fall down my cheeks. "Every. Fucking. Time," I groan, walking back to the side of the bed where Lennon stands. A muscle in my jaw twitches hard. "I can't fucking talk to you about her, Stella. I remember seeing the two of you together, and it just— It hurts too fucking much right now." My lungs constrict, suddenly overwhelmed as sadness swamps me. I can't fucking breathe.

Over on my nightstand, my phone vibrates in the charging stand. My eyes shift toward the ceiling, though I'm not really seeing it. I don't want to fucking answer.

"That's a phone call. I hate calls in the middle of the night."

I shake off the memories that put my emotional state at risk and bring my gaze back to hers. "It's my dad." No doubt the security company has called him to report the alarm being triggered.

"How do you—?" Her brow furrows, but I see it the moment understanding dawns. "Oh, fuck. I'm sorry."

I exhale sharply, holding up a hand. "I told you to stop apologizing for it." It's fucking messing with me to have her saying she's sorry for something that's caused by god knows what. "You aren't setting off the alarm on purpose. Are you?"

"Well, no, but Bear offered to stay with me because he was worried that something would happen." Her eyes flick to mine. "I do some weird shit when I'm stressed out, and yesterday was one thing—"

"After another. I know. Still not your fault." Of course he offered to stay with her.

This time, the phone chirps with several text notifications, and I lunge, snatching it out of the cradle. As I read, the tip of my tongue glides slowly over my upper lip, then back again. It's a nervous habit, one that happens when I'm trying to maintain control and not fly off the handle. My father isn't making it easy on me.

The fuck, Duke.
Just had yet another call from the alarm
company.
Handle. Her.

I let out an annoyed sigh. Lennon watches me carefully, a tiny line running down the middle of her forehead. It mars her otherwise perfect face. "One sec." I shoot him my typical smart response. I don't want to give him the idea that she means a damn thing to me, because if I do, he'll only watch more carefully. He needs to believe I still consider her a thorn in my fucking side. And to be honest, some days she is prickly. But I don't believe she's the problem child my father insists she is. My observations have been very different. He doesn't get to have that information, though. I'm keeping it close to my chest and fucking watching both her and everything that happens around her.

> If you have solutions for sleepwalking,
> I'm all ears.

Maybe I should come get her after all.
It's about time we had her evaluated.

Deep in my gut, I sense there is more to this than simply a girl with a myriad of acute sleep issues. He wants to get her head examined, but I don't think making her feel like a fucking mental case is going to help.

I'd love to know what the fuck is going on, but I'm afraid I'm not the one she'd bare her soul to—not by a long shot.

"Definitely Tristan?"

"Yeah. It's fine." If being a complete dickhead about

his stepdaughter's issues is no big deal. I tap out another response that I hope gets him off our backs.

> She's hardly settled in.
> Give her another week or so.
> If she's still causing trouble then, we'll talk.
> After the auction, okay?
> Lemme get through that.

I toss my phone to the side, completely confused by his suggestion. I call bullshit. I. Call. Fucking. Bullshit.

I glance over at Lennon, waving it off, as if it's nothing.

Her forehead pinches. "What aren't you telling me?"

Unfortunately, sometimes where my father is concerned, I have trouble managing my facial expressions. My features must be ratting me out big-time, because one second, Lennon's calmly waiting for me to answer her, and the next she makes a flying squirrel dive across my body for my phone.

She lands sideways across my chest, knocking me over, and we both topple backward onto the mattress. In her hand, she's got a death grip on the phone, but I've managed to make a grab for her wrist, and I'm not letting go.

Determined to look at the messages, she grunts out, "Duke! Lemme look at it. What's the big deal?"

The big deal is that I know what it's going to look like to her if she does read those messages. "You don't want to look." She squirms on top of me, and truthfully, we're in the worst of positions because her pussy—in those teeny little shorts—is right on top of my dick. I hiss, "Fuuuck. Stop," but she keeps right on struggling, so I bring my free hand down on her ass. I squeeze hard, getting her attention. Then I roll until my body lands atop hers on the mattress, and I use my weight to hold her down. I wrench the phone from her and toss it out of reach.

"Duke!" She strikes out at me, frustration sliding over her pretty features as she slaps at my shoulders. "If he's talking shit about me, I want to know."

I take her hands in mine, threading my fingers with hers—even though it makes my knuckles scream in protest—and hold them over her head. "Seriously," I gasp out with my jaw clenched, "you know how my father is. You don't need to read a word of that trash."

And still, she strains against me, trying to yank her hands from my grip, but all she succeeds in doing is rubbing her tits against my chest. I let out a tortured groan.

We freeze and stare at each other for several seconds,

the awkwardness of our current position on the bed stunning us silent. From the look on her face, I assume, like me, she doesn't want to be the one to say something or move away. I don't have a fucking clue what that means, but my vision tunnels as I look down into pools of blue. All I see is her. And it feels so fucking good to be on top of her, my hips nestled between her slim thighs. So. Fucking. Good. Blood rushes to my dick so fucking fast my head spins.

I've got a raging, massive erection for my stepsister. Fuck. *Fuuuck.*

And even though I definitely shouldn't, I allow my eyes to slam shut for a moment, letting the feel of her beneath me sink into my skin. Into my bones. Into every blasted fucking part of my body. Fuck, the way she smells like tropical fruit and fucking heaven. I want to bury my face in her neck and inhale her like she's a drug, and I need my next hit more than I need air.

Lennon's breaths come shallow and quick, and when I open my eyes, her desire-filled gaze pins me in much the way my body pins hers. I can't fucking move. Don't want to.

And then, out of nowhere, she shifts, and her pussy brushes my dick. My gaze snaps to her eyes, a swirling sea of deep-blue emotion. I can't tell what she's thinking, but fuck. I wanna say she's turned-on. She moves again, the softest of moans escaping her. *No. This is wrong.* But fire sizzles through my veins, and I can't help myself. Out of my mind and letting my dick do all my thinking, I thrust against her. "Fuuuck," I breathe out.

Her eyes are wild, and I imagine mine are, too. We don't say another fucking word, but we begin to move, grinding together like our lives depend on it. I give in to my earlier desire, nudging my nose from her collarbone up her neck. Inhaling deeply, I groan aloud.

I rock against her, and when I come up for air, I see it written all over her face. She's quickly coming un-fuck-ing-done. Her body chases mine, stroke for stroke, seeking friction.

Thrusting roughly against her, I give her what she needs, then lower my head to her breast, sucking her nipple into my mouth through the thin material of her tank top. Her back arches. She's so fucking beautiful.

"Stella. Fuck, you're killing me," I grit out, unable to contain my thoughts anymore.

She blinks and squeezes my hands. Both of our bodies come to an agonizing halt. "Why *do* you call me Stella?" Panted breaths fall from between her lips as she stares up at me in question.

She can't ever fucking know the answer to that. *Fuck.* Anger at my own actions surges through me, but I can't resist taking things one step further. I close my mouth over the wet patch I'd made and bite her breast at the same time I thrust hard against her clit. A gasped moan spills from her lips as she looks at me through dazed eyes.

I push myself off her, climb from the bed, and point to the door. "Get out. I can't fucking do this. Not with you."

And *definitely* not to-*fucking*-day.

EIGHTEEN

BEAR

I STAND in the middle of the hallway, my eyes trained on the ceiling, though I don't know why. I'm not Superman. I don't have X-ray vision, and what I am is goddamn tired. I shake my head, chewing on my lip for a moment.

After Lennon asked if she could be the one to try to speak to Duke, I hadn't exactly wanted to head upstairs to the attic for two distinct reasons. One, with the state Duke had been in, I wasn't sure if I'd have to come to Lennon's rescue or not, if he'd be angry that she wanted to be the one to check on him. Because damn. Mason and Duke? I hadn't seen that coming. Maybe I should have. Hell, I don't know.

And two, I figured Mason would need some time to cool down or flip out on his own or whatever the fuck he decided he needed to do to deal with his shit. I doubt I read things wrong. With a few choice words, Duke rejected whatever went on between the two of them. Harsh. And I think Mason is really hurting.

I can't quite tell what Duke's feeling. Embarrassment? Anxiety over secrets being spilled? Who knows with him, he keeps everything so tight to his chest.

So, with Lennon entering the lion's den to try to soothe Duke and Mason up in the attic doing god knows what, I took the world's fastest shower, then kept an ear out. Leaving my door open, I'd laid on the bed with a book I'd been meaning to get back into. At first, it had been relatively quiet. But then, not only could I hear some muffled sounds from above, like Mason was shoving things across the floor and throwing shit, but also some sharp-toned voices sounded from next door. Which direction do I move first? Who needs me more? This is like one of those comics where the superhero has to decide whether to save his girl or the train of people heading for certain disaster. Like I said, I'm not fucking Superman. I'm not fast enough to be in two places at once, so I don't know how to manage the clusterfuck developing around me.

Duke's door whips open behind me, and I spin on my heel, my heart slamming into my stomach. Lennon emerges, but doesn't see me standing here, that much is obvious from the way she slumps against the closed door, hands over her face. At six foot six, I'm damn hard to miss, which tells me she's way too preoccupied by whatever transpired in that room. After taking a few deep breaths, she drops her hands, shaking her head. As soon as she does, she practically leaps into the air with a terrified shriek.

I grimace, holding my hands palm out in front of me. "Sorry," I grunt, "I was trying not to scare you, but you didn't see me when you came outta there." My gaze travels to the door behind her. "What the fuck happened?"

Lennon huffs out an unamused laugh, her eyes a dull version of the sparkling blue they usually are. "Just my stepbrother being his usual charming self." She presses her lips together, but she can't hide the hurt seeping from her pores. Not from me. She glances down the hallway to be certain we're alone before murmuring in a low voice, "I'm fine. I really don't think he is, though. I don't know how to help him, or if I'm even able to. In fact, I might be the last person who can." A visible tremor moves through her body, and she comes toward me, stopping to tip her chin up so she can look into my eyes. "What kind of shit day *is* this?"

The worst, honestly. And it seems like one crappy event after another is piling up on us. Eventually, the mountain of bullshit will crumble, burying us in the landslide.

I don't say a word but draw her into my arms right as a loud bang sounds overhead. Blowing out a breath, I press my lips into her hair, mumbling, "I haven't been up there yet. I was trying to respect his privacy, but he's starting to worry me."

Her gaze moves between Duke's door and the one to the attic, behind which Mason hides. "You really think ...?"

"Yeah." I rest my head on top of hers. "The more I think about it, yes, I do. I should have seen it before. The tension between them has been thick for a long time."

A huge thud sounds from above, followed by another. And another. Both pairs of our eyes dart to the ceiling. Lennon visibly jerks when something crashes to the floor. "I should go up there," she whispers. Her fingers dig into my abs where she's holding onto me.

I rear back, setting her apart from me, and grasp her chin with my fingers, bending a bit so that we're on a more even eye level. My brows pull together as I stare into her worried eyes. "No. No you fucking shouldn't."

"But—"

"Are you out of your fucking mind?" I growl, cutting her off. She flinches, and my eyes crash shut. I exhale hard as I open them again, reconnecting our gazes.

"I'm sorry, but I think that's a terrible idea after the last two times you've been in his space. I don't want to risk another damn catastrophe smacking us upside the head today." When she purses her lips, and I can see she's getting ready to argue, I bite out, "I'm sorry, Lennon, but look at what we've already had to work through tonight. Duke's upset. You were sleepwalking. The entire brotherhood's yapping their fucking mouths." I swallow hard. "Duke and Mason. And it's only"—I withdraw my phone and glance at the time—"five in the fucking morning. Who knows what else will be thrown our way today. But you could sleep three hours if you go to bed now. You should."

Her chest rises with her inhale, and her eyes flutter shut as she breathes out, "But ... what about you?"

"I'll sleep between practice and whatever brother-hood meeting Duke is planning. He might not be up for it by the end of the day, anyway. Hard to say. I can always tell everyone that they'd better get their asses in line. We can talk about the auction bullshit some other time." I let a gust of air blow past my lips. "As if we don't have enough to worry about this week."

"Wait, you don't want to do it? The auction, I mean?" Her head tilts to the side, and she studies me with all the inquisitiveness I've come to expect from Lennon. And maybe the slightest gleam of hope.

"I don't think it's necessary, but these insane events have always been done at the beginning of the year. I've never really questioned it before because it was out of my control." I let out a strangled groan. "Fuck, it still *is* something we don't get a fucking say in. And frankly, I'm worried about whatever Duke has in his head where Kingston is concerned because this auction puts them in the same room. Two fucking heads of brotherhoods who don't take shit from anyone. It's a fucking disaster waiting to happen." If Duke could just fucking let it go, they'd both be better off. Easy for me to say, though. I'm not the one with the dead girlfriend. Another crash sounds overhead. Glass? *Fuck.* "We can talk about it some other time. I'm going to go up. Go to bed." To soften the blow, I pull her back to me and drop a gentle kiss on her forehead. "Please, Lennon. For me?"

She nods, drawing in a shaky breath. "We just need this day to be over with."

I agree with her, but I also know a change of date isn't going to magically fix everything. Leaving Lennon at the doorway to her room with a tight smile and a wave, I open the attic door. Mason fucking hates surprises, so I bang the door shut behind me and call up the stairs to him. "Mase. I'm coming up. Don't throw shit at me."

Labored breathing sounds from above, like he's

really given himself a workout letting all the chaos and rage inside him out. I'd been hoping he'd just whip out his charcoals and draw, but nope. As I reach the top of the steps, I grip the metal railing to my right and peer through the bars at him. He's pacing, hands in his hair again, tugging hard. He's tossed a bunch of shit around, may have even destroyed some of his work. It's now in a pile in the corner of the room, the wood frames of broken canvases sticking up at bizarre angles. My inner self lets out a low whistle that I don't dare release.

"What do you want?" Mason's voice is rough, like it gets when he's been drinking. Despite all the ruckus he's caused up here, he still seems to be agitated, ready to go off like a bomb at any moment. It'd take very little to light his fuse, that's for fucking sure.

Cautiously, I move closer, reaching out and stopping his motion with a hand to his shoulder. He lets out an anguished roar as he spins in my hold. I catch him against me, clamping both of my arms around his biceps and across his chest. I grapple with him for a few seconds before he gives up, all the fight going out of him.

"Fucking let go. I'm fine."

I gesture toward the bottle he's obviously been downing. "You save any of that vodka for me?"

Apparently, he wasn't expecting that question from me. I release him and he turns around, frowning. His lip curls as he considers me warily. "You never drink during football season."

"It depends, man. I've got five days before another game. I'm sure it'll be fine. And my sleep's already fucked, so may as well, right? Practice is going to suck today either way." I shrug, my eyes drifting over the mess. "Besides. Looks like you could use a drinking buddy."

His jaw works to the side as he rolls his eyes, but he walks over to the table where the vodka bottle sits, waiting for him to demolish it. Reluctantly, he picks up the bottle and hands it to me before dropping himself to the middle of the floor. He sits hunched over with his arms crossed and resting on his knees. A deep, audible sigh leaves him as he lowers his head to his forearm.

Fuck it. Who am I to argue with where he wants to do this? I lower myself across from him, stretching my legs out in front of me. I take a swig of the vodka directly from the bottle before I set it between us and lean back on my hands. Thank goodness Mason likes the good stuff or that would have hurt going down a helluva lot more than it did. I wait a moment before speaking, allowing the alcohol to take a slow, winding path to my stomach. I watch as he snags the bottle and swallows down another shot, then stares at the floor, as if he's burning a hole in it. I grimace. And maybe he wants to. Duke is down there, after all.

I don't even know where to start, so I take the easy route. A simple question. Or so I hope. "What the hell happened tonight? You want to clue me in?"

Ever so slowly, Mason lifts his head, meeting my gaze with deep, dark eyes that hold all the damn secrets to his twisted soul. He scrapes his teeth over his lip, then begins to chew on it. When Mason's up and throwing shit, he's an open book, his seething, wrathful emotions on full display ... but when he gets contemplative like this, he turns inward, and it's really hard to get him to speak freely.

"Take another drink. Maybe it'll help," I grit, my voice raspy. "Or maybe I could try to help you figure out what you want to talk about."

"Who says I want to talk?" He glances at me, a snarl close to the surface of his question.

"You can say that, but I actually think you need a friend tonight more than you do a drinking buddy." I hold out my hand for the bottle. "But I'll be both, if that's what helps."

"I don't need any more help now than I've needed in the last three years."

My eyebrows dart together. I think I understand what he's getting at, but we need to start with tonight.

"You know, I kinda had an idea that you might play for both teams."

He doesn't say anything but lifts a brow and nods. His chest jerks with his silent admission.

Okay, so we're getting somewhere. Sort of. "And I'd gotten a certain vibe from the two of you, but I thought I was imagining it." My eyes flick to his. "I haven't had long to think about it, but I'm a little disappointed neither of you ever said a word about it. We've been friends *forever,* Mase."

This time, he shrugs before taking another drink, eyeing me. His tongue slips out to slide over his recently abraded lower lip, an attempt to soothe the battered skin. "Didn't know what you'd think. Does it bother you?"

"No." I pause, running a hand through my hair. "It doesn't. It's not something I'm into, but I'm cool with it. You should do what feels right to you."

Mason takes that in with a deep breath. "Okay. As for Duke, I know fuck all of what's in his head sometimes." Groaning, he mutters, "Just when I think I've got him on lock, he throws me so bad it—" His lip curls, and he brings the vodka to his lips again. He covers his eyes with his hand for a moment before he mutters, almost to himself, "Hurts just as bad as the first time."

We sit in silence for a few moments, my brain's synapses attempting to fire in its sleep-deprived state.

"Wait. Freshman year, the two of you fell out pretty hard. I remember it vividly. Like one day you were cool with each other, we were getting our bearings here ... and the next you were at each other's throats." My jaw works to the side as I begin to finally piece the puzzle together. "In fact, it was right around September 5."

Mason presses his lips together, and his jaw turns stony. It takes him a moment, but he nods ever so slightly, our eyes connecting. "I thought it'd help him get his mind off shit." He huffs out a laugh at my eyes as they bug out. "Not me. I brought a chick home, and we took turns fucking the hell out of her. She eventually left. We were drunk and naked."

I blink hard. "And you ..."

"Yep." He takes a longer swallow of the vodka. "It was good, but it fucked everything up. I wanted more, and he's been in denial ever since."

"And"—I scrub my hands through my hair, the vodka finally working itself on me—"tonight was? More of the same?"

"His retribution? Payback? A pissy mood? I don't fucking know. But—" His gaze shifts from mine as he mutters, *Jesus.* I didn't go in there with the intent of fucking my friend. I was just trying to crack him open, stop him from throwing up even more unbreachable walls." His dark eyes find mine again. "Did I push too hard? Maybe. Do I regret it? Not in the slightest. He was drowning, Bear, and he needed to use me to keep his head above water. He'll never admit it, but whether I intended it or not, in that moment, he needed me. *Me.* I won't regret helping my friend, even if he hates me for it for another three years. I can handle it."

"Neither of you were drunk tonight, which is different from the last time."

"Nope, no we weren't. Not at the time of the fuckening, anyway. That's what I'm calling it this time, by the way. The fuckening." He snorts out a sad laugh. "I'm plenty fucking drunk now, though."

I try not to laugh because I know damn well he's trying to make light of a situation that's been steadily brewing between them for years now. Seems like maybe they reached the boiling point again tonight.

We go several more minutes in complete silence, and when I could swear Mason has fallen asleep sitting up, he looks up, his lips quirking strangely. "You know, besides fucking the hell out of me, I think he's as messed up over her death as ever. And I obviously didn't help things."

I rub my hands over my thighs, absently playing with the fabric of my joggers. "You weren't trying to do him any harm. But I agree, he's nowhere near over her death. Not that I'd expect him to be."

Huffing out a broken laugh, Mason blurts, "Are you

aware that Lennon and Juliette were friends?" His alcohol-soaked gaze searches mine.

"Yep. Lennon fuckin' told me while we were outside."

Mason nods, this time pushing his hair back from his face, revealing a grim smile. "They worked together. *Worked.* How fucking crazy is it to find out Juliette had a goddamn job with all the money the Hawthorne family has. But from what Lennon said, Jared Hawthorne is a prick and Juliette was trying to save money. She didn't share why, but as the son of a complete asshole, I could make the obvious guess—she wanted to distance herself."

Stella's. Stella Bella. Confused as hell, I shake my head, trying to process. "When did she talk to *you* about this?"

His brows lift on his forehead. "You're gonna fucking love this. That day she ran away from Duke on campus, I found her at Juliette's fucking grave."

My mind bends even farther. "So, they were close enough that Lennon knows where Juliette is buried. *And* visits her there. Uh"—my brow furrows—"does Duke know this?"

"About her and Juliette being friends, *yes.* About me finding Lennon having a meltdown at Juliette's grave then napping there afterward, nope. I didn't see the point. I figured it'd be like rubbing salt in his wounds with how close to *today* we were."

No fucking wonder Lennon is a thorn in his side. She's a goddamn reminder of everything he lost. How had he never mentioned they were friends? "He never fucking said anything about knowing her beyond the stepsibling thing, yet he knew of Lennon before ..."

"Before their parents got married, yep." His eyes droop for a moment. *Fuck,* I can't tell how drunk he is, and his next words don't help at all. "You know what?" He haphazardly throws out his hand, almost knocking over the vodka—*okay, he's fairly fucked up*—and with an agonized groan, he mumbles, "She also said some shit during that nightmare she had—it was about Juliette. It kinda unnerved me."

I rub my hands over my face, now wishing I had a completely clear head. "Like what?"

"It was as if she were talking to her. She kept asking her to wait and why was she scared and who was he?" Mason heaves out a sigh. "It freaked me the fuck out. She sounded so lost and anxious. That's why I woke her up. Then I wish I fuckin' hadn't because—" He exhales sharply, then rubs his temple with a few fingers, clearly disturbed. He's not kidding. And if something is bad enough to unnerve Mason, it's definitely bad. And I do understand where he was going with that, even though he didn't finish. If he hadn't woken her up, they wouldn't have fucked around. And if they hadn't ... well, I'd seen it in his horrified eyes. He's falling for her, even though he knows he shouldn't. Mason struggles with so many demons. I know about some of them, but I believe he hides some things way down deep. And Lennon, without ever meaning to, has brought those demons out to play in a way we couldn't have anticipated.

I grit my teeth, not liking this one bit. "You're positive she was talking about Juliette?"

"Yep. She said her name, I'm sure of it. It knocked me sideways, because I wasn't expecting it. But ... she was also caught in a nightmare. So, who the fuck knows? The mind can be a very strange, distorted place." He lets out another sigh. "Is it worth upsetting her or Duke by bringing it up? I dunno. That's why I haven't said anything about it. It was fuckin' strange, though. And she was so upset, tears were streaming from her eyes, even though they were squeezed shut."

I pinch my lips tightly together. "I think we should sit on it. Definitely not something we need to be bringing up today of all fucking days, you know?"

"Agreed." He takes another sip of vodka and sets the bottle aside. "Fuck, I need to stop drinking that or I'm not going to make it to class."

I snag the bottle and take one more swig, then set it

at my side with plans to take it with me. He doesn't need more, but sometimes he doesn't know when to stop. "You're already going to be drunk in class, so yeah. Maybe it's time to call it quits." I heave out a breath, trying to figure out how to round out this conversation without sending him into a spiral. "I'm glad we talked, though. About all of it."

He catches what I'm saying, and his eyes crash shut. "I hope like fuck I didn't screw things up with him. Or her. Fuuuck."

A bit of a smile twitches to my lips. "Well, Lennon seems pretty open to different kinds of relationships and experiences."

He ponders that statement for only a moment before he shoots me a mischievous grin. "Okay, so you might be right there. I guess we'll find out." But two seconds later, he's right back to clenching his teeth together. "Duke, though?" He huffs out a distressed, unbalanced laugh before shaking his head. "I'm fucked. And not in a pleasurable way."

NINETEEN

LENNON

I MAKE my way downstairs after only two fitful hours of sleep—that's post sleepwalk. I must have gotten around three hours prior to my inadvertent and embarrassing dunk in the pool, so five broken hours total. I groan internally as last night comes flooding back to me, my brain can't help the mental recap. Everything about fight night, Duke's upset over Juliette, Bear and me fucking down at the spa, almost drowning myself, assholes laughing, the Duke-and-Mason discovery, and for the pièce de résistance ... dry humping my stepbrother. I can't even say which is going to cause me the most grief, but my head is swirling around the final two.

Honestly, I'm most worried about how to deal with Duke. I'd been seconds from an explosive orgasm when —like a complete idiot—I'd asked Duke why he calls me

Stella. He'd sprung from the bed almost as if I'd burned him.

I touch my fingers to my cheeks, feeling the flames rising under my skin. That was so bad. Am I attracted to Duke? Of course. He's fucking hot with his cut jaw and piercing blue eyes. He smells delicious, and his body is muscular in all the right places.

He's watched me with both Mason and Bear, and he's kissed me as if it were punishment. Guilt seeps through my veins. I liked all of it. But most of all, I liked the way he called me *baby*. And also that he thought to bring me that damn cinnamon lollipop at fight night. There's not a moment I've spent with Duke that isn't emblazoned in my memory. I can't get him out of my head. I've never been able to.

I blow out a breath. But he's my stepbrother. I have to face facts that last night was his wake-up call, and I can't imagine he'll ever be okay with anything more happening between us. But in each other's arms, for several heart-pounding moments, we'd let go, forgotten who we were, and holy fuck, it'd been hot. His touch ...

My eyes slam shut. I can't think about it, not if I want my panties to remain dry. It's really too bad he'd flipped out on me and reverted to the asshole I've come to know and ... hate?

Setting that aside, Mason and Duke as a twosome is

definitely on my mind. I can't decide whether they'd surprised me or not with the revelation that they're into each other. That day Mason drew on me up in the attic, there'd been a moment while I'd watched them rolling around fighting that I'd thought, *Whoa. This is kinda hot.* But it hadn't actually clicked in my mind why I'd thought they were emitting inferno levels of heat. Had I been ogling two hot guys? Or two hot guys ... *together?* It's hard to say, honestly, and then I'd gotten so caught up in the fact that they were hurting each other, and I was sitting there naked and degraded. What a mess that'd been.

Come to think of it, I'd wondered why it'd seemed like they'd forgotten me the moment they started fighting. I'm going to bet all the Twizzlers in Brendan's candy jar that I've finally figured it out—the push and pull of *will we, won't we* has got to be an all-consuming thing in their heads. I hope they know—both of them—that it doesn't affect how I think of them or even how I feel about either one of them.

I shake my head a bit. I wish there was a straight path forward, but there's not. Not for how to survive this house or Duke, Bear, and Mason. I'm inextricably entwined with all three, and I don't know if there is any getting myself out unscathed. There's so much more to each of them that I want to uncover, so many facets of what we could be to explore. But everything is in a constant state of turmoil, leaving me to feel like I'm falling through air without a safety net. It feels dangerous. Exhilarating. There's no stopping the bastards of Bainbridge Hall from barreling toward me like a fiercely deadly thunderstorm. Mason—he's the crashing thunder roaring furiously through my head, a raging chaotic promise. The pelting rain is Bear, soaking into my very skin, like he has always belonged there inside me. And Duke's the sizzling, electrifying lightning zipping through my veins and setting me on fire. They're a force to be reckoned with. And I think they're coming for my heart.

As I hurry into the kitchen, I find Bear at the stovetop again, this time flipping pancakes. My face infuses with a surge of heat as my stomach rumbles, a strange combination for sure.

Looking around the dining and kitchen areas, I survey the few brothers who are already chowing down on their breakfasts and decide I don't have the energy to deal with any of these people, especially not Arik, with whom I'll have to share a table. Maybe I can convince Bear to let me wait elsewhere.

I step up next to him and murmur, "Morning." Giving another glance over my shoulder, I see both Arik and Brendan's eyes are fully on us. Arik's watching from the table in here and Brendan from over his coffee mug in the dining room. If there's one thing I've decided I really hate around here, it's that some of these asshats seem to be waiting for me to do something wrong like it's their new hobby.

Bear's mouth curves. "Morning, Lennon." Before I can say anything else, he frowns, then lifts his hand, letting the pad of his thumb slide gently under my eye. "Exhausted, huh? Are you okay to go to class?"

"Yeah. I'm fine. I'll be done by lunchtime and come home. Wait." I glance around. "Is Duke going? Mason?" It's just registered that they aren't anywhere in sight.

"Duke, doubtful. Mason said he'd be down soon."

I wrinkle my nose, nodding. "I guess you guys will tell me who will be there to walk with me between classes?"

"Yeah, definitely. Mason and I will handle it. You want to eat before we go?"

My lips twist as I inhale the scent of his seriously delicious-smelling pancakes. "Can I take one with me? I'll roll it up and eat it. I—" I pause, then fidget in place. Trying again, I add, "I was kind of hoping you'd open the door for me so I can sit on the steps and wait for you. Get some fresh air."

He leans in, gripping the back of my neck, sending a jolt of warmth right down my spine.

"They're watching."

Bear raises a brow at my concern but shifts so he's blocking me from everyone else's view but his. "Does that help? I have zero fucks to give any of them after some of the behavior around here lately." His lips press against my forehead just before he speaks in a low voice meant only for me. "You're not going to take off after last night, are you, Little Gazelle?"

I'm sure he's speaking of more than just our encounter, but I blink at his gruff tone, my already-pink cheeks turning blaze red, as he makes me recall how he'd told me to take Daddy's cock like a good little girl last night. If it was his intention to fluster me, he was successful ... and he knows it. His lips twitch with blatant amusement.

Two can play at this game. I catch my bottom lip briefly between my teeth and flutter my eyelashes at him. "No, *Gideon*. I'm not running anywhere. *Daddy* said no."

His hazel eyes twinkle, and with a satisfied grunt, he breathes out, "Good girl."

A grin spreads across my face as my heart flips in my chest. My shoulders lift a fraction before dropping. "I could use a few minutes to myself, and I don't wanna sit with these yahoos to eat my breakfast, anyway, if that's okay."

Satisfied with my answer, he snags a paper towel from the holder and picks up a pancake off the stack before handing it to me. "You sure you don't want to sit down and eat it with butter and syrup?"

"Yep. I just want to go outside."

Bear glances over toward the dining room. Raising his voice, he asks, "Hey, Warren? Would you mind letting Lennon out the front door?"

Warren gives Bear a quizzical look but nods anyway. "Sure. No problem." He gets up from the table with his coffee mug in hand and shoots me a smile.

"Thanks, man. Extra pancakes for you." Bear turns back to me and chucks me under the chin. "See you in a little bit. You've got about twenty minutes."

"Yep. Sounds good. Thank you."

Warren salutes Bear like some goofy soldier addressing a superior as he passes by on his way to the foyer. "Be right back."

I follow him down the long hallway in silence, then Warren steps directly in front of the security panel. "Sorry," he whispers. "It'd be bad if you knew the code when you aren't supposed to."

I can't deny that it hadn't occurred to me to watch him, but that wasn't my intent. "No worries. Maybe one day I'll earn it."

"Of course you will." He winks, opening the door and gesturing with a flourish that I'm free to exit.

I haven't been seated on the steps for more than five minutes when Tristan's sleek, black Escalade edges up the driveway. My heart stumbles to a stop in my chest, my lungs squeezing hard. *Fuck.* Of all the mornings for me to ask to wait outside. There's a slim chance I could have avoided Tristan if only I'd had the stomach to sit with Arik and eat my pancake ... but I hadn't. That guy looks at me like I'm doing him some sort of wrong by existing.

So, now because I've allowed that asshat to make me uncomfortable, I've put myself into this situation instead. What a stellar start to the day this is.

I set the remainder of my pancake and paper towel on the step and peer into the interior of the SUV, hoping on the off chance that my mother is in the passenger seat and can offer a buffer. No luck. He's alone. My brow furrows. He could totally be here for Duke, not me, though I wouldn't actually wish Tristan on anyone, come to think of it. Not even Duke. Especially not today. My teeth grind hard, wondering and worrying about the unknown of this surprise visit.

Tristan parks, leisurely exiting his vehicle, as if he knows damn well I'll sit here, frozen to the spot waiting on him. As usual, my heart rate spikes, despite the fact I tell myself to play it cool. The jerk probably knows he gives me anxiety. Some teenagers hide away in their rooms to play video games or read or video chat with their friends. That was never the case for me, though I spent every moment possible tucked away in the room he'd appointed for me in his home, never leaving unless it was required of me. That place was never my home, no matter that I lived there for three years. He never made me feel welcome, much less wanted.

If I hadn't hidden myself away, Tristan probably would have found a way to break my spirit. It's so entirely fucking weird that he's always treated me like crap. He's the one who decided to marry my mother. He knew what she was like and where we came from— granted, maybe not at first—but they supposedly fell in love, so it didn't matter. Does he regret marrying her, and thereby getting saddled with me? Sure as hell seems like it.

What I do know is that since the day they were married and he officially became my stepfather, he's always been ready with a tongue-lashing. I'm the à la carte daughter he wasn't expecting to come with the enticing meal that is my mother. He didn't want or need another kid. He has an heir to his fortune already, someone to take over all the businesses that he runs and real estate he owns. I serve no purpose but to make him look like a doting stepfather.

With a sigh, I press my lips together, noting that he's as sharply dressed as ever, beard immaculately groomed, and hair combed into place like he prefers it. Frankly, my time here at Bainbridge Hall has been a nice break from him, so to have him appear like this is a tiny bit unnerving.

"Lennon." His voice is gruff. Cold. It sends a shiver through me, which is an odd sensation in the early morning heat.

Refusing to look at him another second, I stare down at my hands and bite out, "Tristan."

"Get up." His tone is an irritated snap. "We need to talk, don't you think?"

My heart wedges in my throat at the same time my palms begin to sweat. My gaze roams his face, traveling over the tightness of his jaw before I flick my eyes to his. "I don't know what about but go right ahead. I have a few minutes before we leave for class."

His unamused eyes roam lethally over me. Like I have most days, I chose to wear a tank top and shorts, and a pair of flip-flops on my feet.

Shit. Is he going to mention the bruises? They're sort of a purplish color now, beginning to fade, but still visible.

I could swear he notices, but he doesn't say a damn word about them. From the way he's stalking toward me, I'd say he's here for a specific reason, and he's not going to be distracted from it. Hell, maybe he thinks I deserved the bruises and doesn't fucking care either way.

"Are you leaving the house at night on purpose to cause trouble? As if the sleepwalking and middle-of-the-night panic attacks aren't enough," he grits out, his eyes flashing angrily. He stops with only a few inches between us, staring down at me. His proximity is meant to intimidate. I can't let him know it's freaking working.

My brows pinch together. "No. Why would you think that? You know I have sleep difficulties." That's how I like to think of them, rather than labeling myself with some disorder or other medical term. I kinda hate him for implying that I have any control over it. I glare up at him. "You really don't like me being here, where you put me, I can still attend the local community college. No problem," I snap.

He chuckles darkly. "No. You can't. It's this or nothing."

Confusion crashes through me as I stare into blue eyes that hold an awful contempt for me. I can't help but want to verbally spar with him. "Why is nothing else suitable? Because the great Tristan Valentine can't have it known that his stepdaughter is attending an inferior college—one that's *not* the esteemed Kingston University?"

"No." An amused spark lights his eyes. "You're simply no longer on their freshman admissions roster. I saw to it."

A roaring begins in my head at his words, and my stomach twists into knots. Surely, he didn't. "What?" My backup plan. *Gone? Motherfucker!*

But I don't even have time to digest that information because he ignores my question, instead cocking his head to the side. "I find it very interesting that I sent you here to see if a fresh start will help, that I've provided you with the best room and board available at KU and the education you could have only dreamed of before this— but you couldn't help yourself. You've continued to cause problems at every turn. Setting off alarms, wrapping my son and his friends around your dirty little finger, acting spiteful and rude to Bainbridge alum."

Derek Pierce? Is that who he's referring to? What is he talking about? At the football game? I wasn't rude to him. He was coming onto me in that sly way he has while we were watching the game, and I left. Period. Or … is my dickhead stepfather talking about himself? My jaw locks and I glare. "What do you mean?"

He ignores my question. Completely ignores it. "Not only that, but you've got my son *lying* for you."

With the speed of a striking snake, his hand darts out and grips me at the juncture of my shoulder and neck. I try to wrench my body away from him but can't free myself from his hold.

"Stop, you're hurting me," I cry out as his fingers bite into the delicate skin of my neck and shoulder, and he grips my upper arm with his other hand, dragging me close and shaking me as he gets right in my face.

Spittle flies as he growls out, "You'll behave yourself while you're here. You fucking keep to yourself and don't cause problems. If you can't handle that, I'll pull you out of here and lock you away."

Tears sting the backs of my eyes as shock reverberates through me to my core. "What are you talking about?"

His hold on me tightens so much that I can feel the tips of his fingernails digging viciously into my skin. He shakes me again, breathing hard in my face like a goddamn dragon or something. As he opens his mouth to come at me again, I close my eyes, unwilling to allow him to see the fear rising within me. Because yes, he's fucking scaring me.

In the next moment, all hell breaks loose.

"Get your fucking hands off her." As if it happens in slow motion, my head turns to the side. I catch a glimpse of blond hair, and all of a sudden, I'm caught between two heaving, angry men. All the breath *whooshes* from my lungs, snatching the ability to cry out as I'm jostled around. Duke grips both of his dad's forearms and squeezes hard, wrestling with me in the middle. "I said let go," he grunts.

Tristan finally releases me, growling through gritted teeth. "Is this how it is? I thought about it at the football game. And then when I was told you were staying with her during the fight, I was a little surer. No fucking wonder you've been so goddamn tight-lipped."

Behind me, Duke's chest heaves. He belts one arm around my waist and the other is slung upward, between my breasts, his palm flat against my chest, fingers splayed out just below my neck as he pulls me backward with him. "Being her stepfather doesn't give you the right to put your hands on her like that." Held tight to him, I feel the rage pouring forth from every cell in his body.

It confuses me.

Setting aside the strange flow of emotion from Duke, I swallow hard, and my eyes flick up to Tristan's cold blue gaze. He. Is. Pissed.

"Inside, Duke. Office. Now." Tristan doesn't mince words, and the second the command is out, he strides past us and up the stairs, his entire body radiating anger.

I bring my arms up, my hands covering Dukes, fingers curling between his. I'm shaking, but the only thing I can do is lean against Duke's chest and try to breathe.

"What the fuck is going on?" Bear's voice is gritty and low as he comes to a skidding stop at our side.

Mason appears only a split second later, takes one look at me with his dark eyes searching mine, and grinds out, "The hell? Kin, are you okay?"

Duke groans at my back. "My *father*. He—" his head drops next to mine, bringing us cheek to cheek. His lips move against the curve of my jaw. "I'm so fuckin' sorry I couldn't get out here faster." His voice hitches. "I-I saw. From upstairs."

"It's fine. I'm fine." I tap his arm, letting him know I want him to loosen his hold, and I turn around, resting my hands on his bare stomach. Looking into his fiery blue eyes, his jaw twitching and popping, I can still sense the animosity toward his father seething directly under the surface. I bite my lip with only one thing on my mind. "Why did he say I have you lying for me? I've never asked you to lie about anything."

His eyes crash shut for a moment, and when he opens them again, I see the fight being waged inside him. He's torn. But what the hell? What's he hiding from me?

"Duke?" My fingers dig into his skin, absorbing his heat, his strength, and wishing he'd answer me but knowing it's fruitless. He won't allow himself to answer me, and I haven't a fucking clue why not.

He rips his gaze from mine and shakes his head, running his hand over his jaw. The anguish is clear in his eyes, but—as I suspected—rather than talk to me, he snaps, "Bear? Mase? Get her the fuck to class." He tears himself from me, both his body and his gaze, striding purposefully up the stairs and into the house where Tristan waits for him.

I may have been thrown by how Tristan treated me a moment ago, but nothing hurts worse than watching Duke's tension-filled back as he walks away from me.

TWENTY

MASON

A CONFRONTATION with Tristan Valentine was not exactly the hangover cure I was hoping for, but opening the front door to see him manhandling Lennon like that and Duke having to wrestle her free of his clutches was enough to snap me out of it and push away most of the fogginess and lethargy.

Who the fuck does he think he is, anyway? She's nineteen. He's supposedly a revered businessman, the owner of a good portion of this fucking town, one who donates to charities and those in need. Most people don't know his businesses are as dirty as hell. But even if he truly were the saint he's known as, that shouldn't matter because no one has the right to put their hands on anyone else the way he just did. I don't give a fucking fuck if Lennon's his stepdaughter or not.

Flames lick at my insides, even though he's no longer in our faces and she's mostly unharmed. Asshole prick with a god complex. That was complete fucking overkill the way he went after her. She didn't deserve it. And we don't even know the filth he spewed before we got out there.

My head steadily thumps as I watch Duke hurry up the steps after him. That's one summons I wouldn't want to answer. I hope he can fucking handle his father because right now, I think the best thing for us to do is follow his direction and get Lennon the hell away from this house. Rubbing my hand over my face, I exhale hard, staring at Bear through my not-quite-sober eyes. "You know he won't want me to intervene after last night, that much I'm sure of. But I also—" My fists clench as my gaze shifts to Lennon. "Fuck." I'm an idiot. She's staring at the ground between us, her hands shaking ever so slightly, giving away the truth of how this has affected her. "Lennon." She glances up at me, blinking rapidly, and not quite meeting my eyes. *Fuck.* I hope her finding out about me and Duke doesn't change things with us. I don't want it to, and the only thing I can think to do is show her. "Come here." I tug her against my chest. "Don't you let that fucking asshole bother you."

She slowly nods, then looks over her shoulder

toward Bear. "Why does he think Duke's been lying to him?"

"Little Gazelle, from the moment you started setting those alarms off, I think they've been watching and waiting. No fucking clue what for." He grits his teeth, stepping up behind her and placing his hands on her shoulders. He buries his nose in the hair at the top of her head, which makes me smirk a bit. Damn, Teddy Bear is so head over heels. His gravelly voice rumbles as he continues. "I'd say Duke's been downplaying some of the shit that's happened lately, and when his father asks how things are going around here, he's been telling him everything's fine. Even though we all fuckin' know there's a whole lot that's not." He squeezes her shoulders. "I'd imagine he's protecting you because he knows in his gut you aren't at fault. He's not blind, Lennon, no matter what other issues the two of you might have with each other. And hell, his dad doesn't know the half of it, only what the stupid fucking security company is making him aware of."

That we know of. I have a sneaking suspicion they have ways of knowing our business, and whether that means there's a rat on the inside, cameras, both, or whatever-the-fuck, I'd like to find out.

"Tristan thinks I'm doing it all on purpose. He

always has—the sleepwalking, the nightmares, all of it. Like a ploy to get attention. But—"

I interrupt her. "You're not. We know. I can't fathom what the fuck his problem is, or any of our fathers', for that matter, but we'll take care of it. Don't worry about it."

Her body trembles between us. "How can I not? You didn't hear what Tristan said. He thinks I'm fucking crazy."

My jaw tightens, irritated at Tristan's manipulation tactics. "You're not." One minute accusing her of making it all up and the next saying she's crazy? He's fucking psychotic. I ease away and tip her chin up, the back of her head coming to rest on Bear's chest. "You've been through a lot, but that doesn't mean you haven't come out stronger and more beautiful, Kintsukuroi. Remember that. I see you." I glance at Bear. "We both do." I wink at her, and her body releases a shuddering exhale as she nods.

"You're right. I shouldn't let him gaslight me."

"Nope. And let's get the fuck out of here before we give him another chance." Bear's voice is gruff and authoritative, spurring Lennon and me both into action. We turn, the three of us heading to our SUV. "I'll drive."

As we walk, Lennon turns to me again. Distress shows itself all over her face, from the downturn of her pretty lips to her shiny eyes to the lines etched into her forehead. "I can't believe Duke—" She stops herself from finishing, eyes closing briefly. When she opens them again, she winces. "Are you sure we should leave? Especially today?"

"I think it's the best course of action right now, yes. He'll deal with his father. I tried to establish that we're here for him last night."

Lennon nods, a funny look slipping over her face that I don't quite understand. She turns her head before I can question her, allowing Bear to help her into the SUV. His gaze sweeps from her over to me. "The bottom line is this: Duke's a big boy. I know you're both concerned, and I am too, don't get me wrong. His asshole father will leave, and hopefully he'll get the space he needs to quiet his thoughts about ... everything." He presses his lips together. "If not, I'll see what I can do when I get home."

I close the door behind her, and as Bear and I walk around the vehicle to the other side, he stops me with a hand to my shoulder and grunts low but quickly, "Something happened with them last night. I don't know what. We ran some man-to-man coverage on the two of you last night. She went to talk to Duke before I came up to see you. She seemed upset when she came out, though she tried to hide it."

I frown. "You didn't say anything." My heart tugs, thinking about her trying to help Duke. I can't imagine it would have gone well, but the fact that she wanted to try says something.

"Yeah, well you were dealing with a lot, too. But I think that's why she's more flustered than she normally would be after an encounter like that with Tristan. Yes, he threw her off her game, but I actually think it's more how Duke came to her defense that's got her all in her head."

"Yeah, okay. Thanks for saying something." I eye him. "Is this fucking weird?" My eyes shift to look at Lennon through the window before bringing them back to Bear.

"Depends on what you mean." His brow raises, waiting for me to explain myself.

Fucker knows this shit is hard for me. He has to know what I'm talking about. I work my jaw to the side. Maybe it's me with the issue. I feel myself falling for her, but it makes me nervous as shit.

He rubs his hand over his thickly stubbled jaw. "I guess it's as weird as we make it. She's—"

I nod, letting myself admit it out loud. "Worth it."

KINGSTON
UNIVERSITY

I GLANCE down at my phone about midway through Lennon's second class to find a text from her.

> Can we go home after this class?
> I can't concentrate.
> And I'm more tired than I thought.

I take a moment to assess the drawing I've been working on. It's her. The way she looked last night as Bear stole every one of her moans with the powerful thrust of his hips. I knew when I got to class today that I wouldn't be able to resist capturing her face in the throes of ecstasy with every stroke of my charcoal.

> I told you, Kintsukuroi.
> Say the word, and I'm there.
> Pick you up in twenty.

> Thanks, Mase.
> Do you wanna walk home?
> Leave the SUV for Bear?

If you're up for it, I'm cool with that.

Fifteen minutes later, I leave class early and head for Broadmore Hall, where Lennon has English lit. I allow the other students to stream out before ducking my head in. She smiles when she sees me, waves at Professor Silverton, and gets to her feet, slinging her bag over her shoulder. Joining me, we walk in silence until we get out of the building. It's not even eleven, but the sun is already beating down hard, and there's no hint of a breeze. "You sure you want to walk?"

She doesn't answer immediately but digs into one of the side pockets of her backpack, coming up with a pencil.

Fuck. I'm adding a package of hair ties to the grocery list for this week. I watch as she skillfully gathers her long mane of hair into her hands, winds it around, and jabs it through the center with the pencil. Fucking sexy, if a little odd.

"There, that's better." With that accomplished, she briefly glances at me. "Mase, I'm not gonna lie—I thought we could use the time alone."

My brows raise on my forehead, but I don't know why they should. I know what's on her mind. Me. Duke. It doesn't get more basic—or more complicated—than that. Especially when she's involved, too. I don't know what the fuck we're doing. I just know I need her and I need to make sure she knows that.

I pull to a stop, catching her forearm in my hand and spin her to face me right in the middle of a crowded walkway, causing her to gasp aloud. Students immediately circumvent us, but I pay them no mind. All I see is her.

Brow furrowing, she opens her mouth to say something, and I take full fucking advantage of it. Pulling her body to mine, I grasp her head in my hands and plunge my tongue between her lips in a vicious, brutal claiming. She lets out a tiny moan as she melts into me, but it doesn't faze me a bit. I nip and pluck at her lip with my teeth, savoring the way it makes her heart race faster. My tongue swoops in again, tasting the sweetness of whatever lollipop she must have sucked on during class. Cherry, I think. Fuuuck. It makes me want to throw her down on the grass, rip her clothes off, and sink inside her pussy. For a fleeting second, I actually consider it. Maybe I'm still drunk. It's a good thing we aren't fucking driving home.

Lennon whimpers as my thumbs slide over her jaw, and I tear myself away to look at her. Her eyes are stormy, radiating nothing but longing and lust. Her breath feathers softly over her lips as she stares at me. "What was that for?"

My lips twitch into a smirk. "Just in case you thought a goddamn thing had changed." I bring our foreheads together, speaking quietly to her as the student body continues diverting around us. No one would dare tell a Bainbridge Hall brother to get the fuck out of their way, though I'm sure it's in their thoughts. "Lennon, you're the only person who understands even a fraction of my damage. It might be selfish, but I don't want to lose that—*you*—even if the way I react to you sometimes scares the fuck out of me. You've dug your way inside my soul, and I don't think you're ever coming out." The admission claws at my heart, the dark chaos inside screaming. *Nooo!* But there's no way to deny it at this point. I feel so desperately connected to her, even if it's in the most twisted part of my heart.

She takes a few deep breaths before she whispers, "Even if there's something very real happening between you and Duke?"

And there it is. I've been nervous, thinking it'd be awkward to discuss him with her. But I wasn't prepared for the understanding look in her eye or the soft expression on her face. I shake my head. "Neither of you is a substitute for the other." I wet my lips when she doesn't say anything, and my lungs constrict, making it hard for me to continue. After another moment, I manage to blurt out, "Am I making any sense, or am I fucking this all up?"

"You aren't fucking up. But you promise, if—"

I shake my head, cutting her off. "Don't. Because that's not happening."

She blinks rapidly, reaching for my hands, but I don't want to hold hands. I want to hold onto *her.* She frowns at first when I let go, but then I wrap my arm around her waist and press a slow kiss to her lips. For once, we're in a really good place.

KINGSTON UNIVERSITY

As we approach the house, she stops in the driveway, glancing upward. She knows which window is Duke's. "Do you think he stayed home?"

I shrug, glancing toward the garage, but the bays are all closed, so it's hard to say if he has one of the other vehicles or if he's sequestered himself in his room.

"I went in to talk to him. After you left," Lennon murmurs, eyes still glued to the window above.

Nodding, I sigh. She needs to be aware that even though the three of us sometimes have issues, we still talk to each other, and definitely keep each other in the loop.

It'd be a piss-poor idea to let her think there are any secrets among us. I huff out a laugh. *Wait, there* was *one big secret, but that seems to be out in the fucking open now.* Slowly, I scrape my teeth over my lip. "Yeah, I know you did." And as I suspected they might, her eyes dart to mine in question. "Bear told me this morning."

She seems to take that information in stride. "Oh. Okay well, I asked him about the Stella thing. He blew me off ... and that's putting it mildly." With her teeth clenched, her gaze finally shifts away from Duke's window to me. Our eyes connect, and I can see in hers that she was disappointed in his reaction ... and continuing lack of explanation.

But to be fair to him, it is *September 5. And we all know it.*

"Maybe it's not the best day to ask about that," I muse, curling my hand around the back of her neck. I brush my fingers briefly over the fingerprints I'd put on her. A thought wanders to the forefront of my mind, one that both disturbs me and arouses me. I actually *like* seeing my mark on her just as much as I liked the feel of my hand circling her neck and the way her pulse jumped against my palm. I'm one sick fuck sometimes.

She pins her eyes on me, a stubborn fire lighting her eyes. "I get that, and I should have known better, but he and I—" She sucks in a breath. "Ugh. Never mind. It's shitty that he keeps calling me Stella if he's not going to admit whatever it means to him. Because I agree with you. It has freaking meaning behind it, and he's let me think all along it was an insult." She reaches up, taking my hand from her neck. "Let's go inside."

My eyes flick to hers, my voice husky and rough when I grit out, "Yep. It's fucking naptime."

With that, we head into the house. As if we're on the same wavelength, Lennon doesn't argue when I take a tour of the lower floor of the house, then peek out back, checking to see if Duke is on the patio. He isn't anywhere obvious, so we climb to the second floor to check his room.

His door is wide open, the room empty. Not much we can do if he isn't here. I have an idea that he may have gone to visit Juliette's grave, so I try not to worry too much. Like Bear said earlier—some space and time to clear his head might be the best thing for him.

We stand in the middle of the hallway semi-awkwardly. I'm unsure what Lennon needs right now from me, if anything. My forehead creases as she squeezes my hand and begins to let go. And at first, I let her, though it hits me square in the chest—it's not what I want. I want her with me, no matter the warning bells that begin to clang furiously in my head.

She takes an uncertain step toward her room, then stops, glancing back toward me. "Mase?"

I clear my throat, setting aside the leaden feeling in my gut. "Yeah?"

"Can I sleep with you? I hate lying there all alone." Her eyes plead with me, even as she tries to hide her anxiety with a smile.

I draw in a breath. "Fuck yeah you can."

TWENTY-ONE

MASON

I'M PULLED out of a peaceful sleep by a deep, gravelly groan. It's followed by a fitful gasp, and then some mumbling I can't quite make heads or tails of in the slumber-induced fog I'm in.

"No. *Nooo.*" The sheer agony in those words is like a punch to the gut and has a frown pulling at my face. But my head is still hazy. *Am I dreaming?* I take a couple of slow, steady breaths, waiting—hoping—I can fall back into a peaceful sleep and I'm not about to veer headlong into a nightmare.

But then, there it is again, the breathless, aching voice behind me. "Why? Why are you here? Why do you do this to me?" Out of nowhere, hands claw at my back and shoulders, then feet push at the backs of my knees as I'm shoved forcefully across the bed.

Oh, fuck. This is not my nightmare. It's Mason's.

I gasp, my back bowing, trying to escape his clutches, because while he's pushing me away, he also doesn't let go. "Mason. Stop," I cry out, but it's as if he doesn't hear me. I struggle, thrashing in the sheets, but he's still got me in his vicious grip.

"You're not fucking real. Get out of my goddamn head," he hisses. "Are you going to haunt me forever? Because I can't fucking handle it." I can tell by his intensity that his jaw is probably tight enough that the muscles twitch and jump. He's overwhelmed by darkness and rage.

Heart pounding furiously, I finally wrench free and manage to roll over, but my long hair is hanging in my face, and he's already grabbed onto my wrists again. The awful truth hits me square in the heart. He thinks I'm his mother, and he won't understand any differently until I can show him it's me. I desperately try to flip my hair so it isn't disguising who I really am. He needs to be able to look into my eyes. "Mase," I gasp out, words tearing from my throat on a sob. "It's me. Look at me."

His uneven breaths are audible as I wrestle with him. I catch slivers of his rage through my dangling hair—dark, fathomless, pain-filled eyes and a jaw clenched so hard, I'm sure he'll break his molars. His nostrils flare as he seethes, "What was I supposed to do? Let him keep hurting you? I couldn't watch him do it anymore! No!" He's in agony, working himself into an unhinged state. He barely takes in air before he huffs it right back out. "I'm sorry. I'm so fucking sorry I couldn't stop him. I'm so sorry I pushed you. Why'd you have to leave me?" His face contorts with a raw heart-wrenching sob that rips from his throat.

His words, his angsty pleas—they tear at my soul.

"Mason!" The weight of another body hits the bed behind him.

At the same time, I cry out, "Mason, it's me. Lennon!"

And now there are two of us battling to get Mason to see past the horror of his nightmare. Me ... and Duke.

I lie there, practically helpless with the vice grip Mason has on my wrists but watch in fascination as Duke curls himself around Mason's back, holding him tightly. His chin rests on Mason's shoulder, and he whispers, "That's Lennon, Mase. Not your mom. Calm the fuck down. Everything is okay." After several nerve-racking seconds, Duke's words seem to get through to Mason, so he continues, his voice gruff. "Let up on her. You don't want to hurt her. I know you don't."

It takes Mason another few moments to digest what Duke's asked of him. He blinks repeatedly. I know what's coming, and it breaks my heart. No matter that he's making his best effort at gaining control over his emotions, a single tear slips from the corner of his eye. Hands shaking, his grip on me relaxes, and I might be crazy, but I slide closer instead of scrambling away like I know I should. I cup his cheek and brush the moisture away with my thumb.

"I-I'm sorry." He sounds absolutely defeated. It makes me so sad for what he's been through, for what he continues to go through all these years later.

I rest my hand on his bare chest. "We've got you, Mase. It's okay." His body shudders between us, and I gently brush his hair out of his eyes. "What can we do?"

"Nothing. I just need a minute," he mumbles, putting his lips into my hair. "I need to forget it, put it out of my head." He exhales harshly, the rise and fall of his chest ragged under my fingertips.

I peek up at Duke from under my lashes. He hasn't moved an inch, his face buried in Mason's neck as he holds on tightly. His cheeks stain pink the longer I keep my eyes trained on the two of them. I definitely see it now. They've simply never allowed anyone to witness this side of their relationship—not that it's an actual relationship. Maybe a better word would be attraction. I'm so freaking curious, but I bite my tongue. Does Duke really not want whatever this is he has with Mason?

Against my better judgment, I slowly bring my hand to rest on Duke's bicep. I give his arm the slightest squeeze so he knows I appreciate what he's doing for his friend right now, no matter what went down between them that had Duke pushing Mason away.

Mason drags in a deep breath, shifting slightly. He guides my face to his, his lips claiming mine in the sweetest kiss he's ever given me. It makes my heart stutter in my chest and has me questioning whether this is the same person who attacked me mere minutes ago. But it is. It's him. The solid beat of his heart and the way his lips move on mine tell me so. He's my very own Dr. Jekyll and Mr. Hyde.

A contented sigh escapes me as we sink into the kiss. His tongue slips into my mouth, slowly curling with mine, and then stroking more desperately, like he's trying to tell me something. A hand grasps my ass as we continue to feast on each other's lips. At first, I think it's Mason's, but when my eyes flutter open, I realize it's Duke's. He grips my panty-covered cheek and tugs me tight against Mason's body. The pounding in my chest accelerates, and my mind races, unsure where this is going.

At a loss for words—and not wanting anything to ruin this moment—I let Duke guide me as the three of us grind together, writhing on the bed. Mason's cock is fully erect behind his boxer briefs, nudging my lower abdomen as we move. Duke's hand slides from my ass to my thigh, and he hitches my leg up over Mason's hip ... and his own. He's adjusted me in such a way that my clit rubs along the hard ridge of Mason's dick with every roll of our collective hips.

Duke shifts momentarily to reach back and yank his shirt over his head. I've seen him shirtless before, but I don't know if I've ever truly let myself appreciate the smoothness of his skin or all those ridges and valleys of muscle. I map them with my eyes, noting how his nipples harden under my gaze. He lies back down and tugs his shorts over his ass before shoving them down his legs and kicking them away. The entire time he's doing that, though, my eyes glue to the faint trail of hair starting just below his belly button and disappearing beneath the waistband of his underwear. From there, they shift to drink in the prominent V of muscle. I'd like to run my tongue over it, taste the salt of his skin, before finally finding out if the dick I'd copped a feel of is really as impressive as I remember. God, I hope it is.

Mason rubs up against me some more, and there's a constant zinging sensation in my core. He palms one of my breasts, and I exhale hard, feeling my heart rate ratchet up about ten notches. The next thing I know, Mason has tugged my tank top over my head, baring my breasts to both of their gazes. We're three pairs of underwear from naked, and the idea of it sends my head spinning.

Mason cups my tit in his hand and immediately dives his head down to lick at my nipple. The expression on Duke's face tells me he isn't sure whether he should be looking at me, watching this. But then in one swift move, Mason pushes me partially onto my back so he can give my other breast attention at the same time he plucks Duke's hand from my leg. He gazes into my eyes for a moment, and I know what he's doing. He's letting me call the shots, just like Bear did that day in the gym. I give an almost imperceptible nod. *Yes. I want this.*

The moment I give consent, Mason puts Duke's hand directly over my full breast. "Touch her. You know you fucking want to, so just do it. She's okay with it." Mason draws in a ragged breath, looking over his shoulder. "I need this, Duke."

Duke grunts a bit and swats Mason's hand out of the way so that he can massage my soft flesh on his own. "Fuuuck," he groans, and I can't say my reaction is any different. I never would have thought we'd get here. I arch my back, reveling in the feel of both of them touching me at once.

A moment later, Duke crawls over us to my other side. His blue eyes sear into mine as he lowers his mouth to my nipple and wets it with his tongue. *Oh, fuck.* Desire tangles with our reality in a relentless tug-of-war. Which will come out on top, our desperate need for each other or the fact that he's technically family?

He flicks that devilish tongue of his over my protruding flesh, circles, and watches for my reaction. I squirm. My panties have to be damn near soaked through, and with them both using their mouths in distinctly different—but equally wicked—ways, my situation is only going to become more dire.

I slide my hands into the hair at the back of their heads, reveling in the idea that they're more than eager to pleasure me. Their hands are everywhere, gliding over my skin, squeezing and touching in a way that has me panting for them. I gasp for air, and soon, their mouths follow their hands, trailing fiery paths of pleasure over my entire body. Their eyes meet over my abdomen, and I don't know whether they silently agreed to what they do next, but they each send a hand south. They skim down to my thighs, and a moment later, they spread my legs and hike them up. Mason jams a pillow under my hips until I'm tilted to a position that will give them better access ... to all of me. Their fingertips slowly track closer and closer to my pussy, and all I can think is that my heart really is going to burst out of my chest at the anticipation of both of them touching me down there.

Mason runs a finger downward, along the hem of my panties, teasing me with one dexterous finger slipping under the fabric. It sets off a cascade of tingles through me that has my body shuddering in a very good way. Duke drags the pad of his thumb directly down the center of the damp patch on my panties. I shiver involuntarily. I know he can see the wetness, know that's why he's specifically touched me right there.

There's a tiny part of me waiting for some sort of smart comment to come flying out of his mouth and knock me on my ass, but I wait, and it never comes. His chest heaves as he looks up at me. What's happening between us is intense and scary and so real I don't quite know what to do with myself.

Mason turns his head, kissing the inside of my thigh, jerking my attention to him. My head reels, and the slightest bit of uncertainty rises within me before I squash it down. I tell myself I'm in control, even as a small whimper falls from my parted lips. Two pairs of eyes follow every hitch of my chest, one blazing-blue and the other sinful and dark.

Mason hooks his fingers in the waistband of my white cotton panties, one eyebrow rising in question.

"Take them off." The voice doesn't even sound like mine, but it *was* me. Somewhere deep inside I know I want this. I want them.

They waste no time peeling the underwear from me, leaving me completely naked and at their mercy. I couldn't stop this now; lust careens through my body at breakneck speed.

It starts simply enough. They take turns playing with me, skimming fingers on either side of my entrance. It feels good, and all my nerve endings spark a needy fire that will flame into a full-blown inferno if we keep going. I writhe between them, waiting with bated breath for more of their touch.

"Please?" The word comes out ragged and desperate. My face flushes.

Mason looks up at me from under his hooded gaze. "Are you begging, Lennon?"

Am I? Fuck yes, I am, and I don't care if they know it. When I nod, he gives me a ghost of a smile before rubbing a few deft fingers over my clit in a circular pattern.

Duke hesitates. His jaw is tight enough to snap, and he's breathing kinda hard. He keeps shaking his head, like he's trying to wake himself up. Only he can't. Because this is happening. He's not dreaming. None of us are anymore.

With Mason still making manic circles around my clit, Duke finally manages to grit out, "What do you want, Lennon?"

I stare at him, wondering if I have the courage to tell him what I really want. I blink, my head in a daze. "I want you to keep touching me." My eyes flick to the hand that is holding my thigh, and I bite my lip. His fingers are long and maybe a little rough. I need them inside me.

He nods, then looks from Mason to my pussy. "She's so fucking wet for us." Taking one fingertip, he slides it down through my slit and teases my entrance before ever so slowly inserting one finger inside me. The reverse motion isn't any faster. He's going to drive me out of my mind because *oh, fuck*. My stepbrother is a tease. He keeps up the same agonizingly slow pace for what could have been one minute or ten. By the time he adds a second finger, sweat pops out on my brow.

A stuttered curse leaves my lips as my body begins to tremble and tension coils inside me. Duke watches my every move as he boldly strokes his fingers inside me. "Does it feel good, Lennon?"

I'm close to combusting, and I can't seem to stop the rock of my hips as my pussy chases those magic fingers of his.

And, as if he doesn't want to be left out of the fun, Mason pushes my leg a little wider and replaces his fingers with his mouth. He covers my clit and sucks on me in time with Duke's ministrations, which now include a beckoning curl of his fingers. Over and over, he rubs a spot that has me moaning aloud. Maybe I should be embarrassed by the noises falling from my lips, but I don't care because these guys are hell-bent on making me feel *so* fucking good. I quickly come undone, hips bucking as my pussy gushes. The orgasm that streaks through me is so powerful my vision goes a little dark and sparkly on the edges. "Fuck. Oh fuck. Yes!"

"I want to taste her."

Duke. My stepbrother. He wants to— Fuck. I can't think, I'm floating on clouds.

While I'm still recovering, they put yet another pillow under my ass, and I glance down to see them holding my legs open and looking at every bit of me with hungry eyes.

My eyes widen as they begin to lick and suck, first one, then the other, and sometimes both at the same time if they can get the right angle. Mouths closing over my clit and kissing my pussy lips. Dips of tongues into my core and swipes over the delicate skin near my ass. The way they work together is like a symphony, only they're playing me, not an instrument.

There's so much sensation down there, I think I may have died or something, because I feel like I'm outside my own body, watching some really fucking lucky girl who is experiencing these men worshipping her. With a jolt, I realize it's definitely me, and my heart squeezes as they both look up at me from between my legs. "You two are so fucking hot."

Mason grunts out, "Agreed." He turns his head, grips the back of Duke's neck, and slams his mouth against Duke's. My mouth drops open, watching the fierceness of their kiss. It's raw, animal ... and beautiful. Their tongues stroke and stroke, and I don't even mind taking the back seat for a bit to watch.

"Fuck, I taste her on you. So fucking good." Duke moans as their mouths slant, and they take the kiss deeper. They don't realize it, but their fingers dig into each of my thighs, and a resulting surge of wetness flows from me. Before I comprehend what I'm doing, my hand drifts down, and I slowly touch my swollen sex, fingers sliding through a mixture of my arousal and their saliva. Mere moments later, I get myself off to the sight of these two men kissing each other like the world could stop, and that'd be okay with them. I come with a loud gasp, my hips rolling through it.

"Fuck, look at you." Mason kneels over me and laps up the juices from my pussy, and licks over my fingers, which I haven't moved.

Duke squeezes my leg, his head tilting to the side. "Did it ... did you—" He stops, a tiny smirk working his way to his lips.

"Watching you got me hot and bothered." My eyes drift down to his gray boxer briefs, which have a wet spot at the front. I gesture with my chin toward his dick. "I think you should touch each other. Let me watch."

Mason rises beside Duke, his lips and chin glistening. He reaches over, firmly grasping Duke's bulge. "I'm game."

Duke's jaw works to the side. He glances at me before searching Mason's eyes. The nod he gives is practically imperceptible, but I catch it, and so does Mason. Moments later, both of them are out of the last of their clothes, kneeling side by side between my spread legs. Their cocks jut out from their bodies, so fucking hard, I feel the answering throb between my legs again. They don't tell me I should move or sit up, so I wait to see what they'll do. Besides, I'm comfortable right where I am. Front-row seat.

Another smirk lifts to Mason's lips as he brings his fingers to my pussy and gathers some of the slick moisture from me. Oh god. I watch as Duke does the same, slowly touching me, our eyes connected. I'm ready for them to get on with it and jack off, but as it happens, I'm totally unprepared for what they apparently have in mind. Mason takes Duke's dick and slowly begins to slide his hand up and down his shaft.

"Fuuuck, Mase." Duke's head drops back on his

shoulders, and he takes a deep, ragged breath. When he returns his gaze to the two of us, he grasps Mason's thick cock in his hand, slicking his tongue over his lower lip, his eyes trained on his own hand stroking his friend's dick.

It's the best thing I've ever witnessed in my entire life.

They work themselves into a frenzy very quickly, and it's arousing as hell to watch the way they experiment, figuring out what the other likes. I touch my fingers to my engorged clit again, enjoying the show way more than I ever thought I would. They're hot enough to burn down the house.

Masculine grunts and groans of pleasure fill the air, mixing with my more feminine moans and cries. I'm really fucking close, but I don't want to miss a second of their action, so I hang on. *Oh god.*

I don't know what I was expecting, or maybe I was so into it I wasn't thinking about the culmination of the action, but when Duke blows, his cum spurts all over me, thick jets of it hitting my hand where I play with myself, my stomach, and even as high as the underside of my breast. My lips drop open in surprised delight.

Duke works Mason's cock in a way that has him groaning and swearing. "Fuck, Duke. Fucking hell.

Fuuuck." He hardly appears to realize he's said anything, he's so into it.

There's an odd glint in Duke's eyes as he watches his friend come undone, and when he unloads on me, Duke manages to aim it directly at my pussy.

Holy shit. All three of us are breathing hard by the end of their fun, and my stare is hot on the two of them. And fuck ... now I'm all wound up again. I bite my lip, not able to foresee what's next.

Mason's breath still comes in fits and starts, heaving from him as he surveys my body. He rubs a hand over his jaw, sneaking a look at Duke. "That was impressive, man. All the way up to her tits."

Duke closes his eyes and works a hard swallow. I'm the tiniest bit worried until a small huff of laughter, mixed with a subtle groan leaves his lips. He opens his eyes and points. "I wasn't sure what the objective was. Distance or a target."

I put a hand lightly over my face, stifling a laugh. Dudes are funny sometimes.

Mason leans over, kissing Duke's jaw. "I think we did pretty good." His lip catches between his teeth. He jerks a thumb over his shoulder. "I'm going to go shower, let you two ..."

My breath stutters. I bring my hand down and focus on him. "Let us what?"

Mason shrugs. "I think maybe you need some time alone." He blinks, looking at us from under his hooded gaze. "Maybe you have unfinished business."

Frozen, Duke and I both follow Mason with our eyes until he closes the door to the bathroom, effectively leaving us on our own. His absence creates an entirely new atmosphere in this room. We're no longer a threesome with our job being to provide comfort and a distraction to Mason. He's removed himself from the equation. And I wouldn't take back a second of what we just did because it worked. Or I assume it did since he hasn't taken off for the attic to ease his chaos.

So, that all seems like a win. Except now, I'm covered in jizz and fully exposed to my stepbrother's eyes. It's not that I wasn't either of those two things before, it just felt different with Mason providing a buffer between us.

My throat feels so thick I don't know if I can speak, and my mouth is dry, furthering the problem.

Duke's gaze swings from the closed door back to me. He shakes his head slowly, exhaling sharply. The tormented expression on his face, the rigid way he's holding his body ... oh god. We fucked up.

My eyes crash shut, and I bring my arms up to cover my chest, then curl myself into a ball as best I can. I try to roll away from him, but Duke still has a hand on my thigh, and his fingers flex, digging into my flesh. He puts his other hand on my knee and spreads my legs open again.

"Don't," he bites out.

My eyes are screwed shut. "Don't what?"

"Hide from me. I'm not close to done with you." His heavy breaths are audible, and I can imagine the rise and fall of his chest as he looks down at my body. Lust is like a sharp-edged knife, and I teeter on the blade, not knowing which way I'll fall. There's something about his tone that is unnerving, making me wonder what's in his head, but I can't deny the heady, potent desire I feel with his eyes drinking me in and how dangerously right it feels when his hands are on me.

His finger trails through the folds of my pussy, made extra slick by the combination of my wetness and Mason's release. My chest jerks when he pushes one cum-covered finger inside me. "Fuuuck." The rumbled word rips from his throat, like he was doing his best to hold it in but lost the fight. He fucks me slowly with that finger, and still, I can't look at him. My chest jerks, and tension coils in my belly with every new sensation. It's not until he removes his finger and trails it down to my ass that my eyes fly open.

I suck in a startled breath as he touches me there. "What are you doing?"

He bites his lip, one brow raising a fraction. "You

like it." He doesn't give me a chance to answer, and I hardly register what he's about to do when he dips down and tentatively flicks his tongue over my pussy. He lets out a guttural moan and pauses, his chest rising and falling fast. I can't tell from the expression on his face what he's thinking, but I can imagine. His breath hitches before he growls out, "Fuck. The taste of you both on my tongue." He inhales deeply, then goes back for more. He's like a wild animal between my thighs, licking and sucking my skin until he's had his fill. I'm writhing, clutching the sheets in my fists.

Duke and I have such a volatile relationship, I'm all spun up, not knowing what to think or how to feel about what's happening. And fuck, it's too much to decipher with his tongue swirling around my clit. I'm so swollen down there and already on the verge that I'm almost as out of control as he is. *Fuck it.* I grab handfuls of his hair, grinding my pussy against his mouth. I don't know what's behind that tormented ice-blue gaze, but I'm too far lost to stop now.

"You want this," he grunts out, then sucks on my clit for a moment. Mumbling against my sensitive skin, he murmurs, "You want me."

On a hard exhale, I cry, "Ye-e-es." My admission has another orgasm ripping right through me, splitting me open with the violence of it. I shake and moan until it's over and I'm nothing more than a quivering mess on the mattress.

While I'm still coming down, he kneels over me, running his hands over the cum he left on my stomach and rubbing it into my skin. Like he wants to make sure he's a part of me, so I won't forget what we've done. My brow furrows. No, wait. That's stupid. Duke and I— This can't be right.

But he's hovering over me, distracting me from my thoughts as he supports himself with his forearms on either side of my head. He stares into my eyes, but I don't understand what I see there. His voice is rough, thick with emotion. "Stella baby ..."

Before I can argue over the usage of *Stella*, his eyes slam shut. Each breath he draws in is ragged. My mind tumbles, unable to read the quickly morphing expressions on his face. He catches my mouth with his and kisses me so fiercely I forget why I wanted to yell at him in the first place.

And then, something splashes on my cheek. I become very still, not even daring to breathe. The truth weighs heavily on me—that was a teardrop.

Duke wrenches his lips from mine and pushes off me to kneel between my legs. He stiffens as he watches me swipe the wetness from my face with my fingers.

Concern flows through me, and I reach for him, whispering, "Duke? Are you okay?"

He jerks away from my touch, climbs from the bed, and slams the door on the way out, taking all the air in the room with him.

TWENTY-TWO

DUKE

A FEW HOURS have passed since I walked away from Lennon and her worried gaze. In that time, I've tried to talk myself down and make myself understand what's in my head. I don't have a great answer because it's difficult to pinpoint whether it's one thing that's bothering me—the crushing reality that my girlfriend has been dead yet another year—or maybe it's that everything else is crashing down on me with the worst possible timing. Hell, the day isn't even over, and things keep piling on. We've had issues with both my father and Derek. I've somehow gotten naked twice with Mason. And then there's Lennon. I all but fucked my stepsister, and I don't know what to do with that.

I glance up from where I've had my head stuck in the refrigerator to see Mason and Lennon come into the kitchen behind me. Sighing deeply, I pull out a bottle of water for myself, then go back for two more before I pivot on my heel.

Lennon leans close to Mason where he's paused at the kitchen island. I can only assume he's waiting for the right moment to say something to me, though I don't know where he'd even begin.

Tipping her head up, she whispers in his ear. Mason nods, his eyes flicking to mine, studying me, no doubt, and assessing the damage. He juts his chin toward me. "Hey."

I hear the unsaid "Is everything okay?" tacked on there but choose to ignore it as I set the bottles of water down. I push two in their direction.

Lennon frowns then picks them up, handing one off to Mason. She unscrews the cap on hers and takes a sip, all the while watching me with a careful eye.

Fuck. I can't believe we did that—all fucking three of us—in Mase's bed. I haven't been able to come to grips with it because the whole thing keeps running around and around on some lusty, sexy loop in my head. *Fuuuck.* Being with either one of them alone fucks with me bad, but both of them together? *Jesus.*

While it's one thing to help Mason through some shit, it's quite another to stay once it was clear we were moving from danger zone to sexy times. I should have left them to it. But then, clear as day, I hear Mase's plea in my head. *I need this, Duke.* I knew he wanted the distraction, something to help distance himself from the nightmare. And when I looked into his eyes, there was no way I could deny him.

Drawing in a steadying breath, I peer at Lennon out of the corner of my eye. What does she think of what we did together? Her expression shows no outward sign of regret or confusion—it's more concern than anything else. The same fucking concern that'd sent me running earlier after I practically lost it. This girl has me so twisted up. If everything we did was supposedly being done to help Mason, then she and I should have fucking stopped the second he walked out of the room, no matter that he'd insinuated we should continue. *Unfinished business*—that's what he'd called it.

I scrub my free hand through my hair, feeling my lungs cave in. It's as if I've been stabbed and they can no longer draw in the fucking air I need to breathe. Having Lennon as a part of my life has always been an issue because I associate her with Juliette, and she'll always be a heart-wrenching reminder. Which is why I've never known how to deal with her.

Then, once my father started putting things in my head, I found it even more difficult to figure her out. But for every instance my father has said she's problematic and a head case, I have equal evidence that he's full of shit. It's confusing as fuck to find out someone is not who you were always told they were.

He's the one who made me believe she was after our money. I shouldn't have trusted him blindly. He makes no fucking sense, though, choosing not to divorce Nikki when he obviously thinks the same of her. Must be some pretty good pussy. I heave out a breath, trying to focus on Lennon again.

What I do know is this: now that I've had a taste of Lennon Bell, there's no fucking going back. In the heat of the moment, I'd almost let my innermost thoughts loose. *She's mine. I will have her.* Heat flares through me, remembering the feel of her naked body beneath me. But she's my stepsister for fuck's sake. That's what keeps hammering around inside my head, making me deny the way I feel when I'm with her.

But what happened today didn't feel wrong, and she hasn't opened up her sassy mouth to question any of it. She's not the one who ran, that was me. But it's possible she could be stewing behind that calm facade, waiting for the perfect moment to lash out at me with that wicked tongue of hers. The kicker is, with the way I've treated her since she arrived on our doorstep, I wouldn't blame her if she did want to take a bite out of me.

My dick stirs in my joggers.

Fuck, is it bad that I wouldn't mind if she did? My jaw locks up, thinking about it. I welcome her fire. I want to be enveloped in her goddamn flames.

From the awkward silence filling the room, it's obvious none of us are in the right headspace to have an actual conversation. Lennon's exhale comes out as an exaggerated huff. "If I make grilled cheese sandwiches, do either of you want one? I'm starving. I think there's some ham in there, too, unless someone ate it." She lets the question hang in the air as she sidesteps me and opens the refrigerator. After a moment, she comes up with ham, sliced cheese, and a tub of butter. She sets them on the kitchen counter and bends down to pull out a cutting mat from one of the lower cabinets. Mase and I both watch her quietly as she turns to get a pan out and sets it on the burner, then fiddles with the stove dial. She spins back around and stops, her eyes sliding to the right. She hesitates, chewing on her lip.

At first, I'm confused, but then it hits me. The fucking bread is in the pantry. It's large for a pantry ... but it's also a small room. The way her face crumples as she winces sets me into motion. I hold up a hand to stop her. "I'll get it."

I retrieve the loaf of bread and set it with everything else on the counter.

"Thank you." She gives me a grateful smile.

I can only make a grunting noise in response. My head is a jammed-up mess where she's concerned. It's ugly. What the fuck made her so anxious about shit like that?

Mason's eyes shift from me to Lennon, and his lips press together. He shrugs. "I'll have one, if you don't mind."

She nods her head. "No problem. I'm famished. We kinda missed eating lunch." She has a slight twinkle in her eye when she glances at him, but when she turns my way, the playful light in her eyes diminishes. Then again, maybe she's nervous that I'll open my dick mouth and say something nasty. I've done it to her before.

Mason's eyes connect with mine, and he gives me a teasing smirk. "We're probably dehydrated, too. Good call on the water."

Bastard. He sure as fuck knows how to push my buttons. My lips twitch, but I can't quite bring myself to smile, especially since my cock is now fully hardening at the not-so-subtle reminder of our earlier adventures. What would it have been like if I'd fucked her like I wanted to? I mean, what we did had been fucking amazing … but now I can't stop thinking about slipping inside her sweet pussy and having it spasm around my cock.

Mason rakes his hand through his hair and points to

the table. "I'm gonna sit in there." Once again, his nonverbal message comes across crystal clear. *Talk to her.*

Why? Have they been talking about me? What about, specifically? My jaw works to the side, and I rest my forearms on the kitchen island, watching her while I try to decide what the fuck I should even say. I have so many options.

Sorry—I wish my father wasn't a complete handsy asshole this morning.

I shouldn't have jizzed on you for the fourth anniversary of my girlfriend's death.

Didn't mean to put my gay AF attraction to my friend on display for you either.

She begins making an assembly line of sandwiches, and her eyes flick to mine. "Do you want one?"

I incline my head. "Yeah." I let loose a deep sigh at the thoughts running through my head. Worst fucking day ever. My chest clenches as a flash of Lennon and Juliette working in that diner infiltrates my mind's eye. I pull in a ragged breath, fighting to keep my emotions under control. *Juliette, why didn't you tell me you were struggling?*

As Lennon works, she peeks up at me from under a thick fringe of lashes. "I-I haven't had a chance to thank you."

My brows dart together, my attention grabbed as she

draws me back to the present. "For what?" I bite out before I have a chance to think about it.

"What happened this morning with your dad." Her mouth pulls into a frown as she assembles the sandwiches and turns to put two of them on the small frying pan. Facing me again, she busies herself digging into a drawer and comes up with a spatula. "I was—" My brow raises as she hesitates. "I was shaken. And when he left, I focused on what he meant about you lying for me—still don't understand that, by the way—but I should have said thank you right then for ..."

Protecting her. From my own douchebag father. After everyone else left for class, I'd met him in the office, as per his demand. He'd been unhinged, pacing the damn room. He'd given me fucking hell for interfering with how he was handling Lennon, then on top of it, as he was raging, he'd made some snide comments about me being way too comfortable with my stepsister. The eye roll I'd given had bought me a bone-jarring backhand from the old man. I reach up, absentmindedly probing with my fingers as I work my jaw.

That side of my mouth twitches up. If only he knew ... He might be right about that last bit, but I'm never going to be okay with him putting his hands on her. What was he trying to do? Scare her? Hurt her? I don't fucking know what was in his head.

I shake my head. "Not fucking necessary." I brace both hands on the counter looking down at them while she flips the sandwiches over to cook the other side.

My father's pitiful excuse about why he'd shown up today has me on high alert. After calming ever so slightly, he'd said he was there to make sure someone would be home to let the set-up and catering crew in on Saturday for the auction, but I don't buy it. Shoot me a fucking text. I have an awful feeling that the real reason behind his visit was Lennon. I don't know why, exactly, but he's way too fucking interested in what she's doing.

She transfers both sandwiches to plates, then takes one over to Mason. When she returns, she slides the other sandwich across the counter to me. Our eyes lock, and the stare down that happens between us is one for the record books. We're unmoving, and I find it hard to breathe with her gaze scanning every nuance of emotion crossing my face. I hate it, but I think she reads me pretty well. The way she seems to know me makes my chest tighten. It makes me fucking ache for the one girl I can never fucking have.

And that's why my father's fucking hands on her had been too much for me to take ... She may not be mine to touch. But she's sure as fuck not *his*.

She wets her lips, pure frustration leaching from her

features. "Duke, why won't you talk to me? What's wrong? Is it your dad or ...?" She grits her teeth.

So many fucking options ... My entire fucking life is blowing up.

With a deep sigh, she picks up the final sandwich and puts it on the pan. She stands with her back to me as she stares at that fucking sandwich, her breaths heaving in and out, like I've upset her.

On a groan, I push away from the counter and close the gap between us in three steps. With my hands firmly planted on her hips, I yank her back against me. Tucking my head near hers, my voice comes out raspy when I whisper, "There's a lot going on today, but if you really want to know what's wrong with me right at this moment? *This.* This is at the forefront of my mind." I shove my stiffening erection up against her ass. A tiny gasp falls from her lips. I grind myself against her, my heart frantically thudding in my chest. Like dragging words over gravel, I grit out, "I shouldn't fucking feel like this about my goddamn stepsister. We shouldn't have done any of that today. I never should have let it happen."

"Duke ..."

My fingers clamp down on her hips and jerk her back onto my cock one more time. "No. I shouldn't have fucking touched y—"

She wrestles free of my grasp and turns around, her confusion boring into me through fiery-blue eyes. All we seem capable of doing is staring at each other as our chests rise and fall together. We're practically nose to nose, and my brain misfires. I want nothing more than to take out all my anger and guilt and grief on her plump lips.

So, I fuckin' *do*. I cover her mouth with mine in a soul-wrenching kiss, my tongue sweeping boldly into her mouth, my cock thick and hard against her belly. I thread my hands into her hair on either side of her head, and I use it to control her. But the part that twists inside my heart is that I don't need to. She clutches me to her, meeting me stroke for greedy stroke.

The sound of a throat clearing has me tearing my mouth from hers and my head whipping around to the source of the noise. Lennon sucks in a gasping breath.

Bear has paused on the threshold of the kitchen, taking in the scene. He blinks, looking first at me, then at Lennon, and shakes his head. But a moment later, he frowns. "What the fuck are you two doing?" He lunges forward, reaching behind us to grab the pan off the stovetop. He immediately drops it to the side with a clatter. "Goddammit," he bites out, grimacing as he nudges us out of the way and turns off the burner.

I study him while he takes in several gulps of air. I

can see the pain etched into his features and scramble to piece together what's happened. At first, I thought he was growling about walking in on the kiss, but maybe it was just the burning sandwich. Fuck, don't kid yourself, it was probably both.

Lennon's eyes are wide, and she makes a pained noise. "Oh my god, I'm an idiot." She steps in to try to help, but Bear gives her a frustrated shake of his head.

With his right arm clamped to his side, he hurriedly flips on the exhaust fan with his left, then waves it over the blackened sandwich to dissipate the smoke.

Mason looks up from his food. "You all setting the house on fire over there?" He tucks his tongue inside his cheek, eyeing Lennon and me before he glances at Bear with a tinge of concern in his gaze. "You okay, man?"

I catch Bear's eye and raise a brow, but he shakes his head again and goes directly to the fridge to pull out a bottle of water before turning on his heel to open the cabinet where he keeps his snacks and assorted medications. He reaches for a bottle of pills way at the top, muscles the cap off, and pours I can't tell how many down his throat before taking a swig of the water.

"What the hell, man? That was—" *A lot.* Far more than any normal person would have downed. I mean, the guy is big, but he's not *that* big.

Mason's brows furrow hard, and he straightens, setting down his phone.

At the same time, Lennon sucks in a breath, and I don't think she's going to say anything, but I squeeze her waist to signal that she definitely shouldn't. I don't care for the storm cloud on the big guy's face, and I definitely think his behavior is odd. Is he just in pain or is it something more? I twist my lips, considering whether to push it further, but Bear heaves out a frustrated breath.

"It's just anti-inflammatories, fuckin' relax. My shoulder is acting up. I'm fine."

He pauses, then huffs out a breath, eyeing my hand on Lennon's hip. "Duke, I was going to ask how you're doing with everything today, but from the looks of what I walked in on, you're doing just fucking fine."

I work my jaw to the side and shake my head. I get it —he's tweaked his shoulder. He's in pain. He's worried about it. But I don't need the attitude today of all days, and he fucking knows it. Blood rushes to my face, anger heating my words. "I'm sorry your shoulder is messed up, but I need you to fuckin' lay off," I growl, dropping my hand from Lennon's waist. I walk over to the table and pull out a chair next to Mason.

Lennon follows with the sandwich she'd made for me and sits on my other side. She takes a big bite of it, then slides the plate in front of me. "Eat."

I huff out a breath, trying to hold myself together. My eyes connect with hers as I force some of it down.

Bear ambles over a minute later with the half-burned sandwich and sits down across from the three of us. "Anyone want this? Otherwise, I'll eat it."

"I could make another." Lennon's brows knit together. Her concern for him is clear in the tone of her voice. "I don't mind."

He groans. "No. That's okay." He rubs his hand—the left, again—over his scalp. "I need a couple minutes." He inhales deeply before letting it all go.

Bear's definitely off his game, and when that happens, it's always one of two responses: unreasonable anger—which we hardly ever see from him—or the need for quiet. Today we get both, which tells me something is really not right.

I take another bite of the sandwich and slowly chew as my gaze and thoughts swing to the guy beside me. Mason sits scrolling idly through who knows what on his phone.

Swallowing without really tasting the sandwich, I allow myself to study him. Between the body made for sin and the full lips that I shouldn't want on mine—but I fucking do—I'm close to done. But then he's got that fucking creative mind that always seems to know just how to push me in all the right ways and those deep, dark eyes that bore into my soul, and that's it. I'm a fucking goner.

Witnessing his terror ... fuck, I couldn't take it. I hadn't intended to jump into his bed—literally *or* figuratively—but when I heard his shouts and saw what was happening, everything in me told me he needed me. And so did Lennon, since she put herself directly in his chaotic, furious path.

These goddamn nightmares of his, the ones that absolutely break him down, they're relentless. This wasn't the first time I've seen him in the throes of one, and I'm certain it won't be the last. The dumb thing is, I've been watching him, and his developing relationship with Lennon and I'm aware he feels very connected to her because they have similar experiences. But shit ... I don't know if I should point out that the two of them sleeping—literal sleep, not fucking—together in the same bed is a bad idea. Unless ... I guess if someone else were to be present, maybe he'd never have a chance to get all wound up and fly off the handle.

My face heats, my mind carrying me right back to the way I'd held him close, felt his body shake. What do I do, offer myself up as their bodyguard? I shake my head. Is that what I want? To be with them both? And ... Bear? He's involved with her, too.

What are we *doing?* We're all tangled up with this girl

who shouldn't have been dumped here in the first place. This girl who I've watched grow into a beautiful woman over the last few years. I may not have seen her often. But I saw her. I heave out a disturbed breath. I don't know. I just don't fucking know how we make sense of what we're becoming.

I rub my chest as memories sneak up on me, despite my best efforts at pushing them down. *Juliette.* I sit, not touching my sandwich for a long moment, trying to reconcile the idea that I have Lennon at my side while I breathe through the pain of Juliette's loss. This shit sneaks up and comes at me in unending, unstoppable waves.

But at least I'm not like fucking Kingston; he couldn't be bothered to visit his sister's grave this morning like he has three years running. There'd been no flowers, no card. He's visited her in the early hours of the morning every year until today. It'd seem like now that he's panting after this girl—one of their initiates—that he's completely forgotten his sister. My teeth grind.

I breathe deeply, attempting to refocus. There will be a day every year where I feel like this. I'd allowed myself to lose it at the graveside, but then Mason's crisis had taken precedence. While it'd been shitty for him and Lennon, it had actually worked in my favor. I'd gone several hours without thinking about losing Juliette.

Maybe I should feel bad about that, but I don't this time around.

My eyes flick up from my plate as there's finally movement from across the table. Bear rubs his hands over his face, but we remain absolutely silent until he drops his hands and reaches for the sandwich again. "I'm sorry. I'm going to be a cranky ass until the meds kick in. Take my mind off it. What've you all been up to today?"

Mason eyes Lennon and me before answering, "That's a loaded fucking question."

TWENTY-THREE

BEAR

MY BROWS SHOOT UP as I work my arm in a slow circle, testing it. Still bad. Not that I'd expected a five-minute miracle. My lips form a tight line, and I breathe slowly in and out through my nose. "Seriously, what the fuck went on here while I was gone?"

Duke lifts one finger. "Hold on." He busily taps out a text, then nods toward the phone when he sets it down. "There. Fuck the meeting. I said what I needed to say in a text. I don't know about you three, but I'm not up to dealing with anything else today."

The anniversary of Juliette's death is always difficult for him. But in addition to that, we had Tristan's appearance this morning, then the strange vibe I'm getting from these three and whatever I'd walked in on with

Duke and Lennon in the kitchen that'd made me give them that bombastic side-eye.

Mason picks up his phone to read Duke's text. He snorts the second his eyes land on what's written. My phone is somewhere in my gym bag by the stairs, where I'd left it when I came in. Fortunately, Mason's more than willing to read it out loud to us. "No meeting tonight. Stay the fuck out of rooms that aren't yours. One more ounce of disrespect toward Lennon—or anyone else in the brotherhood, for that matter—and—" His reading of the message is cut off by the howl of laughter that rips from him. "Oh fuck. I can't." He shakes his head, wheezing with amusement.

Lennon frowns, her forehead pinching. "What's it say? I'm obviously not in that group text."

My eyes roam from her questioning gaze to Duke's. He's trying really fucking hard not to look at her, but he can't even help himself. He shakes his head "I may have threatened to dip their balls in gasoline and make them stand over an open flame."

Her eyes grow wide. "You—" She bites her lip. "You're just fucking with them."

Duke shrugs. "I bet they don't want to fuck around and find out."

I wait until their amusement dies down to growl, "Is

anyone going to answer my question? Seems like you're hiding something."

Duke, Mason, and Lennon exchange glances, and there's a decidedly uncomfortable few moments of quiet before Mason clears his throat. "Um, so, Lennon and I were fucking tired when we came home from class. We took a nap, and I promptly wigged out on her, thinking she was my mom. Again." He shoots me a tight-lipped smile. "That's where it started."

My eyes dart from Mason over to Lennon, and I can feel the blood leaving my head and my hands going clammy. "Fuck. Are you okay? What the hell happened?" I come half out of my seat before Lennon holds her hands up, palms out.

"I'm fine." She takes a fortifying breath, staring at me. Finally, with a wince, she admits, "Duke came to the rescue."

"Tell me," I grit out, unable to keep the bark out of my voice. My demanding gaze flicks over Duke, whose teeth are tightly clenched, before swinging to Mason.

He grimaces. "I was only half awake. Shouted some nonsense in her face as I was trying to wrestle her out of my bed." He scrubs a hand through his hair. "Whatever part of me was awake, looked at the long blonde hair on my pillow and flipped." He swallows hard, looking down at the table for a moment before he meets Lennon's eyes.

"I'm really fucking sorry, Kintsukuroi," he murmurs, his voice gritty and raw.

I wince. He's so fucking troubled by what happened to his mother. I wish we could get him to see someone about it, but he outright refused the last time I suggested it.

Lennon draws in a shaky breath. "I know you are. And you already told me so."

Mason grips chunks of his hair in both hands. "I can't control it. I killed her. I don't want to hurt you, Lennon." His jaw sets hard, and he stares down at the table, his chest heaving with the effort of breathing. He's letting himself get worked up again.

I can't take it when he blames himself like this, and we all fucking know he's struggling with his reaction to having her here in this house. Between him and Duke, I don't know which is fucking worse sometimes, though her physical safety with Mason is a real concern, so that's what I tend to focus on.

Mason's fist slams down on the table, making all the plates jump and clatter.

Before I can say a word, Duke shouts, "For fuck's sake, Mason, how many times do we have to hash this out? You can't keep doing this to yourself. You did *not* kill your mother. You fucking didn't!" He turns and grabs the seat of Mason's chair, pulling him closer. He grasps him by the back of the neck, his thumb sliding over his jaw. Duke guides Mason's head so that their gazes connect. Quietly, he reiterates, "You fucking didn't, Mase."

Mason's dark eyes lock on Duke's, full of sadness. A muscle at the back of his jaw twitches madly, and I absently wonder if Duke can feel it moving under his thumb.

Watching the moment they're having, I slide my tongue over my lower lip, wetting it, finally deciding that something more needs to be said. "He's right, Mase. Your father is in prison for her murder. He was tried and convicted. Period." I slash my uninjured arm angrily through the air. The movement jars the other shoulder anyway, and I suck in a quick breath before I grit out, "The. Fucking. End. It does you no good to torture yourself like this. It's one thing to have nightmares you can't control, flashbacks, all that shit. But you're completely coherent right now. You're *not* to blame. Admit that to yourself."

I don't miss the swift intake of breath from Lennon. Is it possible she wasn't aware of parts of that? Or maybe it's simply hard to hear that your friend's dad is a fucking scumbag. She knows now, at the very least.

Mason looks at all of us with wounded eyes.

Duke's voice comes out rough, sounding as if it's

scraping what he wants to say out of his throat. He levels his concerned stare on Mason. "Accident. Your part in what happened to your mother—it was a fucking accident. You never should have been there at all."

Mason looks at each of us in turn, slowly breathing. In. Out. In. Out. Just like I taught him to, a technique that sometimes works for me. "I—" He hesitates, his eyes crashing shut for a moment. I can tell he's mentally grappling with what he wants to say. He blinks rapidly, and I nod at him, trying to give him some encouragement. "I might"—his voice hitches—"not ever believe that."

Duke tugs Mason closer, resting their foreheads together. He sighs deeply. "Mase." His name comes out on a rasp. "Don't do this to yourself."

Lennon gets up from her chair and slips between Mason's legs, sitting on his thigh and wrapping her arm around his shoulders.

I lean back in the chair, observing the three of them. Suddenly, it hits me like a bolt of lightning. Lennon mentioned Duke coming to the rescue, but none of them had said a damn thing about how that went down, but something tells me whatever happened between Mason's nightmare and me walking in on Duke kissing Lennon in the kitchen is the root of it. I drag in a breath. I'm not asking. They'll tell me if they want me to know. "I'm going to leave the three of you to it."

"Bear? Are you sure you're okay?" Lennon catches the corner of her lip between her teeth as she brings her pretty blue-eyed gaze to mine.

"Yeah. What I am is exhausted. I didn't sleep at all, obviously. Class. Practice. I'm fucking wrecked. I'll catch you tomorrow. Unless you need me, of course."

"I'll always need you"—Lennon shoots me a wink—"but you should rest."

I definitely should, no question about it. But we'll see if I can sleep with thoughts of my Little Gazelle saying she needs me racing through my head.

EARLY THE NEXT MORNING, I wake up in pain, so I dig out the only other bottle of oxy I have, the supply really low, and take one. It crushes my soul to acknowledge I'm slipping, but I don't know how to handle the pain without them. I hate that I need them.

Addict.

The word licks through me like an evil demon whispering in my ear. I draw in an agitated breath, pushing the thought aside. It's just until my shoulder calms the fuck down. I haven't relapsed or anything. I'm not dependent on this shit. I'm not.

But I have been. My chest tightens. I don't want to be that person again.

Against my better judgment, I head downstairs to get in a quick workout. I figure I can concentrate on my legs and give my shoulder a fucking break, and maybe hit the recumbent bike, too.

As I reach the bottom of the steps, I hear Lennon before I see her. "Ow. Fuck!" comes her hissed exclamation.

Frowning, I hurry toward the gym, but stop short in the doorway. With a hint of a smile creeping onto my lips, I lean against the doorframe and watch.

Lennon stands in front of the hanging bag, swatting ineffectively at it. I have to hand it to her—she's really cute in her gray shorts and bright-pink sports bra, but she doesn't even have her hands wrapped. She should have come to me if she wanted to do this.

"Little Gazelle, what the fuck do you think you're doing?" I let my voice rumble out low and smooth, so as to not scare her too badly.

She sucks in a quick breath as she catches the bag to stop the swing before she whirls around. "Oh, uh."

"'Oh, uh,' is right." I shake my head, pushing off the

doorframe and advancing on her. "You're going to injure yourself again going at it like that."

She clenches her teeth together, giving me a rueful smile. "I thought using the bag would be safe enough."

I shake my head, dragging my eyes away from her because fuck—all I want to do is drink her in. "Nope. As a beginner, we'd wrap your hands and have you wear gloves to use a punching bag. There's such a thing as bare-knuckle boxing, but it's something you work up to. Besides, I wouldn't teach you how to punch using a bag. You need proper technique, gotta learn the correct stance, how to hold your hand. I'll teach you how to move your body to give you maximum power."

Her eyes light up like a kid in a candy store—or more specifically, like she has one of her lollipops between her lips. "Are you going to teach me?"

I draw in a breath, unable to say no to her hopeful question or that smile. I rub my hand over my thickly stubbled jawline. "I promised you, didn't I?"

She grins. "You did."

"I can show you a few things to practice this morning, if you want."

When she wrinkles her nose at me, I think it might be the cutest thing I've ever seen. "Don't I get to practice on you?"

I step up close to her, tilting her chin up with my fingers. "Baby girl, I think you might be biting off more than you can chew." I wink at her, then ease back, taking her hand in mine. "So, here's your first lesson. Do you remember when you hit that asshole Chris at the party and what it felt like?"

Her face goes a little pale and her teeth clench. "Yeah. I do." She makes a face. "It fucking hurt."

"Yeah, I know it did." I huff out a quiet laugh. "Show me how you held your hand before you socked him in the nose."

She folds her hand into a fist, thumb tucked inside her fingers.

I shake my head. "You're lucky you didn't break your thumb that night." Her eyes widen, and I take her hand, unfolding it. "Fingers curl down, thumb folded, between the first and second knuckles of your middle and index finger. In other words, keep it out of the way." I show her where her fist is going to make contact, letting my fingertips skim over her soft skin. "You'll be leading with those front two knuckles. Leave your ring finger, pinkie, and thumb out of it."

I take a few more minutes showing her a proper stance, and then take her through how to use her body to her advantage, first teaching her a jab and then a cross.

"You practice those two punches for me—start with the jab. Watch the mirror, make sure your arm's coming out straight, but you're not lunging forward with your body."

She nods and gives it a try, her face the picture of concentration.

"Remember what I said, don't lunge forward." I come in next to her, adjusting her stance ever so slightly. I tap the top of her head. "Imagine there's a pole from the ceiling that extends down through your head and body to the floor. You can't move forward. You can only swivel." I show her a few times in slow motion what I mean, then gesture that she should try.

She does it a few times, perfectly, before muttering, "Yes, sir." She stops, her eyes comically big as she does this little shimmy before she takes her stance again.

I growl. "Fuck you're tempting."

"Should I move on to the cross yet?" She gives me a hopeful look.

"Nope. Keep jabbing."

She pouts but goes at it again while I lie down on the bench of the leg press and plant my feet on the footplate. She's quiet for a moment, then out of nowhere, she blurts, "Were you upset with me yesterday?" She doesn't turn her head, but her eyes have followed me in the mirror as I do a few reps. I'll stay right here so I can watch what she's doing. And apparently, she's decided to be chatty again this morning.

I smoothly push the weights up and down the track. "Upset?" My brows draw together.

"You, um." She drops her arms and turns toward me. "Sorry. You seemed funny when you first got home yesterday. And maybe later, too, before you went upstairs."

I glance over to find she's still standing there, watching me. "I wasn't upset. Just in a bad mood. I told you my shoulder's been acting up. And if you're asking about whatever went on with you, Mason, and Duke— you don't have to explain a damn thing you do to me. I thought you understood that."

"Well, I know. But I don't want you to think I'm a —" She stops and turns back around to face the mirror. "Fuck it," she growls under her breath as she throws a punch.

I watch her for a beat, realizing she's moved on to the cross without saying anything, and doesn't have her form right. Slightly irritated, I let the weights down as fast as I can, get up, and move behind her, grasping her hips in my hands. "Stop." She goes to punch again, and I clamp down harder, yanking her body back against mine so she can't very well do jack shit. I grimace as searing pain shoots through my shoulder and down my arm. "Would you hold it a second?" I whisper harshly in her ear.

She glances quickly over her shoulder, her expression one of frustration. "Why?"

I turn her in my arms and grasp her chin in my hand. "Look at me, Lennon." Her eyes crash shut, and her lips pinch together. *Shit, she's stubborn this morning.* "Don't want me to think you're a what?" I question softly.

Since they weren't being forthcoming about it, I'm going to assume that after Mase had a nightmare they all ended up in the bed. Makes sense to me. And who knows what happened to bring us to where we are now. But it seems like she's worried about where she stands with me, which maybe I can't quite blame her for, what with my surly-ass attitude yesterday.

"I'm aware of what it must look like."

"It looks like whatever you or we want it to look like. Period."

Lennon pulls away, turning back around. She stares into the mirror and resumes the fighting stance I taught her, bringing her right leg back, bending a bit at the knee, and lifting her hands near her face to protect it.

Working my jaw to the side as I consider her words, I watch her pivot properly and throw the right-handed punch. She swivels back and goes again.

I walk around and hold up my hands for her. "Go easy on this, but I want a jab-cross combination."

Her eyes finally flick up and meet mine. "You want me to ...?"

"Hit my hands." I hold them up. "Hit me with the jab and then the cross. See how they work together."

She's a goddamn natural. Jabbing straight out, she follows it with the cross. *Smack, smack. Smack, smack. Smack, smack*. Over and over again she goes. I knew she'd be good at this—she's in tune with her body, she has endurance. It's great.

A little more power begins to come into the punches she's throwing, and I grimace, then hold up a hand. "You're doing great. Time for a break." I exhale deeply. "By the way, I can teach you all the things you want me to, but sometimes, the most effective way to deal with an asshole is to pull your hand into a fist and then"—I make a fist and in slow motion show her what to do, bringing the back of my fist to the tip of her nose—"sharply smack at the nose with the back of your hand."

Her eyes widen. "That's smart." She nods her head. "Doesn't mean I don't want another lesson."

I draw in a breath, moving my arm in a slow, small circle. "I'll sit over here and watch if you want to keep going."

"Your arm hurting?"

"Yeah. This is the one I had surgery on a few years ago." Wide, curious eyes lock on me as her mouth forms an O. I wave it off. "I've just gotta give it a break. It's all good."

She walks over to some mats and sits down, then lies on her back with her legs bent, feet firmly on the ground. She pats the mat beside her. "Lie down here with me."

I do as she asks, unable to deny her simple request. I'm unsure if I'd deny her any damn thing. I take a deep breath before diving back into our earlier conversation. "My relationship with you. It's whatever we want it to be. This shit with Mase and Duke—it's gotta be fucking confusing." I pause, giving her a moment. "I don't know many women who'd want to take on three guys, but you should do what you fucking want, whether it's relation-ships or just sex. You do what works for you."

"I always do. But what if it doesn't work for you?"

"Me specifically? I don't have a problem with what-ever you want."

She rolls over, props her head on her elbow, and when I meet her gaze, I see the concern in her eyes. Her lips seal tightly together.

"Come here."

She hesitates.

Fortunately, she's on my left, so I roll, too, putting us close together. I lift my injured arm—don't fucking care at the moment—and brush a few tendrils of hair from her face, tucking them behind her ear. "Does Mase freak me the hell out where you're concerned? *Yes.* Absolutely. Was I thrown off to see that heat between you and Duke? Again, *yes.* But that's because the two of you have been at each other's throats off and on since you got here. So, if yesterday was you figuring shit out, then so be it."

"It doesn't bother you that I've kinda been with all three of you in some way?"

"It really doesn't."

"Promise?"

"Fuck, here I go again making promises to you."

She bites her sexy-as-hell lip, her eyes scanning my face. To my surprise, a moment later, her smile turns upside down and her face falls. "He made it pretty clear right before you walked in that we shouldn't have let it go as far as we did."

"Duke is all caught up in his head. It sure as hell didn't look like he doesn't want you to me."

"But what if he won't let himself? I wasn't certain if he was just helping Mason or if he wanted—" Her cheeks pick up the rosiest blush I've ever seen. "If he wanted me, too. You have to admit, it's fucking awkward as hell."

She's not wrong. The stepsibling thing is a bit of a gray area, that's for fuckin' sure. I reach out and rest my hand on her hip, giving her a squeeze. "If there's one thing I know about Duke, it's that his actions absolutely speak louder than his words."

"You really think?"

"I know. Fucking think about it, Lennon. Think back to every single thing he's done and said since you've gotten here, and you fucking tell me which you think is real. You have to decide if the way you feel about him outweighs the strain it'll put on you both if you decide to move forward. Only you and Duke can decide that." I lean forward and kiss the tip of her nose. "Good job today, little brawler." And with that, I get up and leave the gym, because I have a feeling she needs time alone with her thoughts.

The secondary reason I take off is that the pain in my shoulder is excruciating, and I need to do something to remedy it. On my way upstairs, I stop in the kitchen, rifling through the cabinet where I'd found the oxy mixed in with the ibuprofen. They look nothing like the anti-inflammatories, and if anyone had looked closely enough, two kinds of pills came out of that bottle. Little orange ibuprofen pills and tiny white oxycodone as well —two of them, to be exact. They seemed more concerned with the quantity of pills I'd taken, which, I suppose taking large amounts of anything isn't a good idea. My head knows this. But I can't stop myself. Yesterday, I'd taken two 10mg tablets. It'd helped some.

I bite back a strangled string of curse words as my eyes crash shut. I give the ibuprofen bottle a shake, but there's simply no more of the white pills hiding in there. In the bottle in my nightstand drawer, there'd only been two more. *Fuck.* That's not gonna fucking do it. How am I going to get through Saturday's game—and worse, Sunday's fight night—if I don't have more?

Heaving out one breath after another, I grimace. I have no fucking choice. I pull my phone from my pocket and put the call through to the only person who can help me, no matter that I fucking hate the thought of him at the moment.

"Son? What can I do for you? I wasn't expecting your call." My father's tone is off-putting, and for a second, I think about ending the call.

Ashamed, I bow my head. "I need more."

TWENTY-FOUR

MASON

I'VE BEEN in the attic for almost three days. I thought I was doing pretty well, but then I wasn't. So I came up here and threw myself into my charcoals, producing a fury of images so messed up, so dirty and dark, I doubt I'll ever show them to anyone.

There have been a few knocks on the attic door, then when I didn't respond, a few texts to check up on me. I finally gave in, sending the same message to all three of them. *I need to be alone.* They know me well enough at this point—Lennon included—that sometimes it's best to let me expel my demons by myself.

I never know what's going to set me off either, so that's fun. Admitting I'm unsure if I can ever believe my mother's death wasn't my fault had thrown me right off the edge of the abyss.

One thing about being a moody asshole no one wants to bother is it gave me plenty of time to sort through the dumpster fire in my head. There's been a lot to sift through since Monday's nightmare episode.

Lennon hadn't flinched in the face of my chaotic storm, and the way Duke had looked beyond the shit we'd been putting each other through to help me had caught me by surprise. Neither of them had to treat me with the kindness they did. It weighs on my heart like a heavy stone that maybe I haven't done enough to be deserving of either one of them. Hell, how will Lennon ever be able to trust me with all I put her through? Duke, too—because I can't really think of anything that requires more trust than what we're doing. I may be comfortable admitting I'm bisexual, but he isn't. I have to respect that if I expect to maintain any sort of relationship—friends, lovers, or something more —with him.

And Bear—fuck. There's something off there, so he's been on my mind, too. We don't see him out of control and unreasonably angry very often, injury or not. It makes me nervous when the caretaker of our group is so clearly troubled. He's the one who makes sure everyone else is okay, so seeing him struggle throws me for a loop. I don't know what to do for him that will help, because he's not the sort to come to us with his problems. Still, there's got to be something I can do. If I ever crawl out of this dark place I've been in, I'll make a point to talk to him.

I let out a heavy sigh as I smudge a stroke of charcoal with my finger to soften it. I haven't bothered with any of my more expensive art paper lately, when I came up here Monday night, I'd unrolled butcher block paper across the length of the attic floor and have been whipping off one sketch after another, drawing on my hands and knees.

Eventually, I'll land on one that feels right, and I'll do a more in-depth study. Right now, I can't seem to find *the one.* I experience a mania about my art that hits every once in a while—and when it does, it overtakes my entire life. When I can't handle being around people, I prefer the company of my charcoals and the quiet solitude of the dark attic.

I haven't been going to my classes, instead choosing to email my professors photos of what I'm working on in the attic, with the request that I be allowed to continue on here at home. They've been more than willing, seeing as how I'm churning out sketch after sketch like some inhuman art fiend. My fingers have practically turned into sticks of charcoal.

I sit back on my heels, looking around. I like the quiet. But I miss Lennon's voice. I like to be alone. But I need the way Lennon looks at me even more. Pushing to my feet, I head down the stairs, fling open the door, and find her bedroom door standing open. Lying sideways across the bed on her stomach, with both a book and a notebook in front of her, she's got that ever-present red lollipop in her mouth.

My lungs practically burst as I hold my breath, watching her. I shift slightly, and the board below my foot creaks. I prepare to have her catch me watching her any second, but she doesn't flinch. Earbuds. She doesn't even know I'm here. Her mouth moves to the words of whatever song she's listening to as she kicks her legs in time to the beat. Just the sight of her has me breathing easier.

"Lennon." I wet my lips, take a quick inhale, then try again, only louder this time. *"Lennon."*

She pulls the lollipop from her mouth and looks over her shoulder. An immediate smile lifts the corners of her lips, and she yanks one earbud out. "Hey, Mase." Her eyes light up.

My heart drops into my stomach. How can she still look at me the way she does when she's learning more and more about how awful my life growing up had been? I hadn't missed the look on her face when she found out my father is in prison for murdering my mother. It makes me sick to think about it. Because I know the truth. I ran at them. She fell. I will never forget the sound she made when she hit the stone patio. I caused that.

It wasn't your fault, Mason. You know it.

But do I? *They* told me all my life it was my fault. My brain twists painfully as I attempt to maintain control.

"Hey. What's going on?" Lennon has risen to her knees on the bed and watches me, a soft but cautious look in her eyes.

I battle back my disturbing thoughts and cross the room. I hold out my hand to her but realize belatedly that my fingers are covered in black charcoal, as is much of my bare torso. I wince ever so slightly, hoping it's not a deal breaker. "Come with me?" I murmur, my voice raspy and unsure. I haven't spoken in days.

To my surprise, she doesn't say a word about my request or the charcoal and climbs from the bed. She steps close and puts her hand in mine, curiosity spreading over her features. "Yeah?"

I nod. "Yeah." I clasp her hand tightly, so she doesn't have a chance to change her mind. To my surprise, though, she doesn't show any signs of misgivings, even when I pull her into the hall and take a right, immediately heading up the attic stairs with her. None of her visits up here have ended particularly well, but there's a first time for everything. I want to show her that I trust her enough to have her up here. The question is can she ever reciprocate that trust again. At the top of the stairs, I stop. When I went downstairs, I just knew it was time —I needed her. But now I don't know how to *show* her.

"What are we doing here?" Her inquisitive gaze meets mine. She gives me a hesitant smile.

"Are you scared to be up here with me?" I grit out in response to her uncertainty.

Her head rears back as she looks me boldly in the eye. "I *never* have been. What's happened up here between us has been unexpected. Maybe a little nerve-racking." She shrugs. "But you invited me up here this time, so ..." I draw in a deep breath. Softly, she murmurs, "I can go if you've changed your mind, but—"

My eyes flick to hers. "But?"

"But I'd like to see what you've been up to. I knew I shouldn't bother you, but I've missed you a lot. I-I didn't know how badly you were struggling. Was it the talk about your mom? Or something else?"

I rub my hand over my heart and nod. "Some days I can talk about it and others I can't. I think I was on overload. It was too much, and my head got all jammed up in the memories." I press my lips tightly together. "It wasn't anyone's fault. I know everyone was trying to help. Too much talk of it, though, and—"

She tugs on my hand, and I step close to her. Her

arms wrap tightly around my middle as my chest jerks with emotion. "It's okay, Mase. You don't have to talk about it right now."

Her eyes travel the room, first landing on the jumbled-up mess from when I lost it the other day. I exhale hard. "I needed room for more recent stuff."

She only nods, then lets me go and turns in a full circle. She takes in everything in this curious way she has. "You've been busy."

"I needed some time to think. This is how I do that."

"I get it." She moves closer to several drawings that I hadn't intended for her to see. She points at them. "These are stunning." Her eyes flick back to them as she moves closer to study them.

I don't know how she can say that, as they're on ripped-up paper and mostly incomplete.

"Does he know you've been drawing him?"

Taking in a deep breath, I shake my head, then focus on the charcoal on my hands.

"If only Duke knew how you see him." When I look up, her lip is clenched between her teeth, and she gives me a little shrug. "It's beautiful, the way you feel about him. He'll come around."

My ears grow hot the longer she looks at the images. I don't even know why I'd drawn them, except ... he'd been on my mind. A lot. "Yeah. Maybe. Maybe not." I shrug my shoulders as if it's no big deal, and another ghost of a smile appears on her face.

"Why am I up here, Mason?"

I scrub my hands through my hair, knowing I'm a black-stained mess. "I was hoping you'd sit for me."

One perfect brow quirks up. "Seriously?"

I lift my hands in a placating gesture in front of me. "I promise I won't do to you what I did last time. Won't even touch you. Not if you don't want me to."

She wrinkles her nose, glancing around at my space, and I find it doesn't even make me panic to have her here. I wonder if she feels the same or if she's looking around and seeing all the places I've hurt her. Degraded her. Threatened her.

My heart picks up speed, and my breathing matches its rapid rhythm.

"Mason." She steps close, gripping my arms right above the elbows, and staring up into my eyes. "Stop. Get out of your head. Look at me. I'm fine." My brows dart together. "Yeah, I understand you pretty fucking well."

I choke on all the things I want to say, my jaw working back and forth as I study her. She lifts onto her toes and brushes her lips over a spot to the side of my chin. I take one slow breath, then another, seeking the calm that I need—and finding it in her.

She nods. "That's it." Moving one hand to my chest, she covers my heart with her palm. "This doesn't need to race unless it's for the right reasons."

Words erupt from me before I truly know what's on my mind or what's been threatening to spill from my mouth. "Kintsukuroi, you are so beautiful to me. Inside and out. Whatever shit you've been through has created you, broken you, and you've put yourself back together." I drag in a ragged breath. "Would you give me a do-over?"

She tilts her head to the side, her eyes narrowing.

"I swear this time will be different." I lift my charcoal-stained finger to my chest, drawing an X over my heart.

Her lips twitch. "Do you want me naked again?"

Images flash in my head of the last time. The reminder of what I did was still capable of making me feel unfathomable shame. But I can't take it back, and at the time, that's what felt right to me. I allow my gaze to roam down her body in her tank and torn-up shorts. "Only if you want to be. Seriously."

In answer, she pulls her tank top over her head. "I'm good with whatever you need, Mase. I have been from the beginning. You should know that by now." She shrugs, pops the button on her shorts, and shoves them down.

Fuck, what did I do to deserve her? I've never had someone look at the madness that sometimes rages inside me and hold out their hand to me. She tells me it's okay to be the way I am and then willingly gives herself over to whatever I need.

So, the answer to my question is I don't know what I did to deserve her, but I sure as fuck *need* her. Standing there in bra and panties, she looks like a fucking wet dream. I swallow hard as blood pumps through my veins and pounds in my head. Suddenly, I know what I want to do. I take her hand and bring her over to the old leather couch that sits out of the way near a big easel. Her eyes shift to look at it at the same time I sit. She gasps as I pull her directly down onto my lap. Smooth legs land on either side of my thighs, and I run my hands over them, smudging her skin with dark streaks. She inhales sharply, then bites down on her lip.

I trace my fingertips over her stomach, then stroke them over each one of her ribs before lifting my hands to her neck. Her pulse races under my thumbs, and her lips part as she stares steadily at me. I swallow, running them up and down before I capture her mouth with mine. I shudder with need, holding her still as I ravage her. My tongue and hers collide, in a furious battle of wills. Over and over again, we clash, desperately seeking the connection we only have with each other. "Need these lips swollen," I grunt, nipping and sucking at them. "Need these cheeks pink. Need these eyes wanton."

A throaty moan escapes her, and she hangs onto my shoulders, her fingers digging into my skin as she grinds on my erection. Her chest heaves as she gasps for air between feverish kisses. All at once, she pulls away, backing off the couch to the floor in front of me. Her hands go for the button on my shorts, then the zipper, and in a flash, she tugs them until I lift my ass and she's able to pull them down.

Her heated gaze locks on my dick, and her tongue flicks out to lick the underside from base to tip. Locking her eyes on mine, she teases the head of my cock, kissing it with her lush pink lips before sucking it into her mouth. She's playing with it like she does one of her goddamn lollipops, and it's going to drive me right over the edge.

Taking my cock in her hand, she jerks me practically as good as I would myself, only it's better—so much fucking better—because her sweet mouth is on me, all pink and wet. Her head bobs in time with her hand, and I'm seeing fucking stars, my head dizzy. My body begins to tremble all over, and I swear all the blood in my body is centered right there at my groin where I'm aching with the need to come.

But this isn't exactly what I'd planned. I want to

capture her with charcoal, post orgasm in a state of goddamn euphoria. "Fuuuck," I hiss, regretting that I'm hitting pause. "Lennon, baby. I want this to be good for you, too."

I grasp her biceps and get her to meet my gaze. The sight of her with my hard-on at full mast right in front of her face does things to me, and I swallow roughly, almost selfish enough to say fuck it and let her keep going. But no. I want her in a state of rapture. She blinks at me, in some sort of daze, and to my surprise, a slight whimper falls from her lips as her focus moves to my cock, but she nods.

I reach down and cup her sex through the scrap of lace between her legs. "You wet for me?" I watch the way her eyes go a little unfocused as I touch her. A flush works its way over her skin. It starts at her chest and sweeps all the way up to her cheeks. I grab her by the waist, swinging myself in one direction to lie back on the couch, and I lift her, bringing her down to straddle my head facing the other direction.

"What are you doing?" she gasps out as one hand finds purchase on the back of the couch, the other gripping my thigh.

"It's not a question of what I'm doing, but more of what you're about to do." I smirk at her as she looks back at me over her shoulder with wide eyes. "The answer is you're going to sit on my fucking face. Let me have that pretty little cunt." I hook my hands over her thighs and pull her to me, squeezing her toned flesh and groaning aloud at the scent of her. My face is fucking buried in her pussy and ass, and my heart gives a sick thud. *Yesss.* I fuckin' love the way she smells all the time, but even more so the scent of her arousal. I kiss her through the lacy panties she's still wearing, using my tongue to dampen the fabric, inhaling deeply as I take another hit of the drug that is Lennon. "Fuck. So fucking sex—"

I don't finish the sentence because Lennon isn't playing this tentatively, and why I thought maybe this position would fluster her, I don't have a fucking clue. She grasps my dick in her hand and strokes me in a way that has me grunting out in pleasure. Taking my cock into her mouth, she swallows me down. That warm wet mouth of hers takes me as deep as she can, and her tongue does wild things, flicking all along my length as she gives me some really spectacular head.

The decadent combination of Lennon squirming over my face as I tease her and the suction of her mouth on my cock have me quickly spiraling until I can't fucking stand the last barrier between us anymore. I grip the skimpy lace underwear with both hands and pull until the ripping sounds of fabric tearing fills the room. She freezes for a moment, but I take that to my full advantage, dipping my tongue into her newly-bared-to-me pussy.

Her entire body jerks as she gets used to me sucking on her clit at the same time she's blowing me. Has she done this before or not? I can't fucking tell, but fuck me, it's so good. Her scent is everywhere, filling my head and making me dizzy. The more I lap at her, the more soaked she becomes.

"Mase, I'm close." She gasps, then slides her hand around to cup my balls, massaging them for a few seconds before giving them an experimental tug. At the same time, she rubs herself over my face, hips rocking in a very precise rhythm.

My fingers dig into her ass cheeks, but I'm not trying to stop her or control her—I'm hanging on for the ride of my life. We pant and moan, writhing together. Hips piston and thrust as legs quake under the force of impending orgasms. "Drench my face, baby. Come for me while your pretty mouth takes my cock like a good girl."

A strangled noise rips from her lips at my demand, and it's not long before her pussy begins to pulse on my tongue. "Oh god, Mase. I'm coming. I'm coming." She pants as her legs quake around my head, her words on repeat. I have no idea how she continues to suck me so fucking good while she's obviously leapt off a cliff and is in a free fall of lust.

"Fuck, Kin. You're so fucking sexy when you come." I suck in a breath, my vision all but blurring. I should have known better. I'm getting the result I wanted from her so that I can draw her in a post-orgasmic haze ... but now I'm going off the deep end myself. This exercise might prove to be more interesting than I had originally planned.

As the waves of her pleasure finally ebb, she lets out a low moan with my dick in her mouth, and that's all it takes to set me off. My balls draw up, and my release shoots in spurts onto her tongue. It's intense, her soaked pussy on my face and her wet mouth taking everything I have to give. I swear, my brains exit my body with the force of that orgasm, and I lie there, stupefied for several long seconds before I can even move again, much less think.

Lennon comes off my dick with a wet pop, then proceeds to lick it and give it a little kiss. I think she's trying to kill me. She carefully turns around and lies on top of me, seeking out my lips with hers. She strokes her tongue into my mouth, and our kiss quickly becomes so fucking dirty and sloppy it makes my dick hard again. Tasting myself on her makes me want to fuck her and keep her and ... everything I've resigned myself to wanting even when I know I shouldn't. I don't fully trust myself with her, yet I can't help but want her. Lennon and I—when we're good, we're so fucking good. And when it's bad, it's scary.

I shove that out of my head. Right now, at this moment, I'm in control, and I want to take advantage of that. "I'm gonna draw you now. Just like this."

The surprise on her face is quickly replaced by acceptance, and she nods. I swear her cheeks take on an even deeper pink hue. "Okay."

I ease myself out from under her, leaving her on her stomach on the couch. After a few minor adjustments to her position, including removing her tattered panties, I move over to the easel, pick up a piece of charcoal, and get to work. I don't usually draw from life because I prefer what's in my head. And my art is how I get some of that craziness *out*. But in this case, I want to capture Lennon as she is—what I did to her just now and how I made her feel. The bliss of her expression makes everything we've been through up to this point worth it. I wonder if she feels the same. Like maybe we're turning a corner together here, today in this dim attic where I exorcise my demons.

My hand moves quickly over the paper, first capturing a rough outline, then going in to add more details. I stroke the charcoal over the paper, smudging certain spots with my pinkie, defining other areas with sharper lines. I even use a soft eraser to draw the blonde highlights into her hair.

Her body. *Jesus.* I take my time and get every delicious part of her right, from the slope of her breast to the curve of her hip. A low growl rumbles in my chest as I notice the streaks and smudges of black all over her skin, everywhere I'd put my hands. They're especially prominent on her ass and thighs from my hands gripping her and holding her pussy to my face. I smirk. I'll include them in the sketch. She's quite literally my dirty girl— because I made her that way.

It doesn't take me long to have a preliminary sketch, and I know I'll be able to do better work when she's not mostly naked and still in a semi-aroused state three feet from me.

The entire time I work, she watches me quietly, a soft look of appreciation on her face. With each glance at her, I feel something stir inside. I was such a fucking fool to think that I could ever push her away. I need this girl. Deep in my soul, I know I do.

Once I'm satisfied with what I've drawn, I put the charcoal on the tray and turn to her, dusting my hands off. I look from what I've drawn to Lennon, rubbing my filthy hand over my heart. There's something I want to say to her, but I don't know how to get the words out. My chest is tight with emotion I wasn't expecting.

"Are you happy with it?"

I drag in a deep breath, tearing my eyes from hers. On paper, she's radiant. Glowing. So effortlessly sexy. But nothing could ever compare to the real thing. I shake my head before I bring my gaze back to her. Quietly, I murmur, "I could try and try and never come close to you."

She frowns, pushing herself to a sitting position. "What do you mean?"

I can see I've made her nervous and huff out a small laugh, then wet my lips. "It's you, Kin. You're the masterpiece. I could draw you all my life, and it'd never be as beautiful as the real thing."

TWENTY-FIVE

DUKE

OUT ON THE PATIO, I sit under one of the wide umbrellas and kick my bare feet up, resting them on the table. From behind my sunglasses, I survey the idiocy going on around me. Arik and Quincy have stopped their game of cornhole and are instead pegging each other with the bean bags. Fuckin' idiots. At least they are smart enough not to have pushed my buttons lately. To my surprise, Warren somehow convinced Maria to show up. She doesn't come around often, but when she does, she always blesses us with her resting bitch face. I would have thought hanging out in the fancy in-ground spa at one of the most exclusive brotherhoods at Kingston U would loosen whatever stick is up her ass, but apparently not. I don't claim to understand their relationship, but from the animated conversation over there, she might not stay very long. Those two break up and get back together more than any other couple I know.

My attention is dragged across the pool to where the sophomores plus Tucker have a game of Spades going at another of the patio tables. I'm somewhat following the game—or at least the reactions to the game play—and I swear, that Kai kid is dumber than a box of rocks. Brendan would do well to pick a different partner next time. Tucker and Pierre have absolutely killed them game after game. I'm surprised there's not more shouting. Maybe they're not drunk enough. It is only Thursday night, after all.

I pour two fingers of whiskey from the bottle I'd brought out with me, then lift the glass to my lips, letting the expensive liquor slide down my throat. I might be drinking because I've had my father breathing down my neck ever since he was here Monday. But it's cool. My life has been pure mayhem lately, but go ahead, pile on, *Dad*. Frankly, this fucking auction is worrying me. He's being very insistent that things are done to their exact specifications. It's no different than events we've held in the past, but I simply hadn't realized how much the OG members had their hands in every aspect of the planning. They're managing everything from the chosen sorority girls to the booze and to the ordering of the masks we're to wear. It fuckin' sounds like it could easily spin right out of our control, kinda like last year when that one dude from Theta house stripped and jumped into the mud pit with the chicks who were wrestling. It'd taken us for fucking ever to get him out because, well, mud. It'd been a slippery, dirty mess. Obviously, the OGs aren't willing to risk a repeat of that this year, hence why the entire event is ... cleaner. And also why we're being completely controlled.

My eyes follow Bear as he cuts through the pool's water like a goddamn machine. He's been quiet this week, mostly kept to himself. Ever since we witnessed him popping the pills on Monday, he's been surly. I'm surprised any of the younger brothers are coming anywhere near him, though they are giving him a wide berth.

I know for a fact he's swimming to allow his shoulder a break. I can't imagine what practice has been like for him the last couple of days, and my concern is that he's in real, genuine pain. I've seen him take hits on the field that would rattle most people's bones and loosen their teeth, but he gets up and continues on like it's nothing. So for this shoulder "tweak" to be bothering him so much that it's altering his mood and how he interacts with others in the house? I think it's gotta be pretty fuckin' bad. A legitimate injury.

In fact, it reminds me of what he was like when he

had a shoulder injury when we were in high school. I wanna ask if he's seen someone about it, if the trainer on staff for the football team is aware because, *fuck*. He shouldn't be playing injured. I don't know if it's worth bringing up. Tough call to make.

I blow out a breath. And last, but sure as hell not least, Lennon and I have been doing this awkward dance around each other. I've tried to get myself to stop fucking looking at her, stop thinking about her. It's hard, though, because I could swear the little minx hangs around wherever I am as a reminder of what I'm missing out on. Kind of like saying, *Fine, you think we made a mistake? I'll show you …*

I'm convinced my hot-as-fuck stepsister is trying to kill me.

Come to think of it, I don't know where she is right now. I swivel my head to glance up toward her room. The balcony door is open, so maybe she's up there doing an assignment for one of her classes. Probably has a lollipop stuck in her mouth. My dick immediately twitches at the thought. I wonder if she realizes where the cinnamon ones are coming from that keep appearing on her nightstand. Has she figured out it's my doing?

I don't know why I'm even making the gesture, to be honest. A peace offering? An apology? A plea? *Please, argue with me and tell me I'm fucking wrong.*

But I've watched her interactions with Bear—she's the only one who hasn't gotten her head bitten off this week—and I think she deserves someone like *him*. She doesn't necessarily need to be taken care of, but she needs someone who cares *about her*. There's a difference.

I huff out a laugh. Someone has to, with the dangerous way she and Mason seem to collide on a semi-regular basis. But those two have a connection as well—they share something she and I couldn't possibly. So again, I like that for her, despite how crazy it's gotten around here at times.

All she and I seem to have is the ability to argue at the drop of a hat and an indescribable tension that is constantly set to detonate at the slightest trigger. She couldn't—shouldn't—want me. There's something about her, though, and the more I interact with her, the harder time I'm having. She's creating a monster. The way I feel about her— I fucking told her we shouldn't have done what we did. Shouldn't have touched each other. Shouldn't have crossed that fucking line. But when I hear myself repeating what I said to her over and over in my head, I don't know if I believe *myself* anymore. I'm close to my breaking point.

Heaving out a sigh, I shake my head and take another swallow of whiskey. Maybe if I drink enough, I'll figure it out. I'm still trying to shake off the swarm of thoughts in my head when a moment later, my phone alerts me to someone at our front door. I frown hard, wondering who the hell it could be. I consider sending one of the grunts to check but they still don't have the security code. I bite the bullet and get up, muttering a curse under my breath.

I must not have been as quiet as I thought because Bear pauses midway across the pool and looks at me questioningly. I shrug, my jaw tense. "Someone's on the front steps. Be right back." He nods and goes back to work, cutting through the water's surface with smooth, efficient strokes.

I stride purposefully through the house, irritated at the interruption. As I approach the door, my steps slow, and I don't know why, but I get an awful feeling of fore-boding. Unwilling to open the door without knowing who is on the other side, I cautiously look out the window next to the door. My eyes narrow at first, but then I blink, my eyes immediately widening. *Oh fuck. No.* My gut clenches with the realization of who stands on the other side.

Hunter Mikaelson. The prick wears a pair of dress pants, a button-down shirt with the collar open, and a shit-eating grin—as if he knows the chaos he's about to bring down on this house if his brother finds out he's at our door. With my head spinning, I take a few deep breaths. *Mason, for once, I don't care. Stay up in that attic as long as you want, buddy.*

I disarm the alarm and pull the door open, and the noise that comes out of my throat is a raspy growl. "What do you want?"

"Little Valentine, is that any way to greet esteemed alumni? Surely not."

My blood boils at his attempt to make me feel inferior. "It's *alumnus*, you dick. There's only one of you. Thank *fuck.*" My teeth bite into my lip to keep me from saying worse.

He chuckles with an uncaring shrug. "You *would* worry about trivial things like Latin grammar. You'll learn soon enough that there's far more important shit to concern yourself with."

I roll my eyes. *What the fuck is this this jerkwad up to? And how fast can I get rid of him?*

"We have something to discuss." There's a certain glint in his eye that tells me trouble has officially arrived on our doorstep ... and not the kind of trouble that Lennon supposedly was. Far, far worse.

I've only opened the door far enough to talk to him, having put my body in the open gap between the door and the frame. I refuse to let this asshole inside when Mason could come down at any moment. My jaw clenches, the need to shield my friend from his brother surging through me. Mason has never fully admitted it, but this abhorrent excuse for a human and his father have contributed to so many of Mason's issues. "So talk, Hunter." I treat him to a patented Valentine look of boredom that suggests without speaking that he should say whatever the fuck he needs to so I can carry on with my life.

He slides an amused look at me before his gaze wanders over my shoulder, and for one heart-stopping moment, I think Mason has come downstairs at the most inopportune time ever. But when I glance behind me, there's no one there.

"My brother home?" His brows raise on his forehead. It's uncanny how much the two brothers are alike, yet still so fucking different. They have the same sharp cheekbones, the same dark eyes. His hair is a little lighter than Mase's ... and he's bigger, bulkier, but his muscles haven't ever been as well-defined as his brother's. He's always relied on his size to intimidate. "Duke? Cat got your tongue?"

My eyes zero in on his thin lips, and I work my jaw to the side. "He's doing some art thing." I'm sure as fuck not telling him that the "thing" he's doing is upstairs in the attic. Hunter doesn't get to be privy to any of that. In fact, he'd have to claw it out of my head before he got any information about Mase at all. I'll be damned if I'll let fucking Hunter mess with him. Sure, Mase is a grown man now, but there's nothing quite like being confronted with someone you grew up being antagonized by to make you feel small again. Vulnerable. I stare at the asshole who is at least partially to blame for some of my friend's ongoing mental health issues and can't find a reason to say another damn thing. "I'm going to ask you one more fucking time. What do you want, Hunter?"

His mouth hikes into a half-smile as he pulls an envelope from behind his back. He holds it out to me. "Your dad and Derek sent me to deliver this personally."

My eyes dart from his sneering expression to the white envelope.

"It's the list of lovely ladies for your auction Saturday night. The OG Bastards thought you should have a heads-up. There were two last-minute additions after their recent meeting."

"You mean their poker game?" I've always had an inkling that their poker nights are more than a fun evening with the guys. Otherwise, they wouldn't be so fucking exclusive about it. Or so secretive. My forehead pinches as I frown.

His head bobs, and I could swear he's trying to hold himself back. "Yeah. *That.* The poker game. See you Saturday. Tell my brother I can't fucking wait to hang out with him so we can talk." He gives me a wink, his eyes twinkling mischievously. "I feel like it's been forever."

That'd be because he avoids you like the goddamn plague. My chest tightens down on my lungs, and I hold my breath as the motherfucker practically skips down the stairs.

As he gets to the bottom of the steps, he spins around on his heel. "I'm very interested to hear what you think of the ladies that will be going up on the auction block. All are guaranteed to be there. Hopefully, you'll help us out with Lennon. She seems like one hell of a wildcat."

My entire body goes rigid. "What the fuck," I grind out to no one in particular because he's already in his fucking asshole Tesla getting on with his asshole life.

Fury whips through me as I open the envelope with shaking hands.

I scan the paper, my eyes immediately drawn to the bottom, where there are actually two names that put me into a confused tailspin.

Lennon Bell - Bainbridge Hall
Elliot Ashford - Hawthorne Hall

TWENTY-SIX

LENNON

My heart does this weird fluttery thing in my chest. Mase is a rather poetic soul, so I don't know why his words up in the attic have sent me spinning.

That's a lie. Deep down, I *do* know why. It's because I'm not used to hearing anyone talk about me the way he did. I've always thought we shared something unique, that the dark moments that shaped us made us understand each other. But to hear him verbalize the way he sees me? It'd damn near been my undoing. And then to have him say the gorgeous, beautiful work he'd created could never compare to the real thing? *Hard swoon*. For me, it was one of those defining moments in our relationship, and I'll keep those words locked away inside me forever, holding onto them should I ever lose my way.

All that tenderness from Mason had me riding a

wave of happiness, especially because he himself seems to be in a much more stable frame of mind than he had been. I let out a sigh of relief as my eyes lock on him where he's hanging out on the balcony. I was hoping maybe he'd go downstairs and join in on some of the antics by the pool, but he seems content to observe from up here for now.

And me, I've gotta finish this psych assignment that he'd interrupted earlier. It's due tomorrow, and it shouldn't be taking me so long, but I've been distracted. I doubt my professor would accept the excuse that I experienced a toe-curling orgasm that'd been so good I couldn't stop thinking about it and therefore had not completed my homework. Not happening. Gotta focus. But god, it'd been good. *So good.*

The slam of the heavy front door has my body jerking in place. I spring from the sprawled-out position on my stomach in front of my textbook to my knees in the time it takes Duke to suck in a breath and shout from the foyer.

"Bear! Mason!" The sharp bite of his words leaves no room for argument.

My brow darts together, and I scramble from the bed. Mason's eyes connect with mine at the same time I hear the patio door open. I hurry to join him on the balcony.

"Hey! Up here. Do I need to come down?" Mason shouts as we watch Duke storm back over toward the pool where Bear has pushed himself out of the water and is standing there like the football god that he is. Water drips down his six-foot-six frame as he gestures to the outdoor shower and begins to move in that direction.

Duke turns and squints as he looks up toward the balcony, and nods, beckoning with one hand. "Get the fuck down here, we've got a problem." He's holding some sort of paper, and I can only imagine that whatever is on it can't be good from the irate expression on his face.

I've seen Duke pissed before, but this is so far beyond that it scares me.

Mase rubs his hand over his jaw and shakes his head, as he ushers me into the bedroom with a hand at my back. "Whatever it is isn't good. Just so you're aware. I don't wanna say he's panicking, but ..."

"I know. You're right."

We make for the hallway, faintly able to hear Duke's agitated voice from here. I don't question Mason's assumption that I should be coming with him. I'm unsure whether Duke wants me down there or not if it's strictly brotherhood business. It won't hurt my feelings to be sent back inside.

But I am curious what the hell has him so worked

up. I peek at Mason out of the corner of my eye as we thunder down the stairs, worried that whatever is going on will adversely affect his state of mind. So far he seems to be managing himself just fine. The question is how long it will last, because who knows what fresh hell is waiting for us. We hurry toward the back of the house where the sound of raised voices is coming through the open patio doors.

From this distance, I can make out Duke shoving the paper into Bear's hands before barking, "This isn't happening." His hands dive into his hair, his body rigid as he stalks around the patio, pacing.

"You've gotta calm down so we can talk about this logically," comes Bear's rough voice in return. In the time it took us to get down here, Bear has wrapped himself in a towel and now sits on one of the patio chairs, resting his forearms on his thighs.

I look nervously up at Mason, who shakes his head, brows drawing together as we approach the others. His expression is that of a thundercloud. I wince. *Shit, whatever this is, we don't need it right now.*

"Elliot Ashford. Hawthorne Hall," Bear mutters, his brow furrowing.

From beside me, Mason growls, "Who the *fuck* is Elliot?"

Elliot Ashford. Hawthorne Hall. It clicks for me a

split second later. "The girl. The one with Kingston and those other guys at the party."

Duke grits his teeth. "She's their initiate."

Those words cause a commotion that doesn't calm for a good thirty seconds, and I have to say, it comes as a surprise to me. These guys may have been told they could treat me like a grunt, but I've never once thought it meant I was actually one of them. But this chick ... is initiating into a brotherhood? That must be wild. Good for her. But ... I kinda see why things are weird. She's not a sorority girl.

Bear looks over the paper again, then eyes Duke. "You're coming at this out of a place of anger, and that's *not* what we fuckin' need right now." His words are forceful, unnecessarily harsh, in my opinion. He's been snappish and downright *mean* to everyone lately. It's concerning. I watch him carefully as he rubs one hand over his face, shaking his head. He's avoiding my eyes, and I don't like it.

Unfortunately, I don't have time to dwell on it because the words that've just come out of Pierre's mouth have my attention flying to him. I run it through my head again to be certain I understood properly. *The sorority houses all put forward girls. Why not us if we have one living here?* And now the pencil-dick fuck is chuckling as he aims his sneer my way.

Wait, what? "You don't mean ...?" I feel like an elephant has taken up residence on my chest. This is about me. My eyes flick back and forth between Duke and Bear, and when they don't immediately answer me, I look to the rest of the brotherhood. It's a mistake.

Brendan stifles a laugh. "Apparently, the powers that be demand we auction you and Elliot off on Saturday with all the other sorority girls."

Seeing red, I don't know whether it's Kai or Pierre who snorts and says, "Have fun with that, grunt. Looks like we're putting your best assets to work for the good of the brotherhood."

I don't give a fuck which one it was, so I aim my glare at both of them as my jaw works to the side. I already said I wouldn't be participating. I don't want any part of it because I have an idea how quickly an event like this will devolve into something ugly and out of my control. I fucking hate the panicky feeling overtaking me.

Meanwhile, Duke's reaction is similar, like he's about to blow his top. "Why do they do this shit? They're on a motherfucking power trip. Why the fuck are they adding girls to this goddamn auction? I don't give a flying fuck if they're the founding fathers of the motherfucking country, never mind this brotherhood!" he roars, then immediately bends at the waist, his hands resting on his thighs for support as he shakes his head. The fact that the OG Bastards are involved makes me even more nervous than I already was. My stomach lurches violently.

With my breaths stuttering faster and faster, Mason wraps an arm around my lower back, pulling me to his side. I lean against him for support. If he feels the tremors running through my body, he doesn't mention it. "Can I see the fucking paper?" Mason asks sharply.

My eyes connect with Bear's. "Is that what it says? That I'm being auctioned off? Because *nope*. No fucking way."

Bear growls, his eyes murderous as he slaps the paper into Mason's palm. Before I can blink, his big body is close to mine, and he grips my chin. Forcing me to look at him, the words that leave his lips are absolutely lethal in tone. "You're not doing anything you don't want to do."

Fuck. The entire house is watching. I look up into his hazel eyes, blinking rapidly, but he doesn't release me until I nod.

"Why does it feel like maybe you guys don't want to let her do it because you want to keep her all to yourselves?" Kai's gaze shifts smoothly from Mason to Bear, who have both had their hands on me, then over to Duke, who is staring daggers at him for asking the question in the first place. Kai lifts his hands. "Just saying."

Duke wets his bottom lip as he stalks over to him, plants his hands on his chest, and shoves hard. "That's enough, you fuckwit. Got it?"

And when the idiot doesn't respond, Bear takes a menacing step in his direction, which results in Kai tripping over his own feet and going down hard on his ass. "What the fuck," he hisses. It's not really a question, and no one bothers—or dares—to say a word.

While he's struggling to stand, Warren groans, throwing his hand out. "It makes no sense. She's just staying here. Why would they add her name to the list?"

The dark-eyed brunette sitting next to Warren gives him the side eye. "Actually, if she's living here, I think it's valid." All eyes dart to her. Warren's girl? There's a little gleam in her eye, and she gives a mild shrug before inspecting her nails, like what we're discussing is completely trivial and beneath her.

I feel the sharp retort rising in me, and sure enough, it flies from my lips before anyone else can say a word. "Sorry, who are you, and why the fuck do you think your opinion means a damn thing?"

"I'm Maria. Warren's girlfriend. And why does yours mean anything either? You're just the house bitch," she counters, staring me down. *Ballsy.* My eyes flick to the side in time to catch Warren as he covers his mouth with his hand with a wince before shooting me an apologetic look.

I had a feeling I wouldn't like Maria if I ever met her. I cross my arms over my chest. "My opinion counts because, as you so boldly pointed out, I live here, unlike you. Not to mention my name is on the motherfucking paper!"

Duke juts his chin at Warren. "Your girl's gotta go."

Maria's mouth drops open as she stares at him, speechless.

"You heard me," Duke grits out. "Get the fuck out. This is brotherhood business."

Her eyes widen, and she exchanges a few whispered words with Warren before she smacks his arm. Hopping up, she storms into the house, presumably to take her leave.

Good riddance. Too bad the rest of our problems aren't so easy to get rid of. As I continue to seethe, from the corner of my eye, I witness Arik and Quincy trying to cover their laughter, and I whirl on them with a pointed finger. "Shut. The fuck. Up."

Bear unclenches his jaw long enough to groan out, "That's e-fucking-nough. All of you." His surly attitude comes in handy in this instance because no one wants to cross him when he's like this.

Duke draws in a breath, eyeing me with what looks way too much like regret for my comfort levels. A dull pounding presents itself between my brows. I can practically see the wheels turning in his head. "Let me be clear. We don't need your fucking opinions. We simply require that you obey and show your loyalty to this house." His face is blotchy with anger. "You'll all be given assignments Saturday morning as to what you need to do at the auction. You'll carry them out exactly as we fucking say. That's all you get to know about it for now. We'll handle the rest."

Brendan raises a hand. "So, no Lennon in the auction?"

Duke's eyes connect with mine briefly before crashing shut. He takes a deep breath before his eyes open again to take in everyone. "I don't know what we're gonna do. The list was handed down from the OG Bastards." His words hang in the air because everyone, including me, understands him. Their word is law. My gut roils. "That said, we aren't nearly done discussing it. We simply don't require input from any of you fucknuts."

"You've gotta admit, though, it'd be amazing." Tucker has the nerve to smirk directly at me. "I guess I might get to bid on you after all, sweet cheeks."

In a split second, Duke lunges at him, fury blazing in

his blue eyes, but Bear clamps a hand on his shoulder, pulling him back. He grunts soft and low near Duke's ear, "Not worth it."

I heard what he said to Duke, but ... I *can't*. Taking three quick steps forward, I cock my head to the side, sizing Tucker up. "Go ahead. You find me on the auction block, bid. I fucking dare you."

"Kintsukuroi, don't ..."

With my eyes locked on Tucker, I look him up and down before grinning. "Don't what, Mase? Tell him that when he wins me he'll have lost his money *and* his dick?" I stare coldly into his eyes, my lips twisting as I draw closer. "Because I'll bite it off, Tuck. *Promise.*"

He snorts with laughter, his slimy gaze wandering all over my body. "Baby, you'll be gagging so hard it'll be impossible to sink your teeth in."

Fucking Tucker. A portion of the brotherhood laughs along with him, but I don't pay much attention to them, nor do I listen to Duke, Bear, or Mason as they use placating words in hopes of stopping me. I hold up a hand to them and give a quick shake of my head. "Nope. I've got this." They know me well enough to recognize my stiff posture for what it is. Tucker's unwittingly entered the danger zone. I have tunnel vision. He doesn't get to make *me* the joke of the brotherhood.

Adrenaline rushes through me like lightning, every

ounce of Bear's training flows through me as my arm shoots out. My knuckles collide with the sharp cut of his jaw, snapping his head back with force. The form of my jab is exactly like Bear taught me—it's sheer perfection. A thing of beauty. Much to my delight the perverted dickwad cries out in pain as the second punch lands with more power behind it than the first. He's in such shock, he never saw the cross coming. He stumbles backward into thin air, and I throw him a smirk of my own as the pool greets him.

Gasps fill the air, followed by laughter as Tucker comes up sputtering and desperately trying to get his hair out of his face while he treads water. His face is red, his eyes sending wave after wave of angry intent in my direction.

"Whoa, stand down, little brawler." Bear steps toward me like I'm a wild animal in need of taming. "Fuck, I should have seen that coming."

At his gravelly words, my gaze shifts, meeting his eyes as my breath shudders from me. My jaw sets, daring him to tell me I shouldn't have done it.

I'm fuming mad and, as a result, hot tears prick at the backs of my eyes. *No. Not now.* I fight back that liquid emotion, knowing that if I allow all these dudes to see me cry, it'll only make things worse. "I'm *not* fucking doing it." I whirl around, running for the patio door with my heart jammed in my throat.

From behind me, I hear Mason's shout first. "Kin!"

"Stella, wait!"

I ignore them, only pausing for a moment at the door when I hear Bear's grumbled curse. "God*dammit*, Little Gazelle."

Alone in my room, I lock the door, breathing hard. My gut instinct is to run, and my head is too clogged up with everything clanging around inside to argue or coherently think the matter through. I dash into the closet and yank out my suitcase, unzipping it and flinging it onto the floor. I open my drawers and begin to scoop clothing out. It doesn't take long because I didn't have that much to start with.

My heart races. Rattled, I force myself to concentrate on the simple act of breathing as I haphazardly pack toiletries. The balcony door is still open, so I can hear bits and pieces of the conversation happening outside.

"Fuck, did you see her haul off and sock him?" *Quincy?*

"Impressive, if you ask me." *Warren.*

"Grunt, get me some ice for my damn face." *Tucker.*

Asshole. My hands shake. But then I think about him anywhere near me, and I know I was right to put him in his place. As if I haven't before. What's it going to take for it to sink into his thick skull?

A knock on the bedroom door has my head whipping up. *Nope.* I open one drawer after another, slamming each shut as I empty it before moving into the bathroom.

A moment later, three bodies fill the doorway, and I come to an abrupt stop. "Stella Bella, what the hell are you doing?"

With my toiletries hugged to my chest, I brush past all of them. My eyes flick to the open balcony door. I'm an idiot. *Doesn't do any good to lock the bedroom door if you're going to leave the balcony door wide open.* I'm not thinking clearly at all.

My breaths leave me in pants as I kneel on the ground, rearranging things, desperately trying to ignore that they're watching me. I'm furious. How dare the OG Bastards get it in their heads that they can force me to participate in that mayhem?

A moment later, hands grip my biceps and lift me to my feet. "Stop!" I turn around, meeting Duke's piercing blue eyes head-on. I shake my head. "I'm not fucking doing it."

"You might not have a choice." His jaw is rigid, his fists clenched.

"I told you when it first came up last week that I

didn't care what anyone else did, but *I* didn't want to be involved. I am *always* in control." I slam my hands to his chest, pushing him from me. "I won't do it, I just wo—"

There's a split second where I see a feral look in his eye, and in the next his hands still the movement of my head, his mouth crashes down on mine, his lips exploring with brutal intent, almost as if he's staking claim. With my heart thrumming in my chest like a manic drummer resides there, I let out a whimper. He swallows it before he thrusts his tongue inside to greet mine in a wicked dance.

Duke. So many things race through my mind at once that I have trouble keeping up. He's kissing the shit out of me despite insisting we'd made a mistake, and he's doing it in front of Mason and Bear. Holy fuck, I can feel their eyes on us, and it sends a jolt of desire down my spine that makes me throb. I shouldn't want this. I grip Duke's forearms as my eyes flutter open for a moment, but he catches my full lower lip between his and sucks it into his mouth.

There's a wildness about the way he tastes and touches that I'm not used to seeing in Duke. This side of him is in direct opposition to his usual controlled self. I'd question it, but I'm far too busy drowning in the kiss I let go on for far too long. As my head catches up with what my body has allowed, I bite down on his lip—hard—then shove him away from me.

I'm breathless from the way he makes me feel, and the stunned look on his face only serves to irritate me. Is it his fault that they want to auction me off? No. But his suggestion that I might have to go along with it makes me irrationally angry.

Duke's chest heaves, his inhale ragged as he touches his fingers to his bite-swollen lip. It gives me a twisted sort of pleasure to know that even if his intention was diversion, he got swept along with me and got what he deserved.

Furious, I seethe, "What? Did you figure you could distract me and everything would be okay?"

Mason stands off to the side, and my eyes flick to his as he emits a deep-throated chuckle. "It's the one fool-proof method he's found to throw you off balance." He hasn't come any closer, but he's eyeing the two of us with his hooded gaze as if he wouldn't mind a repeat of what happened the other day.

I try to ignore the unmistakable sensation of my panties dampening and focus on what he's just said. His assessment of how Duke deals with me isn't wrong. Nearly each of Duke's kisses has been a fucking sneak attack meant to shut me up. My cheeks heat. My step-brother knows how to play me like a fiddle, and it's the tiniest bit embarrassing ... I'm stubborn, though, and there's no way I'm allowing myself to be auctioned off like some prize heifer at a county fair.

As they circle me, I know each of them registers the defiance in my eyes. I shake my head and repeat as my gaze connects with each of them in turn, "I'm not fucking doing it. They can't make me."

Bear steps close to my side and gathers my hair in his big hand, securing it as he uses it to angle my head the way he wants. It's hard to know what's in his head lately, but the way he's looking at me, a feeling of security washes over me. Gruffly, he murmurs, "We'll figure this out." He presses his lips to my temple, letting them linger there a moment before sliding down the curve of my jaw, his scruff tickling my skin.

Something about the way Bear's touching me provides me with a sense of calm and security, but at the same damn time, it makes me hunger for more of him. I know he means it—we'll handle whatever ends up coming our way. He's my rock. My protector. *My* Gideon. And everything about him makes my heart race.

He nips at a particularly sensitive spot, and a gasp stutters from me. He guides my face to his and our lips brush. A rush of tingles moves through me as I open myself to his kiss, and his tongue strokes languidly into my mouth, slowly tasting and teasing until I think I might go out of my mind. My head grows hazy, and an unbidden moan slips from between my lips. The three of them are like a wall of heat and muscle and hunger, surrounding me. Claiming me.

I savor the way Bear's bold, sure lips feel on mine and encourage his groans as our tongues tangle. Still engulfed by his kiss, my body lights up further when the backs of Mason's fingers skim along the tiny sliver of exposed flesh between my tank and shorts. Duke's thumb flicks over the taut peak of my nipple as he cups my breast. It feels so good to have all three of them touching me at once, I'm having trouble believing I'm not asleep in my bed and dreaming. I press another kiss to Bear's lips, then ease back, my eyes wide and pinging from Duke to Mason and then over to Bear. A desperation fills me like nothing I've ever known before. I want them. All of them.

With my head still reeling at that revelation, Mason guides my face to his with a touch of his fingertips under my chin. "Do you trust us, Kintsukuroi?"

I draw in a ragged breath, touch his bare chest with my fingertips, knowing the damaged heart that resides inside this man and wanting it—wanting *him*—anyway. I nod and pull his body closer. "I need you to kiss me, too." I stare into his deep, dark eyes as need rips through me. If he doesn't put his mouth on mine in the next three seconds, I might die.

He doesn't disappoint me. Swooping in, he devours my lips in that way he has that makes my toes curl and has all coherent thoughts flying out of my head. When he kisses me, it's like a warning. He's chaos and fire wrapped up in a brooding, hot package.

Overwhelmed and not quite sure who to focus on next, my eyes land on Duke. As if they orchestrated it, Bear and Mason move as one on either side of me, pulling my tank over my head. Duke wastes no time grazing his fingers over my collarbone, then down, down, down, through the valley of my breasts before finally sweeping them over my stomach with a light touch that makes goose bumps raise on my skin. His jaw twitches. Is he okay with this? Because the last time we found ourselves entwined between the sheets, he took off. He catches my gaze, and I'm trapped in all that ocean blue, mesmerized by the way he's looking so deeply, so intently at me. "Never gonna let anyone hurt you, Lennon."

I wet my lips. "Promise?" I whisper the question, uncertainty clear in my eyes.

He catches my jaw with his hand, his voice husky. "I fuckin' promise."

Bear leans close, his big body solid against me. "No one touches you but us. No one." His dexterous hand skates down my back, then around to my stomach, dipping his fingertips under the waistband of my jean shorts. I lean back into him, taking in those words. Wrapping my head around how the four of us got here to this place in time ... it's too much to comprehend while their eyes and hands roam over me. These guys know me better after two weeks than people who have known me my entire life. And I do believe them. More importantly, I trust them. That knowledge seeps into my brain and squeezes at my heart.

I reach back and undo the clasp of my bra. "Make me yours."

TWENTY-SEVEN

BEAR

OURS. My heart ricochets around in my chest as Lennon's bra slips down her arms and hits the floor at our feet. What we're about to do—or at least what I envision us doing—doesn't surprise me, because from the time she walked through the door of Bainbridge Hall, Lennon Bell's taken what she wanted.

She made me fuckin' want *her*. She made *all* of us want her.

I pop the button on her shorts and unzip them, sliding my hand inside her panties and dipping my fingers into her arousal. Fuck, she's so wet the slickness covers my fingers with one slow drag along her slit. I pull them forward, finding her clit swollen and needy. She lets a heady moan escape her lips, and it's hard to say what's

363

causing her reaction—the pressure I'm applying right where she needs it or Mason's tongue flicking a path up her neck. Probably both.

Lennon trembles, her legs quaking at our attention. She rides my hand, rubbing her wet pussy on my fingers. "Oh god, yes," she breathes out as I dip one thick digit inside her. Her head falls back, and I can tell she's quickly becoming overwhelmed by everything she's physically feeling.

"You get off on me fucking you with my finger?" I murmur, my voice low and gravelly. "You like it when Mason leaves a trail of hickeys all over your skin?"

Her eyes drift shut as she nods, arching to give Mason more room to suck on the delicate skin at the top of her breast. She turns her head toward me, lips parting on a gasp as I pick up the pace, plunging in and out of her wet heat. My thumb flicks back and forth over her clit.

I'm rock-hard and want my dick in her so fucking bad. It hasn't escaped me that I've only got a towel wrapped around my waist and my cock is pitching a rather impressive tent beneath it. A jolt of desire lances through me. It wouldn't take much to whip it off, yank her shorts down, and slide my cock inside her pussy—right where I belong.

And the interesting thing about this situation is that

I don't think it's going to be a problem for me if Duke and Mason watch me fuck Lennon. I sure as hell couldn't have cared less if anyone had witnessed me bending her over the hot tub the other night. In fact, Mase *did* see it, according to Lennon. I hadn't given him a moment's thought because I was too wrapped up in how good Lennon's pussy felt as it spasmed around me.

With my lips in her hair, I steal a peek at Duke. His eyes are laced with an uncertain look that makes me slightly nervous. Is it indecision about her? Is he on board with this? Because I don't want this to turn into another one of those unfortunate occasions where he goes from infatuated idiot to asshole stepbrother— because that wrecks her every time, even if she doesn't want to admit it.

"Duke. Let's get these shorts off her," I grit out, my tone low but commanding.

He snaps out of whatever daze he's in and pushes the denim material off her ass and down her legs, dragging her underwear along with them. I don't miss the rough swallow working its way past his Adam's apple or the intent look in his eye as he brings his gaze back to hers.

There's incredible tension in the room; like we're standing on top of a powder keg, waiting for the spark that sets off the explosion. *Want.* It hangs thick and potent in the air between them. It's supposed to be such a simple thing. Want something? Reach out and take it. But for them, it hasn't been that easy, and something tells me the effects of whatever happens within these four walls will linger for a long time afterward. We stand on a precipice, and I have no fucking clue how this is all going to shake out in the end.

Lennon catches her lip between her teeth. Her eyes are trained on Duke. I can only assume she's waiting for him to say something since things have been horribly strained between the two of them all week long. Fuck, who am I kidding? It's been like that ever since she arrived here.

A moment later, Duke backs away from us and heads for the balcony door.

My stomach churns. *Shit.*

I immediately feel Lennon tense up. She must be disappointed. I rest a hand on her shoulder and give her a reassuring squeeze. Mason steadily watches Duke's retreat, a hint of a wince on his lips, his jaw clenched tight. He doesn't have to say a damn word for me to recognize the distress on his features.

The world stops moving as Duke gets to the balcony door and pauses. Time ticks by at a scarily slow pace. I wish I knew what he was thinking or how to help him.

My head is caught up in how to reassure Lennon and Mason that this isn't about them and how we'll figure out where we go from here when Duke makes the windows in the glass-paned door rattle as he shuts it with a resounding slam.

He takes a few deep breaths, then turns around, eyeing all three of us. His blue eyes burn with a need I've never seen before in them. "I'm not going any-fucking-where. In case you were worried." His brows lift, then he pulls his shirt off. "What are you waiting for? Get her on the bed."

Lennon releases a ragged sigh of relief. I blink, unsure I've heard him right, but Mason shakes his head, a small laugh bursting from his lips. His eyes connect with Duke's across the room, and he walks over to talk to him.

Pep talk maybe? Letting Mason deal with Duke, I bend and hoist Lennon over my good shoulder—thank fuck for the pills I found in my gym bag that allow me to function—and smack her right on the ass. Before I allow her to tumble from my hold, she grabs the towel I'd secured around my waist and yanks. Off it comes, leaving me buck naked, my dick at full attention and weeping for her.

I'm not a modest guy, but this whole thing with three dicks in a bed is nothing we've ever remotely come close to discussing. Sharing Lennon like Mason and I did that one time is a little different than what I assume is being proposed here. The focus was entirely on her, not on our hard-ons. I growl, trying to push it out of my mind, and drop her onto the bed. I would do anything for this girl, give her whatever she needs. And if that's all of us, then so be it. I climb onto the mattress and settle beside her. She's got this half-excited, half-anxious look on her face. "You okay?" I whisper.

"I don't know." She picks up my hand and places it over her heart, which is going a million miles a second. Blinking up at me, her brow furrows as if she's asking what I think of how fast it's going, then her gaze moves to Duke, and she bites her lip, worry sliding over her features.

"I'm going to call that normal for the circumstances." I pause, cupping her cheek, and make sure she's looking at me and really hearing me. "If at any point this becomes uncomfortable or it isn't what you want, you let me know, and that'll be it."

"I know you'll take care of me, Gideon. You always do." She presses a kiss to my mouth, then to my jaw before lying back on the bed. Propped up on my elbow, I stare down at her and run my thumb over her full lower lip. I'm so focused on the plush softness I miss the wicked intent in her eye until she's already taken my thumb into her mouth. My heart gives an oddly pronounced thump in my chest as she sucks, swirling her tongue around. She's watching me for clues, I can tell. Do I like what she's doing? *Umph. Yes.* More blood rushes south, creating an overwhelming heaviness in my balls. *Fuuuck.* My eyes heat as she takes it deeper, withdraws, then takes it back into her mouth again.

If I wasn't already fully hard, I would be now. My needy gaze is trained on what she's doing, and the impish look in her eyes makes me growl deep in my chest. "Baby girl, keep teasing me and I'll have to replace that thumb with my dick." I pick up the heavy appendage and smack it against her thigh. Her eyes widen, but it's not from fear at all. Her expression is steeped in desire and longing.

Before I can say anything else, Mason slips onto the bed on her other side, his mouth immediately going for her tit. I watch the way he nips and bites at her, remembering the mark he left on her, and wonder if he'll endeavor to leave another. She lets out a strangled moan of pleasure as he sucks her nipple deep.

My head spins, thinking about all the ways the three of us could claim her. I cup her cheek and begin to kiss her again at the same time I pinch the other taut bud between my finger and thumb. Needing to taste her, I plunge my tongue into her mouth. I think she must have eaten a lollipop earlier because her mouth tastes a bit like sweet cinnamon. She's nearly killing me, and we're only getting started.

I glance at Mason, who I now realize has also discarded his pants somewhere. His cock is nestled at her side, and with every lick and suck and bite he's also grinding himself against her body. He lifts his head, searching her eyes. "You going to let us claim you, Kin?" There's an ache to his voice. A yearning. Lennon threads her fingers through the strands of his dark hair and nods, then offers me a shaky smile. But only a moment later, an anxious energy slips over her expression as Duke joins us.

The bed dips as he climbs up and kneels. He stares down at her, lust clouding his eyes. He's nervous as fuck, the same way she is. I don't believe for a second it's all four of us together like this that's throwing both of them. It's Duke, himself, and how he pushes her away every time they get the slightest bit close. Something in his head hasn't let him go there mentally, or if he *does*— at least physically, like I suspect happened Monday afternoon—he punishes both of them for it, lashing out to ease his frustration ... or is it guilt? Reaching between his legs, he takes his erection in hand and slowly strokes himself as he watches us with Lennon.

It seems like he needs a minute to acclimate, so I kiss her neck and down the slope of her shoulder before brushing my stubble over her nipple. She gasps aloud. "Oh god. Do that again." So I do, firmly holding her breast in my hand and using my facial hair to drive her wild. Not to be outdone, Mason catches her taut peak between his teeth, scraping over the sensitive skin in a way that has her moaning.

I don't know what the tipping point is, but a moment later, Duke slides his hands up her silky legs to the knee. He stops. "Stella, show me your pretty cunt," he rasps.

Their eyes connect. And just when I don't think it'll ever happen, she slowly lets her legs fall open. "Show me how much you want it."

And with that, he drags her legs over his shoulders and dives in, burying his face in all that sensitive pink skin. Her spine arches at the sudden onslaught of his tongue lashing out against her—only this time, it's not cruel words. It's nothing but pleasure.

She writhes and cries out on a gasped breath, "Duke! F-fuck!"

From here, I can see his tongue as it dips into her pussy. He jams it in as far as he can get it, moving it in and out. She's trembling hard in no time flat. He soon replaces his tongue with his fingers, and shifts his mouth over her clit, alternately lapping at it and sucking. *Yep.* Our friend has something to prove. I'm all for letting him do anything that makes Lennon happy, and right now, oh fuck, she's ecstatic. Actually, that's a piss-poor choice of words. She's one hundred percent blissed-out. Living practically in another realm.

The orgasm starts with a stutter of her breath. Her mouth slackens as her eyes lose focus. "D-Duke ..." But she can't get out another word before she gives in, her body succumbing to the rapture she's feeling.

He rears up, letting her legs fall from his shoulders, and pushes his cock inside her body inch by inch. Mason and I stop, entranced. We watch his dick disappear as her pussy swallows it. Duke groans, eyes pinned on where they're joined. "Fuck, Lennon. Look at you taking my cock like a good girl." He grips her inner upper thighs and pushes her legs as far apart as he can get them. Withdrawing until just the head of his cock is still inside her, he grimaces. She lets out a whimper that is very clear to all of us.

Mason looks up at the sound and murmurs, "She likes it deep." Duke meets his gaze and with a quick nod and a twitch of his lips, plunges back in.

She swallows thickly as she looks down her body to where he's fucking her at the most leisurely pace ever. Nice and deep, slow drags in and out that have her eyes lighting with a fiery glow. "Y-yes. Fill me with that big dick. I know you've wanted to." She wets her lips as she stares at him. "You know it, too."

His eyes burn bright. "Fuck yes I've wanted it." His eyes flick to Mason's and then mine. "Hold her legs for me?"

With a quick glance and a nod at Mason, we get on our knees on either side of her, each of us holding a thigh, as requested. There's no denying that what we're finally seeing happen between Duke and Lennon is way past due … but it's also totally hot. I can only speak for myself, but my engine is revving. I slowly stroke my length, taking in everything before me, and notice Mason is jerking his dick, too.

Lennon bats my hand away from my cock and takes over, her cheeks a rosy pink. I watch, my mouth going dry as her thumb sweeps over the tip where she collects the bead of pre-cum before she begins to stroke me.

My gaze flicks up to where she's doing mostly the same with Mason. His stuttered "F-fuuuck" is followed quickly by my deep grunt of satisfaction. She's a little clumsy at it at first, but who can blame her when she's never jerked two dicks at the same time while getting railed by a third. To her credit, it doesn't take her long to get the hang of it, and within minutes, she has both Mason and me ready to die at her hands.

The groans and moans coming from all of us are

fucking out of control. It's a good thing Duke had the brains to shut the damn balcony door or the entire brotherhood would hear the soundtrack of our lovefest.

My eyes trail back and forth over Lennon, landing on each of my friends, and I try not to think too carefully about what we're doing. But I gotta say, it's a visual feast for the goddamn eyes. Lennon's breasts bounce with each of Duke's measured thrusts. I really fucking hope there's not something wrong with me for being hyper turned-on while watching my friend's cock bring my girl pleasure. My eyes shift to Lennon. Oh, hell yes, she's enjoying this. Her lips are parted, soft little hums and moans escaping.

A moment later, to my surprise, Duke pulls out, drags his fingers through her arousal, and sucks them into his mouth. He glances at me as he licks them clean. "Your turn."

My eyes dart to Lennon's, and she lets go of my dick, her lip caught between her teeth. "Please fuck me."

I scrub my hand through my hair. With half my brain on the girl in front of me, I slide my hands over her soft skin and move between her legs while the other half watches Duke edging closer to Mason.

"Can I taste her?" Mason's brows lift as he grasps the back of Duke's neck, staring into his eyes.

There's a flicker of something that passes between

them, and in answer, Duke's mouth slams down on Mason's. Their tongues duel and stroke, and my head might explode. I knew. I *knew* they'd been together, but I hadn't seen any of this fiery heat with my own two eyes.

Lennon juts her chin toward them as I position myself at her entrance and slide the head of my cock up and down through her arousal. "Hot, aren't they?"

I blink rapidly. "I'm still processing," I say gruffly, holding onto her leg while I grip my fully engorged dick with the other. I smack it against her clit, loving the way she gasps in surprised pleasure.

Lennon sneaks a look at Duke and Mason and, seeing them well-occupied, mouths, "Fuck me, Daddy."

"Fucking hell." Lust burns through me, and I line myself up, thrust deep, and sink in to the hilt.

Her eyes roll back in her head, and her hands clench the sheets at her sides. "Oh, shit, Gid. Fuck. I forgot how big you are." The walls of her pussy clamp down on me as I drive in and withdraw. Her breath stutters.

Mason and Duke break their kiss, both panting raggedly, momentarily distracted by her comment. Heat hits my cheeks as all eyes are now on my massive dick.

"And here I thought the monster cock was probably just a rumor." Mason smirks at me.

"Shut the fuck up. We've changed in locker rooms together half our lives," I growl.

His lips curve, a naughty twinkle in his eye. "Kidding, kidding."

Thrusting inside Lennon, I watch as her body stretches to accept my thick cock, and, as I had surmised, found I don't mind Mason and Duke watching. Fuck, she feels so good, I will gladly wait "my turn" any day of the week if it ends with my dick burrowing inside her.

"Duke." Lennon bites her lip and moans out, "I want to suck you off." His cock is coated with her juices, the same way mine currently is. So slick. My brain hurtles into space as my balls throb with need.

I have no idea how Duke had intended for this to go, but he looks for a moment like he might pass out. He gets over it quickly, though, moving close to where her head is turned. Her eyes flick up to meet his as she grasps the base of his dick, firmly stroking. The look that passes between them is heady, but when she turns and our eyes connect, there's no less electricity there. "Make me come, Bear. While he fucks my mouth."

Jesus, the things that fall from those sweet lips. I grunt, the sounds we're making with every snap of my hips and every wet slap of our bodies together threatens to send me over the edge, make me come. Keeping up a slow but steady pace, I gesture with my chin. "She could use some help if that's going to work, Mase." At my suggestion, her pussy muscles flutter around my dick. My jaw clenches hard, lust raging through my body as I try not to think about what we're doing.

Mason nods in agreement and seats himself behind Lennon, propping her up. He places his hand over hers on Duke's cock, then whispers in her ear. Lennon gulps, her eyes going as wide as saucers. She removes her hand from Duke and lets Mason's hand take the place of hers. Duke groans out, "Oh, fuuuck."

Pushing into her a few more times, my head buzzes with the realization that Mason intends to jerk Duke while Lennon takes him in her mouth. It's a hot minute before I can even wrap my head around what this will be like for Duke, a masculine hand that isn't his own on his cock, paired with Lennon's warm, wet mouth.

I shudder. It's hot. I don't think it'll ever be me, but fucked if I'm not going to enjoy watching how it plays out. My head twists cautiously around the idea that I'll also be participating. I'm the one responsible for making sure she gets off. With that in mind, I pull out and lower my face between her legs, delivering a few long, lapping licks to her cunt, swirling my tongue over every inch of her.

She cries out, "Oh *fuck* yes. Keep doing that."

I groan as Lennon's hips begin to buck against my face, and she lets out a strangled noise as I spear my tongue inside her, licking at her inner walls. She tastes tart but a little sweet—deliciously feminine—and completely aroused by what we're doing.

It's a fact. I feel the words beating within my heart, pounding through my head—I will do anything for her. Anything at all that she asks of me.

And tonight, we've just gotten started.

TWENTY-EIGHT

DUKE

HOLY FUCK. My chest jerks. This thing we're doing, my head won't fuckin' wrap around it. The physical stuff, the emotions ... just *fuck*. I give myself a mental shake and drag in a breath. My skull feels like it's in a vice that keeps tightening, turning everything happening in front of me—fuck, happening *to* me—into some sort of hazy wild dream.

My heart thumps erratically as my gaze skates over Lennon's naked body—the one girl I was never meant to have, much less want. But it's time to admit it—at least to myself—I *do* want her. And the scary part is it's not simply that I want to sink my dick in her again. I've found myself beginning to look for ways to be close to her, to make her see me as more than the asshole step-brother she was forced to move in with. The time I spend thinking about her is damn near all-consuming. My head screams at me, telling me I'm being a fucking idiot, that it'll cause so many problems. But—and here's the kicker—if I'm not supposed to be with her, I'm unsure how we've landed where we have. *Again.* I keep coming back for more. I tried to distance myself, but something inside me is so drawn to her, I simply can't anymore. I'm fucking done denying myself.

I need Lennon. Want to feel her lips on mine. Am dying to have her hands all over me. Need her in any way she'll let me have her. Every way.

A breath heaves from my chest, my attention diverting as Mason begins to stroke my dick with his dexterous hand. Heat fires through me. "F-Fuck," I bite out, trying to keep some semblance of control.

I don't think I'm fooling anyone. I'm about to lose it. This guy. My friend. He's going to fuck me up royally. My heart seizes, clamping down so hard on itself I can hardly breathe. Because I want *him*, too.

Mason's gritty, rough voice finds its way to me through the mire of thoughts bogging me down, and I turn my head toward it, finding myself under the heat of his stare, his eyes piercing mine. "Come closer, D. Feed her your cock."

"Jesus," grunts Bear from between Lennon's legs. His golden eyes flick up, watching, while the lower half of his face is buried in her cunt, making her moan and quake.

My jaw twitches, my brain set to implode. While Bear and I haven't directly talked about what's happening between Mason and me, that mind-bending kiss earlier had left little room for debate as to the truth of our relationship, and the fact that his hand is currently wrapped around my cock has slammed the door shut.

I've known Bear a long-ass time and ... *fuck it,* we're all naked. He knows the score at this point. Honestly, from the way he paused, swore at the sight of us, then reengaged in his fervor to get Lennon off said more than any words ever could. It's not like he got up and left. In fact, it felt like acceptance. *Stop fucking overthinking this.* I look down into Lennon's eyes, so full of ache, it kills me. She pulls me out of my head in a way no one else can.

"Please, Duke." Little panting noises fall from her lips, her breath unsteady. I grip her jaw, and her mouth drops open with zero prompting from me.

"Good girl." I push my hips forward, and her tongue swipes greedily over the crown of my cock before I nudge myself between her puffy, swollen lips. I thrust slowly, watching as she takes so much of my dick that I hit the back of her throat.

Mason's in her ear, his throaty commentary audible. "He's so hard for us, baby." In tandem, the two of them work my cock so fucking good, I'm coming apart at the seams, flying out of my body. All I can do is try to hang onto my sanity as her warm mouth slides up and down, wetting every inch of skin she encounters like she's on a mission to make me come as quickly as possible. She swirls her tongue, tracing along veins and circling the head of my cock before plunging forward again. Mason keeps pace with her, paying careful attention to his movements so it's good for me. I fucking love his rough hand on my dick, the way he knows how tightly to grip me. My chest constricts as I watch the two of them make me lose my goddamn mind.

A moment later, Lennon slows what she's doing, her body shaking. Mason and I both glance at Bear, who is rather masterfully bringing her right to the goddamn edge of sanity. I don't know how she's able to concentrate on me at all with the way he's ravenously feasting on her.

"Such a fucking filthy girl," I growl out. "You're gonna come on his face with my dick in your mouth, aren't you?"

Gasping around my cock for air, she nods, taking me deep again. There are tears at the corners of her eyes, which would be concerning if not for the way her pupils are blown, dilated by lust. Mason's free hand wanders over her chest, pinching at her nipples. She whimpers and cries out around my cock, her hips riding Bear's face of their own volition.

Mason groans. "That's it, baby. You're so beautiful when you come." His face is rigid with suppressed desire. He's helping us find nirvana, but I'll make sure he gets off, too.

I feel the vibration of Lennon's throaty cries all the way up my cock. It does something to me, the aching fullness in my balls now overwhelming. And while she's still shaking from the force of her orgasm, I'll be damned if this girl isn't still curling her tongue around my dick. My gaze darts from her to Mason as I feel the beginning of my orgasm take hold. The corners of his mouth quirk up, and he gives me the barest of nods as he tightens his hold on me. My eyes roll back in my head, beads of sweat popping out on my forehead as I try to hold on but can't. There's no stopping this runaway train. "Fuck, Lennon. Mase," I heave. "Fuck." I thrust forward, unable to hold back the roar I make as cum spurts forcefully from me, and my vision goes dark around the edges. There's a very real possibility that my soul has left my body.

A few moments later, Mason releases me from his

hold, his eyes burning with lust as they lock on mine. "I could feel that. The way your cock pulsed."

My dick twitches in response, releasing a final drop of cum onto Lennon's waiting tongue. I'd respond verbally somehow, but all I can do is breathe and savor how good I feel right now. I let my cock slip free of Lennon's mouth, then bend and kiss her, tasting myself on her sweet lips.

"Lennon," Bear groans, gasping as he strokes himself, his eyes burning as he takes her in, "you're so fucking gorgeous, baby."

A breath stutters from her as his cum shoots all over her thighs and pussy, even as far up as her belly. "Oh god, yes." Her chest heaves as they stare at each other. Bear exhales harshly, blinking fast. The way he looks at her ... he's lost. The connection between them is heady and so fucking real and palpable, I could practically reach out and touch it.

While his chest continues to rise and fall, Lennon begins to sit up. He holds out a hand to her. "Wait. I'll get a towel to clean you up."

"I could just—" She pauses at the look on Bear's face and nibbles at her lip, brows darting together.

"Little Gazelle, we're not done with you yet." He shakes his head, laughing quietly, and climbs from the bed, heading into the bathroom.

I totally fucking agree with him.

Mason does too, apparently, because he wastes no time, shifting back out from behind Lennon, grasping her by the hands and pressing them to the mattress over her head. He kisses her with increasing intensity, which I can't really blame him for, considering he's the only one of us who hasn't gotten off. In between feverish nips and licks, Mason peers at me, groaning aloud. "I taste you on her."

"Is that a problem?" My lips twitch, already knowing the answer.

"I fucking love it." He grunts, shifting a bit. "My dick definitely loves it." Sure enough, he's leaving streaks of pre-cum all over Lennon's hip.

Watching the two of them, my dick is getting hard all over again. Nope, definitely not done. With that thought, when Bear returns with a washcloth for Lennon, I signal to him that I'll be right back.

In my room, I take several seconds to breathe, raking my hands through my hair. I let air fill my lungs in an attempt at defogging my head. Fucking hell. It's so goddamn good, the four of us together. I never would have thought we'd do something like this, but now it seems so fucking right. She said it herself—she wants us to make her *ours*.

Hopefully, I'm not imagining the need for the lube

that I grab from my nightstand. You just never fucking know, and I'd rather not be caught without.

Hurrying, I check for wandering brothers and their prying eyes before I slip back across the hall with my heart a pounding drumbeat in my head. I haven't been gone more than a minute tops, but in that time, Lennon and Mason have pulled a position swap. She's straddling him, her hands resting on his chest as her hips piston over him.

Bear has settled in with his back against the headboard, watching the action with interest, teeth tightly clamped onto his lip. He catches my eye, brows wriggling.

I give a soft chuckle, tossing the lube onto the bed, and lie down on my side next to Mason, alternately watching his face, then hers. The smell of sex permeates the air, and I groan, inhaling. Lennon's concentration is fully on Mason, their eyes locked as they melt together in a frenzy of tangled limbs and pounding hearts. She rides his cock so damn good, Mason isn't going to last much longer.

I can't blame him because her pussy is what dreams are made of.

"Kin." He places his hand on her belly, runs it up between her breasts, and then back down, rubbing her clit. "Love the way your pussy milks my cock, baby."

Her pelvis jerks, and she slows her movements, really grinding down on his fingers. It's hotter than hell the way her body shows us how much she wants us. I love the flush of her skin and her blissed-out expression. "Oh god, Mase. Fuck."

I grunt out, "That's it, baby. Ride him good."

She leans forward, collapsing on his chest as her hips rock. I push myself up to sitting and put my hand on her ass. Across from them, Bear gets the same idea, moving closer and squeezing her other cheek, holding her open the same way I am. My dick is hard again, and all I can think is that I want to slide myself inside her when he's done.

"My fucking god," Bear groans as we take advantage of the up-close view of Lennon's pussy taking Mason's dick, sliding up and down his length over and over.

"Are you watching?" she breathes out, her pants, and his, filling the room.

Mason groans, his voice hoarse with raw desire. "Fuck yes they are, baby. They can see how good you're taking it; how wet you are for us."

A moment later, it's obvious they're both ready to detonate. "Come all over his cock, Lennon," Bear demands gruffly.

And she does, the two of them a quaking mess as he follows her over the edge, unable to hold back.

Bear smooths his hand from Lennon's ass up her back. "Little Gazelle, you have one more round in you?" She turns her head toward him and nods. "Yes."

"Of course she does." Mason cups her cheek, winking at her. "That kitty is purring for more." He puts his head to her ear. "Get on your hands and knees for Duke. I have an idea."

His words are like a lightning strike to my dick. Immediately hard, I take myself in hand and stroke while I watch her climb off Mason and assume the position. I'm so fucking turned-on, I'm already leaking pre-cum … because I'm about to put my cock into her cum-soaked pussy. I can't think coherently; my brain is muddled, my breaths heavy, my vision tunneled. I move behind her. She's shoved her ass into the air and is watching me over her shoulder, intently waiting for my next move.

I can't resist gripping both cheeks and spreading her open so I have a full view of her dripping cunt and puckered pink asshole. It's a fucking sight to see. I bend at the waist, licking her from her clit to her ass, and she bellows at the unexpected contact. *Oh, fuck yes.* Unable to wait another second, I line my cock up with her slit and slip effortlessly inside.

She gasps, so I still.

Bear puts his hand on her back. "You okay?"

All I can see is the vigorous nodding of her head.

Bear's eyes connect with mine, and he nods that I should continue. Mason gets his attention, jutting his chin toward Lennon, communicating without words. Bear's brow raises. All part of the plan, I suppose.

"Lennon," I rasp, "your pussy—" My head is a swirling vortex of complex emotion. "I need this. I—"

She peers at me over her shoulder again. "Duke. I need you, too." The corners of her mouth curve into one of her signature sassy smiles. My fingers depress into her ass cheeks. Those words take hold of my heart and squeeze, begging me to pay attention.

While I slowly move in and out of her tight, cum-slicked pussy, Bear shifts to kneel in front of her, whispering softly. I blink. I swear to fuck I think I heard him ask her if she could take Daddy's cock in her mouth like a good girl. *Fucking yes, sir.* Sure enough, Bear holds her jaw and guides his dick between her lips. I can't see everything, but my god, there's no telling whether the moans she's making have more to do with my cock driving into her relentlessly or because she's teasing Bear and his long-and-girthy-as-fuck dick. I don't care much either way because it's sexy as hell.

Having finally recovered, Mason joins me at my side. "How does it feel to fuck her pussy when it's full of my cum?"

My lips twitch, and I huff out a breath, continuing

to rock into Lennon's cunt. I turn my head, keeping one hand on her hip and grasp him by the back of his neck, tugging him to me so that our lips brush. I see the challenge in his eyes. This is the moment where I can deny him or accept what's happening between us. I don't think he cares if Lennon and Bear hear my response or not. And for the first time ever, neither do I.

With my heart pounding out of control, my chest seizes viciously around it. I stare into his dark eyes, seeing all the lust and want and need—and more emotions I'm not ready to process—reflected in his eyes. Through clenched teeth, I grit out. "You know I fuckin' love it." And with that, I slam my mouth on his, reveling in his soft yet intensely masculine lips.

His hand threads through my hair, fisting the strands at the back of my head. We battle back and forth for control of the lip-lock, and I relish every second of how he licks into my mouth like he's looking for new and uncharted parts of me with every bold stroke of his tongue. With each breath we share, I'm overcome by all the things I want to say but am not ready to divulge.

He tears his mouth away and puts his lips to my ear, his fingers still tangled in my hair as if he's afraid I'll run if he lets go. "Tell me, D. Did you bring that lube in here for a reason?" Mason's voice is gritty and raspy, sending jolts of pleasure rocketing down my spine. "You're fucking her pretty good. Is it your turn to get fucked, too?"

I suck in a steadying breath, turning my head to meet the raging fire in his dark eyes. "Yes."

Other than a quick gasp from Lennon, who is now taking as much of Bear's cock into her mouth as she can, it's deathly quiet in the room, barring the sounds of heavy breathing and the snap of my hips against Lennon's ass cheeks.

It's possible they thought I wouldn't say yes, that I'd panic and freak the fuck out. Or maybe—and I wonder if this isn't where the truth lies—each of them recognizes the importance of this moment for me and no one wants to fuck it up.

Mason opens the lube and drizzles some over his cock. I can't fucking stop watching him, as he strokes himself. My mind tumbles and turns, spinning back, remembering that drunken night, the only other time I've let myself be this vulnerable.

Unfortunately, it hadn't fucking ended well, because I couldn't accept what we'd done, and I hate that thoughts of how damaging it was to our friendship are skipping along the periphery of my mind when all I want is what I've denied myself for three long years.

"Curl your body over hers. Widen your legs." Mason's gravelly command hits me square in the chest, and I do what he says, reveling in the idea of what he's going to do to me while my cock is buried in Lennon. I don't know how I'll be able to focus on anything else, but a moment later, Mason slips his lube-coated fingers between my cheeks, and I'm taken to another level. I suck in a startled breath at the feel of them gliding over my asshole and surrounding area.

"Oh my fuuuck." My heart is close to rupturing from behind my rib cage and bursting out of my chest. "Fuck. Fuck." I can't even come up with another word as Mason's fingers explore my ass, a fingertip gently prodding, then skating away. My brain is buzzing so hard, I don't recognize that he's picked up the lube until the cold, slippery liquid runs between my ass cheeks again.

"Gonna make this good for you, Duke. Promise." He kisses my shoulder, his lips lingering there, then moves behind me.

I can only imagine what he's seeing. My ass. Me fucking Lennon, who's sucking Bear for all she's worth. And the big guy on the end, able to see all of it from the reverse perspective. My breath hitches and my face infuses with blood, flushing hard.

Mason's fingers return, one of his digits breaching the tight ring of muscle. Molten desire flows through me as nerve endings cry out with pleasure. My head is all twisted up. I shouldn't want this. But I do. I want every fucking thing he'll give me. His finger pushes deeper inside me, and I moan, dropping my head and letting out a heavy breath. This thing we're doing, it's a fiery hot pendulum of desire, first my dick sinking into Lennon's soaking-wet pussy, then my ass chasing Mason's finger for more of his touch. Need scorches my blood, making me pliant. I shudder. *Fuck.*

"You okay?" he whispers in my ear. Earlier, he wanted Lennon and Bear to know he wasn't afraid of doing any of this in front of them. But this, checking in with me in a soft voice that's for me alone … My head grows hazy, wondering what all this means to him. What *I* mean to him.

I nod. "Yeah. I'm good."

A second finger slips inside to join the first, and he scissors them, gently plunging in and out, preparing my body to take his cock. Just the feel of him fucking me with his fingers has me ready to explode. I'm nervous as hell, hoping I don't embarrass myself.

When I look up at Bear, he gives me a nod. Approval? It's not like I'm going to ask him for clarification mid thrust, and he goes right back to focusing on Lennon. "That's it, baby girl. Take Daddy's cock to the back of your pretty throat."

My eyes go wide. The way he growled that command

was sexy as hell. Fuck, I think I like that part of their dynamic.

"Ready, D?" Mason's grunted question snatches my attention back to him. His fingers now slide easily in and out of my ass. His breaths behind me are heavy. He wants this every bit as much as I do, I can tell.

I nod. "Fuck, *yes.*" He moves closer and removes his fingers, replacing them with the fat head of his cock. I grip Lennon's hips, my fingers digging into her soft flesh as I pause my movement while Mason pushes into me, inch by careful inch. "Oh god, oh fuck," I heave out, my lips parting of their own volition at the sensation of fullness. "Hold still a sec," I mumble, trying to get my bearings before I come way too fast. I let out one stuttering breath, then another.

Behind me, Mason lips are on my back, coasting over the skin, sometimes stopping to suck or lick. Every jump and twitch of his dick in my ass has me gasping for air. Lennon moves ever so slightly, and it sets off a chain reaction as my ass clamps down on Mason.

"Fuuuck," he rasps, thrusting forward.

We each moan out our pleasure in turn.

At the other end, Bear's jaw has gone rigid, and he looks up at the ceiling as he growls, "Do that a-fucking-gain."

From behind me, Mason chuckles, pulls back to the

point where I almost cry out at the loss before he plows into me again. Lennon makes a breathy noise of enjoyment as my dick ends up deep in her pussy, and her mouth subsequently is stuffed full of Bear's dick.

"Fuck, yes," I mutter.

And from there, we go, like a great rippling wave of madly undulating water, all groans and sighs and moans. Grunts and heavy breaths and raspy cries.

Honestly, it feels so fucking good, I think maybe I've died. All of us linked together like this, it seems impossible, a wholly unusual kind of relationship. But at this moment in time, I don't fucking care. This is the most natural and authentic thing I've ever experienced, and I don't want it to stop. And that's only the emotional aspect of it.

Physically, sensitive nerve endings are being lit up that I wasn't aware—or hadn't wanted to remember—I possessed. I hadn't known that engaging in sex with more than one person would feel like this. My dick is wet and my ass is full in the best way possible. Yep, I'm going to go off like a geyser any minute.

"Duke, goddamn." Mason grasps my hip with one hand, letting the other roam, sliding over my sweaty skin, fingers alternately groping and clawing at me as he fucks me so good I can hardly stand it.

I heave out a breath and then another. Jesus, I'm

fucking panting, overwhelmed and swamped by sensation after sensation. I'm definitely not lasting much longer. I reach around to tease Lennon's clit, and she lets out a choked moan.

I look up when a hiss from Bear catches me off guard, and the ecstasy on his face tells me all I need to know.

"That's it," he rasps, "milk every last drop, sweetheart."

A moment later he slips from her mouth, a dazed grin on his face and falls to the side. With nothing stopping her, Lennon moans long and low as my fingers continue to brush over her clit. "Oh god. I'm gonna—" She throws her head back, hips bucking against me as her pussy spasms. "I'm coming on your cock, Duke."

And that's all it takes for me, my dick throbs hard, then I'm painting my stepsister's cunt with my cum, and something about that seems dirty as hell but oh so satisfying.

Mason groans, pumping slowly in and out of my body. He whispers raggedly, "Fucking fuck, baby."

My heart thumps wildly, two quick, hard beats in response to the endearment that I don't even know if he meant.

More words tear from his lips as he pushes himself fully inside me. "Your ass is pulsing around my—" He never finishes that thought, and I swear I can feel his hot cum spurting deep inside me.

Lennon cranes her neck around and meets my eyes, then Mason's. "You guys are seriously so f-fucking hot. All of you."

Jesus. Fuck. What a ride that was.

TWENTY-NINE

DUKE

THOROUGHLY SATED, it'd been a while before we got moving again. Once we were able to untangle ourselves from each other, we'd taken turns in the bathroom cleaning up. Lennon is still in there, blow-drying her hair, while Mason and Bear have taken it upon themselves to put fresh sheets on the bed.

Trying to figure out if there's something I could do that would be useful, I turn a full three-sixty, my eyes finally landing on something sitting to the side of Lennon's dresser. I huff out a mildly disgruntled laugh under my breath. There sits the box of clothing that started World War Three. I purse my lips and walk over to stand in front of it. My stepsister is a stubborn woman. As I rub my hand over my stubbled jaw, my brows knit together. It's slightly amusing she hasn't figured out I'm just as stubborn, if not more so.

With a shake of my head, I kneel down in front of the box and open it, then proceed to pull out the zillion things I'd purchased for her that are still in their bags. She may have poked around in here, but she definitely didn't remove anything. I wonder what the fuck was in her head when she opened it and realized I hadn't given her sorority girl cast-offs. I give a slight shrug, stand up with a multitude of bags in hand, and begin the process of unpacking them on the bed now that it's made.

Sensing eyes on me, I look up to find Bear's thick brows hitched up on his forehead. Mason's mouth has twisted into a smirk that I'd kinda like to kiss right off his face, but I don't have time for that. "Help me, would you? Pull tags off and put stuff in drawers or if they need to be hung up, we can do that when she comes out."

"You think she'll be okay with that?" Bear's head tips to the side, as he considers his own question.

I wet my lips as my eyes slide to the closed bathroom door. "We just engaged in a four-way fuckfest. I think she'll be okay with whatever at this point, don't you?"

Mason scrubs his hand through his wild hair. "Fuck it. I'm in." He digs into a bag, pulling out some pricy underwear, bras, and the hotter-than-sin white nightie that I've been dreaming of seeing Lennon in ever since I bought it—even though she'd more than likely have used it as a torture device against me until just recently. Mason is intently removing all the little tags and leaving them in a pile on the nightstand.

"The dress I want her to wear on Saturday night is in here somewhere. It's sexy. Black. Has this amazing drape in the back." I take a deep breath, looking around, and when I finally locate it, all I can do is shake my head in utter disbelief at how perfect the dress is for her.

Mason lets out a low whistle. "Yeah. She's going to look so good in that."

Eyeing me, Bear drags a few of the bags across the bed, raising a brow as he pulls out several skirts and shorts that I thought were similar in style to what she wears. He works his jaw back and forth, then finally relents. "Okay, I'm going to help, but be prepared for her reaction to go one of two ways." He meets my gaze across the mountain of clothing now covering the bed.

My lips quirk up on one side. "And what do you think are the likely scenarios?" I would have thought I'd be embarrassed to stand here idly chatting with someone who just saw—and heard—me get railed, but it's Bear. My friend. And he's not acting any differently toward me than he ever has. Relief courses through me.

"She'll either kiss you or punch you. And I guarantee you won't like the punch." He winks at me as he hurriedly pulls more garments from bags. "That kiss, though, that's the real knockout."

"You're definitely not kidding." I shake my head and turn around to pull the last of the bags from the box.

With all three of us working on it, we have everything put away before Lennon rejoins us. She comes out wearing nothing but a towel, a soft smile curving her lips. Her gaze bounces among the three of us, as if she can tell we were talking about her. "What's going on?"

Before I can answer, she opens the top drawer of her dresser where she keeps her lingerie. My teeth clench together, grinding. Her movements halt, her back to us as she stares down at her newfound clothing. "What's this?"

I glance over to Bear and Mason, both of whom put their hands up. *This is all me. Got it.* I step up beside her, resting my hand on her back. She peers at me from the corner of her eye, fingers clutching the towel between her breasts. Her pink tongue slides over her lower lip.

"Please accept the clothes I bought for you." I pause to clear my throat. "Please trust that I picked them out and gave them to you because I thought you'd like them." I grimace. "And maybe I was trying to prove I could be a good stepbrother or some shit like that. I dunno. There was something in here"—I claw at my chest, watching her, searching for some glimmer of understanding to cross her features—"I didn't want you to think I was a complete asshole, even if that's exactly what it seemed like."

"That's what you *were.*" She takes several breaths, then turns her head toward me, a flicker of something I haven't seen before in her eyes. Her lips twist as she glances into the drawer again. "You picked out everything yourself? For me?"

I nod, gesturing to the bed. "Including the dress over there that needs to be hung up." She turns around, and Mason picks it up to show her, then walks into the bathroom with it. He comes back a moment later without it. "I put it in the closet, on the left near the door for you."

Her breath skitters out as she looks at me again. "What if I say no, I don't want any of it?" Her eyes dart to the drawer again for a split second. She doesn't want to say no, she's just afraid to admit that she's been a tiny bit in the wrong, too—she hiked up the mound of beautiful clothing she's been denying herself and had intended to die on that very hill.

I exhale and shake my head. "You could. But you don't want to. And I think you've come to trust me ... at least more than you used to." I pluck the nightgown out to show her.

She chews on her lip and lets go of the towel. Damp, it drops to the floor at her feet. "Help me into it?"

I know I've already seen her naked, was just inside her not long ago, but *goddamn.* I suck in a breath. "You got it." I hold it up so she can slip it over her head.

It's undeniably made for her, the frothy material practically floating around her. She makes my heart stop in my chest.

"I still think you're an asshole sometimes," she quips as she goes up on tiptoe, pressing her body against mine, her taut nipples poking my chest as she grasps the back of my neck with both hands and tugs until she can attack my mouth with hers.

Bear was right. It's a fucking knockout from the moment she slides her tongue past my lips. This girl can make all logical thoughts fly out of my head. I thread one hand through the hair at the side of her head and tilt her to a better angle, but I'm not fooled—she's totally in control here with the way she's got my tongue chasing hers.

I could easily kiss her for hours, but I ease back with a small laugh. "I don't know how I thought I could ever fucking resist you."

She shrugs, lunging forward again and sucking my lip into her mouth for a moment, her eyes sparkling. "I don't either." She gives me a saucy wink, then, as she's climbing onto the bed between Bear and Mason, ass in the air, she glances back over her shoulder. "Thanks for the clothes, Duke. I mean it."

"You're welcome." As she settles in, I note that her dusky nipples are visible through the white fabric, and it sends a jolt straight to my dick. She looks so good I want to tear the damn thing right back off her. I laugh internally at myself as I join everyone on the bed. I never saw her coming. Not any of this.

I take the space at the end of the bed, lying on my side. I haven't even gotten comfortable when I catch an odd look on Bear's face as he grits out, "Little brawler, lemme see your hand."

She folds them together, a funny expression cast across her face. "I'm fine."

I'd all but forgotten she'd hauled off and punched Tucker a few hours ago. We were so consumed with making sure she didn't walk out on us, her attack on Tucker kinda got tossed to the wayside. But now ... I frown, trying to get a look at whatever Bear's seeing from this angle.

He tilts his head to the side. "Show me." His voice is low and demanding. Not one I'd deny if I were her, that's for fuckin' sure.

"Kin?" Mason questions, his brow furrowing as he shifts on the bed. "Let us see."

Like a viper strike, Bear's hand darts out, grasping

her wrist. I'm so surprised by his action, my gaze flies to his face, just in time to see him wince, his jaw setting hard. He doesn't let on, but I think that gambit really fucking hurt his shoulder.

He glances down, inspecting her knuckles before clearing his throat. "These look a bit swollen. Why didn't you say something?" His eyes flick up to meet hers, but she shakes her head.

"It's nothing." She drags in a ragged breath, her gaze moving to each of us in turn. "I'm sorry that happened, but I'm fine."

"Don't you dare be sorry," I grit out.

A muscle in Bear's jaw twitches as he studies her hand. "Tucker was being an asshole and he knows it. Too bad for him, you have a fucking excellent coach."

Mason smirks. "You surprised the shit out of him." He reaches out, patting Lennon's thigh. "I'm going to get you some ibuprofen or something. Do you have any in your bathroom?"

Lennon sighs. "Yeah, okay. I guess it wouldn't hurt, maybe they're a little sore. There should be something in the medicine cabinet."

Mason is busy concentrating on Lennon, but I don't like the tightness around Bear's eyes and the way he keeps readjusting his arm and shoulder. I jut my chin, grabbing his attention. "You need some, too?"

"No," he huffs, irritation lacing his tone. "I have prescription stuff in my room. And I'll run down to get some ice for your knuckles, Lennon. Be right back." He drops a quick kiss to her forehead and climbs from the bed. I watch his quiet exit and wonder what the fuck is going on with my friend that he's not willing to share.

I push it aside as Mason returns. He hands Lennon a paper cup of water, then shakes a few pills out of a bottle, and puts them in her palm. He eyes her warily, and because I do know him that well, I fully read that he has something else on his mind. A moment later, he proves me right. "Speaking of being sore, maybe you should soak in a tub or something. That was some marathon sex."

She smirks and throws the pills back along with the water. "Maybe later. I just want to be with you guys right now."

"Is that so?" A blush hits her cheeks, and I reach out, grab her foot, and kiss the arch.

Bear reenters the room, quickly reclaiming his spot beside Lennon on the bed. He picks up her hand and kisses the back of it before handing her a baggie of ice. "What are we talking about?"

Mason leans in on her other side, nipping at her ear. "She said she'd rather hang with us than soak in a tub."

She lifts her shoulders to her ears. "Can you blame me? Look at the three of you."

I don't get a chance to fire off any witty remarks because my phone vibrates on the table next to her bed.

A second later, Bear's and Mason's go off as well.

What the fuck?

I get to mine first, dread slithering down my spine as I realize we've all received the same text from my father. My jaw goes rigid as I rub a hand over my chest.

"What is it?" Lennon plucks at the hem of her nightie, worrying it between her fingers absentmindedly.

Mason's head rears back as he glances at the disturbing message on the screen. "What's that about?"

With her eyes moving wildly from one to the other of us, she murmurs, "Seriously. You're freaking me out."

Bear growls, his face a thunderous storm cloud as he reads the message for her benefit. "Country club—tomorrow evening at nine. No questions. No excuses."

THIRTY

LENNON

THIS MORNING, I almost fell asleep during my nine o'clock class and by the time I was done with all my classes for the day, I'd been so tired that I'd crawled into bed to read and had promptly fallen asleep. There are three very energetic men who are to blame for my current state. Except ... maybe it's me who is at fault. I told them to make me theirs, and that's exactly what they'd done.

Waking up hours later in the dark, I half wonder if the guys went to the country club without me since I zonked out. But when I consider the shitstorm that seems to follow me around like a bad omen every time I'm alone, I kinda doubt they'd do that. They've been very careful to escort me to and from classes and haven't left me alone at the house. And because of those precautions, it's been mostly quiet around here—with the distinct exception of me using Tucker as a punching bag yesterday. That was nothing that the guys could have avoided. The minute that dickhead opened his foul mouth, I knew he'd have an unfortunate meeting with my fists. I don't know where he gets off thinking he can call me "sweet cheeks" or talk about how he'd like to buy me in the auction.

And I still have no idea why I've been added to the list of sorority girls being auctioned off anyway. I don't get it, but I don't get anything the OG Bastards do ... especially my stepfather.

Thinking back to the way the guys had closed ranks when the text message summons from Tristan had come in has me worrying all over again. They'd been so close-mouthed about it, I hadn't wanted to push. To be honest, I couldn't quite tell if they knew the reason they were being so suddenly and urgently called upon. I got the sense that bringing the guys in and not just dropping by may mean we're talking about meeting with more than just the two OG Bastards. That's just a guess, though.

I don't know where anyone is, but the whole damn house is dark as I wander through it—with the exception of the dim light over the cooktop. What the hell time *is* it? How long had I slept? I pat myself down, relieved to find my phone in the pocket of my leggings because I thought I'd left it upstairs. It's only eight thirty.

"There you are. We're getting ready to go." Mason strides into the room in dark jeans and a plain black T-shirt. For once, he doesn't look like he's been rolling around in charcoal all day. He cocks his head to the side, his intense, dark eyes scanning my features. "What's wrong, Kintsukuroi? You look confused."

"Um. Nothing. I just woke up, I guess I'm a little disoriented. I wasn't sure if I was supposed to come with you tonight or not, and if not, how we'd handle it." I give him a tight smile and tuck my hair behind my ears. "Stay here and deal with the brotherhood or go with you and chance an encounter with Tristan and his buddies. Great options I've got."

Just then, Tucker comes in from the patio, shooting a disgruntled look in my direction. The bruising on his face stands out against the light tone of his skin. His eyes are trained on me, the roll of his eyes and the clenching of his jaw telling me plenty. It's safe to say he's not going to forgive me anytime soon for embarrassing him in front of the brotherhood. My fists bunch, remembering what it felt like to handle him on my own. A whisper of a smile reaches my lips at the memory. A moment later, Tucker tears his eyes from mine and hurries away down the back hall.

Mason clears his throat. "You okay?"

"Yeah. That dude is acting like a pissy little bitch."

Snorting at my evaluation, he nods. "Agreed. And no way are we leaving you here with him or any of these assholes."

I let out a heavy breath. "I think that's probably the right call."

Bear's gravelly voice flows over me like a smooth whiskey as he approaches. "If you're talking about tonight, I think our best bet is to take you with us." He reaches out, skimming a few fingers along the curve of my jaw. "Don't worry, there's no way in hell we're bringing you into the lion's den."

Duke wanders in just in time to hear that last bit. "Yeah, that'd be a bad idea tonight." His expression is grim as he meets Bear's and Mason's eyes. They carry the same disturbed concern. It doesn't do anything to calm my nerves.

A crease etches into my forehead, and I purse my lips. "Okay. So, I come with ... but I stay in the SUV?"

Mason hooks his arms around my neck from behind and pulls me back against his chest, kissing the top of my head. "Take your phone and whatever else you need to entertain yourself. We shouldn't be too long."

Twenty minutes later, Mason pulls our SUV into the driveway of a fancy country club. It's got the same Southern charm of so many of the homes in the area, only on a grander scale. The odd part is the area surrounding the building is relatively dark with only a few pedestals topped with ornate lights lending any illumination at all. If I didn't know better, I'd say no one is here.

I draw in a breath, trying to brush off the apprehensive sensation rattling down my spine. "This place is beautiful. What I can see of it, anyway." My brows pinch together as I continue to peek out the window, searching for some sign of life in there.

"It's the OG Bastards playground." Bear shrugs from the front seat. "They spend a lot of time here."

"Oh yeah?" I turn and give Duke a questioning stare.

He nods. "Yep. They own it. One of their many business establishments."

Jesus, how many pots do the OG Bastards have their fingers in? "Are you guys here a lot?"

"No." Mason's voice is unusually clipped. "Brothers are not invited to participate in events here until they've graduated." He clears his throat, glancing at Bear. "We've all been here before, but always just to run errands for them for one thing or another. Half the time, the shit they ask of us is illogical and impractical."

It doesn't take me long to understand what he's saying. It's all some sort of test to prove they're worthy. "Show your loyalty. Obey. Keep your mouth shut," I whisper.

Duke gives me a grim smile before tapping Mason's shoulder and pointing to a more secluded area. "Why don't we park over there? It's a little more out of the way, and anyone who comes outside is less likely to notice Lennon and ask questions."

Bear's brows knit together. "I'd say park right here, but it's not like we can keep an eye out any easier. You're right. I'd rather not draw attention to the fact that she's here at all."

"Done." Mason hits the gas, taking us over to the suggested lot. Once parked, he reaches back, squeezing my knee. "We won't be but ten minutes, okay?"

I nod, and a moment later, Bear grunts as he turns in his seat. "We'll text you if it looks like it'll be longer than expected."

"Seriously. Don't worry about me. I have a fully charged phone and a book on my Kindle app. I'm good." I wave my hand in a shooing motion, but at the same time, I study the anxious looks on their faces. It's obvious they're unsure about what they're walking into. What the hell is the purpose behind this visit? Is it the auction? Something more? I have no fucking clue, but none of them are happy to be here. My stomach twists into knots *for* them.

With uneasy nods and an air of disquiet, Mason and Bear exit the vehicle.

I expect Duke to follow suit, but instead, he turns toward me, his blue eyes piercing mine. My heart gives a jump when he takes my hand. His thumb skims over the back of it in what would be a soothing manner if everything about this visit didn't have warning bells ringing in my head. Finally, his voice thick, he murmurs, "Whatever you do, don't come into the club. Promise me you'll stay right here, Stella Bella." He's so insistent, concern flowing steadily from him that I don't even mind the usage of the nickname.

"You're freaking me out." My worry increases at the troubled look in his eyes, and I tug my hand away. "I promise. Just go do what you need to do so we can go home," I murmur. "Be safe."

He exhales hard at my words, his chin dropping to his chest. I watch him with no idea what's in that blond head of his, but all at once he refocuses on me. "Will do. See you in a few."

I wish with everything in me that I hadn't drank that entire bottle of water, because the guys have been gone a while and no one has texted me to say how much longer I'll be waiting.

I have to pee, dammit. I've held it, crossed my legs, jiggled up and down, but nothing is working to take my mind off it. The knowledge that there are toilets right inside that building is enough to make me want to scream. Relief within reach ... but not an actual option.

The pressure on my bladder increases, becoming an issue of epic, emergent proportions. Biting my lip, I come to the conclusion that I have two choices.

One, deliberately disobey. Go inside. Find the bathroom.

Or two ... my eyes flick to the huge bushes lining the side of the building ... do the most embarrassing thing ever and cop a squat in the bushes.

Ugh. Fuck my life. I don't want to flagrantly go and do exactly what they asked me not to by sneaking in to find a toilet. So I let myself out of the SUV, and after a quick look to see if anyone is watching me, I dart to the bushes. As I shove my leggings and panties down around my knees, I practically moan with relief as my bladder empties. Remembering where I am, though, I clamp my lips shut. I stay there doing an awkward shimmy and shake before I call it good and stand, pulling my clothing back into place. I feel so much better, it takes me a moment before it registers that there's a window above the bushes.

A gasp heaves from my throat when my eyes lock on the people inside the room. It's kinda dark, but there are two figures I can make out—Tristan and Duke. I have no idea what they're saying, but their words are obviously heated. Angry. One second, they're in each other's faces, and the next, Tristan backhands Duke. He must have really packed a wallop because Duke's head snaps to the side.

I gasp again, my eyes widening in horror, as I stumble away from the window. I want to distance myself from this, but I can't tear my eyes from the scene before me. They continue to lock horns, and my heart is pumping so hard it hurts. When the second hit lands and Tristan goes in for the kill, I don't think, I don't hesitate. *I run.*

Desperation streaks through me, and my blood *whooshes* through my head so loudly, I can hardly hear a thing. I race to the nearest door and slip inside despite

Duke's warning and the promise I made him. I have to get to him.

The door opens to a long corridor somewhere deep in the bowels of the country club, and it's strangely gloomy. I don't see a light switch anywhere, but a light flickers from a room at the end of the hallway. Dread slithers down my spine the farther I go. This place has a distinctive, aromatic smell—mossy and earthy. Dense and pungent. It makes my stomach pitch and groan.

Shuddering hard, I take a few cautious steps toward the light. There's something about this place. Something I don't like. My mind reaches out to grab hold of a memory that floats the surface, but then it's gone. A rumble of voices has my heart clenching hard, as if someone has reached into my chest and is intent on viciously squeezing it with every beat. Fear coats my skin like an unwelcome lover, its hands all over me, and terror lances through my body, keeping me in its tight grip.

My breaths heave from me faster and faster. I'm in trouble and I know it but can't do anything to stop it. Dark whispers fill my ears. I spin around, becoming disoriented, so dizzy I might throw up. My vision tunnels until all I see is a black void and the twinkling of silvery stars.

THIRTY-ONE

BEAR

"FUCK THIS. We should get the hell out of here," I growl, glancing around the dimly lit room. I trace my finger over the rim of the tumbler of whiskey in front of me. We've never been invited to the country club before for poker night, then again, we aren't truly invited guests on this occasion, either, which is probably why I'm not keen on sticking around any longer than we have to.

We've been summoned.

This is yet another of the prestigious Bainbridge alumni events that my father runs. High-stakes poker. Men with very deep pockets and no care of blowing thousands of dollars in an evening for entertainment. I recognize a few of them, but there are new faces, too—possibly alum from other frats. It's a pay-to-play situation, so anyone with a fat stack of cash would merit an invitation. Old money, new money, dirty money. Doesn't matter. All this kind of shit is right up my dad's alley, and I'm positive Derek Pierce makes it lucrative for himself.

Upon arrival, we'd been ushered into a room where several poker games were already in progress. We were told to sit and have a drink, that someone would be out to get us shortly. After five minutes, a guy I recognized as one of the many goons on my father's payroll came out but said only Duke was to follow.

"I don't get why we're here." Mason shakes his head, throwing back the vodka he'd requested before leaning toward me and whispering, "Where the fuck do they get these girls? They can't be more than fifteen or sixteen."

The muscle at the back of my jaw twitches and jumps. "I don't know," I grit out, surveying the large room. The club has always had an air of wealth, and I suppose tonight is no different—there's a haze of cigar smoke, free-flowing alcohol, raucous laughter, and plenty of testosterone. But there's also something prickling along my spine that my subconscious mind is picking up on. Maybe it's the underage waitstaff. Or, more specifically, the way these old bastards follow the girls with their eyes.

I have zero desire to be here. We have a fuckin' early afternoon away game before I can even think about the auction tomorrow night and the mess that will be. And now, not only do we have to deal with whatever they've deemed important enough to command our presence tonight, but I also have to have a conversation with my drug-supplying father. He knows I need more oxy to get through the game tomorrow, but he hadn't immediately said yes, just that he'd see what he could do. While it's highly doubtful he's had a crisis of conscience, I also can't figure out why he'd change his tune.

I take full responsibility for taking the pills from him in the first place. I was the one who ingested them. No one forced me. But fuck, now he's making me nervous because without anything to help me through the game, it's doubtful I'll be able to fight Sunday. And wouldn't you know it, some badass from Sigma Iota Nu is scheduled. It's a huge fucking deal. The entire thing is getting to me. Releasing a heavy sigh, I hang my head. I never should have gone back down this fucking road.

A moment later, Mason nudges me. Another one of the lackeys has shown up and is beckoning us to follow him. Mason gives me a wary look, and I can't deny I feel the same. I leave my whiskey on the table, untouched. Booze and oxy don't mix well. Maybe I should pat myself on the back for not being too out of control that I don't recognize that. I scrub my hand over my face. *Fuck.*

I grit my teeth and follow the man with Mason at my side.

We're led down a hallway and around a corner before being brought into a large room lined with bookshelves. All the furnishings are plush and expensive, exactly as I expected them to be, the lighting soft and low.

Duke glances at us out of the corner of his eye without turning his head. I frown. *What the fuck is going on here?* He's seated on a couch across from two armchairs. My father is seated in one of them, Tristan in the other. They are every inch what I'd expect of them— cool, calm, and collected with secrets hidden behind their eyes that they may or may not deem us worthy enough to know.

I step past Duke, as does Mason, and take the far cushion, leaving Mason to sit between us. When I look back toward Duke, I notice the redness on his cheek, like a bad sunburn ... or the rosy hue left by a smart slap to the face. Mason must see it at the same time because he lifts his hand, as if he's going to touch him. Before Mason can follow through, Duke gives him a severe look and jerks his head. I let out a steadying breath. *Fuck.* How awkward would it be for Duke and Mason if their fathers were to find out about their relationship? The only reason it flashes through my mind is because I know what they demand of their sons. They're expected to marry nice girls and supply their families with the new generation of bastards to keep the dirty-as-hell legacy going strong.

Dad clears his throat, shifting to cross his foot over his knee while eyeing Mason. There's a faint smirk on his lips that I don't care for, and in the next moment, I know why. "Nice to have both Mikaelsons under the same roof for a bit."

Oh, fuck.

Mason tenses, his eyes immediately scanning the room, like an animal that senses a predator is nearby. His fists clench on his thighs. "Hunter's here?"

Hunter. Fucking apt name, if you ask me.

"Somewhere." Dad nods, his smile not meant to reassure any of us, least of all Mason. He has to know something about why Mason can't stand his brother. They can't have been so blind as to miss the bad blood between them. It's existed for years and years but was particularly bad after Lily Mikaelson's death. The way Hunter got on Mason, it's not a wonder he thinks like he does. They practically brainwashed him into taking the blame, and no matter how much Duke and I have tried to pull him out of it, the damage has proven irreversible. Who can compete with a dead mother who shows up? The idea that he was at fault is lodged so deep in his psyche, I don't know if it's ever coming out.

I draw in a deep breath. There's enough tension in the room already to make my head spin. The crazy part is I don't believe it has anything to do with Hunter. Not with the storm brewing on Tristan's face. *The fuck is going on here?* He wears a contemplative smirk as he watches the three of us. "I'm going to get right to the point, boys. We know you don't want to auction Lennon off tomorrow." He stops and leans forward, resting his elbows on his knees. "But you're going to. That girl needs to earn her place, and she'll bring a pretty fucking penny. I'm sick of her giving me trouble with no return."

Sweat dampens my back. First, how the fuck did they know how we feel? That I'm aware of, none of us have said a damn word since we got that list of girls for the auction. Do we have a fuckin' leak? Or cameras we don't know about? Second, what a way to speak about your stepdaughter ... as if Lennon is some milk cow that isn't producing like it should.

Duke grimly shakes his head but before he's formulated his thoughts, Tristan chuckles, scrubbing his hand over his neatly-trimmed beard. "I can see what you're about to say son, but you *will* put her up there. I don't care if the three of you have made her your personal slut."

Mason jerks as if he's about to lunge across the coffee

table and take him out. I swallow hard, grasping his arm so he doesn't make that mistake. I squeeze. He continues to breathe hard, his eyes narrowed on them, but he remains on the couch.

Duke huffs out a breath, his voice rough as he asks, "What about this Elliot girl?"

I can't fucking tell what my grief-stricken friend is thinking, and I do remember the anger in his eyes while he watched Kingston following the pretty brunette out of that party. I worry that he'd probably love nothing more than to agree to putting her up for auction just to piss Kingston off. But it makes no fucking sense for the OG Bastards to be demanding it. And that's probably got him thinking twice about following through with it. At least I fuckin' hope it does.

Clearing his throat, Dad looks pointedly at each of us. "Elliot Ashford being auctioned off is one small part of our plan to get Murdock out of the prison he's been caged in." He works his jaw back and forth, his gaze landing on Mason, who is practically vibrating, he's so shaken by this very fucking unexpected news. "But that's nothing you need to worry about. Just trust us that we know what we're fucking doing."

My teeth grind. "What the fuck do you want from us? Why are we here? Because I'm about done with this conversation."

Dad levels me with a lethal stare. "You're done when we say you're done, son."

And this is where I bite my tongue because if I don't, things won't go well for me, and I can't risk that, now more than ever.

Tristan picks up where Dad leaves off. "At the moment, we're not too fucking sure we like how you're handling things as the heads of that damn house. What we need from you is pretty simple. *Be* the fucking Bastards of Bainbridge Hall—the ones we've raised you to be so that one day you can have all this." He gestures with an agitated hand around the room, but I know we're supposed to be envisioning their filthy business empire. He exhales hard through his nostrils. "Remind everyone who you really are and why we command their respect. Prove yourselves to us, prove that you're worthy members of our brotherhood. Fucking do what we're asking." His lips twist. "Hunter will be there to watch every damn move you make tomorrow night and to make sure the event is carried through in the way we need it to be.

"It's an important fucking night, as it is every year, but even more so this year with what we have planned. You will work that motherfucking crowd; you will make sure we get out of it what we need. And if you can't fucking do that, then maybe you don't deserve the life-long benefits of being one of the brothers of Bainbridge Hall. You'll lose the respect that's already slipping away. You'll be banned."

I blink. "Fucking hell," I mutter under my breath. He's dead fucking serious. My stomach sinks like a stone into my gut.

Duke runs his hand over his face, then meets his father's stern gaze. "I don't know about this Elliot girl but Lennon can't be controlled the way you think."

"Don't tell me you can't handle some little girl, son." Tristan's teeth clamp down so hard I can practically hear them grind together.

I run my hand over my jaw, scrubbing my fingers through the growth of hair. I glare hard at both of them, irritated because my goddamn hands are tied.

Dad leans back in his seat, crossing his arms over his chest. Low and dangerous, he grits out, "The three of you will put those little bitches up for auction. Period. Or face the fucking consequences." I don't like the gleam in his eye, especially when his gaze dips to my shoulder. "Get the fuck out of here."

I blink, then stand. Duke also gets up, his jaw popping. I can totally tell he's holding back everything he wants to say. But it comes down to this—we don't want to deal with the potential fallout because we *know*. All three of us. Our fathers are really fucking bad men.

Bad enough that I'm beginning to suspect they don't care if their sons will be around to carry on their twisted legacy.

A cold sweat breaks out on my forehead, which is due to one of two things: the current situation or perhaps the lack of oxy I've had today. I draw in a stabilizing breath. I'm going to be fine. I'm going to be fucking okay. But at the moment, there's someone worse off than I am, and my eyes and thoughts drift to him.

Mason sits stock-still, staring at his hands, as he clenches and unclenches his fists over and over. I don't know how the fuck they plan to get his father out of prison or what this Elliot girl has to do with it, but it's fucking thrown Mason bad. Combine that with telling him that Hunter is lurking around here somewhere and will be in our home tomorrow? *Fuck.*

"Mase. Let's go." Duke puts his hand on his shoulder and bends at the waist to murmur something in his ear. I don't know what he says, but Mason shoots up off the couch, flips off both my dad and Tristan with a double bird and storms away. Wide-eyed, Duke lets out a heavy breath, running his hand over his jaw.

I track Mason with my eyes as he stalks out. Under my breath, I murmur, "Go with him. I'll be right there."

"You sure?" Duke's gaze flicks from me to my dad.

The sudden sick grin on my old man's face is making me ten kinds of nervous.

I nod. "There's something I need to speak to my dad about. I'll be thirty seconds behind you. *Go.* We've been here too long already."

Duke shoots me an agonized look, but takes off after Mason.

Once he's left the room, Tristan stands, winking at me. "I'll leave you to ... your transaction."

Anger shoots through me as he ambles away, not a care in the fucking world. Slowly, I twist around to meet my father's gaze. "You fucking told him?" I hiss out.

"I needed some help procuring what you needed." He tosses a baggie at me. "Should be enough to get you through the game tomorrow. We'll see how things go at the auction before I allow any more. I'll send it with Hunter."

Hand shaking, I shove the pills into my pocket, staring at him incredulously. "So you're threatening me. *Again.*"

"Whatever works, kid. You'll get the job done at the game and tomorrow night. I know you will. Because you don't have a choice. Now, fuck off home."

Humiliation burns through me like wildfire.

But I don't have time to respond despite the rage simmering within me, because there are agonized shouts

But the thing I'm most disturbed by? Hands down, it was my inability to stay with Lennon in the moment when we found her on the floor like we did. Instead, I dove headlong into the hazy, gut-wrenching recollections of kneeling beside my mother as life bled from her.

Everything I touch becomes a disaster.

Duke's whispered words after we'd returned to the house last night echo through my mind: "Mase. She needs you." And my answer of "I'm sorry, I can't help her like this," had twisted a knife in my heart. The two of us in meltdown mode at the same time is no fucking good.

I don't know what happened after that. I'd been too wrecked and emotionally battered to deal. And I hate that. Because even while I was losing it, I was longing for the one who understands something of the darkness in my head.

It's killing me that I haven't even checked in with her today.

I'll get my chance, now, maybe. But what kind of conversation can we have with this motherfucking auction hanging over our damn heads?

Securing my belt around my waist, I give myself one last look in the mirror. I've dressed up as much as I ever do for stuff like this—white button-down with the collar open and sleeves rolled up. Charcoal-gray dress pants.

Ready for whatever is coming our way, I run a hand through the hair that consistently falls into my face. Unsure if I'll get a chance to come back up once I'm swallowed by the pre-event hustle going on downstairs, I grab the mask I'll wear later. Just as I'm putting my phone into the pocket of my pants, it vibrates, so I pull it back out. It's Duke.

You okay?

I've been better, but I'll survive.

A few moments go by, like he's trying to decide how to respond to my misery.

Could you meet us outside Lennon's room?
Bear is just back from his game.
And we have to fuckin' talk to her.
She's holed herself up in there all day.

I wet my lips, my tongue sliding slowly as I process his words. I can't decide if I'm ticked that he didn't react more to my response or if it's just one of those fucking days. We have a lot of shit on our minds. And he's not wrong. We've gotta make sure Lennon can handle what we're about to ask of her. Duke and Bear had both texted me last night to make sure we were on the same fucking page for tonight. I don't even want to think about what we'll do if she won't go along with everything. I grasp my hair in my fist and tug as my jaw twitches incessantly.

I close my eyes and let out a huffed breath. There's a tender piece of my heart that wanted more from Duke, but maybe I'm being a fucking needy asshole. Brushing off the hurt, I swallow past the thickness in my throat and tap out a short response.

Agreed. I'm dressed already.
Be right there.

I slip my phone back into my pocket and stride from my bathroom to the door, already able to hear their hushed voices outside in the hall. Taking a deep breath, I join them, tossing them one of my usual smirks. "Imagine seeing you two here."

Duke is dressed much the same as I am—button-down and dress pants—but he added a black tie. He looks really fucking good, and I have to drag my eyes from him. Bear hasn't changed yet and is still in joggers and T-shirt, his hair wet from his post-game shower. Both give me odd half-smiles, and I'm positive I know why.

I press my lips together, eyeing them carefully. "What, did you think another instance of my brain tricking me, along with the appearance of my dickhead brother was going to send me to the psych ward?"

"Our concern was warranted, Mason," Bear grumbles as he scrubs a hand over his face.

I shrug off their apprehension. "Can we just do this?"

"Hang on." Duke glances from Bear to me. "We ask her to play along, knowing it's all a load of bullshit. We're in agreement that's our best strategy?"

With a roll of my eyes, I knock on her door. "We're about to find out." I clear my throat. "Kintsukuroi! We need to talk to you. Can we come in?"

To my surprise, the door opens quickly, a vision in black on the other side with her hair half up and curled in soft waves. Lennon's applied a tiny bit more makeup than she usually does, the most notable being the bright-pink gloss that's slicked over her luscious lips. My eyes travel downward, noting the way the dress Duke bought her hugs her body like nothing I've ever seen before, and when she turns and heads back into the room, my jaw drops. The dress scoops low on her back, sitting no more than an inch above her ass. She's ... *stunning*. A beautiful compilation of all her broken pieces.

My eyes feast on her. "I feel like one of those

cartoon characters whose eyes turn into hearts and bug out of their heads." I chuckle. "It's a good thing you don't walk around like this all the time." Blood rushes to places it definitely doesn't need to right at this moment.

Beside me, Bear runs a hand over his face, shaking his head like he can't quite believe his eyes. "You look gorgeous, Lennon."

Her cheeks stain pink at our compliments, then her eyes cast down to the floor.

My gaze trails over to Duke, and I almost laugh at his dumbfounded expression. The poor guy has been rendered speechless.

Finally, he takes a stuttered breath. "Fuck. You look amazing. I wasn't sure if you'd wear it. Thank you."

She gives him a slight inclination of her head. Bear moves in closer and collars the back of her neck with his big hand, tugging her close so he can press a kiss to her temple. "Are you okay? After last night, I mean?"

She fidgets for a moment before mumbling, "It was just another embarrassing panic attack. I told you I didn't need to talk about it."

My brows dart sharply together.

Bear takes the words right out of my mouth. "But why were you there in the first place?"

Her mouth drops open, and her eyes dart to Duke as

she chews on her lip. She looks down at her hands, fisting them, then unclenching.

Oh, fuck. What's this?

She presses those pouty lips together, finally swallowing and finding Duke's eyes. "I saw." She pauses to take a quick breath. "I saw what he did to you." And then the words come in a waterfall-like rush. "I know you said to stay in the car and not come in, but I had to pee so bad, and so I did. In the bush. But I was under the window. You were in that room with Tristan."

Both my head and Bear's simultaneously whip from her to Duke. My chest clenches savagely. "D? Care to enlighten us?" I murmur softly, already aware of what she's referring to. I'd been so worked up by the time we got home, I hadn't brought up the goddamn handprint his father left on his face.

He hangs his head, his tongue coming out to slide across his upper lip as he looks away toward the pool. "It was just my father being the prick he always is." There's a faint tremor to his hand as he raises it to his jaw. "He gets off on smacking me around. You know that." His blue eyes meet mine for a split second. In that short time, though, I see the immense pressure he's under.

Lennon steps close to him, tugging his hand away from his face and gently sliding her fingertips along his jaw. "I'm sorry he did that to you. I could say he's an insufferable asshole, but you already know that." She gives him a little smirk before she touches her lips to his cheek.

Bear crosses his arms over his chest, studying Duke. "You okay?"

"I'm fine." He gives a swift jerk of his head. Huffing a bit, he focuses on Lennon. "I want to know what happened to *you* in there."

She sucks in a breath, her gaze shifting to take in each of us in turn. "I told you. A panic attack. You know how susceptible I am to them. Dark hallway, maybe I felt closed in or something." She shrugs. "I don't know. I'm just a freak, I guess."

That's so much bullshit I almost can't stand it, and from the looks Duke and Bear shoot me, I know they're thinking the same. She should know by now this shit isn't her fault. We've only scratched the surface of the things she's dealt with in her life—of that I'm sure. I work my jaw to the side. She shouldn't have to put on pretenses with us. I wonder what it was that set her off this time, and it almost feels like she's hiding something, but now's not the time to ask. We just need to know that she's okay. "Kin—" I begin, but she throws a hand up to stop me.

"I'm really fine." She looks up at me from under her long lashes. *"You're* okay?"

I grit my teeth. "You noticed my freak-out, huh? I was hoping you missed it in your dash to escape."

"No. I was aware." She clutches at a spot over her heart. "I always know." Tearing her eyes from me, she gives all of us a brief smile. "I'm not quite ready yet, so I guess we'd better get on with whatever you're about to tell me."

The tension in the room thickens to the point where we're all suffocating on it. Duke points toward the balcony door and jerks his head in that direction, too. He's right. We don't know how our fathers are getting their intel, but it'd be a shame to make things easy on them.

We shuffle out the door, all four of us onto the balcony. Duke shuts the door behind him and leans against it.

I glance over the balcony, checking for eavesdroppers. "This is safer."

Lennon mouths, "Is my room bugged or something?"

Bear shrugs, shaking his head. "We don't know," he says in a low voice.

Duke draws in a steadying breath as he focuses on Lennon. "I know this has the potential to make you mad, but we need you to do as we say tonight." He pauses, his eyes closing on a wince. Dragging his gaze back to hers a moment later, he very matter-of-factly states, "We need to follow through with putting you up for auction."

Lennon's brow raises, and she squares her shoulders. "Obey." The inhale through her nose that jerks her chest is the only outward sign of her unease.

Bear growls deep in his chest, leaning against the balcony railing. "No. We're *asking* you to go along with it. We'll try to find a distraction or a way to keep things from escalating. But if you end up being auctioned, we'll make sure we have the highest bid. We won't let it go any other way. If we can distract, though, and bypass ever having to bring you up on the stage with us, we will. In that case, I'll make eye contact with you, I'll blink a bunch of times, and when you see that, get the hell out of the ballroom and up to your bedroom as fast as you can. Lock yourself in, both sets of doors. Don't open them for anyone. We'll come to you through the balcony door when it's safe. That way you can see that it's us. But whichever way this goes down, you're going to be fine."

"You're sure?" Her delicate brow furrows.

I rake my teeth over my lower lip as I step forward and take her hand in mine. "We're going to be putting on one hell of a show tonight. You can expect us to be assholes, bastards really, and you're not going to like it. We *need* you to go along with it. You don't have to like it.

In fact, fight the fuck back and *be* pissed." I let out a heavy sigh. "But when it comes down to it, we've got you. Don't forget that."

"Obviously, this has to do with last night." She knows it does, it's not even a question.

Bear pulls her against him. "It does. The OG Bastards have their own agenda, unfortunately, and because we're bound to them, sometimes we have to do shit that we don't want to do." He lifts one of her curls, playing with it while he looks into her eyes. "Can you trust us? We'd never let anyone hurt you."

Her gaze flits rapidly to each of us in turn, and she cocks her head to the side. "Okay. One pissed-off Lennon, coming right up." She rolls her eyes. "It probably won't take much. Be the bastards your fathers expect you to be."

THIRTY-THREE

DUKE

IT'S time to get this shit over with. I hurry down the hall toward the gigantic ballroom where everything is set up to do a last-minute check. We've got about twenty minutes before our guests descend. My gut is churning over this whole fucking thing. The mess with the OG Bastards demanding Lennon be included in the auction is one thing, but the addition of Elliot Ashford is something I don't understand. The second Derek said it had something to do with Murdock Mikaelson ... just *fuck*. I don't see the connection yet, and that has me very leery. But now my eyes are wide open, waiting for someone to misstep and give us some clue what's happening.

I pause outside the door when voices drift to me from inside. *Oh, fuck.* It's Mason and ... when the hell did Hunter get here? *Goddammit!* I almost barge in but hold myself back. If he says something about their dad, I'm interested in having firsthand knowledge of it, but if things begin to go south, I'll step in. Hunter has a way of getting under Mason's skin. It's ugly.

"You wouldn't be so fucking crazy if you weren't to blame, and we all know it. Your cooperation is essential in getting Dad released for a crime we both know he's not responsible for committing."

There's an awful silence, and I imagine a hateful stare down happening between them. *Come on, Mason. Stand up to that fucker.*

Mason's voice comes out gravelly, as if he's holding back. "I don't fucking understand what is going on tonight. Maybe if I did, I would help." My fists clench for him, wanting to stroll in and sock Hunter in his wicked mouth.

Hunter makes a disgusted noise. "You're fucking lying. But you can bet if you don't follow through, I'll make your last year here a living fucking hell. Do what's asked so Dad can get out, and maybe I won't set fire to your life."

"You know nothing."

Maniacal laughter trips out of him that chills me to the bone. "You have no idea how much I know, little brother."

Unable to stand this anymore, I barrel in, fiery wrath

shooting through my veins. "Leave him the fuck alone," I snarl. "You're here to make sure we get the job done, not antagonize him."

Hunter laughs again, his eyes glinting from behind his mask. "Ah, but if I can do both at the same time, that's too sweet a deal for me to resist."

I step forward, shoving his shoulder. "You get off on causing him distress. You're sick, Hunter. So, do what you need to do, but stay the fuck away from us while we do what *we* need to."

Hunter shrugs, putting his hands up as he winks and begins to back away. "Just remember to have fun tonight. But don't fuck things up or you're fucked." He smirks, pinning his eyes on Mason. "Hey, I hear there's a total babe named Lennon being auctioned this year. I think I'll bid on her. Make her take my cock down her throat right in the middle of this fucking room, in front of everyone. I think she'll be all over it, don't you?"

I sense the dark rage flowing through him, so it doesn't surprise me when Mason throws himself at his brother, pounding his fist into his jaw before I'm able to grab him and drag him away. Mason's body is vibrating, but he narrows his eyes. "I will fucking kill you, Hunter."

"That's what you're good at." Hunter turns on his heel, rubbing his hand over the spot where Mason's punch landed, and walks away. His shoulders shake with laughter.

I step directly in front of Mason, but he won't meet my eyes. He stares stonily at the floor, his jaw locked. With a quick look around, I find us alone, so I grasp his head with both my hands and force him to look at me, tugging him in close. There's pain and confusion and—more than anything else—hate swimming in his brown eyes. I quietly whisper, "Baby, he's goading you, and he's so fucking good at it. Don't listen to a goddamn word he says."

"He's got his eye on her." His words catch in his throat as he blinks at me from under his inky dark lashes. "He'll hurt her."

I give him a shake, my gaze drifting to his lips. My mouth goes dry. I want to kiss him so fucking bad. "We won't let him. She's ours. No way is he coming near her."

MORE AND MORE OF the elite brotherhoods on campus spill through the main doors of the ballroom. I'm keeping tabs on who has arrived, waiting, of course, for one group in particular—the brothers of Hawthorne Hall. Kingston, Archer, and Cannon—and Elliot, can't forget her—have yet to show their faces, though some of the other brothers are present.

That Alec kid, the one with the loose lips who's in my statistics class, is already here, wandering around with a couple of his buddies. He raises his hand in greeting and, assuming my Bainbridge bastard persona, I give a vague nod in his direction.

A moment later, Bear rumbles under his breath. "They're here. Time for the shit show." His eyes roam the room. "Where's Lennon?"

Mason locks his hands around the back of his neck, tugging. "She said she'd be waiting to come in until the last minute." His eyes meet mine. "I'm watching Hunter. He's over near the bar."

Bear grits his teeth. "I haven't had the pleasure of talking with him yet. Maybe later," he mutters, clamping one of his hands down on each of our shoulders. "Deep breaths. Time to turn on bastard mode."

I nod, then stride quickly to the stage and mount the stairs. Over at the side, there's a microphone, and I pick it up. *Thud, thud, thud,* it sounds against my finger, getting everyone's attention. I scan the room, taking in the sea of elite brothers in their suits and ties and the glitter and sparkle of the sorority girls who chose to join us tonight in a bid to up their social status.

My perusal of the room stops short when my eyes land on Kingston with the dark-haired girl, Elliot. She's pretty, I'll give him that, and her dress is killer, strapless and black. He tugs her to him, whispering in her ear. I press my lips together. The way he touches her makes it very obvious that they're together.

I take a deep, steadying breath, then slowly release it. Here we go. Holding the mic up, I give our guests my signature cocky smirk. "Welcome. I bet you've all got questions as to what we're doing tonight. So far, it's an elegant party, wouldn't you say? Everyone enjoying the food and drink?" My brows raise as they answer my question with applause. "But before we let you in on the details"—I smirk again, my gaze drifting over everyone—"a few housekeeping tips for the night."

Mason steps up next to me, relieving me of the mic. I'm hardly listening as he mentions that they're to eat, drink, and be merry ... and that there will be an auction this evening. My eyes crash shut for a moment, my jaw going rigid. When my eyes open again, they lock on Lennon. I suck in a breath. I can fault Kingston for a lot of things. But maybe it's going a bit far to begrudge him happiness now. Lennon's head tilts to the side, questioning my slip into awkwardness. She's turned my damn world upside down, made me fall for her, despite all the anger and grief that still lives inside me. *Fuck.* This is going to be a difficult evening.

Mason crosses his arms over his chest as the rumble of the crowd grows, a sly grin on his face that almost slips when he glances at me.

Fuck. Do not mess this up, Duke.

Sensing that I still need a second, Bear takes over. He gives them a feral smile. "And we hope you'll join us in all the *sexy* this auction has to give." His arm swings out, pointing out a few people—sorority girls—in the crowd. "There are many lovely ladies here this evening who were gracious enough to join us tonight. They come from all the best sororities, houses, and halls on campus, and they would love to show you a good time." The big guy grins, nodding as he gestures with his hand that he hopes they brought cash with them. "But you gotta pay up. Gotta beat out everyone else to get the girl you want." He glances at me, then his eyes scan the crowd, landing on Lennon as he grunts out, "And let's face it, these ladies you've been mingling with ... they are hot and ready."

My eyes dart to Lennon as her brow raises. Well, that's one way to do it. I can't tell if she's pissed or amused at our asshole behavior yet. The only thing for sure is that we are behaving exactly as we promised her we would—like bastards.

I'm distracted by Elliot up front, who has just accepted a drink from Cannon ... and kisses him on the jaw as a thank you. My brain clicks and whirs, then shoves that information aside as I realize I've missed whatever Bear was saying.

Blowing out a breath, I regroup. I need to get my fucking head in the game. Make this look fucking good. My eyes cut across the room to Hunter, who nods with a sick grin on his lips. I take the mic from Bear. These brothers are anxious to get fucking started, so it's time to give them what they want—and give the OGs what they want. My stomach curls in on itself. "Almost done. Once you've won a lady for the evening, anything goes so long as it's *consensual*." I turn my head, taking in the guests. Shocked gasps and excited murmurs fill the room. "Make use of one of the rooms along the back hall with a black ribbon tied on the doorknob. Get your cock sucked on the patio. Fornicate right here in front of everyone. As long as you're both into it, do what you want."

The sorority girls know that's their cue and file over to the steps at the side of the stage. Mason throws an arm around my shoulders, pulling me in so he can get at the microphone. "And, of course, all proceeds go to charity. This year we're giving to a local women's shelter. So, see? It's for an excellent cause." His hand squeezes the ball of my shoulder, and I read it as *Are you ready for this?* I don't know. Am I? *Fuck.* But there's literally no way out. All we can do is put on the best fucking show we can and hope it's enough to satisfy Hunter.

It's obvious that I haven't been paying attention because all at once there's a girl next to me. I slide my gaze down her body, then give my lip a little bite. "Tell us about yourself, honey. Why do you think one of these men will bid on you? What's the most compelling reason you can think of as to why these fine men"—I wave my hand in the general direction of the salivating crowd— "would want to pay big bucks to have you for the next two hours?"

I notice Kingston whisper to Elliot, who is frowning hard. Dear fucking god, I don't know how Hunter expects to get her up here, but he promised he had it covered. My teeth grind hard as the brunette on stage with me shoots me a grin, then winks as she says, "Hi, I'm Kelly. I'm a psych major and a sister at Sigma Nu. And ... I give the best blow jobs around."

I clear my throat. Let the games begin ... "Bidding starts at one hundred dollars."

One girl after another comes up and does her best to tease and tempt the men in the room. I've seen more tits, ass, and pussy tonight than I have in a very long time.

Lennon's face is unreadable as all of this is happening. She's stiff, her arms crossed over her chest. I've seen several dudes look at her as if wondering why the fuck she isn't in line to be auctioned, and a few more blatantly question her. It makes me go rigid every time one of them steps into her personal space, like they have the right. They don't. She's *ours,* dammit. She's done a good job of flicking them away like annoying gnats, but as we get closer and closer to the end of the line, I get more and more nervous about how this is going to go down.

I peek at Bear out of the corner of my eye, and he shakes his head. He's in a fucking mood tonight, and I wonder if it has something to do with his damn shoulder again. We'd been so consumed with talking to Lennon about how to handle things tonight that I hadn't even asked how the game went. Bad fucking friend I am.

I huff out a breath, glad to let Mason take over as the auctioneer for a bit.

Tucker ends up bidding on some girl and winning. He hauls off with his prize over his shoulder, heading toward the hallway of rooms with black ribbons on the doorknobs. Maybe that fucker realized bidding on Lennon wouldn't be such a hot idea. Nice of him to pull his head out of his ass finally. My eyes swing back to the crowd in time to see Elliot and Archer take off together. At first, I inwardly cheer, thinking maybe it's a good thing that she leaves of her own accord. That is, until one by one, *our* underclassmen slink away from the room, each giving a brief nod to Hunter on their way out.

My jaw works to the side as I try not to make it obvious that I'm glaring at Mason's dickhead brother. He gives a soft chuckle that I obviously can't hear, but it hits me in the gut like a cannonball. This is it. As the final few girls are auctioned off, I feel it in my bones that Hunter's plan to get Elliot up here is going to be successful. Trying to appear calm, I laugh along with the crowd, throw them smirks, and wriggle my brows where appropriate.

The last girl has just been claimed when the ballroom door opens. Arik and Quincy stride through with a struggling Elliot between them. Poor thing, I can tell she's trying not to make a big deal of it, but she really, really doesn't want to be involved, it's written all over her face. I guess that's the problem with being an initiate. There's always a part of you that wonders what is an actual test of your merit versus what's simply brotherhood bullshit to put up with. So, she's unsure what to do, and meanwhile, Kingston and Cannon are just standing there, watching her be brought up to the stage. They're probably internally freaking out while trying to figure out how to get her out of this without creating a huge scene at one of the biggest events of the year.

They're all about their traditions and image. *Good luck with that.*

There's some back-and-forth between our grunts and Elliot as they get her up the stairs. Clearly displeased, she tries to wrench herself free, but they've got her in a vice grip, singularly focused on the task Hunter gave them. Once she's finally on stage, Arik and Quincy both give us grins and little salutes.

Playing my part, I grin wickedly at Elliot. "Well, aren't you a pretty thing?"

She doesn't respond, her eyes instead search the crowd. Hard to say what's in her head, but it's obvious she's spotted Cannon and Kingston. I glance around the room, noting that Archer is still missing, as are Kai, Brendan, and Pierre. No doubt they had the job of securing Archer, thereby ensuring Elliot could be snatched.

She looks for all the world as if she's going to attempt to flee. I catch Mason's eye and subtly jerk it in her direction. Bear catches on as well, and all three of us move closer to her. She's not going anywhere. We need this girl to cooperate. Looking into her eyes, I can't figure out what the hell she has to do with our fathers at all. She's young. Eighteen probably. A freshman.

A moment later, Kingston shouts, "What the fuck! She came with us. She's not for fuckin' sale."

454

I press my lips together, hating to do this, especially when I spot Lennon rolling her eyes at me. I shout, "Opening bid starts at two—"

"Two hundred dollars." Alec from my math class bids first.

Jesus, the way Elliot trembles when he shoots her an ugly grin makes my teeth clench. There's obvious animosity between them. She stutters, "N-no," her breaths shallow.

"Two twenty-five." Mason catches her by the shoulder. "What's the matter, baby? It's for charity, remember?" He leans close and whispers loudly, "Don't worry, I'll be gentle."

"Three hundred." Archer has come out of nowhere. His mask is askew, and now that I take a second to look around the room again, Pierre, Kai, and Brendan have all returned. They're hanging out, rather nonchalantly, as if they hadn't just grabbed Archer to hold him hostage while Elliot was forced on stage.

Some idiot shouts, "Four hundred! How many times do you think she'll suck my dick in two hours?"

Kingston immediately grits out, "Five hundred." He's fucking seething, his eyes glittering mad.

Bear catches my eye right before he looks down at Elliot, then grips her by the waist, lifting her for a moment. He nods, letting out a huffed growl. "Yep, you'll do. Six hundred." Elliot immediately elbows Bear in the gut, which makes him back away, hands up. He gives her a crazy-eyed look, which, because she doesn't know him, might be scary as fucking hell. And she's definitely unnerved since she's shaking like a leaf.

The bids come in fast and furious, and I finally snap to and pay attention when we hit two thousand.

Hunter is watching me so fucking carefully that I sidle up to Elliot and throw my arm around her shoulders. "Come on, guys." I trace my fingertips over her collarbone. I receive an immediate glare from Lennon as I shift Elliot forward. "She's worth more than that to you, isn't she?"

"Four thousand," growls a gritty, rough voice.

Well, damn. I don't think I've ever heard Cannon speak before, and from the dead quiet in the room, neither have many other people. There's also the fact that he looks like a raging fucking bull about to charge up here and impale me on his horns.

Kingston bellows, "Duke, I think it's gone fuckin' high enough."

I slide my tongue over my lower lip, my gaze bouncing in so many directions, it makes my head pound. That's when I realize Hunter is not where he was before. *Holy fuck, where is he?* Sweat trickles between my shoulder blades and down my spine. I don't care where he's gone. This is our fucking chance to create the diversion to get Lennon out of here. My heart begins to hammer hard in my chest, a harsh surge of adrenaline rushing through my body. I meet Bear's eyes and give him a nearly imperceptible nod. Mason, who is standing just behind me, puts his hand on my back and pats twice, as if to say, *Finish it.*

Lennon's angry eyes are on us, and I hope like fuck she's watching Bear for the signal. I keep my eyes steady on Kingston. "This isn't your playground, Hawthorne." I give a horrible, wicked-sounding chuckle. "Forty-one hundred." The end of auction buzzer goes off. My eyes flick to Lennon's, and hers widen as she sees Bear blink rapidly at her.

Unease rolls through my body. While it's given Lennon a chance to escape, I don't like that we no longer have eyes on Hunter. What's that fucker up to? With my heart in my throat, I watch as Lennon hesitates. *Please, Stella Bella. Don't let anything we've done or said sway you. Just* run.

THIRTY-FOUR

LENNON

CHAOS ENSUES AT MY BACK, but my feet carry me swiftly away from it. I knew Elliot would probably not have been warned that she was about to be auctioned off as some dude's cum bucket for the night. And sure enough, it'd been cringeworthy to witness her reaction to being pulled up on that stage. Girlfriend hadn't wanted any part of it, and what'd been more interesting to me was watching those guys from Hawthorne Hall frantically bidding on her. They hadn't won, though, and my stomach roils, unsure of what's about to happen, how everything will pan out. My face burns. The guys told me everything I saw and heard would be an elaborate act ... but how far are they willing to go? Did they want me out of there and up in my room on purpose?

Without fully understanding everything at play here

458

tonight, I make a mad dash for the exit, passing by one brother after another, all in masks. They're a blur, including one outside the door, deep in an agitated phone conversation. I kick off my heels and snatch them up, then race for the stairs, my heart thumping unevenly in my chest. Stepping onto the upstairs landing, I dart down the hall to my bedroom with Bear's command ringing through my head. *Lock yourself in, both sets of doors. Don't open them for anyone.* Out of breath, I yank the door open, slip into my room, and turn to shut the heavy wood door behind me.

I jerk backward, my brain not registering at first what's happening. A tall, burly man—in a mask, of course—has appeared out of nowhere. Had he followed me? I try to slam the door shut on him, but he wedges his foot in between the door and the frame.

I'm so surprised, I stumble back a pace, dropping my shoes to the floor in the process. His lips curl into an ugly smile, his brown eyes glinting at me from behind his devious-looking black mask. "What do you think you're doing? Get the fuck out. The party is downstairs."

He huffs out a disturbing laugh and steps into my room, shutting the door behind him. "Really? I think the party is right fucking here. You made it so easy for me, too, racing up here the way you did. I'll remember to thank the guys for that."

An uneasy, sick feeling overwhelms me, causing bile to rise in my throat and sweat to slick my palms. *They wouldn't have. No. They didn't.* My breathing becomes more and more shallow as anxiety overtakes me, but I bite down on my lip to prevent its wobble. *What kind of elaborate hoax is this?*

A moment later, though, something else takes precedence in my thoughts. This predatory fuck has something in his hand that glints in the moonlight coming in from the balcony doors. I blink hard, staring at it, and my eyes widen in alarm.

A knife. He has a knife. The blood drains from my face, not that he can see that in the darkened room. "Who the *fuck* are you? What do you want?" I try to keep my tone even and sharp, but fear crawls its way into my every movement, my body beginning to shake.

He wets his lips, acting like he's pondering my question. One corner of his mouth lifts. "We've met before. You might not remember. Did you really think you'd get out of the auction tonight?"

My head spins, and I don't have time to process what he said because he stalks relentlessly toward me. Every backward step I take, he advances.

"You didn't really want to play with the little boys tonight, did you?" He cocks his head to the side, leering at me. "That's okay. You'll have more fun with the big boys instead."

What? I spin on my heel to get away, but he lunges, grabs me, and pulls me to him, my back to his front.

He whispers in my ear as he holds the knife near my throat, the blade grazing my skin. "Where do you think you're running to?" I hold my breath, afraid to even breathe. My chest jerks from the effort, and he chuckles darkly in my ear before he moves us past the end of the bed.

Right in plain view sits the frilly, frothy white nightie I'd worn for the guys. My heart jackhammers as he picks it up with the tip of the knife. "I think you need to wear this for us."

I don't even know how to answer, and I definitely don't like where this is going. Swallowing hard, I take it from him. He releases me, pushing me slightly, and as I turn to face him, he growls, "Take off the dress," the rumble in his voice lethal.

I shake my head. "No."

It doesn't take him a split second to have the blade poking at my chest. He gives me a perverted, menacing smile as he applies pressure with the blade, making me gasp out in pain. "Do it. *Now.*"

My eyes crash shut, and with jerky movements, I lift my hands to the straps of the beautiful dress I'll never look at the same way again and slip them from my shoulders. The garment falls easily from my body, pooling at my feet on the hardwood floor.

His filthy gaze follows, taking in my bare breasts and the tiny pair of lace panties—the same pair Mason had seen me in from the balcony—before traveling down my trembling legs and back up. He picks up the nightie, assessing it. "Yep, that'll do. Put it on." He throws it at me, and I only catch it because it hits me square in the chest. With shaking hands, I pull it over my head.

He gives me a lascivious grin. "Like sex on a stick, baby."

A commotion makes both of us jump, doors opening and closing, one after another outside my bedroom. Someone is systematically checking the rooms, coming closer and closer.

My masked captor grabs me, hauls me over toward the window seat, and shoves me onto it. "Sit right fucking there."

I blink but quickly do what he says, drawing my legs close to my chest. My breath catches as out of the corner of my eye, I spot Bear heading into the pool house with Elliot over his shoulder.

Through his mask, his eyes glint as he gets in my face, his hot breath making me feel sick. "You say a motherfucking thing, I'll slit your fucking throat." Another door opens, then slams shut. Whoever is out there is close. He tilts his head to the side and whispers harshly, "You'd better hope that's not one of your lover boys or they're dead." He slips behind the thick floor-length damask curtain to hide.

My hand covers the painful spot on my chest that he jabbed. If he had pushed any harder, he'd have sliced into my skin. I don't know who's coming through that door, but I can't even entertain the idea of crying out for help. This guy is certifiable.

The door flies open, taking what's left of my breath with it. One of the Hawthorne Hall brothers, the one who bid four-thousand dollars on Elliot, bursts into the room, then stops short, staring at me. He's a big guy, maybe slightly shorter than Bear but just as broad and muscular, probably the kind who spends his spare time working out.

My heart rate ratchets up, and my automatic response is to scoot back on the window seat at this newcomer's arrival into my unpredictable situation. I can't keep my eyes from darting everywhere, calculating whether a run for it would be worthwhile in the end. But no, he's hiding not a foot from me, and I have no doubt he'll follow through on his threats. *Don't panic, don't panic, don't panic.* Outwardly, I'm frozen in fear, but on the inside, I'm screaming. I need to slow my breathing before my anxiety gets the best of me.

Looking at this guy, I can only assume he wants to know if I've seen Elliot, but why doesn't he just come out with it? He takes his time, wetting his lips and squeezing his eyes shut, and I sense the concealed asshole with the knife becoming more and more irritated at the interruption. This guy needs to get the fuck out of here before we're both killed.

Finally, the big guy blurts out in a rough voice, "A girl was t-taken." He pauses to clear his throat. "Do you know where?"

I study him, unsure what this masked dickhead wants me to do, but he told me not to speak, so I look out the window toward the pool house and hope this guy looks out the balcony windows. But he doesn't. *Oh, fuck. Oh, shit.* He walks a few paces forward, coming close to the edge of the bed, intent on looking out the same window I am, and everything inside me flies apart. I flinch hard, on purpose, to get him to stop.

He—thank fuck—halts in his tracks, holding his hands up. "Not here to hurt you." His gaze wanders out the window, then his eyes widen before they swing back to me. He rasps out roughly, "Thank you," then spins on his heel and sprints from the room. His shout is probably heard throughout the house as he thunders down the steps. "Kingston! Archer! Out back!"

There's quite a commotion downstairs, and when I shift like I'm going to get up from the window seat, the scary fuck with the knife emerges from his hiding place, shaking his head. "Don't fucking move an inch. We wait."

Shuddering there in my white nightie, I nod my understanding and attempt to take deep, slow breaths. I can't let myself have a full-blown panic attack. Not now. I press my lips together and look out the window again, noting that there are three of them out there at the pool house door, including the one I recognize as Kingston.

As they break the door in, I simultaneously cry out. Something stuck me, and an odd, tingling sensation flows under the skin of my upper arm. *No.* I try to wrench it away, only to be forcefully removed from the window seat a second later. "Turn around, or I'll gut you."

At my sharp inhale, he slides his palms down the outside of my arms, and before I realize what he's doing, secures both wrists in one hand. A moment later, he ties them behind my back with some sort of smooth, silky material. *Maybe his tie?* And then immediately after, he obscures my vision with a blindfold, adding the mask on top for good measure.

My heart sinks, not understanding what is happening or why. I'm relieved for a moment that he doesn't gag me, but what he does is worse. He puts his arm around me, securing his hand over my mouth and nose, then shuffles me from the room.

I try to keep track of where we're going, but I feel like this is some sadistic child's game where the victim is spun around and around until they don't know which end is up anymore. Or maybe it's simply whatever he put in my arm. Some sort of drug, obviously, because I'm dizzy and out of it, completely disoriented. I don't have any concept of where we are or where the hell he's taking me. He picks me up, throwing me over his shoulder, and I bounce around as he jogs down a flight of stairs. This is like being in a nightmarish fun house, only without the fun part.

The sound of a latch being disengaged and the creak of a door sends my heart pounding even harder. I try to speak, but words won't come out. More stairs. Up? Down? I can't freaking tell.

Another door opens, and there's a murmur of voices on the other side. My breathing is more erratic than ever as I'm set back on my feet and whirled around, which causes me to lose my sense of balance. Harsh, unforgiving hands grasp me by the arms just above my elbows. Sick dread curls around my spine as whispered words drift toward me. *Oh, no. No, no, no. Where am I?* My heart thumps out of control, pounding loudly in my ears.

The blindfold is removed a moment later, and I blink hard in the dimly candlelit room. My vision blurs but not so much that I can't see the small group of men in black masks sitting in a semicircle, all eyes on me. My head is so foggy, I can't focus. Everything spins. I might vomit from that sensation alone.

"Well, she's not who we were expecting."

"Yeah, but she grew up fucking good, didn't she?"

TO BE CONTINUED ...